The Way of a Man

Emerson Hough

Grace Shows a Lack of Sympathy.

The Way Of A Man

by Emerson Hough

Author of *The Covered Wagon*, etc.

ILLUSTRATED WITH SCENES FROM THE PHOTOPLAY
A PATHÉ PICTURE

Grosset & Dunlap

1907

Contents

Chapter I - The Kissing Of Miss Grace Sheraton

I admit I kissed her.

Perhaps I should not have done so. Perhaps I would not do so again. Had I known what was to come I could not have done so. Nevertheless I did.

After all, it was not strange. All things about us conspired to be accessory and incendiary. The air of the Virginia morning was so soft and warm, the honeysuckles along the wall were so languid sweet, the bees and the hollyhocks up to the walk so fat and lazy, the smell of the orchard was so rich, the south wind from the fields was so wanton! Moreover, I was only twenty-six. As it chances, I was this sort of a man: thick in the arm and neck, deep through, just short of six feet tall, and wide as a door, my mother said; strong as one man out of a thousand, my father said. And then—the girl was there.

So this was how it happened that I threw the reins of Satan, my black horse, over the hooked iron of the gate at Dixiana Farm and strode up to the side of the stone pillar where Grace Sheraton stood, shading her eyes with her hand, watching me approach through the deep trough road that flattened there, near the Sheraton lane. So I laughed and strode up—and kept my promise. I had promised myself that I would kiss her the first time that seemed feasible. I had even promised her—when she came home from Philadelphia so lofty and superior for her stopping a brace of years with Miss Carey at her Allendale Academy for Young Ladies—that if she mitigated not something of her haughtiness, I would kiss her fair, as if she were but a girl of the country. Of these latter I may guiltily confess, though with no names, I had known many who rebelled little more than formally.

She stood in the shade of the stone pillar, where the ivy made a deep green, and held back her light blue skirt daintily, in her high-bred way; for never was a girl Sheraton who was not high-bred or other than fair to look upon in the Sheraton way—slender, rather tall, long cheeked, with very much dark hair and a deep color under the skin, and something of long curves withal. They were ladies, every one, these Sheraton girls; and as Miss Grace presently advised me, no milkmaids wandering and waiting in lanes for lovers.

When I sprang down from Satan Miss Grace was but a pace or so away. I put out a hand on either side of her as she stood in the shade, and so prisoned her against the pillar. She flushed at this, and caught at my arm with both hands, which made me smile, for few men in that country could have put away my arms from the stone until I liked. Then I bent and kissed her fair, and took what revenge was due our girls for her Philadelphia manners.

When she boxed my ears I kissed her once more. Had she not at that smiled at me a little, I should have been a boor, I admit. As she did — and as I in my innocence supposed all girls did — I presume I may be called but a man as men go. Miss Grace grew very rosy for a Sheraton, but her eyes were bright. So I threw my hat on the grass by the side of the gate and bowed her to be seated. We sat and looked up the lane which wound on to the big Sheraton house, and up the red road which led from their farm over toward our lands, the John Cowles farm, which had been three generations in our family as against four on the part of the Sheratons' holdings; a fact which I think always ranked us in the Sheraton soul a trifle lower than themselves.

We were neighbors, Miss Grace and I, and as I lazily looked out over the red road unoccupied at the time by even the wobbling wheel of some negro's cart, I said to her some word of our being neighbors, and of its being no sin for neighbors to exchange the courtesy of a greeting when they met upon such a morning. This seemed not to please her; indeed I opine that the best way of a man with a maid is to make no manner of speech whatever before or after any such incident as this.

"I was just wandering down the lane," she said, "to see if Jerry had found my horse, Fanny."

"Old Jerry's a mile back up the road," said I, "fast asleep under the hedge."

"The black rascal!"

"He is my friend," said I, smiling.

"You do indeed take me for some common person," said she; "as though I had been looking for—"

"No, I take you only for the sweetest Sheraton that ever came to meet a Cowles from the farm yonder." Which was coming rather close home, for our families, though neighbors, had once had trouble over some such meeting as this two generations back; though of that I do not now speak.

"Cannot a girl walk down her own carriage road of a morning, after hollyhocks for the windows, without—"

"She cannot!" I answered. I would have put out an arm for further mistreatment, but all at once I pulled up. What was I coming to, I, John Cowles, this morning when the bees droned fat and the flowers made fragrant all the air? I was no boy, but a man grown; and ruthless as I was, I had all the breeding the land could give me, full Virginia training as to what a gentleman should be. And a gentleman, unless he may travel all a road, does not set foot too far into it when he sees that he is taken at what seems his wish. So now I said how glad I was that she had come back from school, though a fine lady now, and no doubt forgetful of her friends, of myself, who once caught young rabbits and birds for her, and made pens for the little pink pigs at the orchard edge, and all of that. But she had no mind, it seemed to me, to talk of these old days; and though now some sort of wall seemed to me to arise between us as we sat there on the bank blowing at dandelions and pulling loose grass blades, and humming a bit of tune now and then as young persons will, still, thickheaded as I was, it was in some way made apparent to me that I was quite as willing the wall should be there as she herself was willing.

My mother had mentioned Miss Grace Sheraton to me before. My father had never opposed my riding over now and then to the Sheraton gates. There were no better families in our county than these two. There was no reason why I should feel troubled. Yet as I looked out into the haze of the hilltops where the red road appeared to leap off sheer to meet the distant rim of the Blue Ridge, I seemed to hear some whispered warning. I was young, and wild as any deer in those hills beyond. Had it been any enterprise scorning settled ways; had it been merely a breaking of orders and a following of my own will, I suppose I might have gone on. But there are ever two things which govern an adventure for one of my sex. He may be a man; but he must also be a gentleman. I suppose books might be written about the war between those two things. He may be a gentleman sometimes and have credit for being a soft-headed fool, with no daring to approach the very woman who has contempt for him; whereas she may not know his reasons for restraint. So much for civilization, which at times I hated because it brought such problems. Yet these problems never cease, at least while youth lasts, and no community is free from them, even so quiet a one as ours there in the valley of the old Blue Ridge, before the wars had rolled across it and made all the young people old.

I was of no mind to end my wildness and my roaming just yet; and still, seeing that I was, by gentleness of my Quaker mother and by sternness of my Virginia father, set in the class of gentlemen, I had no wish dishonorably to engage a woman's heart. Alas, I was not the first to learn that kissing is a most difficult art to practice!

When one reflects, the matter seems most intricate. Life to the young is barren without kissing; yet a kiss with too much warmth may mean overmuch, whereas a kiss with no warmth to it is not worth the pains. The kiss which comes precisely at the moment when it should, in quite sufficient warmth and yet not of complicating fervor, working no harm and but joy to both involved — those kisses, now that one pauses to think it over, are relatively few.

As for me, I thought it was time for me to be going.

Chapter II - The Meeting Of Gordon Orme

I had enough to do when it came to mounting my horse Satan. Few cared to ride Satan, since it meant a battle each time he was mounted. He was a splendid brute, black and clean, with abundant bone in the head and a brilliant eye—blood all over, that was easy to see. Yet he was a murderer at heart. I have known him to bite the backbone out of a yearling pig that came under his manger, and no other horse on our farm would stand before him a moment when he came on, mouth open and ears laid back. He would fight man, dog, or devil, and fear was not in him, nor any real submission. He was no harder to sit than many horses I have ridden. I have seen Arabians and Barbary horses and English hunters that would buck-jump now and then. Satan contented himself with rearing high and whirling sharply, and lunging with a low head; so that to ride him was a matter of strength as well as skill. The greatest danger was in coming near his mouth or heels. My father always told me that this horse was not fit to ride; but since my father rode him—as he would any horse that offered—nothing would serve me but I must ride Satan also, and so I made him my private saddler on occasion.

I ought to speak of my father, that very brave and kindly gentleman from whom I got what daring I ever had, I suppose. He was a clean-cut man, five-eleven in his stockings, and few men in all that country had a handsomer body. His shoulders sloped—an excellent configuration for strength—as a study of no less a man than George Washington will prove—his arms were round, his skin white as milk, his hair, like my own, a sandy red, and his eyes blue and very quiet. There was a balance in his nature that I have ever lacked. I rejoice even now in his love of justice. Fair play meant with him something more than fair play for the sake of sport—it meant as well fair play for the sake of justice. Temperate to the point of caring always for his body's welfare, as regular in his habits as he was in his promises and their fulfillments, kindling readily enough at any risk, though never boasting—I always admired him, and trust I may be pardoned for saying so. I fear that at the time I mention now I admired him most for his strength and courage.

Thus as I swung leg over Satan that morning I resolved to handle him as I had seen my father do, and I felt strong enough for that. I remembered, in the proud way a boy will have, the time when my father and I, riding through the muddy streets of Leesburg town together, saw a farmer's wagon stuck midway of a crossing. "Come, Jack," my father called me, "we must send Bill Yarnley home to his family." Then we two dismounted, and stooping in the mud got our two shoulders under the axle of the wagon, before we were done with it, our blood getting up at the laughter of the townsfolk. When we heaved together, out came Bill Yarnley's wagon from the mud, and the laughter ended. It was like him—he would not stop when once he started. Why, it was so he married my mother, that very sweet Quakeress from the foot of old Catoctin. He told me she said him no many times, not liking his wild ways, so contrary to the manner of the Society of Friends; and she only consented after binding him to go with her once each week to the little stone church at Wallingford village, near our farm, provided he should be at home and able to attend. My mother I think during her life had not missed a half dozen meetings at the little stone church. Twice a week, and once each Sunday, and once each month, and four times each year, and also annually, the Society of Friends met there at Wallingford, and have done so for over one hundred and thirty-five years. Thither went my mother, quiet, brown-haired, gentle, as good a soul as ever lived, and with her my father, tall, strong as a tree, keeping his promise until at length by sheer force of this kept promise, he himself became half Quaker and all gentle, since he saw what it meant to her.

As I have paused in my horsemanship to speak thus of my father, I ought also to speak of my mother. It was she who in those troublous times just before the Civil War was the first to raise the voice in the Quaker Meeting which said that the Friends ought to free their slaves, law or no law; and so started what was called later the Unionist sentiment in that part of old Virginia. It was my mother did that. Then she asked my father to manumit all his slaves; and he thought for an hour, and then raised his head and said it should be done; after which the servants lived on as before, and gave less in return, at which my father made wry faces, but said nothing in regret. After us others also set free their people, and presently this part of Virginia was a sort of Mecca for escaped blacks. It was my mother did that; and I believe that it was her influence which had much to do with the position of East Virginia on the question of the war. And this also in time had much to do with this strange story of mine, and much to do with the presence thereabout of the man whom I was to meet that very morning; although when I started to mount my horse Satan I did not know that such a man as Gordon Orme existed in the world.

When I approached Satan he lunged at me, but I caught him by the cheek strap of the bridle and swung his head close up, feeling for the saddle front as he reached for me with open mouth. Then as he reared I swung up with him into place, and so felt safe, for once I clamped a horse fair there was an end of his throwing me. I laughed when Miss Grace Sheraton called out in alarm, and so wheeled Satan around a few times and rode on down the road, past the fields where the blacks were busy as blacks ever are, and so on to our own red pillared-gates.

Then, since the morning was still young, and since the air seemed to me like wine, and since I wanted something to subdue and Satan offered, I spurred him back from the gate and rode him hard down toward Wallingford. Of course he picked up a stone en route. Two of us held his head while Billings the blacksmith fished out the stone and tapped the shoe nails tight. After that I had time to look around.

As I did so I saw approaching a gentleman who was looking with interest at my mount. He was one of the most striking men I have ever seen, a stranger as I could see, for I knew each family on both sides the Blue Ridge as far up the valley as White Sulphur.

"A grand animal you have there, sir," said he, accosting Me. "I did not know his like existed in this country."

"As well in this as in any country," said I tartly. He smiled at this.

"You know his breeding?"

"Klingwalla out of Bonnie Waters."

"No wonder he's vicious," said the stranger, calmly.

"Ah, you know something of the English strains," said I. He shrugged his shoulders. "As much as that," he commented indifferently.

There was something about him I did not fancy, a sort of condescension, as though he were better than those about him. They say that we Virginians have a way of reserving that right to ourselves; and I suppose that a family of clean strain may perhaps become proud after generations of independence and comfort and freedom from care. None the less I was forced to admit this newcomer to the class of gentlemen. He stood as a gentleman, with no resting or bracing with an arm, or crossing of legs or hitching about, but balanced on his legs easily—like a fencer or boxer or fighting man, or gentleman, in short. His face, as I now perceived, was long and thin, his chin square, although somewhat narrow. His mouth, too, was narrow, and his teeth were narrow, one of the upper teeth at each side like the tooth of a carnivore, longer than its fellows. His hair was thick and close cut to his head, dark, and if the least bit gray about the edges, requiring close scrutiny to prove it so. In color his skin was dark, sunburned beyond tan, almost to parchment dryness. His eyes were gray, the most remarkable eyes that I have ever seen—calm, emotionless, direct, the most fearless eyes I have ever seen in mortal head, and I have looked into many men's eyes in my time. He was taller than most men, I think above the six feet line. His figure was thin, his limbs thin, his hands and feet slender. He did not look one-tenth his strength. He was simply dressed, dressed indeed as a gentleman. He stood as one, spoke as one, and assumed that all the world accepted him as one. His voice was warmer in accent than even our Virginia speech. I saw him to be an Englishman.

"He is a bit nasty, that one"; he nodded his head toward Satan.

I grinned. "I know of only two men in Fairfax County I'd back to ride him."

"Yourself and—"

"My father."

"By Jove! How old is your father, my good fellow?"

"Sixty, my good fellow," I replied. He laughed.

"Well," said he, "there's a third in Fairfax can ride him."

"Meaning yourself?"

He nodded carelessly. I did not share his confidence. "He's not a saddler in any sense," said I. "We keep him for the farms."

"Oh, I say, my friend," he rejoined—"my name's Orme, Gordon Orme—I'm just stopping here at the inn for a time, and I'm deucedly bored. I've not had leg over a decent mount since I've been here, and if I might ride this beggar, I'd be awfully obliged."

My jaw may have dropped at his words; I am not sure. It was not that he called our little tavern an "inn." It was the name he gave me which caused me to start.

"Orme," said I, "Mr. Gordon Orme? That was the name of the speaker the other evening here at the church of the Methodists."

He nodded, smiling. "Don't let that trouble you," said he.

None the less it did trouble me; for the truth was that word had gone about to the effect that a new minister from some place not stated had spoken from the pulpit on that evening upon no less a topic than the ever present one of Southern slavery. Now, I could not clear it to my mind how a minister of the gospel might take so keen and swift an interest in a stranger in the street, and that stranger's horse. I expressed to him something of my surprise.

"It's of no importance," said he again. "What seems to me of most importance just at present is that here's a son of old Klingwalla, and that I want to ride him."

"Just for the sake of saying you have done so?" I inquired.

His face changed swiftly as he answered: "We owned Klingwalla ourselves back home. He broke a leg for my father, and was near killing him."

"Sir," I said to him, catching his thought quickly, "we could not afford to have the horse injured, but if you wish to ride him fair or be beaten by him fair, you are welcome to the chance."

His eye kindled at this. "You're a sportsman, sir," he exclaimed, and he advanced at once toward Satan.

I saw in him something which awakened a responsive chord in my nature. He was a man to take a risk and welcome it for the risk's sake. Moreover, he was a horseman; as I saw by his quick glance over Satan's furniture. He caught the cheek strap of the bridle, and motioned us away as we would have helped him at the horse's head. Then ensued as pretty a fight between man and horse as one could ask to see. The black brute reared and fairly took him from the ground, fairly chased him about the street, as a great dog would a rat. But never did the iron hold on the bridle loosen, and the man was light on his feet as a boy. Finally he had his chance, and with the lightest spring I ever saw at a saddle skirt, up he went and nailed old Satan fair, with a grip which ridged his legs out. I saw then that he was a rider. His head was bare, his hat having fallen off; his hair was tumbled, but his color scarcely heightened. As the horse lunged and bolted about the street, Orme sat him in perfect confidence. He kept his hands low, his knees a little more up and forward than we use in our style of riding, and his weight a trifle further back; but I saw from the lines of his limbs that he had the horse in a steel grip. He gazed down contemplatively, with a half serious look, master of himself and of the horse as well. Then presently he turned him up the road and went off at a gallop, with the brute under perfect control. I do not know what art he used; all I can say is that in a half hour he brought Satan back in a canter.

This was my first acquaintance with Gordon Orme, that strange personality with whom I was later to have much to do. This was my first witnessing of that half uncanny power by which he seemed to win all things to his purposes. I admired him, yet did not like him, when he swung carelessly down and handed me the reins.

"He's a grand one," he said easily, "but not so difficult to ride as old Klingwalla. Not that I would discount your own skill in riding him, sir, for I doubt not you have taken a lot out of him before now."

At least this was generous, and as I later learned, it was like him to give full credit to the performance of any able adversary.

Chapter III - The Art Of The Orient

"Come," said Orme to me, "let us go into the shade, for I find your Virginia morning warm."

We stepped over to the gallery of the little tavern, where the shade was deep and the chairs were wide and the honeysuckles sweet. I threw myself rather discontentedly into a chair. Orme seated himself quietly in another, his slender legs crossed easily, his hands meeting above his elbows supported on the chair rails, as he gazed somewhat meditatively at his finger tips.

"So you did not hear my little effort the other night?" he remarked, smiling.

"I was not so fortunate as to hear you speak. But I will only say I will back you against any minister of the gospel I ever knew when it comes to riding horses."

"Oh, well," he deprecated, "I'm just passing through on my way to Albemarle County across the mountains. You couldn't blame me for wanting something to do—speaking or riding, or what not. One must be occupied, you know. But shall we not have them bring us one of these juleps of the country? I find them most agreeable, I declare."

I did not criticise his conduct as a wearer of the cloth, but declined his hospitality on the ground that it was early in the day for me. He urged me so little and was so much the gentleman that I explained.

"Awhile ago," I said, "my father came to me and said, 'I see, Jack, that thee is trying to do three things—to farm, hunt foxes, and drink juleps. Does thee think thee can handle all three of these activities in combination?' You see, my mother is a Quakeress, and when my father wished to reprove me he uses the plain speech. Well, sir, I thought it over, and for the most part I dropped the other two, and took up more farming."

"Your father is Mr. John Cowles, of Cowles' Farms?"

"The same."

"No doubt your family know every one in this part of the country?"

"Oh, yes, very well."

"These are troublous times," he ventured, after a time. "I mean in regard to this talk of secession of the Southern States."

I was studying this man. What was he doing here in our quiet country community? What was his errand? What business had a julep-drinking, horse-riding parson speaking in a Virginia pulpit where only the gospel was known, and that from exponents worth the name?

"You are from Washington?" I said at length.

He nodded.

"The country is going into deep water one way or the other," said I. "Virginia is going to divide on slavery. It is not for me, nor for any of us, to hasten that time. Trouble will come fast enough without our help."

"I infer you did not wholly approve of my little effort the other evening. I was simply looking at the matter from a logical standpoint. It is perfectly clear that the old world must have cotton, that the Southern States must supply that cotton, and that slavery alone makes cotton possible for the world. It is a question of geography rather than of politics; yet your Northern men make it a question of politics. Your Congress is full of rotten tariff legislation, which will make a few of your Northern men rich—and which will bring on this war quite as much as anything the South may do. Moreover, this tariff disgusts England, very naturally. Where will England side when the break comes? And what will be the result when the South, plus England, fights these tariff makers over here? I have no doubt that you, sir, know the complexion of all these neighborhood families in these matters. I should be most happy if you could find it possible for me to meet your father and his neighbors, for in truth I am interested in these matters, merely as a student. And I have heard much of the kindness of this country toward strangers."

It was not our way in Virginia to allow persons of any breeding to put up at public taverns. We took them to our homes. I have seen a hundred horses around my father's barns during the Quarterly Meetings of the Society of Friends. Perhaps we did not scrutinize all our guests over-closely, but that was the way of the place. I had no hesitation in saying to Mr. Orme that we should be glad to entertain him at Cowles' Farms. He was just beginning to thank me for this when we were suddenly interrupted.

We were sitting some paces from the room where landlord Sanderson kept his bar, so that we heard only occasionally the sound of loud talk which came through the windows. But now came footsteps and confused words in voices, one of which I seemed to know. There staggered through the door a friend of mine, Harry Singleton, a young planter of our neighborhood, who had not taken my father's advice, but continued to divide his favor between farming, hunting and drinking. He stood there leaning against the wall, his face more flushed than one likes to see a friend's face before midday.

"Hullo, ol' fel," he croaked at me. "Hurrah for C'fedrate States of America!"

"Very well," I said to him, "suppose we do hurrah for the Confederate States of America. But let us wait until there is such a thing."

He glowered at me. "Also," he said, solemnly, "Hurrah for Miss Grace Sheraton, the pretties' girl in whole C'federate States America!"

"Harry," I cried, "stop! You're drunk, man. Come on, I'll take you home."

He waved at me an uncertain hand. "Go 'way, slight man!" he muttered. "Grace Sheraton pretties' girl in whole C'federate States America."

According to our creed it was not permissible for a gentleman, drunk or sober, to mention a lady's name in a place like that. I rose and put my hand across Harry's mouth, unwilling that a stranger should hear a girl's name mentioned in the place. No doubt I should have done quite as much for any girl of our country whose name came up in that way. But to my surprise Harry Singleton was just sufficiently intoxicated to resent the act of his best friend. With no word of warning he drew back his hand and struck me in the face with all his force, the blow making a smart crack which brought all the others running from within. Still, I reflected, that this was not the act of Harry Singleton, but only that of a drunken man who to-morrow would not remember what had been done.

"That will be quite enough, Harry," said I. "Come, now, I'll take you home. Sanderson, go get his horse or wagon, or whatever brought him here."

"Not home!" cried Harry. "First inflict punishment on you for denyin' Miss Gracie Sheraton pretties' girl whole C'fedrate States America. Girls like John Cowles too much! Must mash John Cowles! Must mash John Cowles sake of Gracie Sheraton, pretties' girl in whole wide worl'!"

He came toward me as best he might, his hands clenched. I caught him by the wrist, and as he stumbled past, I turned and had his arm over my shoulder. I admit I threw him rather cruelly hard, for I thought he needed it. He was entirely quiet when we carried him into the room and placed him on the leather lounge.

"By Jove!" I heard a voice at my elbow. "That was handsomely done—handsomely done all around."

15

I turned to meet the outstretched hand of my new friend, Gordon Orme.

"Where did you learn the trick?" he asked.

"The trick of being a gentleman," I answered him slowly, my face red with anger at Singleton's foolishness, "I never learned at all. But to toss a poor drunken fool like that over one's head any boy might learn at school."

"No," said my quasi-minister of the gospel, emphatically, "I differ with you. Your time was perfect. You made him do the work, not yourself. Tell me, are you a skilled wrestler?"

I was nettled now at all these things which were coming to puzzle and perturb an honest fellow out for a morning ride.

"Yes," I answered him, "since you are anxious to know, I'll say I can throw any man in Fairfax except one."

"And he?"

"My father. He's sixty, as I told you, but he can always beat me."

"There are two in Fairfax you cannot throw," said Orme, smiling.

My blood was up just enough to resent this challenge. There came to me what old Dr. Hallowell at Alexandria calls the "*gaudium certaminis.*" In a moment I was little more than a full-blooded fighting animal, and had forgotten all the influences of my Quaker home.

"Sir," I said to him hotly, "I propose taking you home with me. But before I do that, and since you seem to wish it, I am going to lay you on your back here in the road. Frankly, there are some things about you I do not like, and if that will remedy your conceit, I'm going to do it for you—for any sort of wager you like."

16

"Money against your horse?" he inquired, stripping to his ruffled shirt as he spoke. "A hundred guineas, five hundred?"

"Yes, for the horse," I said. "He's worth ten thousand. But if you've two or three hundred to pay for my soiling the shoulders of your shirt, I'm willing to let the odds stand so."

He smiled at me simply—I swear almost winningly, such was the quality of the man.

"I like you," he said simply. "If all the men of this country resembled you, all the world could not beat it."

I was stripped by this time myself, and so, without pausing to consider the propriety on either side of our meeting in this sudden encounter in a public street, we went at it as though we had made a rendezvous there for that express purpose, with no more hesitation and no more fitness than two game cocks which might fall fighting in a church in case they met there.

Orme came to me with no hurry and no anxiety, light on his feet as a skilled fencer. As he passed he struck for my shoulder, and his grip, although it did not hold, was like the cutting of a hawk's talons. He branded me red with his fingers wherever he touched me, although the stroke of his hand was half tentative rather than aggressive. I went to him with head low, and he caught me at the back of the neck with a stroke like that of a smiting bar; but I flung him off, and so we stepped about, hands extended, waiting for a hold. He grew eager, and allowed me to catch him by the wrist. I drew him toward me, but he braced with his free arm bent against my throat, and the more I pulled, the more I choked. Then by sheer strength I drew his arm over my shoulder as I had that of Harry Singleton. He glided into this as though it had been his own purpose, and true as I speak I think he aided me in throwing him over my head, for he went light as a feather, and fell on his feet when I freed him. I was puzzled not a little, for the like of this I had not seen in all my meetings with good men.

As we stepped about cautiously, seeking to engage again, his eye was fixed on mine curiously, half contemplatively, but utterly without concern or fear of any kind. I never saw an eye like his. It gave me not fear, but horror! The more I encountered him, the more uncanny he appeared. The lock of the arm at the back of the neck, those holds known as the Nelson and the half-Nelson, and the ancient "hip lock," and the ineffectual schoolboy "grapevine"—he would none of things so crude, and slipped out of them like a snake. Continually I felt his hands, and where he touched there was pain— on my forehead, at the edge of the eye sockets, at the sides of my neck, in the middle of my back—whenever we locked and broke I felt pain, and I knew that such assault upon the nerve centers of a man's body might well disable him, no matter how strong he was. But, as for him, he did not breathe the faster. It was system with him. I say, I felt not fear only but a horror of him.

By chance I found myself with both hands on his arms, and I knew that no man could break that hold when once set, for vast strength of forearm and wrist was one of the inheritances of all men of the Cowles family. I drew him steadily to me, pulled his head against my chest, and upended him fair, throwing him this time at length across my shoulder. I was sure I had him then, for he fell on his side. But even as he fell he rose, and I felt a grip like steel on each ankle. Then there was a snake-like bend on his part, and before I had time to think I was on my face. His knees were astride my body, and gradually I felt them pushing my arms up toward my neck. I felt a slight blow on the back of my head, as though by the edge of the hand—light, delicate, gentle, but dreamy in its results. Then I was half conscious of a hand pushing down my head, of another hand reaching for my right wrist. It occurred to me in a distant way that I was about to be beaten, subdued—I, John Cowles!

This had been done, as he had said of my own work with Singleton, as much by the momentum of my own fall as by any great effort on his part. As he had said regarding my own simple trick, the time of this was perfect, though how far more difficult than mine, only those who have wrestled with able men can understand.

For the first time in my life I found myself about to be mastered by another man. Had he been more careful he certainly would have had the victory over me. But the morning was warm, and we had worked for some moments. My man stopped for a moment in his calm pinioning of my arms, and perhaps raised his hand to brush his face or push back his hair. At that moment luck came to my aid. He did not repeat the strange gentle blow at the back of my head—one which I think would have left unconscious a man with a neck less stiff—and as his pressure on my twisted arm relaxed, I suddenly got back my faculties. At once I used my whole body as a spring, and so straightened enough to turn and put my arm power against his own, which was all I wanted.

He laughed when I turned, and with perfect good nature freed my arm and sprang to his feet, bowing with hand upreached to me. His eye had lost its peculiar stare, and shone now with what seemed genuine interest and admiration. He seemed ready to call me a sportsman, and a good rival, and much as I disliked to do so, I was obliged to say as much for him in my own heart.

"By the Lord! sir," he said—with a certain looseness of speech, as it seemed to me, for a minister of the gospel to employ, "you're the first I ever knew to break it."

"'Twas no credit to me," I owned. "You let go your hand. The horse is yours."

"Not in the least," he responded, "not in the least. If I felt I had won him I'd take him, and not leave you feeling as though you had been given a present. But if you like I'll draw my own little wager as well. You're the best man I ever met in any country. By the Lord! man, you broke the hold that I once saw an ex-guardsman killed at Singapore for resisting—broke his arm short off, and he died on the table. I've seen it at Tokio and Nagasaki—why, man, it's the yellow policeman's hold, the secret trick of the Orient. Done in proper time, and the little gentleman is the match of any size, yellow or white."

I did not understand him then, but later I knew that I had for my first time seen the Oriental art of wrestling put in practice. I do not want to meet a master in it again. I shook Orme by the hand.

"If you like to call it a draw," said I, "it would suit me mighty well. You're the best man I ever took off coat to in my life. And I'll never wrestle you again unless"—I fear I blushed a little—"well, unless you want it."

"Game! Game!" he cried, laughing, and dusting off his knees. "I swear you Virginians are fellows after my own heart. But come, I think your friend wants you now."

We turned toward the room where poor Harry was mumbling to himself, and presently I loaded him into the wagon and told the negro man to drive him home.

For myself, I mounted Satan and rode off up the street of Wallingford toward Cowles' Farms with my head dropped in thought; for certainly, when I came to review the incidents of the morning, I had had enough to give me reason for reflection.

Chapter IV - Wars And Rumors Of War

We sent our carriage down to Wallingford that evening and had my new friend, Mr. Orme, out to Cowles' Farms for that night. He was a stranger in the land, and that was enough. I often think to-day how ready we were to welcome any who came, and how easily we might have been deceived as to the nature of such chance guests.

Yet Orme so finely conducted himself that none might criticise him, and indeed both my father and mother appeared fairly to form a liking for him. This was the more surprising on the part of both, since they were fully advised of the nature of his recent speech, or sermon, or what you choose to call it, at the Methodist church, the sentiments of which scarce jumped with their own. Both my parents accepted Orme for what he purported to be, a minister of the gospel; and any singularity of his conduct which they may have noticed they ascribed to his education in communities different from our own quiet one. I remember no acrimonious speech during his visit with us, although the doctrine which he had pronounced and which now and again, in one form or another, he renewed, was not in accord with ours. I recall very well the discussions they had, and remember how formally my mother would begin her little arguments: "Friend, I am moved to say to thee"; and then she would go on to tell him gently that all men should be brothers, and that there should be peace on earth, and that no man should oppress his brother in any way, and that slavery ought not to exist.

"What! madam," Orme would exclaim, "this manner of thought in a Southern family!" And so he in turn would go on repeating his old argument of geography, and saying how England must side with the South, and how the South must soon break with the North. "This man Lincoln, if elected," said he, "will confiscate every slave in the Southern States. He will cripple and ruin the South, mark my words. He will cost the South millions that never will be repaid. I cannot see how any Virginian can fail to stand with all his Southern brothers, front to front against the North on these vital questions."

"I do not think the South would fight the North over slavery alone. The South loves the flag, because she helped create it as much or more than the North. She will not bear treason to the flag." Thus my father.

"It would be no treason," affirmed Orme, "but duty, if that flag became the flag of oppression. The Anglo-Saxon has from King John down refused to be governed unjustly and oppressively."

And so they went on, hour after hour, not bitterly, but hotly, as was the fashion all over the land at that time. My father remained a Whig, which put him in line, sometimes, with the Northern men then coming into prominence, such as Morrill of New England, and young Sherman from across the mountains, who believed in the tariff in spite of what England might say to us. This set him against the Jefferson clans of our state, who feared not a war with the North so much as one with Europe. Already England was pronouncing her course; yet those were not days of triumphant conclusions, but of doubtful weighing and hard judgment, as we in old Virginia could have told you, who saw neighbors set against each other, and even families divided among themselves.

For six years the war talk had been growing stronger. Those of the South recoiled from the word treason—it had a hateful sound to them—nor have they to this day justified its application to themselves. I myself believe to-day that that war was much one of geography and of lack of transportation. Not all the common folk of the North or of the South then knew that it was never so much a war of principle, as they were taught to think, but rather a war of self-interest between two clashing commercial parties. We did not know that the unscrupulous kings of the cotton world, here and abroad, were making deliberate propaganda of secession all over the South; that secession was not a thing voluntary and spontaneous, but an idea nourished to wrong growth by a secret and shrewd commercial campaign, whose nature and extent few dreamed, either then or afterward. It was not these rich and arrogant planters of the South, even, men like our kin in the Carolinas, men like those of the Sheraton family, who were the pillars of the Confederacy, or rather, of the secession idea. Back of them, enshrouded forever in darkness—then in mystery, and now in oblivion which cannot be broken—were certain great figures of the commercial world in this land and in other lands. These made a victim of our country at that time, even as a few great commercial figures seek to do to-day, and we, poor innocent fools, flew at each other's throats, and fought, and slew, and laid waste a land, for no real principle and to no gain to ourselves. Nothing is so easy to deceive, to hoodwink, to blind and betray, as a great and innocent people that in its heart loves justice and fair play.

I fear, however, that while much of this talk was going on upon the galleries at Cowles' Farms, I myself was busier with the training of my pointer than I was with matters of politics. I was not displeased when my mother came to me presently that afternoon and suggested that we should all make a visit to Dixiana Farm, to call upon our neighbors, the Sheratons.

"Mr. Orme says he would like to meet Colonel Sheraton," she explained, "and thee knows that we have not been to see our neighbors for some time now. I thought that perhaps Colonel Sheraton might be moved to listen to me as well as to Mr. Orme, if I should speak of peace—not in argument, as thee knows, but as his neighbor."

She looked at me a moment, her hand dusting at my coat. "Thee knows the Sheratons and the Cowles have sometimes been friends and sometimes enemies—I would rather we were friends. And, Jack, Miss Grace is quite thy equal—it any may be the equal of my boy. And some day thee must be thinking, thee knows—"

"I was already thinking, mother," said I gravely; and so, indeed, I was, though perhaps not quite as she imagined.

At least that is how we happened to ride to the Sheratons that afternoon, in our greater carriage, my father and Mr. Orme by the side of my mother, and I alongside on horseback. In some way the visit seemed to have a formal nature.

Colonel Sheraton met us at his lawn, and as the day was somewhat warm, asked us to be seated in the chairs beneath the oaks. Here Miss Grace joined us presently, and Orme was presented to her, as well as to Mrs. Sheraton, tall, dark, and lace-draped, who also joined us in response to Colonel Sheraton's request. I could not fail to notice the quick glance with which Orme took in the face and figure of Grace Sheraton; and, indeed he had been a critical man who would not have called her fair to look upon.

The elder members of the party fell to conversing in their rocking-chairs there on the lawn, and I was selfish enough to withdraw Miss Grace to the gallery steps, where we sat for a time, laughing and talking, while I pulled the ears of their hunting dog, and rolled under foot a puppy or two, which were my friends. I say, none could have failed to call Grace Sheraton fair. It pleased me better to sit there on the gallery steps and talk with her than to listen once more to the arguments over slavery and secession. I could hear Colonel Sheraton's deep voice every now and then emphatically coinciding with some statement made by Orme. I could see the clean-cut features of the latter, and his gestures, strongly but not flamboyantly made.

As for us two, the language that goes without speech between a young man and a maid passed between us. I rejoiced to mock at her, always, and did so now, declaring again my purpose to treat her simply as my neighbor and not as a young lady finished at the best schools of Philadelphia. But presently in some way, I scarce can say by whose first motion, we arose and strolled together around the corner of the house and out into the orchard.

Chapter V - The Madness Of Much Kissing

"That was a very noble thing of you," Miss Grace Sheraton was saying to me, as we passed slowly among the big trees of the Sheraton apple orchard. Her eyes were rather soft and a slight color lay upon her cheeks, whose ivory hue was rarely heightened in this way.

"I am in ignorance, Miss Grace," I said to her.

"Fie! You know very well what I mean — about yesterday."

"Oh, that," said I, and went rather red of the face, for I thought she meant my salutation at the gate.

She, redder now than myself, needed no explanation as to what I meant. "No, not that," she began hastily, "that was not noble, but vile of you! I mean at the tavern, where you took my part —"

So then I saw that word in some way had come to her of the little brawl between Harry Singleton and myself. Then indeed my face grew scarlet. "It was nothing," said I, "simply nothing at all." But to this she would not listen.

"To protect an absent woman is always manly," she said. (It was the women of the South who set us all foolish about chivalry.) "I thank you for caring for my name."

Now, I should have grown warmer in the face and in the heart at this, but the very truth is that I felt a chill come over me, as though I were getting deeper into cold water. I guessed her mind. Now, how was I, who had kissed her at the lane, who had defended her when absent, who called now in state with his father and mother in the family carriage — how was I to say I was not of the same mind as she? I pulled the ears of the hunting dog until he yelped in pain.

We were deep in the great Sheraton orchard, across the fence which divided it from the house grounds, so far that only the great chimney of the house showed above the trees. The shade was gracious, the fragrance alluring. At a distance the voices of singing negroes came to us. Presently we came to a fallen apple tree, a giant perhaps planted there generations before. We seated ourselves here, and we should have been happy, for we were young, and all about us was sweet and comforting. Yet, on my honor, I would rather at that moment have been talking to my mother than to Grace Sheraton. I did not know why.

For some time we sat there, pulling at apple blossoms and grass stems, and talking of many things quite beside the real question; but at last there came an interruption. I heard the sound of a low, rumbling bellow approaching through the trees, and as I looked up I saw, coming forward with a certain confidence, Sir Jonas, the red Sheraton bull, with a ring in his nose, and in his carriage an intense haughtiness for one so young. I knew all about Sir Jonas, for we had bred him on our farm, and sold him not long since to the Sheratons.

Miss Grace gathered her skirts for instant flight, but I quickly pushed her down. I knew the nature of Sir Jonas very well, and saw that flight would mean disaster long before she could reach any place of safety.

"Keep quiet," I said to her in a low voice. "Don't make any quick motions, or he'll charge. Come with me, slowly now."

Very pale, and with eyes staring at the intruder, she arose as I bade her and slowly moved toward the tree which I had in mind. "Now— quick!" I said, and catching her beneath the arms I swung her up into the low branches. Her light lawn gown caught on a knotty limb, somewhat to her perturbation, and ere I could adjust it and get her safe aloft Sir Jonas had made up his mind. He came on with head down, in a short, savage rush, and his horn missed my trouser leg by no more than an inch as I dodged around the tree. At this I laughed, but Miss Grace screamed, until between my hasty actions I called to her to keep quiet.

Sir Jonas seemed to have forgotten my voice, and though I commanded him to be gone, he only shook his curly front and came again with head low and short legs working very fast. Once more he nearly caught me with a side lunge of his wicked horns as he whirled. He tossed up his head then and bolted for the tree where Miss Grace had her refuge. Then I saw it was the red lining of her Parisian parasol which had enraged him. "Throw it down!" I called out to her. She could not find it in her heart to toss it straight down to Sir Jonas, who would have trampled it at once, so she cast it sidelong toward me, and inch by inch I beat Sir Jonas in the race to it. Then I resolved that he should not have it at all, and so tossed it into the branches of another tree as I ran.

"Come," called the girl to me, "jump! Get up into a tree. He can't catch you there."

But I was in no mind to take to a tree, and wait for some inglorious discovery by a rescue party from the house. I found my fighting blood rising, and became of the mind to show Sir Jonas who was his master, regardless of who might be his owner.

His youth kept him in good wind still, and he charged me again and again, keeping me hard put to it to find trees enough, even in an orchard full of trees. Once he ripped the bark half off a big trunk as I sprang behind it, and he stood with his head still pressed there, not two feet from where I was, with my hand against the tree, braced for a sudden spring. His front foot dug in the sod, his eyes were red, and between his grumbles his breath came in puffs and snorts of anger. Evidently he meant me ill, and this thought offended me.

Near by me on the ground lay a ragged limb, cut from some tree by the pruners, now dry, tough and not ill-shaped for a club. I reached back with my foot and pulled it within reach, then stooped quickly and got it in hand, breaking off a few of the lesser branches with one foot, as we still stood there eying each other. "Now, sir," said I to Sir Jonas at last, "I shall show you that no little bull two years old can make me a laughing stock." Then I sprang out and carried the war into Africa forthwith.

Sir Jonas was surprised when I came from behind the tree and swung a hard blow to the side of his tender nose; and as I repeated this, he grunted, blew out his breath and turned his head to one side with closed eyes, raising his muzzle aloft in pain. Once more I struck him fair on the muzzle, and this time he bawled loudly in surprise and anguish, and so turned to run. This act of his offered me fair hold upon his tail, and so affixed to him, I followed smiting him upon the back with blows which I think cut through his hide where the pointed knots struck. Thus with loud orders and with a voice which he ought better to have remembered, I brought him to his senses and pursued him entirely out of the orchard, so that he had no mind whatever to return. After which, with what dignity I could summon, I returned to the tree where Grace Sheraton was still perched aloft. Drawing my riding gloves from my pocket I reached up my hands, somewhat soiled with the encounter, and so helped her down to earth once more. And once more her gaze, soft and not easily to be mistaken, rested upon me.

"Tell me, Jack Cowles," she said, "is there anything in the world you are afraid to do?"

"At least I'm not afraid to give a lesson to any little Sir Jonas that has forgot his manners," I replied. "But I hope you are not hurt in any way?" She shook her head, smoothing out her gown, and again raised her eyes to mine.

We seated ourselves again upon our fallen apple tree. Her hand fell upon my coat sleeve. We raised our eyes. They met. Our lips met also—I do not know how.

I do not hold myself either guilty or guiltless. I am only a man now. I was only a boy then. But even then I had my notions, right or wrong, as to what a gentleman should be and do. At least this is how Grace Sheraton and I became engaged.

Chapter VI - A Sad Lover

I shall never forget the scene there under the oak of the Sheraton front yard, which met my gaze when Miss Grace and I came about the corner of the house.

Before us, and facing each other, stood my father and Colonel Sheraton, the former standing straight and tall, Colonel Sheraton with tightly clenched hand resting on his stick, his white hair thrown back, his shaggy brows contracted. My mother sat in the low rocker which had been brought to her, and opposite her, leaning forward, was Mrs. Sheraton, tall, thin, her black eyes fixed upon the men. Orme, also standing, his hands behind him, regarded the troubled men intently. Near at hand was the Sheratons' Jim, his face also fixed upon them; and such was his own emotion that he had tipped his silver tray and dropped one of the Sheraton cut glass julep glasses to the sod.

It was mid-afternoon, or evening, as we call it in Virginia, and the light was still frank and strong, though the wind was softening among the great oaks, and the flowers were sweet all about. It was a scene of peace; but it was not peace which occupied those who made its central figures.

"I tell you, Cowles," said Colonel Sheraton, grinding his stick into the turf, "you do not talk like a Virginian. If the North keeps on this course, then we Southerners must start a country of our own. Look, man—" He swept about him an arm which included his own wide acres and ours, lying there shimmering clear to the thin line of the old Blue Ridge—"We must fight for these homes!"

My mother stirred in her chair, but she made no speech, only looked at my father.

"You forget, Colonel," said my father in his low, deep voice, "that this man Lincoln has not yet been elected, and that even if elected he may prove a greater figure than we think. He has not yet had chance to learn the South."

Orme had been standing silent, his face indifferent or faintly lighted with an habitual cynicism. Now he broke in. "He will never be elected," he said emphatically. "It would ruin the entire industry of the South. I tell you Lincoln is thinking of his own political advancement and caring nothing for this country. The South *must* secede, gentlemen—if you will allow me as a stranger to venture an opinion."

My mother turned her gaze to him, but it was Sheraton who spoke.

"It goes back to the old Articles of Federation, our first compact," he said. "From the very first the makers of this country saw that by reason of diverse industries the South was separated from the North. This secession has been written in the sky from the beginning of the world."

"Nay, brother Sheraton," broke in my mother eagerly "it was the union of brothership that was written first in the sky."

He turned to her with the bow of a gentleman. "It is you ladies who knit the world together with kindness," he said. "Alas, that men must rend it with fighting."

"Alas!" whispered she.

Sheraton's own face was sad as he went on with the old justification. "Jefferson would turn over in his grave if he saw Virginia divided as it is. Why, Cowles, we've all the world we need here. We can live alone here, each on his own acres, a gentleman, and all he needs of government is protection and fair laws. Calhoun was right. Better give us two peaceful countries, each living happily and content, than one at war with itself. Clay was a great man, but both he and Webster were fighting against the inevitable."

"That is true," interrupted Orme; "unquestionably true. Texas came near becoming a colony of England because this country would not take her. She declared for slavery, and had that right. The Spaniards had made California a slave state, but the gold seekers by vote declared her free. They had that right to govern themselves. As to the new lands coming in, it is their right also to vote upon the question of slavery, each new state for itself."

"The war has already begun on the border," said my father. "My friend and partner, Colonel Meriwether of Albemarle, who is with the Army in the West, says that white men are killing white men all across the lands west of the Missouri."

"At least, Cowles," said Colonel Sheraton, pacing a short way apart, his hands behind his back, "we can wait until after this election."

"But if the Government takes action?" suggested Orme.

Sheraton whirled quickly, "Then war! war!" he cried, "War till each Virginian is dead on his doorstep, and each woman starved at her fireside. John Cowles, you and I will fight—I *know* that you will fight."

"Yes," said my father, "I will fight."

"And with us!"

"No," said my father, sighing; "no, my friend, against you!" I saw my mother look at him and sink back in her chair. I saw Orme also gaze at him sharply, with a peculiar look upon his face.

But so, at least, this argument ended for the time. The two men, old neighbors, took each other solemnly by the hand, and presently, after talk of more pleasant sort on lesser matters, the servants brought our carriage and we started back for Cowles' Farms.

There had been no opportunity for me to mention to Colonel and Mrs. Sheraton something that was upon my mind. I had small chance for farewell to Miss Grace, and if I shall admit the truth, this pleased me quite as well as not.

We rode in silence for a time, my father musing, my mother silent also. It was Orme who was the first I heard to speak.

"By the way, Mr. Cowles," he said, "you spoke of Colonel Meriwether of Albemarle County. Is he away in the West? It chances that I have letters to him, and I was purposing going into that country before long."

"Indeed, sir?" replied my father. "I am delighted to know that you are to meet my friend. As it chances, he is my associate in a considerable business enterprise—a splendid man, a splendid man, Meriwether. I will, if you do not mind, add my letter to others you may have, and I trust you will carry him our best wishes from this side of the mountains."

That was like my father—innocent, unsuspicious, ever ready to accept other men as worthy of his trust, and ever ready to help a stranger as he might. For myself, I confess I was more suspicious. Something about Orme set me on edge, I knew not what. I heard them speaking further about Meriwether's being somewhere in the West, and heard Orme also say carelessly that he must in any case run over to Albemarle and call upon some men whom he was to meet at the University of Virginia. We did not ask his errand, and none of us suspected the purpose of his systematic visiting among the more influential centers of that country. But if you will go now to that white-domed building planned by Thomas Jefferson at Charlottesville, and read the names on the brazen tablets by the doors, names of boys who left school there to enter a harder school, then you will see the results of the visit there of Gordon Orme.

My little personal affairs were at that time so close to me that they obscured clear vision of larger ones. I did not hear all the talk in the carriage, but pulled my horse in behind and so rode on moodily, gazing out across the pleasant lands to the foot of old Catoctin and the dim Blue Ridge. A sudden discontent assailed me. Must I live here always—must I settle down and be simply a farmer forever? I wanted to ride over there, over the Rock Fish Gap, where once King Charles' men broke a bottle in honor of the king, and took possession of all the lands west of the Pacific. The West—the word in some way thrilled in my blood—I knew not why. I was a boy. I had not learned to question any emotion, and introspection troubled me no more than it did my pointer dog.

Before we had separated at the door of our house, I motioned to my mother, and we drew apart and seated ourselves beneath our own oaks in the front yard of Cowles' Farms. Then I told her what had happened between Miss Grace and myself, and asked her if she was pleased.

"I am very content with thee," she answered, slowly, musingly. "Thee must think of settling, Jack, and Miss Grace is a worthy girl. I hope it will bring peace between our families always." I saw a film cross her clear, dark eye. "Peace!" she whispered to herself. "I wish that it might be."

But peace was not in my heart. Leaving her presently, I once more swung leg over saddle and rode off across our fields, as sad a lover as ever closed the first day of his engagement to be wed.

Chapter VII - What Cometh In The Night

When I rode up our lane in the dusk, I found my father and mother sitting in the cool of the front gallery, and giving my rein to one of our boys, I flung myself down on the steps near by, and now and again joined in their conversation.

I was much surprised to learn that our whilom guest, Gordon Orme, had taken sudden departure during my absence, he having been summoned by a messenger from the village, who he stated brought him word that he must forthwith be on his way to Albemarle. He had asked my father if he cared to sell the black horse, Satan, to which he had taken a fancy, but this had been declined. Then it seems there had come up something of our late meeting at the village, and Orme, laughing, had told of our horse breaking and wrestling in a way which it seemed had not detracted from my standing in my parents' eyes. None of us three was willing to criticise our guest, yet I doubt if any one of us failed to entertain a certain wonder, not to say suspicion, regarding him. At least he was gone.

Our talk now gradually resolved itself to one on business matters. I ought to have said that my father was an ambitious man and one of wide plans. I think that even then he foresaw the day when the half-patriarchial life of our State would pass away before one of wider horizons of commercial sort. He was anxious to hand down his family fortune much increased, and foreseeing troublous times ahead as to the institution of slavery in the South, he had of late been taking large risks to assure success in spite of any change of times. Now, moved by some strange reasons which he himself perhaps did not recognize, he began for the first time, contrary to his usual reticence, to explain to my mother and me something of these matters. He told us that in connection with his friend, Colonel William Meriwether, of Albemarle, he had invested heavily in coal lands in the western part of the State, in what is now West Virginia. This requiring very large sums of money, he for his part had encumbered not only the lands themselves, but these lands of

Cowles' Farms to secure the payment. The holder of these mortgages was a banking firm in Fredericksburg. The interest was one which in these times would be considered a cruel one, and indeed the whole enterprise was one which required a sanguine courage, precisely as his; for I have said that risk he always held as challenge and invitation.

"Does thee think that in these times thee should go so deeply in debt," asked my mother of him.

"Elizabeth," he said, "that is why I have gone in debt. Two years from now, and the value of these lands here may have been cut in half. Ten years from now the coal lands yonder will be worth ten times what they are to-day."

"John," she said to him suddenly, "sell those coal lands, or a part of them."

"Now, that I could not do," he answered, "for half their value. The country now is fuller of war than of investment. But come peace, come war, there lies a fortune for us all. For my share there remains but one heavy payment; and to-morrow I ride to raise funds for that among our tenants and elsewhere. I admit that my bankers are shrewd and severe—in fact, I think they would rather see the payments forfeited than not. As Meriwether is away, it is with me to attend to this business now."

And so, with this prelude, I may as well tell without more delay what evil fortune was in store for us.

That coming day my father rode abroad as he had planned, taking black Satan for his mount, since he needed to travel far. He had collected from various sources, as his account book later showed, a sum of over five thousand dollars, which he must have had in gold and negotiable papers in his saddle-bags. During his return home, he came down the deep trough road which ran in front of the Sheraton farms and ours. He passed near to a certain clump of bushes at the roadside. And there that happened which brought to a sudden end all the peace and comfort of our lives, and which made me old before my time.

I heard the horse Satan whinny at our lane gate, wildly, as though in fright; and even as I went out my heart stopped with sudden fear. He had leaped the gate at the lower end of the lane. His bridle rein was broken, and caught at his feet as he moved about, throwing up his head in fright as much as viciousness. I hastily looked at the saddle, but it bore no mark of anything unusual. Not pausing to look farther, I caught the broken reins in my hand, and sprung into the saddle, spurring the horse down the lane and over the gate again, and back up the road which I knew my father must have taken.

There, at the side of the road, near the clump of blackberry vines and sumac growth, lay my father, a long dark blot, motionless, awesome, as I could see by the light of the moon, now just rising in a gap of the distant mountains. I sprang down and ran to him, lifted his head, called to him in a voice so hoarse I did not recognize it. I told him that it was his son had come to him, and that he must speak. So at last, as though by sheer will he had held on to this time, he turned his gray face toward me, and as a dead man, spoke.

"Tell your mother," he said; "Tell Meriwether—must protect—good-by."

Then he said "Lizzie!" and opened wide his arms.

Presently he said, "Jack, lay my head down, please." I did so. He was dead, there in the moon.

I straightened him, and put my coat across his face, and spurred back down the road again and over the gate. But my mother already knew. She met me at the hall, and her face was white.

"Jack," she said, "I know!"

Then the servants came, and we brought him home, and laid him in his own great room, as the master of the house should lie when the end comes, and arrayed him like the gentleman he was.

Now came that old wire-hair, Doctor Bond, his mane standing stiff and gray over a gray face, down which tears rolled the first time known of any man. He sent my mother away and called me to him. And then he told me that in my father's back were three or four pierced wounds, no doubt received from the sharp stubs of underbrushes when he fell. But this, he said, could hardly have been the cause of death. He admitted that the matter seemed mysterious to him.

Up to this time we had not thought of the cause of this disaster, nor pondered upon motives, were it worse than accident. Now we began to think. Doctor Bond felt in the pockets of my father's coat; and so for the first time we found his account book and his wallets. Doctor Bond and I at once went out and searched the saddle pockets my father had carried. They were quite empty.

All this, of course, proved nothing to us. The most that we could argue was that the horse in some way had thrown his rider, and that the fall had proved fatal; and that perhaps some wandering negro had committed the theft. These conclusions were the next day bad for the horse Satan, whom I whipped and spurred, and rode till he trembled, meting out to him what had been given old Klingwalla, his sire, for another murdering deed like this. In my brutal rage I hated all the world. Like the savage I was, I must be avenged on something. I could not believe that my father was gone, the man who had been my model, my friend, my companion all my life.

But in time we laid him away in the sunny little graveyard of the Society of Friends, back of the little stone church at Wallingford. We put a small, narrow, rough little slab of sandstone at his head, and cut into it his name and the dates of his birth and death; this being all that the simple manners of the Society of Friends thought fit. "His temple is in my heart," said my mother; and from that day to her death she offered tribute to him.

Thus, I say, it was that I changed from a boy into a man. But not the man my father had been. Life and business matters had hitherto been much a sealed book for me. I was seized of consternation when a man came riding over from the little Wallingford bank, asking attention to word from Abrams & Halliday, bankers of Fredericksburg. I understood vaguely of notes overdue, and somewhat of mortgages on our lands, our house, our crops. I explained our present troubles and confusion; but the messenger shook his head with a coldness on his face I had not been accustomed to see worn by any at Cowles' Farms. Sweat stood on my face when I saw that we owed over fifteen thousand dollars—a large sum in those simple days—and that more would presently follow, remainder of a purchase price of over a hundred thousand dollars for lands I had never seen. I looked about me at the great house of Cowles' Farms, and a coldness came upon my heart as I realized for the first time that perhaps this home was not ours, but another's. Anger again possessed me at this thought, and with small adieu I ordered the man from the place, and told him I would horsewhip him if he lingered but a moment. Then, too late, I thought of more business-like action, and of following the advice my father had given me, at once to see his associate, Colonel Meriwether. Thereafter I consulted my mother.

In the chaotic state of affairs then existing, with the excitement of a turbulent election approaching, it may be supposed that all commercial matters were much unsettled. None knew what might be the condition of the country after the fall elections; but all agreed that now was no time to advance money upon any sort of credit. As to further pledges, with a view to raising these sums now due, I found the matter hopeless.

Colonel Sheraton might, perhaps, have aided us, but him I would not ask. Before this time I had acquainted him of my intentions in regard to his daughter; and now I went to him and placed the matter before him, explaining to him the nature of our affairs and announcing my intention to make a quick journey to the West, in order to obtain assistance from Colonel Meriwether, of whom I hoped to find instant solution of the financial problems, at least. It seemed wise for me to place before Miss Grace's father the question of advisability of allowing her to remain pledged to a man whose fortunes were in so sad a state. I asked him what was right for me to do. His face was very grave as he pondered, but he said, "If my girl's word has been passed, we will wait. We will wait, sir." And that was all I knew when I made my hurried preparations for the longest journey I had at that time ever known.

Chapter VIII - Beginning Adventures In New Lands

In those days travel was not so easy as it is now. I went by carriage to Washington, and thence by stage to the village of York in Pennsylvania, and again by stage thence to Carlisle Barracks, a good road offering thence into the western countries. In spite of all my grief I was a young man, and I was conscious of a keen exhilaration in these my earliest travels. I was to go toward that great West, which then was on the tongue of all the South, and indeed all the East. I found Pennsylvania old for a hundred years. The men of Western Pennsylvania, Ohio and New York were passing westward in swarms like feeding pigeons. Illinois and Iowa were filling up, and men from Kentucky were passing north across the Ohio. The great rivers of the West were then leading out their thousands of settlers. Presently I was to see those great trains of white-topped west-bound wagons which at that time made a distinguishing feature of American life.

At this Army post, which then was used as a drilling ground for the cavalry arm, one caught the full flavor of the Western lands, heard the talk of officers who had been beyond the frontier, and saw troops passing out for the Western service. Here I heard also, and to my consternation, quiet conversation among some of the officers, regarding affairs at our National capital. Buchanan, it seems, was shipping arms and ordnance and supplies to all the posts in the South. Disaffection, fomented by some secret, unknown cause, was spreading among the officers of the Army. I was young; this was my first journey; yet none the less these matters left my mind uneasy. I was eager to be back in Virginia, for by every sign and token there certainly was trouble ahead for all who dwelt near the Potomac.

Next I went on to Harrisburg, and thence took rail up the beautiful Susquehanna valley, deep into and over the mountains. At Pittsburg I, poor provincial, learned that all this country too was very old, and that adventures must be sought more than a thousand miles to the westward, yet a continual stir and bustle existed at this river point. A great military party was embarking here for the West—two companies of dragoons, their officers and mounts. I managed to get passage on this boat to Louisville, and thence to the city of St. Louis. Thus, finally, we pushed in at the vast busy levee of this western military capital.

At that time Jefferson Barracks made the central depot of Army operations in the West. Here recruits and supplies were received and readjusted to the needs of the scattered outposts in the Indian lands. Still I was not in the West, for St. Louis also was old, almost as old as our pleasant valley back in Virginia. I heard of lands still more remote, a thousand miles still to the West, heard of great rivers leading to the mountains, and of the vast, mysterious plains, of which even yet men spoke in awe. Shall I admit it—in spite of grief and trouble, my heart leaped at these thoughts. I wished nothing so much as that I might properly and fitly join this eager, hurrying, keen-faced throng of the west-bound Americans. It seemed to me I heard the voice of youth and life beyond, and that youth was blotted out behind me in the blue Virginia hills.

I inquired for Colonel Meriwether about my hotel in the city, but was unable to get definite word regarding his whereabouts, although the impression was that he was somewhere in the farther West. This made it necessary for me to ride at once to Jefferson Barracks. I had at least one acquaintance there, Captain Martin Stevenson of the Sixth Cavalry, a Maryland man whom we formerly met frequently when he was paying suit to Kitty Dillingham, of the Shenandoah country. After their marriage they had been stationed practically all of the time in Western posts.

I made my compliments at Number 16 of Officers' Row, their present quarters at Jefferson. I found Kitty quite as she had been in her youth at home, as careless and wild, as disorderly and as full of good-heartedness. Even my story, sad as it was, failed to trouble her long, and as was her fashion, she set about comforting me, upon her usual principle that, whatever threatened, it were best be blithe to-day.

"Come," she said, "we'll put you up with us, right here. Johnson, take Mr. Cowles' things; and go down to the city at once for his bags."

"But, my dear Mrs. Kitty," I protested, "I can't. I really must be getting on. I'm here on business with Colonel Meriwether."

"Never mind about Colonel Meriwether," rejoined my hostess, "we'll find him later—he's up the river somewhere. Always take care of the important things first. The most important thing in the whole world just now is the officers' ball to-night. Don't you see them fixing up the dancing platform on Parade? It's just as well the K.O.'s away, because to-night the mice certainly are going to play."

It seemed good to hear the voice of friends again, and I was nothing loath to put aside business matters for the time and listen to Kitty Stevenson's chatter. So, while I hesitated, Johnson had my hat and stick.

The city of St. Louis, I repeat, was then the richest and gayest capital of the West, the center of the commercial and social life of West and South alike. Some of the most beautiful women of the world dwelt there, and never, I imagine, had belles bolder suitors than these who passed through or tarried with the Army. What wonder the saying that no Army man ever passed St. Louis without leaving a heart, or taking one with him? What wonder that these gay young beauties emptied many an Army pocket for flowers and gems, and only filled many an Army heart with despondency in return? Sackcloth lay beyond, on the frontier. Ball followed ball, one packed reception another. Dinings and sendings of flowers, and evening love-makings—these for the time seemed the main business of Jefferson Barracks. Social exemptions are always made for Army men, ever more gallant than affluent, and St. Louis entertained these gentlemen mightily with no expectation of equivalent; yet occasionally the sons of Mars gave return entertainments to the limits, or more than the limits, of their purses. The officers' balls at these barracks were the envy of all the Army; and I doubt if any regimental bands in the service had reason for more proficiency in waltz time.

Of some of these things my hostess advised me as we sat, for the sake of the shade, on the gallery of Number 16, where Stevenson's man of all work had brought a glass-topped table and some glasses. Here Captain Stevenson presently joined us, and after that escape was impossible.

"Do you suppose Mr. Cowles is engaged?" asked Kitty of her husband impersonally, and apropos of nothing that I could see.

"I don't think so. He looks too deuced comfortable," drawled Stevenson. I smiled.

"If he isn't engaged he will be before morning," remarked Kitty, smiling at me.

"Indeed, and to whom, pray?" I inquired.

"How should I know? Indeed, how should you know? Any one of a dozen—first one you see—first one who sees you; because you are tall, and can dance."

"I hardly think I should dance."

"Of course you will dance. If you refuse you will be put in irons and taken out to-morrow and shot. It will do you no good to sit and think, poor boy."

"I have no clothes," I protested.

"Johnson will have your boxes out in time. But you don't want your own clothes. This is *bal masque*, of course, and you want some sort of disguise, I think you'd look well in one of Matt's uniforms."

"That's so," said Stevenson, "we're about of a size. Good disguise, too, especially since you've never been here. They'll wonder who the new officer is, and where he comes from. I say, Kitty, what an awfully good joke it would be to put him up against two or three of those heartless flirts you call your friends—Ellen, for instance."

"There won't be a button left on the uniform by morning," said Kitty contemplatively. "To-night the Army entertains."

"And conquers," I suggested.

"Sometimes. But at the officers' ball it mostly surrenders. The casualty list, after one of these balls, is something awful. After all, Jack, all these modern improvements in arms have not superceded the old bow and arrow." She smiled at me with white teeth and lazy eyes. A handsome woman, Kitty.

"And who is that dangerous flirt you were talking about a moment ago?" I asked her, interested in spite of myself.

"I lose my mess number if I dare to tell. Oh, they'll all be here to-night, both Army and civilians. There's Sadie Galloway of the Eighth, and Toodie Devlin of Kentucky, and the Evans girl from up North, and Mrs. Willie Weiland—"

"And Mrs. Matthew Stevenson."

"Yes, myself, of course; and then besides, Ellen."

"Ellen who?"

"Never mind. She is the most dangerous creature now at large in the Western country. Avoid her! Pass not by her! She stalketh by night. She'll get you sure, my son. She has a string of hearts at her will as long as from here to the red barn."

"I shall dance to-night," I said. "If you please, I will dance with her, the first waltz."

"Yes?" She raised her eyebrows. "You've a nice conceit, at least. But, then, I don't like modest men."

"Listen to that," chuckled Stevenson, "and yet she married me! But what she says is true, Cowles. It will be worse than Chapultepec in the crowd anywhere around Ellen to-night. You might lose a leg or an arm in the crush, and if you got through, you'd only lose your heart. Better leave her alone."

"Lord, what a night it'll be for the ball," said Kitty, sweeping an idle arm toward Parade, which was now filling up with strings of carriages from the city. We could see men now putting down the dancing floor. The sun was sinking. From somewhere came the faint sound of band music, muffled behind the buildings.

"Evening gun!" said Stevenson presently, and we arose and saluted as the jet of smoke burst from a field piece and the roar of the report brought the flag fluttering down. Then came strains of a regimental band, breaking out into the national air; after which the music slid into a hurrying medley, and presently closed in the sweet refrain of "Robin Adair," crooning in brass and reeds as though miles away. Twilight began to fall, and the lamps winked out here and there. The sound of wheels and hoofs upon the gravel came more often. Here and there a bird twittered gently in the trees along the walks; and after a time music came again and again, for four bands now were stationed at the four corners of the Parade. (And always the music began of war and deeds, and always it ended in some soft love strain.) Groups gathered now upon the balconies near the marquees which rose upon the Parade. Couples strolled arm in arm. The scene spoke little enough of war's alarms or of life's battles and its sadness.

A carriage passed with two gentlemen, and drew up at the Officers' Club. "Billy Williams, adjutant," commented Captain Stevenson lazily. "Who's the other?"

"Yes, who's the tall one?" asked Kitty, as the gentlemen descended from the carriage. "Good figure, anyhow; wonder if he dances."

"Coming over, I believe," said Stevenson, for now the two turned our way. Stevenson rose to greet his fellow officer, and as the latter approached our stoop, I caught a glance at his companion.

It was Gordon Orme!

Orme was as much surprised on his own part. After the presentations all around he turned to me with Kitty Stevenson. "My dear Madam," he said, "you have given me the great pleasure of meeting again my shadow, Mr. Cowles, of Virginia. There is where I supposed him now, back home in Virginia."

"I should expect to meet Mr. Orme if I landed on the moon," I replied.

"Er—Captain Orme," murmured Adjutant Williams to me gently.

So then my preacher had turned captain since I saw him last!

"You see, Stevenson," went on Williams easily, "Captain Orme was formerly with the British Army. He is traveling in this country for a little sport, but the old ways hang to him. He brings letters to our Colonel, who's off up river, and meantime. I'm trying to show him what I can of our service."

"So good of you to bring Captain Orme here, Major. I'm sure he will join us to-night?" Kitty motioned toward the dancing pavilion, now well under way. Orme smiled and bowed, and declared himself most happy. Thus in a few moments he was of our party. I could not avoid the feeling that it was some strange fate which continually brought us two together.

"The Army's rotten for want of service," grumbled Williams, following out his own pet hobby. "Nothing in the world to do for our fellows here. Sport? Why, Captain Orme, we couldn't show you a horse race where I'd advise you to bet a dollar. The fishing doesn't carry, and the shooting is pretty much gone, even if it were the season. Outside of a pigeon match or so, this Post is stagnant. We dance, and that's all. Bah!"

"Why, Major, you old ingrate," reproved Kitty Stevenson. "If you talk that way we'll not let you on the floor to-night."

"You spoke of pigeon shooting," said Orme lazily, "Blue rocks, I imagine?"

"No," said Williams, "Natives—we use the wild birds. Thousands of them around here, you know. Ever do anything at it?"

"Not in this country," replied Orme. "Sometimes I have taken on a match at Hurlingham; and we found the Egyptian pigeons around Cairo not bad."

"Would you like to have a little match at our birds?"

"I shouldn't mind."

"Oh, you'll be welcome! We'll take your money away from you. There is Bardine—or say, Major Westover. Haskins of the Sixth got eighty-five out of his last hundred. Once he made it ninety-two, but that's above average, of course."

"You interest me," said Orme, still lazily. "For the honor of my country I shouldn't mind a go with one of your gentlemen. Make it at a hundred, for what wagers you like."

"And when?"

"To-morrow afternoon, if you say; I'm not stopping long, I am afraid. I'm off up river soon."

"Let's see," mused Williams. "Haskins is away, and I doubt if Westover could come, for he's Officer of the Day, also bottle-washer. And—"

"How about my friend Mr. Cowles?" asked Orme. "My acquaintance with him makes me think he'd take on any sort of sporting proposition. Do you shoot, sir?"

"All Virginians do," I answered. And so I did in the field, although I had never shot or seen a pigeon match in all my life.

"Precisely. Mrs. Stevenson, will you allow this sort of talk?"

"Go on, go on," said Kitty. "I'll have something up myself on Mr. Cowles." ("Don't let him scare you, Jack," she whispered to me aside.)

That was a foolish speech of hers, and a foolish act of mine. But for my part, I continually found myself doing things I should not do.

Orme passed his cigarette case. "In view of my possibly greater experience," he said, "I'd allow Mr. Cowles six in the hundred."

"I am not looking for matches," said I, my blood kindling at his accustomed insolence; "but if I shot it would be both men at scratch."

"Oh, very well," smiled Orme. "And should we make a little wager about it—I ask your consent, Mrs. Stevenson?"

"America forever!" said Kitty.

What could I do after that? But all at once I thought of my scanty purse and of the many troubles that beset me, and the strange unfitness in one of my present situation engaging in any such talk. In spite of that, my stubborn blood had its way as usual.

"My war chest is light," I answered, "as I am farther away from home than I had planned. But you know my black horse, Mr. Orme, that you fancied?"

"Oh, by Jove! I'll stake you anything you like against him—a thousand pounds, if you like."

"The odds must be even," I said, "and the only question is as to the worth of the horse. That you may not think I overvalue him, however, make it half that sum, or less, if these gentlemen think the horse has not that value."

"A son of old Klingwalla is worth three times that," insisted Orme. "If you don't mind, and care to close it, we'll shoot to-morrow, if Major Williams will arrange it."

"Certainly," said that gentleman.

"Very well," I said.

"And we will be so discourteous to the stranger within our gates," said the vivacious Kitty, "as to give you a jolly good beating, Captain Orme. We'll turn out the Post to see the match. But now we must be making ready for the serious matters of the evening. Mr. Orme, you dance, of course. Are you a married man—but what a question for me to ask—of course you're not!"

Orme smiled, showing his long, narrow teeth. "I've been a bit busy for that," he said; "but perhaps my time has come."

"It surely has," said Kitty Stevenson. "I've offered to wager Mr. Cowles anything he liked that he'd be engaged before twelve o'clock. Look, isn't it nicely done?"

We now turned toward the big square of the Parade, which had by this time wholly been taken over for the purposes of military occupation. A vast canopy covered the dancing floor. Innumerable tents for refreshments and wide flapped marquees with chairs were springing up, men were placing the decorations of flags, and roping about the dancing floor with braided ribbons and post rosettes. Throngs now filled the open spaces, and more carriages continually came. The quarters of every officer by this time were packed, and a babel of chatter came from every balcony party. Now and again breathed the soft music from the distant military bands. It was a gay scene, one for youth and life, and not for melancholy.

"Now, I wonder who is this Ellen?" mused I to myself.

Gordon Orme Laughs At Ellen's Accusation Of His Treachery

Chapter IX - The Girl With The Heart

Captain Stevenson left us soon after dinner, he being one of the officers' committee on preparations for the ball, so that I spent a little time alone at his quarters, Orme and Major Williams having gone over to the Officers' Club at the conclusion of their call. I was aroused from the brown study into which I had fallen by the sound of a loud voice at the rear of Number 16, and presently heard also Kitty's summons for me to come. I found her undertaking to remove from the hands of Annie, her ponderous black cook, a musket which the latter was attempting to rest over the window sill of the kitchen.

"Thar he goes now, the brack rascal!" cried Annie, down whose sable countenance large tears were coursing. "Lemme get one good shot at him. I can shore hit him that clost."

"Be silent! Annie," commanded Kitty, "and give me this gun. If I hear of your shooting at Benjie any more I'll certainly discharge you.

"You see," explained Kitty to me, "Annie used to be married to Benjie Martin, who works for Colonel Meriwether, at the house just beyond the trees there."

"I'se married to him *yit*," said Annie, between sobs. "Heap more'n that taller-faced yaller girl he done taken up with now."

"I think myself," said Kitty, judicially, "that Benjie might at least bow to his former wife when he passes by."

"That'd be all I *wanted*," said Annie; "but I kaint stand them horty ways. Why, I mended the very shirt he's got on his back right now; and I *bought* them shoes fer him."

"Annie's *such* a poor shot!" explained Kitty. "She has taken a pot-shot at Benjie I don't know how many times, but she always misses. Colonel Meriwether sent a file down to see what was going on, the first time, but when I explained it was my cook, he said it was all right, and that if she missed Benjie it harmed no one, and if she happened to kill him it would be only what he deserved. Annie's the best cook in the Army, and the Colonel knows it. Aren't you, Annie?"

"Ef I could only shoot as good as I ken cook," remarked Annie, "it would be a powerful sight o' res' to my soul. I shorely will git that nigger yet."

"Of course you will," said Kitty. "Just wait till to-morrow morning, Annie, and when he starts around in the yard, you take a rest over the window sill. You see," she resumed to me, "we try to do everything in the world to keep our servants happy and comfortable, Mr. Cowles.

"But now, as to you, sir, it is time you were getting ready for the serious business of the evening. Go into Matt's room, there, and Johnson will bring you your disguise."

So finally I got into Captain Stevenson's uniform, which I did not dislike, although the coat was a trifle tight across the back. At the domino mask they fetched I hesitated, for anything like mummery of this sort was always repugnant to me. Not to comply with the order of the day, however, would now have made me seem rather churlish, so presently, although with mental reservations, I placed myself in the hands of my hostess, who joined me in full ball costume, mask and all.

"You may know me," said Kitty, "by the pink flowers on my gown. They're printed on the silk, I suspect. When Matt and I are a major, we'll have them hand embroidered; but a captain's pay day doesn't come half often enough for real hand embroidery."

"I should know you anywhere, Mrs. Kitty," I said. "But now as to this Ellen? How shall I know *her*?"

"You will not know her at all."

"Couldn't you tell me something of how she will look?"

"No, I've not the slightest idea. Ellen doesn't repeat herself. There'll be a row of a dozen beauties, the most dangerous girls in all St. Louis. You shall meet them all, and have your guess as to which is Ellen."

"And shall I never know, in all the world?"

"Never in all the world. But grieve not. To-night joy is to be unconfined, and there is no to-morrow."

"And one may make mad love to any?"

"To any whom one madly loves, of course; not to twelve at once. But we must go. See, isn't it fine?"

Indeed the scene on Parade was now gayer than ever. Laughter and chatter came from the crowded galleries all about the square, whose houses seemed literally full to overflowing. Music mingled with the sound of merry voices, and forsooth now and again we heard the faint popping of corks along Officers' Row. The Army entertained.

At once, from somewhere on Parade, there came the clear note of a bugle, which seemed to draw the attention of all. We could see, ascending the great flagstaff at the end of its halyard, the broad folds of the flag. Following this was hoisted a hoop or rim of torches, which paused in such position that the folds of the flag were well illuminated. A moment of silence came at that, and then a clapping of hands from all about the Parade as the banner floated out, and the voices of men, deep throated, greeting the flag. Again the bands broke into the strains of the national anthem; but immediately they swung into a rollicking cavalry air. As they played, all four of the bands marched toward the center of the Parade, and halted at the dancing pavilion, where the lighter instruments selected for the orchestra took their places at the head of the floor.

The throngs at the galleries began to lessen, and from every available roof of the Post there poured out incredible numbers of gayly-dressed ladies and men in uniform or evening garb, each one masked, and all given over fully to the spirit of the hour.

"To-night," said Kitty to me, "one may be faithless, and be shriven by the morning sun. Isn't it funny how these things go? Such a lot of fuss is made in the world by ignoring the great fact that man is by nature both gregarious and polygamous. Believe me, there is much in this doctrine of the Mormons, out there in the West!"

"Yes, look at Benjie, for instance," I answered. "It is the spell of new faces."

"You see a face on the street, in the church, passing you, to be gone the next instant forever," she mused. "Once I did myself. I was mad to follow the man. I saw him again, and was yet madder. I saw him yet again, and made love to him madly, and then—"

"You married him," said I, knowing perfectly well the devotion of these two.

"Yes," said Mrs. Kitty, sighing contentedly, "it was Matt, of course. There's something in that 'Whom God hath joined together.' But it ought to be God, and not man, that does the joining."

"Suppose we talk philosophy rather than dance."

"Not I! We are here to-night to be young. After all, Jack, you are young, and so is—"

"Ellen?"

"Yes, and so is Ellen."

The floor now was beginning to fill with dancers. There moved before us a kaleidoscope of gay colors, over which breathed the fragrance of soft music. A subtle charm emanated from these surroundings. Music, the sight and odor of sweet flowers, the sound of pleasant waters, the presence of things beautiful — these have ever had their effect on me. So now I felt come upon me a sort of soft content, and I was no longer moved to talk philosophy.

Sighing, I said to myself that I was young. I turned to speak to my hostess, but she was gone on business of her own. So there I stood for half an hour, biting my thumb. I had as yet seen nothing of the mysterious Ellen, although many a score of eyes, in license of the carnival, had flashed through their masks at me, and many others as their owners passed by in the dance or promenade near where I stood. Presently I felt a tug at my sleeve.

"Come with me," whispered a voice.

It was Kitty. We passed to the opposite side of the dancing floor, and halted at the front of a wide marquee, whose flaps were spread to cover a long row of seats.

"Count them," whispered Kitty hoarsely. "There are twelve!"

And so indeed there were, twelve beautiful young girls, as one might pronounce, even though all were masked with half-face dominos. Half of them were dressed in white and half in black, and thus they alternated down the row. Twelve hands handled divers fans. Twelve pairs of eyes looked out, eyes merry, or challenging, or mysterious, one could not tell. About these young belles gathered the densest throng of all the crowd. Some gentlemen appeared to know certain of the beauties, but these had hard work to keep their places, for continually others came, and one after another was introduced in turn, all down the line, as presently it was to be my fortune to be.

"Is she here, Mrs. Kitty?" I whispered.

"You shall guess. Come." And so, as occasion offered, I was put through this ordeal, by no means an easy one. At each fair charmer, as I bowed, I looked with what directness I dared, to see if I might penetrate the mask and so foil Kitty in her amiable intentions. This occupation caused me promptly to forget most of the names which I heard, and which I doubt not were all fictitious. As we passed out at the foot of the row I recalled that I had not heard the name of Ellen.

"Now then, which one is she?" I queried of my hostess.

"Silly, do you want me to put your hand in hers? You are now on your own resources. Play the game." And the next moment she again was gone.

I had opportunity, without rudeness, the crowd so pressing in behind me, to glance once more up the line. I saw, or thought I saw, just a chance glance toward where I stood, near the foot of the Row of Mystery, as they called it. I looked a second time, and then all doubt whatever vanished.

If this girl in the black laces, with the gold comb in her hair, and the gold-shot little shoes just showing at the edge of her gown, and the red rose at her hair, held down by the comb—half hidden by the pile of locks caught up by the ribbon of the mask—if this girl were not the mysterious Ellen, then indeed must Ellen look well to her laurels, for here, indeed, was a rival for her!

I began to edge through the ranks of young men who gathered there, laughing, beseeching, imploring, claiming. The sparkle of the scene was in my veins. The breath of the human herd assembled, sex and sex, each challenging the other, gregarious, polygamous.

I did not walk; the music carried me before her. And so I bowed and murmured, "I have waited hours for my hostess to present me to Miss Ellen." (I mumbled the rest of some imaginary name, since I had heard none.)

The girl pressed the tip of her fan against her teeth and looked at me meditatively.

"And ours, of course, is *this* dance," I went on.

"If I could only remember all the names—" she began hesitatingly.

"I was introduced as Jack C., of Virginia."

"Yes? And in what arm?"

"Cavalry," I replied promptly. "Do you not see the yellow?" I gestured toward the facings. "You who belong to the Army ought to know."

"Why do you think I belong to the Army?" she asked, in a voice whose low sweetness was enough to impel any man to catch the mask from her face and throw it down the nearest well.

"You belong to the Army, and to Virginia," I said, "because you asked me what is my arm of the service; and because your voice could come from nowhere but Virginia. Now since I have come so far to see you and have found you out so soon, why do you not confess that you are Miss Ellen? Tell me your name, so that I may not be awkward!"

"We have no names to-night," she answered. "But I was just thinking; there is no Jack C. in the *Gazette* who comes from Virginia and who wears a captain's straps. I do not know who you are."

"At least the game then is fair," said I, disappointed. "But I promise you that some time I shall see you face to face, and without masks. To-morrow—"

"Tut, tut!" she reproved. "There is no to-morrow!"

I looked down on her as I stood, and a certain madness of youth seized hold upon me. I knew that when she rose she would be just tall enough; that she would be round, full, perfect woman in every line of her figure; that her hair would be some sort of dark brown in the daylight; that her eyes would also be of some sort of darkness, I knew not what, for I could not see them fully through the domino. I could see the hair piled back from the nape of as lovely a neck as ever caught a kiss. I could see at the edge of the mask that her ear was small and close to the head; could see that her nose must be straight, and that it sprang from the brow strongly, with no weak indentation. The sweep of a strong, clean chin was not to be disguised, and at the edge of the mask I caught now and then the gleam of white, even teeth, and the mocking smile of red, strongly curved lips, hid by her fan at the very moment when I was about to fix them in my memory, so that I might see them again and know. I suspect she hid a smile, but her eyes looked up at me grandly and darkly. Nineteen, perhaps twenty, I considered her age to be; gentle, and yet strong, with character and yet with tenderness, I made estimate that she must be; and that she had more brains than to be merely a lay figure I held sure, because there was something, that indefinable magnetism, what you like to call it, which is not to be denied, which assured me that here indeed was a woman not lightly to accept, nor lightly to be forgotten. Ah, now I was seized and swept on in a swift madness. Still the music sang on.

"My hostess said it would be a lottery to-night in this Row of Mystery," I went on, "but I do not find it so."

"All life is lottery," she said in answer.

"And lotteries are lawful when one wins the capital prize. One stretches out his hand in the dark. But some one must win. I win now. The game of masks is a fine one. I am vastly pleased with it. Some day I shall see you without any mask. Come. We must dance. I could talk better if we were more alone."

As I live, she rose and put her hand upon my arm with no further argument; why, I cannot say, perhaps because I had allowed no other man to stand thus near her.

We stepped out upon the crowded floor. I was swept away by it all, by the waltz, by the stars above, by the moon, by the breath of women and the scent of their hair, and the perfume of roses, by the passion of living, by youth, youth! Ah, God! ah, God! — I say to you, it was sweet. Whatever life brings to us of age and sorrow, let us remember our youth, and say it was worth the while. Had I never lived but that one night, it had been worth while.

She danced as she stood, with the grace of a perfect young creature, and the ease of a perfect culture as well. I was of no mind to look further. If this was not Ellen, then there was no Ellen there for me!

Around and around we passed, borne on the limpid shining stream of the waltz music, as melancholy as it was joyous; music that was young; for youth is ever full of melancholy and wonder and mystery. We danced. Now and again I saw her little feet peep out. I felt her weight rest light against my arm. I caught the indescribable fragrance of her hair. A gem in the gold comb now and then flashed out; and now and again I saw her eyes half raised, less often now, as though the music made her dream. But yet I could have sworn I saw a dimple in her cheek through the mask, and a smile of mockery on her lips.

I have said that her gown was dark, black laces draping over a close fitted under bodice; and there was no relief to this somberness excepting that in the front of the bodice were many folds of lacy lawn, falling in many sheer pleats, edge to edge, gathered at the waist by a girdle confined by a simple buckle of gold. Now as I danced, myself absorbed so fully that I sought little analysis of impressions so pleasing, I became conscious dimly of a faint outline of some figure in color, deep in these folds of lacy lawn, an evanescent spot or blur of red, which, to my imagination, assumed the outline of a veritable heart, as though indeed the girl's heart quite shone through! If this were a trick I could not say, but for a long time I resisted it. Meantime, as chance offered in the dance — to which she resigned herself utterly — I went on with such foolish words as men employ.

"Ah, nonsense!" she flashed back at me at last. "Discover something new. If men but knew how utterly transparent they are! I say that to-night we girls are but spirits, to be forgot to-morrow. Do not teach us to forget before to-morrow comes."

"I shall not forget," I insisted.

"Then so much the worse."

"I cannot."

"But you must."

"I will not. I shall not allow—"

"How obstinate a brute a man can be," she remonstrated.

"If you are not nice I shall go at once."

"I dreamed I saw a red heart," said I. "But that cannot have been, for I see you have no heart."

"No," she laughed. "It was only a dream."

"To-night, then, we only dream."

She was silent at this. "I knew you from the very first," I reiterated.

"What, has Kitty talked?"

It was my turn to laugh. "Ah, ha!" I said. "I thought no names were to be mentioned! At least, if Kitty has talked, I shall not betray her. But I knew you directly, as the most beautiful girl in all the city. Kitty said that much."

"Oh, thank thee, kind sir!"

"Then you knew I was a Quaker? Kitty has talked again? I had forgotten it to-night, and indeed forgotten that Quakers do not dance. I said I ought not to come here to-night, but now I see Fate said I must. I would not have lived all my life otherwise. To-night I hardly know who I am."

"Officer and gentleman," she smiled.

The chance compliment came to me like a blow. I was not an officer. I was masking, mumming, I, John Cowles, who had no right. Once more, whither was my folly carrying me? Suddenly I felt saddened.

"I shall call you The Sorrowful Knight," chided my fair companion."

"Quite as well as any name, my very good friend."

"I am not your friend."

"No, and indeed, perhaps, never may be."

Her spirit caught the chill of this, and at once she motioned the edge of the floor.

"Now I must go," she said. "There are very many to whom I am promised." I looked at her and could very well believe the truth of that. Many things revolved in my mind. I wondered whether if after all Kitty had had her way; wondered if this was the mysterious Ellen, and if after all she had also had her way! Ah, I had fallen easily!

"Sir Sorrowful," she said, "take me back." She extended a little hand and a round arm, whose beauty I could fully catch. The long mousquetaires of later days were then not known, but her hands stood perfectly the trying test of white kids that ended short at the wrist.

Reluctantly I moved away with her from the merry throng upon the pavilion floor. At the edge of the better lighted circle she paused for a moment, standing straight and drawing a full, deep breath. If that were coquetry it was perfect. I swear that now I caught the full outline of a red, red heart upon her corsage!

"Mademoiselle," I said, as I left her, "you are Ellen, and you have a heart! At half past ten I shall come again. Some day I shall take away your mask and your heart."

"Oh, thank thee!" she mocked again.

At half past ten I had kept my word, and I stood once more at the Row of Mystery. The chairs were vacant, for the blue coats had wrought havoc there! A little apart sat a blonde beauty of petite figure, who talked in a deep contralto voice, astonishing for one so slight, with a young lieutenant who leaned close to her. I selected her for Tudie Devlin of Kentucky. She whom I fancied to be the "Evans girl from up North," was just promenading away with a young man in evening dress. A brunette whom I imagined to be Sadie Galloway of the Ninth was leaning on the back of a chair and conversing with a man whom I could not see, hidden in the shade of a tent fold. I looked behind me and saw a row of disgruntled gentlemen, nervously pacing up and down. At least there were others disappointed!

I searched the dancing floor and presently wished I had not done so. I saw her once more—dancing with a tall, slender man in uniform. At least he offered no disguise to me. In my heart I resented seeing him wear the blue of our government. And certainly it gave me some pang to which I was not entitled, which I did not stop to analyze, some feeling of wretchedness, to see this girl dancing with none less than Gordon Orme, minister of the Gospel, captain of the English Army, and what other inconsistent things I knew not!

"Buck up, Jack," I heard a voice at my side. "Did she run away from you?"

I feigned ignorance to Kitty. "They are all alike," said I, indifferently. "All dressed alike—"

"And I doubt not all acted alike."

"I saw but one," I admitted, "the one with a red heart on her corsage."

Kitty laughed a merry peal. "There were twelve red hearts," she said. "All there, and all offered to any who might take them. Silly, silly! Now, I wonder if indeed you did meet Ellen? Come, I'll introduce you to a hundred more, the nicest girls you ever saw."

"Then it was Ellen?"

"How should I know? I did not see you. I was too busy flirting with my husband—for after awhile I found that it was Matt, of course! It seems some sort of fate that I never see a handsome man who doesn't turn out to be Matt."

"I must have one more dance," I said.

"Then select some other partner. It is too late to find Ellen now, or to get a word with her if we did. The last I saw of her she was simply persecuted by Larry Belknap of the Ninth Dragoons—all the Army knows that he's awfully gone over Ellen."

"But we'll find her somewhere—"

"No, Jack, you'd better banish Ellen, and all the rest. Take my advice and run over home and go to bed. You forget you've the match on for to-morrow; and I must say, not wanting to disturb you in the least, I believe you're going to need all your nerve. There's Scotch on the sideboard, but don't drink champagne."

The scene had lost interest to me. The lights had paled, the music was less sweet.

Presently I strolled over to Number 16 and got Johnson to show me my little room. But I did very little at the business of sleeping; and when at last I slept I saw a long row of figures in alternate black and white; and of these one wore a red rose and a gold comb with a jewel in it, and her hair was very fragrant. I did not see Grace Sheraton in my dreams. Clearly I reasoned it out to myself as I lay awake, that if I had seen Ellen once, then indeed it were best for me I should never see Ellen again!

Chapter X - The Supreme Court

If remorse, mental or physical, affected any of the dwellers at Jefferson Barracks on the morning following the officers' ball, at least neither was in evidence. By noon all traces of the late festivities had been removed from the parade ground, and the routine of the Post went on with the usual mechanical precision. The Army had entertained, it now labored. In a few hours it would again be ready to be entertained; the next little event of interest being the pigeon match between Orme and myself, which swift rumor seemed to have magnified into an importance not wholly welcome to myself.

We had a late breakfast at Number 16, and my friend Stevenson, who was to handle me in the match, saw to it that I had a hard tubbing before breakfast and a good run afterward, and later a hearty luncheon with no heavy wines. I was surprised at these business-like proceedings, which were all new to me, and I reflected with no satisfaction that my hot-headedness in accepting Orme's challenge might result in no glory to myself, and worse than that, let in my friends for loss; for Stevenson informed me that in spite of the fact that I had never shot in a race, a number of wagers were backing me against the Englishman. I reasoned, however, that these responsibilities should not be considered by one who needed perfect command of himself. Moreover, although I had never shot at trapped birds, I reasoned that a bird in the air was a flying bird after all, whether from trap or tree. Then, again, I was offended at Orme's air of superiority. Lastly, though it might be the fault of the Cowles' blood to accept any sort of challenge, it was not our way to regret that so soon as the day following.

The grounds for the match had been arranged at the usual place, near to the edge of the military reservation, and here, a half hour before the time set, there began to gather practically all of the young officers about the Post, all the enlisted men who could get leave, with cooks, strikers, laundresses, and other scattered personnel of the barracks. There came as well many civilians from the city, and I was surprised to see a line of carriages, with many ladies, drawn up back of the score. Evidently our little matter was to be made a semi-fashionable affair, and used as another expedient to while away ennui-ridden Army time.

My opponent, accompanied by Major Williams, arrived at about the same time that our party reached the grounds. Orme shook hands with me, and declared that he was feeling well, although Williams laughingly announced that he had not been able to make his man go to bed for more than an hour that morning, or to keep him from eating and drinking everything he could lay his hands upon. Yet now his eye was bright, his skin firm, his step light and easy. That the man had a superb constitution was evident, and I knew that my work was cut out for me, for Orme, whatever his profession, was an old one at the game of speedy going. As a man I disliked and now suspected him. As an opponent at any game one was obliged to take account of him.

"What boundary do we use, gentlemen?" Orme asked, as he looked out over the field. This question showed his acquaintance, but none the less his confidence and his courtesy as well, for in closely made matches all details are carefully weighed before the issue is joined. "I am more used to the Monaco bounds of eighteen yards," he added, "but whatever is your custom here will please me. I only want to have a notion of your sport."

"Our races here have usually been shot at fifty yards bounds," said Stevenson.

"As you like," said Orme, "if that pleases Mr. Cowles."

"Perfectly," said I, who indeed knew little about the matter.

Orme stepped over to the coops where the birds were kept—splendid, iridescent creatures, with long tails, clean, gamy heads and all the colors of the rainbow on their breasts. "By Jove!" he said, "they're rippers for looks, and they should fly a bit, I'm thinking. I have never seen them before, much less shot a race at them."

"Still your advantage," said I, laughing, "for I never shot a race at any sort in my life."

"And yet you match against me? My dear fellow, I hardly like—"

"The match is made, Captain Orme, and I am sure Mr. Cowles would not ask for any readjustment," commented Stevenson stiffly.

"Don't understand me to wish to urge anything," said Orme. "I only wish it so we shall all have a chance at revenge. Is there any one who wishes to back me, perhaps, or to back Mr. Cowles? Sometimes in England we shoot at a guinea a bird or five, or ten." Stevenson shook his head. "Too gaited for me at this time of the month," he said; "but I'll lay you a hundred dollars on the issue."

"Five if you like, on the Virginian, sir," said young Belknap of the Ninth to Orme.

"Done, and done, gentlemen. Let it be dollars and not guineas if you like. Would any one else like to lay a little something? You see, I'm a stranger here, but I wish to do what will make it interesting for any of you who care to wager something."

A few more wagers were laid, and the civilian element began to plunge a bit on Orme, word having passed that he was an old hand at the game, whereas I was but a novice. Orme took some of these wagers carelessly.

"Now as to our referee, Captain," said Stevenson. "You are, as you say, something of a stranger among us, and we wish your acquaintance were greater, so that you might name some one who would suit you."

"I'm indifferent," said Orme politely. "Any one Mr. Cowles may name will please me."

His conduct was handsome throughout, and his sporting attitude made him many friends among us. I suspect some Army money went on him, quietly, although little betting was now done in our presence.

"I see Judge Reeves, of the Supreme Court of the State, over there in a carriage," suggested Major Williams. "I've very much a notion to go and ask him to act as our referee."

"God bless my soul!" said Orme, "this is an extraordinary country! What—a judge of the Supreme Court?"

Williams laughed. "You don't know this country, Captain, and you don't know Judge Reeves. He's a trifle old, but game as a fighting cock, and not to mention a few duels in his time, he knows more even about guns and dogs to-day than he does about law. He'll not be offended if I ask him, and here goes."

He edged off through the crowd, and we saw him engaged in earnest conversation with the judge. To our surprise and amusement we observed the judge climb hastily down out of his carriage and take Major Williams' arm.

Judge Reeves was a tall, thin man, whose long hair and beard were silvery white, yet his stature was erect and vigorous. It was always said of him that he was the most dignified man in the State of Missouri, and that he carried this formality into every detail of his daily life. The story ran that each night, when he and his aged consort retired, they stood, each with candle in hand, on either side of the great bed which all their married life they had occupied in harmony. She, formally bowing to him across the bed, said "Good-night, Judge Reeves"; whereat he, bowing with yet greater formality, replied, "Good-night, Mrs. Reeves." Each then blew out the candle, and so retired! I cannot vouch as to the truth of this story, or of the further report that they carried out their ceremony when seating themselves at table, each meal of the day; but I will say that the appearance of this gentleman would have given such stories likelihood.

We uncovered as the judge approached us, and he shook hands with us in the most solemn way, his own wide black hat in his hand. "A—a—hem, gentlemen," he said, "a somewhat unusual situation for one on the bench—most unusual, I may say. But the Court can see no harm in it, since no law of the land is violated. Neither does the Court hold it beneath the dignity of its office to witness this little trial of skill between gentlemen. Further speaking, the Court does not here pass upon questions of law, but sits rather as jury in matters of ocular evidence, with the simple duty of determining whether certain flying objects fall upon this or the other side of that certain line marked out as the boundaries. Gentlemen, I am, a—hem, yours with great pleasure." If there was a twinkle in his eye it was a very solemn one. I venture to say he would have lost no votes at the next election were he up for office.

"Is the case ready for argument?" presently asked the judge, benignly. Williams and Stevenson both replied "All ready."

"I suggest that the gentlemen place their ammunition and loading tools upon the head of the cask at my right," said the judge. "I presume it to be understood that each may employ such charge as he prefers, and that each shall load his own piece?" The seconds assented to this. Of course, in those days only muzzle loaders were used, although we had cut-felt wads and all the improvements in gunnery known at that time. My weapon was supplied me by Captain Stevenson—a good Manton, somewhat battered up from much use, but of excellent even pattern. Orme shot a Pope-made gun of London, with the customary straight hand and slight drop of the English makes. I think he had brought this with him on his travels.

"Shall the firing be with the single barrel, or with both barrels?" inquired our referee. In those days many American matches were shot from plunge traps, and with the single barrel.

"I'm more used to the use of both barrels," suggested Orme, "but I do not insist."

"It is the same to me," I said. So finally we decided that the rise should be at twenty-eight yards, the use of both barrels allowed, and the boundary at fifty yards—such rules as came to be later more generally accepted in this country.

"Gentlemen, I suggest that you agree each bird to be gathered fairly by the hand, each of you to select a gatherer. Each gentleman may remunerate his gatherer, but the said remuneration shall in each case remain the same. Is that satisfactory?" We agreed, and each tossed a silver dollar to a grinning darky boy.

"Now, then, gentlemen, the Court is informed that this match is to be for the sum of twenty-five hundred dollars, wagered by Captain Orme, against a certain black stallion horse, the same not introduced in evidence, but stated by Mr. Cowles to be of the value of twenty-five hundred dollars in the open market. As the match is stated to be on even terms, the said John Cowles guarantees this certain horse to be of such value, or agrees to make good any deficit in that value. Is that understood, gentlemen?"

"I did not ask any guarantee," said Orme. "I know the horse, and he is worth more than twice that sum. You are using me very handsomely, gentlemen."

"Judge Reeves is right," said I. "The match is to be even." We bowed to each other.

The judge felt in his pockets. "Ahem, gentlemen," he resumed. "The Court being, as it were, broke, will some one be so good as to lend the Court a silver coin? Thank you," to Williams, "and now, gentlemen, will you toss for the order of precedence?"

We threw the coin, and I lost the toss. Orme sent me to the score first, with the purpose, as I knew, of studying his man.

I loaded at the open bowls, and adjusted the caps as I stepped to the score. I was perhaps a bit too tense and eager, although my health and youth had never allowed me to be a victim of what is known as nervousness. Our birds were to be flown by hand from behind a screen, and my first bird started off a trifle low, but fast, and I knew I was not on with the first barrel, the hang of Stevenson's gun being not quite the same as my own. I killed it with the second, but it struggled over the tape.

"Lost bird!" called out Judge Reeves sharply and distinctly; and it was evident that now he would be as decisive as he had hitherto been deliberate.

Under the etiquette of the game no comment was made on my mishap, and my second, Stevenson, did not make the mistake of commiserating me. No one spoke a word as Orme stepped to the score. He killed his bird as clean as though he had done nothing else all his life, and indeed, I think he was half turned about from the score before the bird was down. "Dead bird!" called the referee, with jaw closing like a steel trap.

Stevenson whispered to me this time. "Get full on with your first," he said. "They're lead-packers—old ones, every one, and a picked lot."

I was a trifle angry with myself by this time, but it only left me well keyed. My bird fell dead inside of Orme's. A murmur of applause ran down the line. "Silence in the court," thundered Judge Reeves.

We shot along for ten birds, and Orme was straight, to my nine killed. Stevenson whispered to me once more. "Take it easy, and don't be worried about it. It's a long road to a hundred. Don't think about your next bird, and don't worry whether he kills his or not. Just you kill 'em one at a time and kill each one dead. You mustn't think of anything on earth but that one bird before you."

This was excellent advice in the game, and I nodded to him. Whatever the cause, I was by this time perfectly calm. I was now accustomed to my gun, and had confidence in it. I knew I could shoot to the top of my skill, and if I were beaten it would be through no fault of my own nerves and muscles, but through the luck of the birds or the greater skill of the other man.

Orme went on as though he could kill a hundred straight. His time was perfect, and his style at the trap beautiful. He shot carelessly, but with absolute confidence, and more than half the time he did not use his second barrel.

"Old Virginia never tires," whispered Stevenson. "He'll come back to you before long, never fear."

But Orme made it twenty straight before he came back. Then he caught a strong right-quarterer, which escaped altogether, apparently very lightly hit. No one spoke a word of sympathy or exultation, but I caught the glint of Stevenson's eye. Orme seemed not in the least disturbed.

We were now tied, but luck ran against us both for a time, since out of the next five I missed three and Orme two, and the odds again were against me. It stood the same at thirty, and at thirty-five. At forty the fortune of war once more favored me, for although Orme shot like a machine, with a grace and beauty of delivery I have never seen surpassed, he lost one bird stone dead over the line, carried out by a slant of the rising wind, which blew from left to right across the field. Five birds farther on, yet another struggled over for him, and at sixty-five I had him back of me two birds. The interest all along the line was now intense. Stevenson later told me that they had never seen such shooting as we were doing. For myself, it did not seem that I could miss. I doubt not that eventually I must have won, for fate does not so favor two men at the same hour.

We went on slowly, as such a match must, occasionally pausing to cool our barrels, and taking full time with the loading. Following my second's instructions perfectly, I looked neither to the right nor to the left, not even watching Orme. I heard the confusion of low talk back of us, and knew that a large crowd had assembled, but I did not look toward the row of carriages, nor pay attention to the new arrivals which constantly came in. We shot on steadily, and presently I lost a bird, which came in sharply to the left.

The heap of dead birds, some of them still fluttering in their last gasps, now grew larger at the side of the referee, and the negro boys were perhaps less careful to wring the necks of the birds as they gathered them. Occasionally a bird was tossed in such a way as to leave a fluttering wing. Wild pigeons decoy readily to any such sign, and I noticed that several birds, rising in such position that they headed toward the score, were incomers, and very fast. My seventieth bird was such, and it came straight and swift as an arrow, swooping down and curving about with the great speed of these birds when fairly on the wing. I covered it, lost sight of it, then suddenly realized that I must fire quickly if I was to reach it before it crossed the score. It was so close when I fired that the charge cut away the quills of a wing. It fell, just inside the line, with its head up, and my gatherer pounced upon it like a cat. The decision of the referee was prompt, but even so, it was almost lost in the sudden stir and murmur which arose behind us.

Some one came pushing through the crowd, evidently having sprung down from one of the carriages. I turned to see a young girl, clad in white lawn, a thin silver-gray veil drawn tight under her chin, who now pushed forward through the men, and ran up to the black boy who stood with the bird in his hand, hanging by one wing. She caught it from him, and held it against her breast, where its blood drabbled her gown and hands. I remember I saw one drop of blood at its beak, and remember how glad I was that the bird was in effect dead, so that a trying scene would soon be ended.

"Stop this at once!" cried the girl, raising an imperative hand. "Aren't you ashamed, all of you? Look, look at this!" She held out the dying bird in her hand. "Judge Reeves," she cried, "what are you doing there?"

Our decisive referee grew suddenly abashed. "Ah—ah, my dear young lady—my very dear young lady," he began.

"Captain Stevenson," exclaimed the girl, whirling suddenly on my second, "stop this at once! I'm ashamed of you."

"Now, now, my dear Miss Ellen," began Stevenson, "can't you be a good fellow and run back home? We're off the reservation, and really—this, you see, is a judge of the Supreme Court! We're doing nothing unlawful." He motioned toward Judge Reeves, who looked suddenly uncomfortable.

Major Williams added his counsel. "It is a little sport between Captain Orme and Mr. Cowles, Miss Ellen."

"Sport, great sport, isn't it?" cried the girl, holding out her drabbled hands. "Look there"—she pointed toward the pile of dead birds—"hundreds of these killed, for money, for sport. It *isn't* sport. You had all these birds once, you owned them."

And there she hit a large truth, with a woman's guess, although none of us had paused to consider it so before.

"The law, Miss Ellen," began Judge Reeves, clearing his throat, "allows the reducing to possession of animals *feroe naturoe*, that is to say, of wild nature, and ancient custom sanctions it."

"They were already *reduced*" she flashed. "The sport was in getting them the first time, not in butchering them afterward."

Stevenson and Williams rubbed their chins and looked at each other. As for me, I was looking at the girl; for it seemed to me that never in my life had I seen one so beautiful.

Her hair, reddish brown in the sunlight, was massed up by the binding veil, which she pushed back now from her face. Her eyes, wide and dark, were as sad as they were angry. Tears streamed from them down her cheek, which she did not dry. Fearless, eager, she had, without thought, intruded where the average woman would not have ventured, and she stood now courageously intent only upon having the way of what she felt was right and justice. There

74

came to me as I looked at her a curious sense that I and all my friends were very insignificant creatures; and it was so, I think, in sooth, she held us.

"Captain Orme," said I to my opponent, "you observe the actual Supreme Court of America!" He bowed to me, with a questioning raising of his eyebrows, as though he did not like to go on under the circumstances.

"I am unfortunate to lead by a bird," said I, tentatively. For some reason the sport had lost its zest to me.

"And I being the loser as it stands," replied Orme, "do not see how I can beg off." Yet I thought him as little eager to go on as I myself.

"Miss Ellen," said Judge Reeves, removing the hat from his white hair, "these gentlemen desire to be sportsmen as among themselves, but of course always gentlemen as regards the wish of ladies. Certain financial considerations are involved, so that both feel a delicacy in regard to making any motion looking to the altering of the original conditions of this contract. Under these circumstances, then, appeal is taken from this lower Court"—and he bowed very low—"to what my young friend very justly calls the Supreme Court of the United States. Miss Ellen, it is for you to say whether we shall resume or discontinue."

The girl bowed to Judge Reeves, and then swept a sudden hand toward Stevenson and Williams. "Go home, all of you!" she said.

And so, in sooth, much shamefaced, we did go home, Judge of the Supreme Court, officers of the Army, and all, vaguely feeling we had been caught doing some ignoble thing. For my part, although I hope mawkishness no more marks me than another, and although I made neither then nor at any time a resolution to discontinue sports of the field, I have never since then shot in a pigeon match, nor cared to see others do so, for it has never again seemed to me as actual sport. I think the intuitive dictum of the Army girl was right.

"Now *wasn't* that like Ellen!" exclaimed Kitty, when finally we found ourselves at her carriage—"just *like* that girl. Just *wasn't* it *like* that *girl*! To fly in the face of the Supreme Court of the State, and all the laws of sport as well! Jack, I was keeping count," she held out her ivory tablets. "You'd have beaten him sure, and I wanted to see you do it. You were one ahead, and would have made it better in the next twenty-five. Oh, won't I talk to that girl when I see her!"

"So that was Ellen!" I said to Kitty.

"The very same. Now you've seen her. What you think I don't know, but what she thinks of you is pretty evident."

"You were right, Mrs. Kitty," said I. "She's desperately good looking. But that isn't the girl I danced with last night. In the name of Providence, let me get away from this country, for I know not what may happen to me! No man is safe in this neighborhood of beauties."

"Let's all go home and get a bite to eat," said Stevenson, with much common sense. "You've got glory enough just the way it stands."

So that was Ellen! And it moreover was none less than Ellen Meriwether, daughter of my father's friend and business associate, whom I had traveled thus far to see, and whom, as I now determined, I must meet at the very first possible opportunity. Perhaps, then, it might very naturally come about that—but I dismissed this very rational supposition as swiftly as I was able.

Chapter XI - The Morning After

Events had somewhat hurried me in the two days since my arrival at Jefferson Barracks, but on the morning following the awkward ending of my match with Orme I had both opportunity and occasion to take stock of myself and of my plans. The mails brought me two letters, posted at Wallingford soon after my departure; one from Grace Sheraton and one from my mother. The first one was—what shall I say? Better perhaps that I should say nothing, save that it was like Grace Sheraton herself, formal, correct and cold. It was the first written word I had ever received from my fiancée, and I had expected—I do not know what. At least I had thought to be warmed, comforted, consoled in these times of my adversity. It seemed to my judgment, perhaps warped by sudden misfortune, that possibly my fiancée regretted her hasty promise, rued an engagement to one whose affairs had suddenly taken an attitude of so little promise. I was a poor man now, and worse than poor, because lately I had been rich, as things went in my surroundings. In this letter, I say, I had expected—I do not know what. But certainly I had not expected to see sitting on the page written in my fiancée's hand, the face of another woman. I hated myself for it.

The second letter was from my mother, and it left me still more disconcerted and sad. "Jack," it said, "I grieve unspeakably. I am sad beyond all imaginings of sadness. I need thee. Come back the first day thee can to thy mother."

There was indeed need for me at home. Yet here was I with my errand not yet well begun; for Captain Stevenson told me this morning that the Post Adjutant had received word from Colonel Meriwether saying that he would be gone for some days or weeks on the upper frontier. Rumor passed about that a new man, Sherman, was possibly to come on to assume charge of Jefferson, a man reported to be a martinet fit to stamp out any demonstration in a locality where secession sentiment was waxing strong. Meriwether, a Virginian, and hence suspected of Southern sympathy, was like many other Army officers at the time, shifted to points where his influence would be less felt, President Buchanan to the contrary notwithstanding. The sum of all which was that if I wished to meet Colonel Meriwether and lay before him my own personal request, I would be obliged to seek for him far to the West, in all likelihood at Fort Leavenworth, if not at the lower settlements around the old town of Independence. Therefore I wrote at once both to my fiancée and to my mother that it would be impossible for me to return at the time, nor at any positive future time then determinable. I bade a hasty good-by to my host and hostess, and before noon was off for the city. That night I took passage on the *River Belle*, a boat bound up the Missouri.

Thus, somewhat against my will, I found myself a part of that motley throng of keen-faced, fearless American life then pushing out over the frontiers. About me were men bound for Oregon, for California, for the Plains, and not a few whose purpose I took to be partisanship in the border fighting between slavery and free soil. It was in the West, and on the new soils, that the question of slavery was really to be debated and settled finally.

The intenseness, the eagerness, the compelling confidence of all this west-bound population did not fail to make the utmost impression upon my own heart, hitherto limited by the horizon of our Virginia hills. I say that I had entered upon this journey against my will. Our churning wheels had hardly reached the turbid flood of the Missouri before the spell of the frontier had caught me. In spite of sadness, trouble, doubt, I would now only with reluctance have resigned my advance into that country which offered to all men, young and old, a zest of deeds bold enough to banish sadness, doubt and grief.

Chapter XII - The Wreck On The River

I made friends with many of these strange travelers, and was attracted especially by one, a reticent man of perhaps sixty odd years, in Western garb, full of beard and with long hair reaching to his shoulders. He had the face of an old Teuton war chief I had once seen depicted in a canvas showing a raid in some European forest in years long before a Christian civilization was known—a face fierce and eager, aquiline in nose, blue of eye; a figure stalwart, muscular, whose every movement spoke courage and self-confidence. Auberry was his name, and as I talked with him he told me of days passed with my heroes—Fremont, Carson, Ashley, Bill Williams, Jim Bridger, even the negro ruffian Beckwourth—all men of the border of whose deeds I had read. Auberry had trapped from the St. Mary's to the sources of the Red, and his tales, told in simple and matter-of-fact terms, set my very blood atingle. He was bound, as he informed me, for Laramie; always provided that the Sioux, now grown exceedingly restless over the many wagon-trains pushing up the Platte to all the swiftly-opening West, had not by this time swooped down and closed all the trails entirely. I wished nothing then so much as that occasion might permit me to join him in a journey across the Plains.

Among all these west-bound travelers the savage and the half-civilized seemed to me to preponderate; this not to say that they were so much coarse and crude as they were fierce, absorbed, self-centered. Each man depended upon himself and needed to do so. The crew on the decks were relics from keel-boat days, surly and ugly of temper. The captain was an ex-pilot of the lower river, taciturn and surly of disposition. Our pilot had been drunk for a week at the levee of St. Louis and I misdoubt that all snags and sandbars looked alike to him.

Among the skin-clad trappers, hunters and long-haired plainsmen, I saw but one woman, and she certainly was fit to bear them company. I should say that she was at least sixty years of age, and nearly six feet in height, thin, angular, wrinkled and sinewy. She wore a sunbonnet of enormous projection, dipped snuff vigorously each few moments, and never allowed from her hands the long squirrel rifle which made a part of her equipage. She was accompanied by her son, a tall, thin, ague-smitten youth of perhaps seventeen years and of a height about as great as her own. Of the two the mother was evidently the controlling spirit, and in her case all motherly love seemed to have been replaced by a vast contempt for the inefficiency and general lack of male qualities in her offspring. When I first saw them she was driving her son before her to a spot where an opening offered near the bow of the boat, in full sight of all the passengers, of whose attention she was quite oblivious.

"Git up, there, Andy Jackson!" she said. "Stan' up!"

The boy, his long legs braiding under him, and his peaked face still more pale, did as he was bid. He had no sooner taken his position than to my surprise I saw his mother cover him with the long barrel of a dragoon revolver.

"Pull your gun, you low-down coward," she commanded, in tones that might have been heard half the length of the boat. Reluctantly the boy complied, his own revolver trembling in his unready hand.

"Now, whut'd you do if a man was to kivver you like I'm a-doin' now?" demanded his mother.

"G-g-g-Gawd, Maw, I dunno! I think I'd j-j-j-jump off in the river," confessed the boy.

"Shore you would, and good luck if you'd git plumb drownded, you white-livered son of misery. Whatever in Gawd A'mighty's world you was borned for certainly is more'n I can tell—and I your Maw at that, that orto know if anybody could."

"Madam," I interrupted, astonished at this discourse, "what do you mean by such talk to your son—for I presume he is your son. Why

80

do you abuse him in this way?" I was sorry for the shivering wretch whom she had made the object of her wrath.

"Shut up, and mind yore own business," answered the virago, swiftly turning the barrel of her weapon upon me. "Whut business is this here of yores?"

"None, madam," I bowed, "but I was only curious."

"You keep your own cur'osity to yourself ef you'r goin' to travel in these parts. That's a mighty good thing for you to learn."

"Very true, madam," said I, gently disengaging the revolver barrel from the line of my waist, "but won't you tell me why you do these things with your son?"

"It's none of your damned business," she answered, "but I don't mind tellin' you. I'm tryin' to make a man out'n him."

"Ah, and this is part of the drill?"

"Part of it. You, Andrew Jackson, stick yore pistol up agin your head the way I tol' you. Now snap it, damn you! Keep *on* a-snappin'! Quit that jumpin', I tell you! Snap, it till you git through bein' scared of it. Do it now, or by Gawd, I'll chase you over the side of the boat and feed you to the catfish, you low-down imertation of a he-thing. Mister," she turned to me again, "will you please tell me how come me to be the mother of a thing like this—me, a woman of ole Missoury; and me a cousin of ole Simon Kenton of Kentucky beside?"

"My good woman," said I, somewhat amused by her methods of action and speech, "do you mind telling me what is your name?"

"Name's Mandy McGovern; and I come from Pike," she answered, almost before the words were out of my mouth. "I've been married three times and my first two husbands died a-fightin, like gentlemen, in diffikilties with friends. Then along come this Danny Calkins, that taken up some land nigh to me in the bottoms—low-downest coward of a, man that ever disgraced the sile of yearth—and then I married *him*."

"Is he dead, too, my dear woman?" I asked.

"Don't you 'dear woman' me—I ain't free to merry agin yit," said she. "Naw, he ain't dead, and I ain't deevorced either. I just done left him. Why, every man in Pike has whupped Danny Calkins one time or other. When a man couldn't git no reputation any other way, he'd come erlong and whupped my husband. I got right tired of it."

"I should think you might."

"Yes, and me the wife of two real men befo' then. If ever a woman had hard luck the same is me," she went on. "I had eight chillen by my two husbands that was real men, and every one of them died, or got killed like a man, or went West like a man—exceptin' this thing here, the son of that there Danny Calkins. Why, he's afraid to go coon huntin' at night for fear the cats'll get him. He don't like to melk a keow for fear she'll kick him. He's afraid to court a gal. He kaint shoot, he kaint chop, he kaint do nothin'. I'm takin' him out West to begin over again where the plowin's easier; and whiles we go along, I'm givin' him a 'casional dose of immanuel trainin', to see if I can't make him part way intoe a man. I dunno!" Mrs. McGovern dipped snuff vigorously.

Thereafter she looked at me carefully. "Say, mister," said she, "how tall are you?"

"About six feet, I think."

"Hum! That's just about how tall my first husband was. You look some like him in the face, too. Say, he was the fightin'est man in Pike. How come him to get killed was a diffikilty with his brother-in-law, a Dutchman that kept a saloon and couldn't talk English. Jim, he went in there to get a bite to eat and asked this Dutchman what he could set up. Paul—that was the Dutchman's name—he says, 'Well, we got dawg—mallard dawg, and red head dawg, and canvas back dawg—what's the kind of dawg you like, Chim?'

"My husband thought he was pokin' fun at him, talkin' about eatin' dawg—not knowin' the Dutchman was tryin' to say 'duck,' and couldn't. 'I might have a piece of duck,' said Jim, 'bit I ain't eatin' no dawg.'

"'I *said* dawg,' says Paul, still a-tryin' to say 'duck.'

"'I know you did,' says Jim, and then they clinched. Jim He broke his knife off, and the Dutchman soaked him with a beer mallet. 'But Mandy,' says Jim to me, jest before he shet his eyes, 'I die content. That there fellow was the sweetest cuttin' man I ever did cut in all my life—he was jest like a ripe pumpkin.' Say, there was a man for you, was Jim—you look some like him." She dipped snuff again vigorously.

"You compliment me very much, Mrs. McGovern," I said.

"Say," she responded, "I got two thousand head o' hawgs runnin' around in the timber down there in Pike."

At the moment I did not see the veiled tenderness of this speech, but thought of nothing better than to tell her that I was going no further up the river than Fort Leavenworth.

"Um-hum!" she said. "Say, mister, mebbe that's yore wife back there in the kebbin in the middle of the boat?"

"No, indeed. In fact I did not know there was any other lady on the boat besides yourself. I am not much interested in young ladies, as it happens."

"You lie," said Mrs. McGovern promptly, "there ain't nothin' in the whole world you are ez much interested in as young wimmin. I'm a married woman, and I know the signs. If I had a deevorce I might be a leetle jealous o' that gal in there. She's the best lookin' gal I ever did see in all my time. If I was merried to you I dunno but I'd be a leetle bit jealous o' you. Say, I may be a widder almost any day now. Somebody'll shore kill Danny Calkins 'fore long."

"And, according to you, I may be a married man almost any day," I replied, smiling.

"But you ain't married yit."

"No, not yet," I answered.

"Well, if you git a chanct you take a look at that gal back there in the kebbin."

Opportunity did not offer, however, to accept Mrs. McGovern's kindly counsel, and, occupied with my own somewhat unhappy reflections, I resigned myself to the monotony of the voyage up the Missouri River. We plowed along steadily, although laboriously, all night, all the next day and the next night, passing through regions rich in forest growth, marked here and there by the many clearings of the advancing settlers. We were by this time far above the junction of the Missouri River with the Mississippi—a point traceable by a long line of discolored water stained with the erosion of the mountains and plains far up the Missouri. As the boat advanced, hour after hour, finally approaching the prairie country beyond the Missouri forests, I found little in the surroundings to occupy my mind; and so far as my communings with myself were concerned, they offered little satisfaction. A sort of shuddering self-reproach overcame me. I wondered whether or not I was less coarse, less a thing polygamous than these crowding Mormons hurrying out to their sodden temples in the West, because now (since I have volunteered in these pages to tell the truth regarding one man's heart), I must admit that in the hours of dusk I found myself dreaming not of my fiancée back in old Virginia, but of other women seen more recently. As to the girl of the masked ball, I admitted that she was becoming a fading memory; but this young girl who had thrust through the crowd and broken up our proceedings the other day—the girl with the white lawn gown and the silver gray veil and the tear-stained eyes—in some way, as I was angrily obliged to admit, her face seemed annoyingly to thrust itself again into my consciousness. I sat near a deck lamp. Grace Sheraton's letter was in my pocket. I did not draw it out to read it and re-read it. I contented myself with watching the masked shadows on the shores. I contented myself with dreams, dreams which I stigmatized as unwarranted and wrong.

We were running that night in the dark, before the rising of the moon, a thing which cautious steamboat men would not have ventured, although our pilot was confident that no harm could come to him. Against assurance such as this the dangerous Missouri with its bars and snags purposed a present revenge. Our whistle awakened the echoes along the shores as we plowed on up the yellow flood, hour after hour. Then, some time toward midnight, while most of the passengers were attempting some sort of rest, wrapped in their blankets along the deck, there came a slight shock, a grating slide, and a rasping crash of wood. With a forward churning of her paddles which sent water high along the rail, the *River Belle* shuddered and lay still, her engines throbbing and groaning.

In an instant every one on the boat was on his feet and running to the side. I joined the rush to the bows, and leaning over, saw that we were hard aground at the lower end of a sand bar. Imbedded in this bar was a long white snag, a tree trunk whose naked arms, thrusting far down stream, had literally impaled us. The upper woodwork of the boat was pierced quite through; and for all that one could tell at the moment, the hull below the line was in all likelihood similarly crushed. We hung and gently swung, apparently at the mercy of the tawny flood of old Missouri.

Chapter XIII - The Face In The Firelight

Sudden disaster usually brings sudden calm, the pause before resolution or resignation. For the first instant after the shock of the boat upon the impaling snag I stood irresolute; the next, I was busy with plans for escape. Running down the companionway, I found myself among a crowd of excited deck hands, most of whom, with many of the passengers, were pushing toward the starboard rail, whence could be seen the gloom of the forest along shore. The gangway door on the opposite side of the boat was open, and as I looked out I could see the long white arms of the giant snag reaching alongside. Without much plan or premeditation I sprang out, and making good my hold upon the nearest limb as I plunged, found myself, to my surprise, standing in not more than four feet of water, the foot of the bar evidently running down well under the boat.

Just as I turned to call to others I saw the tall figure of my plainsman, Auberry, appear at the doorway, and he also, with scarcely a moment's deliberation, took a flying leap and joined me on the snag. "It's better here than there," he said, "if she sinks or busts, and they're allus likely to do both."

As we pulled ourselves up into the fork of the long naked branch we heard a voice, and saw the face of a woman leaning over the rail of the upper deck. I recognized my whilom friend, Mandy McGovern. "Whut you all doin' down there?" she called. "Wait a minute; I'm comin', too." A moment later she appeared at the opening of the lower deck and craned out her long neck. I then saw at her side the figure of a young woman, her hair fallen from its coils, her feet bare, her body wrapped apparently only in some light silken dressing to be thrown above her nightwear. She, too, looked out into the darkness, but shrank back.

"Here, you," called out Mandy McGovern, "git hold of the end of this rope."

She tossed to me the end of the gang-plank rope, by which the sliding stage was drawn out and in at the boat landings. I caught this and passed it over a projection on the snag.

"Now, haul it out," commanded she; and as we pulled, she pushed, so that presently indeed we found that the end reached the edge of the limb on which we sat. Without any concern, Mrs. McGovern stepped out on the swaying bridge, sunbonnet hanging down her back, her long rifle under one arm, while by the other hand she dragged her tall son, Andrew Jackson, who was blubbering in terror.

This bridge, however, proved insecure, for as Mandy gave Andrew Jackson a final yank at its farther end, the latter stumbled, and in his struggles to lay hold upon the snag, pushed the end of the planks off their support. His mother's sinewy arm thrust him into safety, and she herself clambered up, very wet and very voluble in her imprecations on his clumsiness.

"Thar, now, look what ye did, ye low-down coward," she said. "Like to 'a' drownded both of us, and left the gal back there on the boat!"

The gang plank, confined by the rope, swung in the current alongside the snag, but it seemed useless to undertake to restore it to its position. The girl cowered against the side of the deck opening, undecided. "Wait," I called out to her; and slipping down into the water again, I waded as close as I could to the door, the water then catching me close to the shoulders.

"Jump!" I said to her, holding out my arms.

"I can't—I'm afraid," she said, in a voice hardly above a whisper.

"Do as I tell you!" I roared, in no gentle tones, I fear. "Jump at once!" She stooped, and sprang, and as I caught her weight with my arms under hers, she was for the moment almost immersed; but I staggered backwards and managed to hold my footing till Auberry's arms reached us from the snag, up which we clambered, the girl dripping wet and catching her breath in terror.

"That's right," said Mandy McGovern, calmly, "now here we be, all of us. Now, you men, git hold of this here rope an' haul up them boards, an' make a seat for us."

Auberry and I found it difficult to execute this order, for the current of old Missouri, thrusting against so large an object, was incredibly strong; but at last, little by little edging the heavy staging up over the limb of the snag, we got its end upon another fork and so made a ticklish support, half in and half out of the water.

"That's better," said Mandy, climbing upon it. "Now come here, you pore child. You're powerful cold." She gathered the girl between her knees as she sat. "Here, you man, give me your coat," she said to me; and I complied, wishing it were not so wet.

None on the boat seemed to have any notion of what was going on upon our side of the vessel. We heard many shouts and orders, much trampling of feet, but for the most part on the opposite part of the boat. Then at once we heard the engines reverse, and were nearly swept from our insecure hold upon the snag by the surges kicked up under the wheel. The current caught the long underbody of the boat as she swung. We heard something rip and splinter and grate; and then the boat, backing free from the snag, gradually slipped down from the bar and swept into the current under steam again.

Not so lucky ourselves, for this wrenching free of the boat had torn loose the long imbedded roots of the giant snag, and the plowing current getting under the vast flat back of matted roots, now slowly forced it, grinding and shuddering, down from the toe of the bar. With a sullen roll it settled down into new lines as it reached the deeper water. Then the hiss of the water among the branches ceased. Rolling and swaying, we were going with the current, fully afloat on the yellow flood of the Missouri!

I held my breath for a moment, fearing lest the snag might roll over entirely; but no concern seemed to reach the mind of our friend Mrs. McGovern. "It's all right," said she, calmly. "No use gittin' skeered till the time comes. Boat's left us, so I reckon we'd better be gittin' somewhere for ourselves. You, Andrew Jackson, dem yer fool soul, if you don't quit snivelin' I'll throw you off into the worter."

Looking across the stream I could see the lights of the *River Belle* swing gradually into a longer line, and presently heard the clanging of her bells as she came to a full stop, apparently tied up along shore. From that direction the current seemed to come toward us with a long slant, so that as we dropped down stream, we also edged away.

We had traveled perhaps three quarters of a mile, when I noticed the dim loom of trees on our side of the stream, and saw that we were approaching a long point which ran out below us. This should have been the deep side of the river, but no one can account for the vagaries of the Missouri. When we were within a hundred yards or so of the point, we felt a long shuddering scrape under us, and after a series of slips and jerks, our old snag came to anchor again, its roots having once more laid hold upon a bar. The sand-wash seemed to have been deflected by the projecting mass of a heap of driftwood which I now saw opposite to us, its long white arms reaching out toward those of our floating craft. Once more the hissing of the water began among the buried limbs, and once more the snag rolled ominously, and then lay still, its giant, naked trunk, white and half submerged, reaching up stream fifty feet above us. We were apparently as far from safety as ever, although almost within touch of shore.

It occurred to me that as I had been able to touch bottom on the other bar, I might do so here. I crawled back along the trunk of the snag to a place as near the roots as I could reach, and letting myself down gently, found that I could keep my footing on the sand.

"Look out there! boy," cried Auberry to me. "This river's dangerous. If it takes you down, swim for the shore. Don't try to get back here." We could see that the set of the current below ran close inshore, although doubtless the water there was very deep.

Little by little I edged up the stream, and found presently that the water shoaled toward the heap of driftwood. It dropped off, I know not how deep, between the edge of the bar and the piled drift; but standing no more than waist deep; I could reach the outer limbs of the drift and saw that they would support my weight. After that I waded back to the snag carefully, and once more ordered the young woman to come to me.

She came back along the naked and slippery trunk of the snag, pulling herself along by her hands, her bare feet and limbs deep in the water alongside. I could hear the sob of her intaken breath, and saw that she trembled in fright.

"Come," I said, as she finally reached the mass of the roots. And more dead than alive, it seemed to me, she fell once more into my arms. I felt her grasp tighten about my neck, and her firm body crowd against me as we both sank down for an instant. Then I caught my feet and straightened, and was really the steadier for the added weight, as any one knows who has waded in fast water. Little by little I edged up on the bar, quite conscious of her very gracious weight, but sure we should thus reach safety.

"Put me down," she said at length, as she saw the water shoaling. It was hip deep to me, but waist deep to her; and I felt her shudder as she caught its chill. Her little hand gripped tight to mine.

By this time the others had also descended from the snag. I saw old Auberry plunging methodically along, at his side Mrs. McGovern, clasping the hand of her son. "Come on here, you boy," she said. "What ye skeered of? Tall as you air, you could wade the whole Missouri without your hair gettin' wet. Come along!"

"Get up, Auberry," I said to him as he approached, and motioned to the long, overhanging branches from the driftwood. He swung up, breaking off the more insecure boughs, and was of the belief that we could get across in that way. As he reached down, I swung the young woman up to him, and she clambered on as best she could. Thus, I scarce know how, we all managed to reach the solid drift, and so presently found ourselves ashore, on a narrow, sandy beach, hedged on the back by a heavy growth of willows.

"Now then, you men," ordered Mandy McGovern, "get some wood out and start a fire, right away. This here girl is shaking the teeth plumb out'n her head."

Auberry and I had dragged some wood from the edge of the drift and pulled it into a heap near by, before we realized that neither of us had matches.

"Humph!" snorted our leader, feeling in her pockets. She drew forth two flasks, each stoppered with a bit of corncob. The one held sulphur matches, thus kept quite dry, and this she passed to me. The other she handed to the young woman.

"Here," said she, "take a drink of that. It'll do you good."

I heard the girl gasp and choke as she obeyed this injunction; and then Mandy applied the bottle gurglingly to her own lips.

"I've got a gallon of that back there on the boat," said Auberry ruefully.

"Heap of good it'll do you there," remarked Mandy. "Looks to me like you all never did travel much. Fer me, I always go heeled. Wherever I gits throwed, there my rifle, and my matches, and my licker gits throwed *too*! Now I'll show you how to, light a fire."

Presently we had a roaring blaze started, which added much to the comfort of all, for the chill of night was over the river, despite the fact that this was in the springtime. Mandy seated herself comfortably upon a log, and producing a corncob pipe and a quantity of natural leaf tobacco, proceeded to enjoy herself in her own fashion. "This here's all right," she remarked. "We might be a heap worse off'n we air."

I could not help pitying the young woman who crouched near her at the fireside, still shivering; she seemed so young and helpless and so out of place in such surroundings. As presently the heat of the flame made her more comfortable, she began to tuck back the tumbled locks of her hair, which I could see was thick and dark. The firelight showed in silhouette the outlines of her face. It seemed to me I had never seen one more beautiful. I remembered the round firmness of her body in my arms, the clasp of her hands about my neck, her hair blown across my cheek, and I reflected that since fortune had elected me to be a rescuer, it was not ill that so fair an object had been there for the rescuing.

Perhaps she felt my gaze, for presently she turned and said to me, in as pleasant a speaking voice as I had ever heard, "Indeed, it might be worse. I thank you so much. It was very brave of you."

"Listen at that!" grunted Mandy McGovern. "What'd them men have to do with it? Where'd you all be now if it wasn't for me?"

"You'd be much better off," I ventured, "if I hadn't done any rescuing at all, and if we'd all stayed over there on the boat." I pointed to the lights of the *River Belle*, lying on the opposite shore, something like a mile above us.

"We're all right now," said old Auberry after a time. "If we can't get across to the boat, it's only four or five miles up to the settlements on this side, opposite the old Independence landing."

"I couldn't walk," said the girl. She shyly looked down at the edge of her thin wrapper, and I saw the outline of an uncovered toe.

"Here, ma'am," said Auberry, unknotting from his neck a heavy bandana. "This is the best I can do. You and the woman see if you can tie up your feet somehow."

The girl hesitated, laughed, and took the kerchief. She and Mandy bent apart, and I heard the ripping of the handkerchief torn across. The girl turned back to the fire and put out a little foot for us to see, muffled now in the red folds of the kerchief. Her thin garments by this time were becoming dry, and her spirits now became more gay. She fell into a ready comradeship with us.

As she stood at the fire, innocent of its defining light, I saw that she was a beautiful creature, apparently about twenty years of age. Given proper surroundings, I fancied, here was a girl who might make trouble for a man. Eyes like hers, I imagined, had before this set some man's heart astir; and one so fair as she never waited long in this world for admirers.

She stooped and spread out her hands before the flames. I could see that her hands were small and well formed, could see the firelight shine pink at the inner edges of her fingers. On one finger, as I could not avoid noticing, was a curious ring of plain gold. The setting, also of gold, was deeply cut into the figure of a rose. I recalled that I had never seen a ring just similar. Indeed, it seemed to me, as I stole a furtive glance at her now and then, I had never seen a girl just similar.

They Fought Furiously The Yelling Charging Redskin Warriors

The Wagons Draw Into A Defensive Circle

We had waited perhaps not over an hour at our fireside, undecided what to do, when Auberry raised a hand. "Listen," he said. "There's a boat coming"; and presently we all heard the splash of oars. Our fire had been seen by one of the boats of the *River Belle*, out picking up such stragglers as could be found.

"Hello, there!" called a rough voice to us, as the boat grated at our beach. Auberry and I walked over and found that it was the mate of the boat, with a pair of oarsmen in a narrow river skiff.

"How many's there of you?" asked the mate—"Five?—I can't take you all."

"All right," said Auberry, "this gentleman and I will walk up to the town on this side. You take the women and the boy. We'll send down for our things in the morning, if you don't come up."

So our little bivouac on the beach came to an end. A moment later the passengers were embarked, and Auberry and I, standing at the bow, were about to push off the boat for them.

"A moment, sir," exclaimed our friend of the fireside, rising and stepping toward me as I stood alongside the boat. "You are forgetting your coat."

She would have taken it from her shoulders, but I forbade it. She hesitated, and finally said, "I thank you so much"; holding out her hand.

I took it. It was a small hand, with round fingers, firm of clasp. I hate a hard-handed woman, or one with mushy fingers, but this, as it seemed to me, was a hand excellently good to clasp—warm now, and no longer trembling in the terrors of the night.

"I do not know your name, sir," she said, "but I should like my father to thank you some day."

"All ready!" cried the mate.

"My name is Cowles," I began, "and sometime, perhaps—"

"All aboard!" cried the mate; and so the oars gave way.

So I did not get the name of the girl I had seen there in the firelight. What did remain—and that not wholly to my pleasure, so distinct it seemed—was the picture of her high-bred profile, shown in chiaroscuro at the fireside, the line of her chin and neck, the tumbled masses of her hair. These were things I did not care to remember; and I hated myself as a soft-hearted fool, seeing that I did so.

"Son," said old Auberry to me, after a time, as we trudged along up the bank, stumbling over roots and braided grasses, "that was a almighty fine lookin' gal we brung along with us there."

"I didn't notice," said I.

"No," said Auberry, solemnly, "I noticed you didn't take no notice; so you can just take my judgment on it, which I allow is safe. Are you a married man?"

"Not yet," I said.

"You might do a heap worse than that gal," said Auberry.

"I suppose you're married yourself," I suggested.

"Some," said Auberry, chuckling in the dark. "In fact, a good deal, I reckon. My present woman's a Shoshone—we're livin' up Horse Creek, below Laramie. Them Shoshones make about the best dressers of 'em all."

"I don't quite understand—"

"I meant hides. They can make the best buckskin of any tribe I know." He walked on ahead in the dark for some time, before he added irrelevantly, "Well, after all, in some ways, women is women, my son, and men is men; that bein' the way this world is made just at these here present times. As I was sayin', that's a powerful nice lookin' gal."

I shuddered in my soul. I glanced up at the heavens, studded thick with stars. It seemed to me that I saw gazing down directly at me one cold, bright, reproving star, staring straight into my soul, and accusing me of being nothing more than a savage, nothing better than a man.

Chapter XIV - Au Large

At our little village on the following morning, Auberry and I learned that the *River Bell* would lie up indefinitely for repairs, and that at least one, perhaps several days would elapse before she resumed her journey up stream. This suited neither of us, so we sent a negro down with a skiff, and had him bring up our rifles, Auberry's bedding, my portmanteaus, etc., it being our intention to take the stage up to Leavenworth. By noon our plans were changed again, for a young Army officer came down from that Post with the information that Colonel Meriwether was not there. He had been ordered out to the Posts up the Platte River, had been gone for three weeks; and no one could tell what time he would return. The Indians were reported very bad along the Platte. Possibly Colonel Meriwether might be back at Leavenworth within the week, possibly not for a month or more!

This was desperate news for me, for I knew that I ought to be starting home at that very time. Still, since I had come hither as a last resort, it would do no good for me to go back unsuccessful. Should I wait here, or at Leavenworth; or should I go on still farther west? Auberry decided that for me.

"I tell you what we can do," he said. "We can outfit here, and take the Cut-off trail to the Platte, across the Kaw and the Big and Little Blue—that'll bring us in far enough east to catch the Colonel if he's comin' down the valley. You'd just as well be travelin' as loafin', and that's like enough the quickest way to find him."

The counsel seemed good. I sat down and wrote two more letters home, once more stating that I was not starting east, but going still farther west. This done, I tried to persuade myself to feel no further uneasiness, and to content my mind with the sense of duty done.

Auberry, as it chanced, fell in with a party bound for Denver, five men who had two wagons, a heavy Conestoga freight wagon, or prairie schooner, and a lighter vehicle without a cover. We arranged with these men, and their cook as to our share in the mess box, and so threw in our dunnage with theirs, Auberry and I purchasing us a good horse apiece. By noon of the next day we were on our way westward, Auberry himself now much content.

"The settlements for them that likes 'em," said he. "For me, there's nothing like the time when I start west, with a horse under me, and run *au large*, as the French traders say. You'll get a chance now to see the Plains, my son."

At first we saw rather the prairies than the Plains proper. We were following a plainly marked trail, which wound in and out among low rolling hills; and for two days we remained in touch with the scattered huts of the squalid, half-civilized Indians and squaw men who still hung around the upper reservations. Bleached bones of the buffalo we saw here and there, but there was no game. The buffalo had long years since been driven far to the westward. We took some fine fish in the clear waters of the forks of the Blue, which with some difficulty we were able to ford. Gradually shaking down into better organization, we fared on and on day after day, until the grass grew shorter and the hills flatter. At last we approached the valley of the Platte.

We were coming now indeed into the great Plains, of which I had heard all my youth. A new atmosphere seemed to invest the world. The talk of my companions was of things new and wild and strange to me. All my old life seemed to be slipping back of me, into a far oblivion. A feeling of rest, of confidence and of uplift came to me. It was difficult to be sad. The days were calm, the nights were full of peace. Nature seemed to be loftily above all notice of small frettings. Many things became more clear to me, as I rode and reflected. In some way, I know not how, it seemed to me that I was growing older.

We had been out more than two weeks when finally we reached the great valley along which lay the western highway of the old Oregon trail, now worn deep and dusty by countless wheels. Our progress had not been very rapid, and we had lost time on two occasions in hunting up strayed animals. But, here at last, I saw the road of the old fur traders, of Ashley and Sublette and Bridger, of Carson and Fremont, later of Kearney, Sibley, Marcy, one knew not how many Army men, who had for years been fighting back the tribes and making ready this country for white occupation. As I looked at this wild, wide region, treeless, fruitless, it seemed to me that none could want it. The next thought was the impression that, no matter how many might covet it, it was exhaustless, and would last forever. This land, this West, seemed to all then unbelievably large and limitless.

We pushed up the main trail of the Platte but a short distance that night, keeping out an eye for grazing ground for our horses. Auberry knew the country perfectly. "About five or six miles above here," he said, "there's a stage station, if the company's still running through here now. Used to be two or three fellers and some horses stayed there."

We looked forward to meeting human faces with some pleasure; but an hour or so later, as we rode on, I saw Auberry pull up his horse, with a strange tightening of his lips. "Boys," said he, "there's where it *was!*" His pointing finger showed nothing more than a low line of ruins, bits of broken fencing, a heap of half-charred timbers.

"They've been here," said Auberry, grimly. "Who'd have thought the Sioux would be this far east?"

He circled his horse out across the valley, riding with his head bent down. "Four days ago at least," he said, "and a bunch of fifty or more of them. Come on, men."

We rode up to the station, guessing what we would see. The buildings lay waste and white in ashes. The front of the dugout was torn down, the wood of its doors and windows burned. The door of the larger dugout, where the horses had been stabled, was also torn away. Five dead horses lay near by, a part of the stage stock kept there. We kept our eyes as long as we could from what we knew must next be seen—the bodies of the agent and his two stablemen, mutilated and half consumed, under the burned-out timbers. I say the bodies, for the lower limbs of all three had been dismembered and cast in a heap near where the bodies of the horses lay. We were on the scene of one of the brutal massacres of the savage Indian tribes. It seemed strange these things should be in a spot so silent and peaceful, under a sky so blue and gentle.

"Sioux!" said Auberry, looking down as he leaned on his long rifle. "Not a wheel has crossed their trail, and I reckon the trail's blocked both east and west. But the boys put up a fight." He led us here and there and showed dried blotches on the soil, half buried now in the shifting sand; showed us the bodies of a half-dozen ponies, killed a couple of hundred yards from the door of the dugout.

"They must have shot in at the front till they killed the boys," he added. "And they was so mad they stabbed the horses for revenge, the way they do sometimes. Yes, the boys paid their way when they went, I reckon."

We stood now in a silent group, and what was best to be done none at first could tell. Two of our party were for turning back down the valley, but Auberry said he could see no advantage in that.

"Which way they've gone above here no one can tell," he said. "They're less likely to come here now, so it seems to me the best thing we can do is to lay up here and wait for some teams comin' west. There'll be news of some kind along one way or the other, before so very long."

So now we, the living, took up our places almost upon the bodies of the dead, after giving these the best interment possible. We hobbled and side-lined our horses, and kept our guards both day and night; and so we lay here for three days.

The third day passed until the sun sank toward the sand dunes, and cast a long path of light across the rippling shallows among the sand bars of the Platte; but still we saw no signs of newcomers. Evening was approaching when we heard the sound of a distant shot, and turning saw our horse-guard, who had been stationed at the top of a bluff near by, start down the slope, running toward the camp. As he approached he pointed, and we looked down the valley toward the east.

Surely enough, we saw a faint cloud of dust coming toward us, whether of vehicles or horsemen we could not tell. Auberry thought that it was perhaps some west-bound emigrant or freight wagon, or perhaps a stage with belated mails.

"Stay here, boys," he said, "and I'll ride down and see." He galloped off, half a mile or so, and then we saw him pause, throw up his hand, and ride forward at full speed. By that time the travelers were topping a slight rise in the floor of the valley, and we could see that they were horsemen, perhaps thirty or forty in all. Following them came the dust-whitened top of an Army ambulance, and several camp wagons, to the best of our figuring at that distance. We hesitated no longer and quickly mounting our horses rode full speed toward them. Auberry met us, coming back.

"Troop of dragoons, bound for Laramie," he said. "No Indians back of them, but orders are out for all of the wagons and stages to hole up till further orders. This party's going through. I told them to camp down there," he said to me aside, "because they've got women with 'em, and I didn't want them to see what's happened up here. We'll move our camp down to theirs to-night, and like enough go on with them to-morrow."

By the time I was ready to approach these new arrivals, they had their plans for encampment under way with the celerity of old campaigners. Their horses were hobbled, their cook-fires of buffalo "chips" were lit, their wagons backed into a rude stockade. Guards were moving out with the horses to the grazing ground. They were a seasoned lot of Harney's frontier fighters, grimed and grizzled, their hats, boots and clothing gray with dust, but their weapons bright. Their leader was a young lieutenant, who approached me when I rode up. It seemed to me I remembered his blue eyes and his light mustaches, curled upward at the points.

"Lieutenant Belknap!" I exclaimed. "Do you remember meeting me down at Jefferson?"

"Why, Mr. Cowles!" he exclaimed. "How on earth did you get here? Of course I remember you."

"Yes, but how did you get here yourself—you were not on my boat?"

"I was ordered up the day after you left Jefferson Barracks," he said, "and took the *Asia*. We got into St. Joe the same day with the *River Belle*, and heard about your accident down river. I suppose you came out on the old Cut-off trail."

"Yes; and of course you took the main trail west from Leavenworth."

He nodded. "Orders to take this detachment out to Laramie," he said, "and meet Colonel Meriwether there."

"He'll not be back?" I exclaimed in consternation. "I was hoping to meet him coming east."

"No," said Belknap, "you'll have to go on with us if you wish to see him. I'm afraid the Sioux are bad on beyond. Horrible thing your man tells me about up there," he motioned toward the ruined station. "I'm taking his advice and going into camp here, for I imagine it isn't a nice thing for a woman to see."

He turned toward the ambulance, and I glanced that way. There stood near it a tall, angular figure, head enshrouded in an enormous sunbonnet; a personality which it seemed to me I recognized.

"Why, that's my friend, Mandy McGovern," said I. "I met her on the boat. Came out from Leavenworth with you, I suppose?"

"That isn't the one," said Belknap. "No, I don't fancy that sister McGovern would cut up much worse than the rest of us over that matter up there; but the other one—"

At that moment, descending at the rear of the ambulance, I saw the other one.

Chapter XV - Her Infinite Variety

It was a young woman who left the step of the ambulance and stood for a moment shading her eyes with her hand and looking out over the shimmering expanse of the broad river. All at once the entire landscape was changed. It was not the desert, but civilization which swept about us. A transfiguration had been wrought by one figure, fair to look upon.

I could see that this was no newcomer in the world of the out-of-doors, however. She was turned out in what one might have called workmanlike fashion, although neat and wholly feminine. Her skirt was short, of good gray cloth, and she wore a rather mannish coat over a blue woolen shirt or blouse. Her hands were covered with long gauntlets, and her hat was a soft gray felt, tied under the chin with a leather string, while a soft gray veil was knotted carelessly about her neck as kerchief. Her face for the time was turned from us, but I could see that her hair was dark and heavy, could see, in spite of its loose garb, that her figure was straight, round and slender. The swift versatility of my soul was upon the point of calling this as fine a figure of young womanhood as I had ever seen. Now, indeed, the gray desert had blossomed as a rose.

I was about to ask some questions of Belknap, when all at once I saw something which utterly changed my pleasant frame of mind. The tall figure of a man came from beyond the line of wagons—a man clad in well-fitting tweeds cut for riding. His gloves seemed neat, his boots equally neat, his general appearance immaculate as that of the young lady whom he approached. I imagine it was the same swift male jealousy which affected both Belknap and myself as we saw Gordon Orme!

"Yes, there is your friend, the Englishman," said Belknap rather bitterly.

"I meet him everywhere," I answered. "The thing is simply uncanny. What is he doing out here?"

"We are taking him out to Laramie with us. He has letters to Colonel Meriwether, it seems. Cowles, what do you know about that man?"

"Nothing," said I, "except that he purports to come from the English Army."

"I wish that he had stayed in the English Army, and not come bothering about ours. He's prowling about every military Post he can get into."

"With a special reference to Army officers born in the South?" I looked Belknap full in the eye.

"There's something in that," he replied. "I don't like the look of it. These are good times for every man to attend to his own business."

As Orme stood chatting with the young woman, both Belknap and I turned away. A moment later I ran across my former friend, Mandy McGovern. In her surprise she stopped chewing tobacco, when her eyes fell on me, but she quickly came to shake me by the hand.

"Well, I dee-clare to gracious!" she began, "if here ain't the man I met on the boat! How'd you git away out here ahead of us? Have you saw airy buffeler? I'm gettin' plumb wolfish fer something to shoot at. Where all you goin', anyhow? An' whut you doin' out here?"

What I was doing at that precise moment, as I must confess, was taking a half unconscious look once more toward the tail of the ambulance, where Orme and the young woman stood chatting. But it was at this time that Orme first saw or seemed to see me. He left the ambulance and came rapidly forward.

"By Jove!" he said, "here you are again! Am I your shadow, Mr. Cowles, or are you mine? It is really singular how we meet. I'm awfully glad to meet you, although I don't in the least see how you've managed to get here ahead of us."

Belknap by this time had turned away about his duties, and Orme and I spoke for a few minutes. I explained to him the changes of my plans which had been brought about by the accident to the *River Belle*. "Lieutenant Belknap tells me that you are going through to Laramie with him," I added. "As it chances, we have the same errand—it is my purpose also to call on Colonel Meriwether there, in case we do not meet him coming down."

"How extraordinary! Then we'll be fellow travelers for a time, and I hope have a little sport together. Fine young fellow, Belknap. And I must say that his men, although an uncommonly ragged looking lot and very far from smart as soldiers, have rather a workmanlike way about them, after all."

"Yes, I think they would fight," I remarked, coolly. "And from the look of things, they may have need to." I told him then of what he had discovered at the station house near by, and added the caution not to mention it about the camp. Orme's eyes merely brightened with interest. Anything like danger or adventure had appeal to him. I said to him that he seemed to me more soldier than preacher, but he only laughed and evaded.

"You'll eat at our mess to-night, of course" said he. "That's our fire just over there, and I'm thinking the cook is nearly ready. There comes Belknap now."

Thus, it may be seen, the confusion of these varied meetings had kept me from learning the name or identity of the late passenger of the ambulance. I presume both Orme and Belknap supposed that the young lady and I had met before we took our places on the ground at the edge of the blanket which served as a table. She was seated as I finally approached, and her face was turned aside as she spoke to the camp cook, with whom she seemed on the best of terms. "Hurry, Daniels," she called out. "I'm absolutely starved to death!"

There was something in her voice which sounded familiar to me, and I sought a glance at her face, which the next instant was hid by the rim of her hat as she looked down, removing her long gloves. At least I saw her hands—small hands, sun-browned now. On one finger was a plain gold ring, with a peculiar setting—the figure of a rose, carved deep into the gold!

"After all," thought I to myself, "there are some things which can not be duplicated. Among these, hair like this, a profile like this, a figure like this." I gazed in wonder, then in certainty.

No there was no escaping the conclusion. This was not another girl, but the same girl seen again. A moment's reflection showed how possible and indeed natural this might be. My chance companion in the river accident had simply gone on up the river a little farther and then started west precisely as Mandy McGovern had explained.

Belknap caught the slight restraint as the girl and I both raised our eyes. "Oh, I say, why—what in the world—Mr. Cowles, didn't you—that is, haven't you—"

"No," said I, "I haven't and didn't, I think. But I think also—"

The girl's face was a trifle flushed, but her eyes were merry. "Yes," said she, "I think Mr. Cowles and I have met once before." She slightly emphasized the word "once," as I noticed.

"But still I may remind you all, gentlemen," said I, "that I have not yet heard this lady's name, and am only guessing, of course, that it is Miss Meriwether, whom you are taking out to Laramie."

"Why, of course," said Belknap, and "of course," echoed everybody else. My fair *vis-a-vis* looked me now full in the face and smiled, so that a dimple in her right cheek was plainly visible.

"Yes," said she, "I'm going on out to join my father on the front. This is my second time across, though. Is it your first, Mr. Cowles?"

"My first; and I am very lucky. You know, I also am going out to meet your father, Miss Meriwether."

"How singular!" She put down her tin cup of coffee on the blanket.

"My father was an associate of Colonel Meriwether in some business matters back in Virginia—"

"Oh, I know—it's about the coal lands, that are going to make us all rich some day. Yes, I know about that; though I think your father rarely came over into Albemarle."

Under the circumstances I did not care to intrude my personal matters, so I did not mention the cause or explain the nature of my mission in the West. "I suppose that you rarely came into our county either, but went down the Shenandoah when you journeyed to Washington?" I said simply, "I myself have never met Colonel Meriwether."

All this sudden acquaintance and somewhat intimate relation between us two seemed to afford no real pleasure either to Belknap or Orme. For my part, with no clear reason in the world, it seemed to me that both Belknap and Orme were very detestable persons. Had the framing of this scene been left utterly to me, I should have had none present at the fireside save myself and Ellen Meriwether. All these wide gray plains, faintly tinged in the hollows with green, and all this sweeping sky of blue, and all this sparkling river, should have been just for ourselves and no one else.

But my opportunity came in due course, after all. As we rose from the ground at the conclusion of our meal, the girl dropped one of her gloves. I hastened to pick it up, walking with her a few paces afterward.

"The next time we are shipwrecked together," said I, "I shall leave you on the boat. You do not know your friends!"

"Why do you say that?"

"And yet I knew you at once. I saw the ring on your hand, and recognized it—it is the same I saw in the firelight on the river bank, the night we left the *Belle*."

"How brilliant of you! At least you can remember a ring."

"I remember seeing the veil you wear once before—at a certain little meeting between Mr. Orme and myself."

"You seem to have been a haberdasher in your time, Mr. Cowles! Your memory of a lady's wearing apparel is very exact. I should feel very much nattered." None the less I saw the dimple come in her cheek.

She was pulling on her glove as she spoke. I saw embroidered on the gauntlet the figure of a red heart.

"My memory is still more exact in the matter of apparel," said I. "Miss Meriwether, is this your emblem indeed—this red heart? It seems to me I have also seen *it* somewhere before!"

The dimple deepened. "When Columbus found America," she answered, "it is said that the savages looked up and remarked to him, 'Ah, we see we are discovered!'"

"Yes," said I, "you are fully discovered—each of you—all of you, all three or four of you, Miss *Ellen Meriwether*."

"But you did not know it until now—until this very moment. You did not know me—could not remember me—not even when the masks were off! Ah, it was good as a play!"

"I have done nothing else but remember you."

"How much I should value your acquaintance, Mr. Cowles of Virginia! How rare an opportunity you have given me of seeing on the inside of a man's heart." She spoke half bitterly, and I saw that in one way or other she meant revenge.

"I do not understand you," I rejoined.

"No, I suppose you men are all alike—that any one of you would do the same. It is only the last girl, the nearest girl, that is remembered. Is it not so?"

"It is not so," I answered.

"How long will you remember me this time—me or my clothes, Mr. Cowles? Until you meet another?"

"All my life," I said; "and until I meet you again, in some other infinite variety. Each last time that I see you makes me forget all the others; but never once have I forgotten *you*."

"In my experience," commented the girl, sagely, "all men talk very much alike."

"Yes, I told you at the masked ball," said I, "that sometime I would see you, masks off. Was it not true? I did not at first know you when you broke up my match with Orme, but I swore that sometime I would know you. And when I saw you that night on the river, it seemed to me I certainly must have met you before—have known you always—and now—"

"You had to study my rings and clothing to identify me with myself!"

"But you flatter me when you say that you knew me each time," I ventured. "I am glad that I have given you no occasion to prove the truth of your own statement, that I, like other men, am interested only in the last girl, the nearest girl. You have had no reason—"

"My experience with men," went on this sage young person, "leads me to believe that they are the stupidest of all created creatures. There was never once, there is never once, when a girl does not notice a man who is—well, who is taking notice!"

"Very well, then," I broke out, "I admit it! I did take notice of four different girls, one after the other—but it was because each of them was fit to wipe out the image of all the others—and of all the others in the world."

This was going far. I was a young man. I urge no more excuse. I am setting down simply the truth, as I have promised.

The girl looked about, gladly, I thought, at the sound of a shuffling step approaching. "You, Aunt Mandy?" she called out. And to me, "I must say good-night, sir."

I turned away moodily, and found the embers of the fire at my own camp. Not far away I could hear the stamp of horses, the occasional sound of low voices and of laughter, where some of the enlisted men were grouped upon the ground. The black blur made by the wagon stockade and a tent or so was visible against the lighter line of the waterway of the Platte. Night came down, brooding with its million stars. I could hear the voices of the wolves calling here and there. It was a scene wild and appealing. I was indeed, it seemed to me, in a strange new world, where all was young, where everything was beginning. Where was the old world I had left behind me?

I rolled into my blankets, but I could not sleep. The stars were too bright, the wind too full of words, the sweep of the sky too strong. I shifted the saddle under my head, and turned and turned, but I could not rest. I looked up again into the eye of my cold, reproving star.

But now, to my surprise and horror, when I looked into the eye of my monitor, my own eye would not waver nor admit subjection! I rebelled at my own conscience. I, John Cowles, had all my life been a strong man. I had wrestled with any who came, fought with any who asked it, matched with any man on any terms he named. Conflict was in my blood, and always I had fought blithely. But never with sweat like this on my forehead! Never with fear catching at my heart! Never with the agony of self-reproach assailing me!

Now, to-night, I was meeting the strongest antagonist of all my life, the only one I had ever feared.

It was none other than I myself, that other John Cowles, young man, and now loose in the vast, free, garden of living.

Yet I fought with myself. I tried to banish her face from my heart — with all my might, and all my conscience, and all my remaining principles, I did try. I called up to mind my promises, my duties, my honor. But none of these would put her face away. I tried to forget the softness of her voice, the fragrance of her hair, the sweetness of her body once held in my arms, all the vague charm of woman, the enigma, the sphinx, the mystery-magnet of the world, the charm that has no analysis, that knows no formula; but I could not forget. A rage filled me against all the other men in the world. I have said I would set down the truth. The truth is that I longed to rise and roar in my throat, challenging all the other men in the world. In truth it was my wish to stride over there, just beyond, into the darkness, to take this woman by the shoulders and tell her what was in my blood and in my heart — even though I must tell her even in bitterness and self-reproach.

It was not the girl to whom I was pledged and plighted, not she to whom I was bound in honor — that was not the one with the fragrant hair and the eyes of night, and the clear-cut face, and the graciously deep-bosomed figure — that was not the one. It was another, of infinite variety, one more irresistible with each change, that had set on this combat between me and my own self.

I beat my fists upon the earth. All that I could say to myself was that she was sweet, sweet, and wonderful — here in the mystery of this wide, calm, inscrutable desert that lay all about, in a world young and strong and full of the primeval lusts of man.

Chapter XVI - Buffalo!

Before dawn had broken, the clear bugle notes of reveille sounded and set the camp astir. Presently the smokes of the cook fires arose, and in the gray light we could see the horse-guards bringing in the mounts. By the time the sun was faintly tinging the edge of the valley we were drawn up for hot coffee and the plain fare of the prairies. A half hour later the wagon masters called "Roll out! Roll out!" The bugles again sounded for the troopers to take saddle, and we were under way once more.

Thus far we had seen very little game in our westward journeying, a few antelope and occasional wolves, but none of the herds of buffalo which then roamed the Western plains. The monotony of our travel was to be broken now. We had hardly gone five miles beyond the ruined station house—which we passed at a trot, so that none might know what had happened there—when we saw our advance men pull up and raise their hands. We caught it also—the sound of approaching hoofs, and all joined in the cry, "Buffalo! Buffalo!" In an instant every horseman was pressing forward.

The thunderous rolling sound approached, heavy as that of artillery going into action. We saw dust arise from the mouth of a little draw on the left, running down toward the valley, and even as we turned there came rolling from its mouth, with the noise of a tornado and the might of a mountain torrent, a vast, confused, dark mass, which rapidly spilled out across the valley ahead of us. Half hid in the dust of their going, we could see great dark bulks rolling and tossing. Thus it was, and close at hand, that I saw for the first time in my life these huge creatures whose mission seemed to have been to support an uncivilized people, and to make possible the holding by another race of those lands late held as savage harvest grounds.

We were almost at the flanks of the herd before they reached the river bank. We were among them when they paused stupidly, for some reason not wishing to cross the stream. The front ranks rolled back upon those behind, which, crowded from the rear, resisted. The whole front of the mass wrinkled up mightily, dark humps arising in some places two or three deep. Then the entire mass sensed the danger all at once, and with as much unanimity as they had lacked concert in their late confusion, they wheeled front and rear, and rolled off up the valley, still enveloped in a cloud of white, biting dust.

In such a chase speed and courage of one's horse are the main essentials. My horse, luckily for me, was able to lay me alongside my game within a few hundred yards. I coursed close to a big black bull and, obeying injunctions old Auberry had often given me, did not touch the trigger until I found I was holding well forward and rather low. I could scarcely hear the crack of the rifle, such was the noise of hoofs, but I saw the bull switch his tail and push on as though unhurt, in spite of the trickle of red which sprung on his flank. As I followed on, fumbling for a pistol at my holster, the bull suddenly turned, head down and tail stiffly erect, his mane bristling. My horse sprang aside, and the herd passed on. The old bull, his head lowered, presently stopped, deliberately eying us, and a moment later he deliberately lay down, presently sinking lower, and at length rolled over dead.

I got down, fastening my horse to one of the horns of the dead bull. As I looked up the valley, I could see others dismounted, and many vast dark blotches on the gray. Here and there, where the pursuers still hung on, blue smoke was cutting through the white. Certainly we would have meat that day, enough and far more than enough. The valley was full of carcasses, product of the wasteful white man's hunting. Later I learned that old Mandy, riding a mule astride, had made the run and killed a buffalo with her own rifle!

I found the great weight of the bull difficult to turn, but at length I hooked one horn into the ground, and laying hold of the lower hind leg, I actually turned the carcass on its back. I was busy skinning when my old friend Auberry rode up.

"That's the first time I ever saw a bull die on his back," said he.

"He did not die on his back," I replied. "I turned him over."

"You did—and alone? It's rarely a single man could do that, nor have I seen it done in all my life with so big a bull."

I laughed at him. "It was easy. My father and I once lifted a loaded wagon out of the mud."

"The Indians," said Auberry, "don't bother to turn a bull over. They split the hide down the back, and skin both ways. The best meat is on top, anyhow"; and then he gave me lessons in buffalo values, which later I remembered.

We had taken some meat from my bull, since I insisted upon it in spite of better beef from a young cow Auberry had killed not far above, when suddenly I heard the sound of a bugle, sharp and clear, and recognized the notes of the "recall." The sergeant of our troop, with a small number who did not care to hunt, had been left behind by Belknap's hurried orders. Again and again we heard the bugle call, and now at once saw coming down the valley the men of our little command.

"What's up?" inquired Auberry, as we pulled up our galloping horses near the wagon line.

"Indians!" was the answer. "Fall in!" In a moment most of our men were gathered at the wagon line, and like magic the scene changed.

We could all now see coming down from a little flattened coulee to the left, a head of a line of mounted men, who doubtless had been the cause of the buffalo stampede which had crossed in front of us. The shouts of teamsters and the crack of whips punctuated the crunch of wheels as our wagons swiftly swung again into stockade. The ambulance was hurriedly driven into the center of the heavier wagons, which formed in a rude half circle.

After all, there seemed no immediate danger. The column of the tribesmen came on toward us fearlessly, as though they neither dreaded us nor indeed recognized us. They made a long calvacade, two hundred horses or more, with many travaux and dogs trailing on behind. They were all clad in their native finery, seemingly hearty and well fed, and each as arrogant as a king. They passed us contemptuously, with not a sidelong glance.

In advance of the head men who rode foremost in the column were three or four young women, bearing long lance shafts decorated with feathers and locks of human hair, the steel tips shining gray in the sun. These young women, perhaps not squires or heralds of the tribe, but wives of one or more of the head men, were decorated with brass and beads and shining things, their hair covered with gauds, their black eyes shining too, though directed straight ahead. Their garb was of tanned leather, the tunics or dresses were of elk skin, and the white leggins of antelope hide or that of mountain sheep. Their buffalo hide moccasins were handsomely beaded and stained. As they passed, followed by the long train of stalwart savage figures, they made a spectacle strange and savage, but surely not less than impressive.

Not a word was spoken on either side. The course of their column took them to the edge of the water a short distance above us. They drove their horses down to drink scrambled up the bank again, and then presently, in answer to some sort of signal, quietly rode on a quarter of a mile or so and pulled up at the side of the valley. They saw abundance of meat lying there already killed, and perhaps guessed that we could not use all of it.

"Auberry," said Belknap, "we must go talk to these people, and see what's up."

"They're Sioux!" said Auberry. "Like enough the very devils that cleaned out the station down there. But come on; they don't mean fight right now."

Belknap and Auberry took with them the sergeant and a dozen troopers. I pushed in with these, and saw Orme at my side; and Belknap did not send us back. We four rode on together presently.

Two or three hundred yards from the place where the Indians halted, Auberry told Belknap to halt his men. We four, with one private to hold our horses, rode forward a hundred yards farther, halted and raised our hands in sign of peace. There rode out to us four of the head men of the Sioux, beautifully dressed, each a stalwart man. We dismounted, laid down our weapons on the ground, and approached each other.

"Watch them close, boys," whispered Auberry. "They've got plenty of irons around them somewhere, and plenty of scalps, too, maybe."

"Talk to them, Auberry," said Belknap; and as the former was the only one of us who understood the Sioux tongue, he acted as interpreter.

"What are the Sioux doing so far east?" he asked of their spokesman, sternly.

"Hunting," answered the Sioux, as Auberry informed us. "The white soldiers drive away our buffalo. The white men kill too many. Let them go. This is our country." It seemed to me I could see the black eyes of the Sioux boring straight through every one of us, glittering, not in the least afraid.

"Go back to the north and west, where you belong," said Auberry. "You have no business here on the wagon trails."

"The Sioux hunt where they please," was the grim answer. "But you see we have our women and children with us, the same as you have—and he pointed toward our camp, doubtless knowing the personnel of our party as well as we did ourselves.

"Where are you going?" asked our interpreter.

The Sioux waved his arm vaguely. "Heap hunt," he said, in broken English now. "Where you go?" he asked, in return.

Auberry was also a diplomat, and answered that we were going a half sleep to the west, to meet a big war party coming down the Platte, the white men from Laramie.

The Indian looked grave at this. "Is that so?" he asked, calmly. "I had not any word from my young men about a war party coming down the river. Many white tepees on wheels going up the river; no soldiers coming down this way."

"We are going on up to meet our soldiers," said Auberry, sternly. "The Sioux have killed some of our men below here. We shall meet our soldiers and come and wipe the Sioux off the land if they come into the valley where our great road runs west."

"That is good," said the Sioux. "As for us, we harm no white man. We hunt where we please. White men go!"

Auberry now turned to us. "I don't think they mean trouble, Lieutenant," he said, "and I think the best thing we can do is to let them alone and go on up the valley. Let's go on and pull on straight by them, the way they did us, and call it a draw all around."

Belknap nodded, and Auberry turned again to the four Sioux, who stood tall and motionless, looking at us with the same fixed, glittering eyes. I shall remember the actors in that little scene so long as I live.

"We have spoken," said Auberry. "That is all we have to say."

Both parties turned and went back to their companions. Belknap, Auberry and I had nearly reached our waiting troopers, when we missed Orme, and turned back to see where he was. He was standing close to the four chiefs, who had by this time reached their horses. Orme was leading by the bridle his own horse, which was slightly lame from a strain received in the hunt.

"Some buck'll slip an arrer into him, if he don't look out," said Auberry. "He's got no business out there."

We saw Orme making some sort of gestures, pointing to his horse and the others.

"Wonder if he wants to trade horses!" mused Auberry, chuckling. Then in the same breath he called, "Look out! By God! Look!"

We all saw it. Orme's arm shot out straight, tipped by a blue puff of smoke, and we heard the crack of the dragoon pistol. One of the Sioux, the chief who by this time had mounted his horse, threw his hand against his chest and leaned slightly back, then straightened up slightly as he sat. As he fell, or before he fell, Orme pushed his body clear from the saddle, and with a leap was in the dead man's place and riding swiftly toward us, leading his own horse by the rein!

It seemed that it was the Sioux who had kept faith after all; for none of the remaining three could find a weapon. Orme rode up laughing and unconcerned. "The beggar wouldn't trade with me at all," he said. "By Jove, I believe he'd have got me if he'd had any sort of tools for it."

"You broke treaty!" ejaculated Belknap—"you broke the council word."

"Did that man make the first break at you?" Auberry blazed at him.

"How can I tell?" answered Orme, coolly. "It's well to be a trifle ahead in such matters." He seemed utterly unconcerned. He could kill a man as lightly as a rabbit, and think no more about it.

Within the instant the entire party of the Sioux was in confusion. We saw them running about, mounting, heard them shouting and wailing.

"It's fight now!" said Auberry. "Back to the wagons now and get your men ready, Lieutenant. As soon as the Sioux can get shut of their women, they'll come on, and come a boilin', too. You damned fool!" he said to Orme. "You murdered that man!"

"What's that, my good fellow?" said Orme, sharply. "Now I advise you to keep a civil tongue in your head, or I'll teach you some manners."

Even as we swung and rode back, Auberry pushed alongside Orme, his rifle at ready. "By God! man, if you want to teach *me* any manners, begin it now. You make your break," he cried.

Belknap spurred in between them. "Here, you men," he commanded with swift sternness. "Into your places. I'm in command here, and I'll shoot the first man who raises a hand. Mr. Orme, take your place at the wagons. Auberry, keep with me. We'll have fighting enough without anything of this."

"He murdered that Sioux, Lieutenant," reiterated Auberry.

"Damn it, sir, I know he did, but this is no time to argue about that. Look there!"

At Every Turn Forced To Hide Their Tracks

A long, ragged, parti-colored line, made up of the squaws and children of the party, was whipping up the sides of the rough bluffs on the left of the valley. We heard wailing, the barking of dogs, the crying of children. We saw the Sioux separate thus into two bands, the men remaining behind riding back and forth, whooping and holding aloft their weapons. We heard the note of a dull war drum beating the clacking of their rattles and the shrill notes of their war whistles.

"They'll fight," said Auberry. "Look at 'em!"

"Here they come," said Belknap, coolly. "Get down, men."

Chapter XVII - Sioux!

The record of this part of my life comes to me sometimes as a series of vivid pictures. I can see this picture now — the wide gray of the flat valley, edged with green at the coulee mouths; the sandy spots where the wind had worked at the foot of the banks; the dotted islands out in the shimmering, shallow river. I can see again, under the clear, sweet, quiet sky, the picture of those painted men — their waving lances, their swaying bodies as they reached for the quivers across their shoulders. I can see the loose ropes trailing at the horses' noses, and see the light leaning forward of the red and yellow and ghastly white-striped and black-stained bodies, and the barred black of the war paint on their faces. I feel again, so much almost that my body swings in unison, the gathering stride of the ponies cutting the dust into clouds. I see the color and the swiftness of it all, and feel its thrill, the strength and tenseness of it all. And again I feel, as though it were to-day, the high, keen, pleasant resolution which came to me. We had women with us. Whether this young woman was now to die or not, none of us men would see it happen.

They came on, massed as I have said, to within about two hundred and fifty yards, then swung out around us, their horse line rippling up over the broken ground apparently as easily as it had gone on the level floor of the valley. Still we made no volley fire. I rejoiced to see the cool pallor of Belknap's face, and saw him brave and angry to the core. Our plainsmen, too, were grim, though eager; and our little band of cavalry, hired fighters, rose above that station and became not mongrel private soldiers, but Anglo-Saxons each. They lay or knelt or stood back of the wagon line, imperturbable as wooden men, and waited for the order to fire, though meantime two of them dropped, hit by chance bullets from the wavering line of horsemen that now encircled us.

"Tell us when to fire, Auberry," I heard Belknap say, for he had practically given over the situation to the old plainsman. At last I heard the voice of Auberry, changed from that of an old man into the quick, clear accents of youth, sounding hard and clear. "Ready now! Each fellow pick his own man, and kill him, d'ye hear, *kill* him!"

We had no further tactics. Our fire began to patter and crackle. Our troopers were armed with the worthless old Spencer carbines, and I doubt if these did much execution; but there were some good old Hawkin rifles and old big-bored Yagers and more modern Sharps' rifles and other buffalo guns of one sort or another with us, among the plainsmen and teamsters; and when these spoke there came breaks in the flaunting line that sought to hedge us. The Sioux dropped behind their horses' bodies, firing as they rode, some with rifles, more with bows and arrows. Most of our work was done as they topped the rough ground close on our left, and we saw here a half-dozen bodies lying limp, flat and ragged, though presently other riders came and dragged them away.

The bow and arrow is no match for the rifle behind barricades; but when the Sioux got behind us they saw that our barricade was open in the rear, and at this they whooped and rode in closer. At a hundred yards their arrows fell extraordinarily close to the mark, and time and again they spiked our mules and horses with these hissing shafts that quivered where they struck. They came near breaking our rear in this way, for our men fell into confusion, the horses and mules plunging and trying to break away. There were now men leaning on their elbows, blood dripping from their mouths. There were cries, sounding far away, inconsequent to us still standing. The whir of many arrows came, and we could hear them chuck into the woodwork of the wagons, into the leather of saddle and harness, and now and again into something that gave out a softer, different sound.

I was crowding a ball down my rifle with its hickory rod when I felt a shove at my arm and heard a voice at my ear. "Git out of the way, man—how can I see how to shoot if you bob your head acrost my sights all the time?"

There stood old Mandy McGovern, her long brown rifle half raised, her finger lying sophisticatedly along the trigger guard, that she might not touch the hair trigger. She was as cool as any man in the line, and as deadly. As I finished reloading, I saw her hard, gray face drop as she crooked her elbow and settled to the sights—saw her swing as though she were following a running deer; and then at the crack of her piece I saw a Sioux drop out of his high-peaked saddle. Mandy turned to the rear.

"Git in here, git in here, son!" I heard her cry. And to my wonder now I saw the long, lean figure of Andrew Jackson McGovern come forward, a carbine clutched in his hand, while from his mouth came some sort of eerie screech of incipient courage, which seemed to give wondrous comfort to his fierce dam. At about this moment one of the Sioux, mortally wounded by our fire, turned his horse and ran straight toward us hard as he could go. He knew that he must die, and this was his way—ah, those red men knew how to die. He got within forty yards, reeling and swaying, but still trying to fit an arrow to the string, and as none of us would fire on him now, seeing that he was dying, for a moment it looked as though he would ride directly into us, and perhaps do some harm. Then I heard the boom of the boy's carbine, and almost at the instant, whether by accident or not I could not tell, I saw the red man drop out of the forks of his saddle and roll on the ground with his arms spread out.

Perhaps never was metamorphosis more complete than that which now took place. Shaking off detaining hands, Andrew Jackson sprang from our line, ran up to the fallen foe and in a frenzy of rage began to belabor and kick his body, winding up by catching him by the hair and actually dragging him some paces toward our firing line! An expression of absolute beatitude spread over the countenance of Mandy McGovern. She called out as though he were a young dog at his first fight. "Whoopee! Git to him, boy, git to him! Take him, boy! Whoopee!"

We got Andrew Jackson back into the ranks. His mother stepped to him and took him by the hand, as though for the first time she recognized him as a man.

"Now, boy, *that's* somethin' *like*." Presently she turned to me. "Some says it's in the Paw," she remarked. "I reckon it's some in the Maw; an' a leetle in the trainin'."

Cut up badly by our fire, the Sioux scattered and hugged the shelter of the river bank, beyond which they rode along the sand or in the shallow water, scrambling up the bank after they had gotten out of fire. Our men were firing less, frequently at the last of the line, who came swiftly down from the bluff and charged across behind us, sending in a scattering flight of arrows as they rode.

I looked about me now at the interior of our barricade. I saw Ellen Meriwether on her knees, lifting the shoulders of a wounded man who lay back, his hair dropping from his forehead, now gone bluish gray. She pulled him to the shelter of a wagon, where there had been drawn four others of the wounded. I saw tears falling from her eyes—saw the same pity on her face which I had noted once before when a wounded creature lay in her hands. I had been proud of Mandy McGovern. I was proud of Ellen Meriwether now. They were two generations of our women, the women of America, whom may God ever have in his keeping.

I say I had turned my head; but almost as I did so I felt a sudden jar as though some one had taken a board and struck me over the head with all his might. Then, as I slowly became aware, my head was utterly and entirely detached from my body, and went sailing off, deliberately, in front of me. I could see it going distinctly, and yet, oddly enough, I could also see a sudden change come on the face of the girl who was stooping before me, and who at the moment raised her eyes.

"It is strange," thought I, "but my head, thus detached, is going to pass directly above her, right there!"

Then I ceased to take interest in anything, and sank back into the arms of that from which we come, calmly taking bold of the hand of Mystery.

Chapter XVIII - The Test

I awoke, I knew not how much later, into a world which at first had a certain warm comfort and languid luxury about it. Then I felt a sharp wrenching and a great pain in my neck, to which it seemed my departed head had, after all, returned. Stimulated by this pain, I turned and looked up into the face of Auberry. He stood frowning, holding in his hand a feathered arrow shaft of willow, grooved along its sides to let the blood run free, sinew-wrapped to hold its feathers tight—a typical arrow of the buffalo tribes. But, as I joined Auberry's gaze, I saw the arrow was headless! Dully I argued that, therefore, this head must be somewhere in my neck. I also saw that the sun was bright. I realized that there must have been a fight of some sort, but did not trouble to know whence the arrow had come to me, for my mind could grasp nothing more than simple things.

Thus I felt that my head was not uncomfortable, after all. I looked again, and saw that it rested on Ellen Meriwether's knees. She sat on the sand, gently stroking my forehead, pushing back the hair. She had turned my head so that the wound would not be pressed. It seemed to me that her voice sounded very far away and quiet.

"We are thinking," said she to me. I nodded as best I could. "Has anything happened?" I asked.

"They have gone," said she. "We whipped them." Her hand again lightly pressed my forehead.

I heard some one else say, behind me, "But we have nothing in the world—not even opium."

"True," said another voice, which I recognized as that of Orme; "but that's his one chance."

"What do you know about surgery?" asked the first voice, which I knew now was Belknap's.

"More than most doctors," was the answer, with a laugh. Their voices grew less distinguishable, but presently I heard Orme say, "Yes, I'm game to do it, if the man says so." Then he came and stooped down beside me.

"Mr. Cowles," said he, "you're rather badly off. That arrow head ought to come out, but the risk of going after it is very great. I am willing to do what you say. If you decide that you would like me to operate for it, I will do so. It's only right for me to tell you that it lies very close to the carotid artery, and that it will be an extraordinarily nice operation to get it out without—well, you know—"

I looked up into his face, that strange face which I was now beginning so well to know—the face of my enemy. I knew it was the face of a murderer, a man who would have no compunction at taking a human life.

My mind then was strangely clear. I saw his glance at the girl. I saw, as clearly as though he had told me, that this man was as deeply in love with Ellen Meriwether as I myself; that he would win her if he could; that his chance was as good as mine, even if we were both at our best. I knew there was nothing at which he would hesitate, unless some strange freak in his nature might influence him, such freaks as come to the lightning, to the wild beast slaying, changes for no reason ever known. Remorse, mercy, pity, I knew did not exist for him. But with a flash it came to my mind that this was all the better, if he must now serve as my surgeon.

He looked into my eye, and I returned his gaze, scorning to ask him not to take advantage of me, now that I was fallen. His own eye changed. It asked of me, as though he spoke: "Are you, then, game to the core? Shall I admire you and give you another chance, or shall I kill you now?" I say that I saw, felt, read all this in his mind. I looked up into his face, and said:

"You cannot kill me. I am not going to die. Go on. Soon, then."

A sort of sigh broke from his lips, as though he felt content. I do not think it was because he found his foe a worthy one. I do not think he considered me either as his foe or his friend or his patient. He was simply about to do something which would test his own nerve, his own resources, something which, if successful, would allow him to approve his own belief in himself. I say that this was merely sport for him. I knew he would not turn his hand to save my life; but also I knew that he would not cost it if that could be avoided, for that would mean disappointment to himself. What he did he did well. I said then to myself that I would pay him if he brought me through—pay him in some way.

Presently I heard them on the sand again, and I saw him come again and bend over me. All the instruments they could find had been a razor and a keen penknife; and all they could secure to staunch the blood was some water, nearly boiling. For forceps Orme had a pair of bullet molds, and these he cleansed as best he could by dipping them into the hot water.

"Cowles," he said, in a matter-of-fact voice, "I'm going after it. But now I tell you one thing frankly, it's life or death, and if you move your head it may mean death at once. That iron's lying against the big carotid artery. If it hasn't broken the artery wall, there's a ghost of a chance we can get it out safely, in which case you would probably pull through. I've got to open the neck and reach in. I'll do it as fast as I can. Now, I'm not going to think of you, and, gad!—if you can help it—please don't think of me."

Ellen Meriwether had not spoken. She still held my head in her lap.

"Are you game—can you do this, Miss Meriwether?" I heard Orme ask. She made no answer that I could hear, but must have nodded. I felt her hands press my head more tightly. I turned my face down and kissed her hand. "I will not move," I said.

I saw Orme's slender, naked wrist pass to my face and gently turn me into the position desired, with my face down and a little at one side, resting in her lap above her knees. Her skirt was already wet with the blood of the wound, and where my head lay it was damp with blood. Belknap took my hands and pulled them above my head, squatting beyond me. Between Orme's legs as he stooped I could see the dead body of a mule, I remember, and back of that the blue sky I and the sand dunes. Unknown to her, I kissed the hem of her garment; and then I said a short appeal to the Mystery.

I felt the entrance of the knife or razor blade, felt keenly the pain when the edge lifted and stretched the skin tight before the tough hide of my neck parted smoothly in a long line. Then I felt something warm settle under my cheek as I lay, and I felt a low shiver, whether of my body or that of the girl who held me I could not tell; but her hands were steady. I felt about me an infinite kindness and carefulness and pitying—oh, then I learned that life, after all, is not wholly war—that there is such a thing as fellow-suffering and loving kindness and a wish to aid others to survive in this hard fight of living; I knew that very well. But I did not gain it from the touch of my surgeon's hands.

The immediate pain of this long cutting which laid open my neck for some inches through the side muscles was less after the point of the blade went through and ceased to push forward. Deeper down I did not feel so much, until finally a gentle searching movement produced a jar strangely large, something which grated, and nearly sent all the world black again. I knew then that the knife was on the base of the arrow head; then I could feel it move softly and gently along the side of the arrow head—I could almost see it creep along in this delicate part of the work.

Then, all at once, I felt one hand removed from my neck. Orme, half rising from his stooping posture, but with the fingers of his left hand still at the wound, said: "Belknap, let go one of his hands. Just put your hand on this knife-blade, and feel that artery throb! Isn't it curious?"

I heard some muttered answer, but the grasp at my wrists did not relax. "Oh, it's all right now," calmly went on Orme, again stooping.

"I thought you might be interested. It's all over now but pulling out the head."

I felt again a shiver run through the limbs of the girl. Perhaps she turned away her head, I do not know. I felt Orme's fingers spreading widely the sides of the wound along the neck, and the boring of the big headed bullet molds as they went down after a grip, their impact softened by the finger extended along the blade knife.

The throbbing artery whose location this man knew so well was protected. Gently feeling down, the tips of the mold got their grip at last, and an instant later I felt release from a certain stiff pressure which I had experienced in my neck. Relief came, then a dizziness and much pain. A hand patted me twice on the back of the neck.

"All right, my man," said Orme. "All over; and jolly well done, too, if I do say it myself!"

Belknap put his arm about me and helped me to sit up. I saw Orme holding out the stained arrow head, long and thin, in his fingers.

"Would you like it?" he said.

"Yes," said I, grinning. And I confess I have it now somewhere about my house. I doubt if few souvenirs exist to remind one of a scene exactly similar.

The girl now kept cloths wrung from the hot water on my neck. I thanked them all as best I could. "I say, you men," remarked Mandy McGovern, coming up with a cob-stoppered flask in her hand, half filled with a pale yellow-white fluid, "ain't it about time for some of that thar anarthestic I heerd you all talking about a while ago?"

"I shouldn't wonder," said Orme. "The stitching hurts about as much as anything. Auberry, can't you find me a bit of sinew somewhere, and perhaps a needle of some sort?"

Chapter XIX - The Quality Of Mercy

A vast dizziness and a throbbing of the head remained after they were quite done with me, but something of this left me when finally I sat leaning back against the wagon body and looked about me. There were straight, motionless figures lying under the blankets in the shade, and under other blankets were men who writhed and moaned. Belknap passed about the place, graver and apparently years older than at the beginning of this, his first experience in the field. He put out burial parties at once. A few of the Sioux, including the one on whom Andrew Jackson McGovern had vented his new-found spleen, were covered scantily where they lay. Our own dead were removed to the edge of the bluff; and so more headstones, simple and rude, went to line the great pathway into the West.

Again Ellen Meriwether came and sat by me. She had now removed the gray traveling gown, for reasons which I could guess, and her costume might have been taken from a collector's chest rather than a woman's wardrobe. All at once we seemed, all of us, to be blending with these surroundings, becoming savage as these other savages. It might almost have been a savage woman who came to me.

Her skirt was short; made of white tanned antelope leather. Above it fell the ragged edges of a native tunic or shirt of yellow buck, ornamented with elk teeth, embroidered in stained quills. Her feet still wore a white woman's shoes, although the short skirt was enforced by native leggins, beaded and becylindered in metals so that she tinkled as the walked. Her hair, now becoming yellower and more sunburned at the ends, was piled under her felt hat, and the modishness of long cylindrical curls was quite forgot. The brown of her cheeks, already strongly sunburned, showed in strange contrast to the snowy white of her neck, now exposed by the low neck aperture of the Indian tunic. Her gloves, still fairly fresh, she wore tucked through her belt, army fashion. I could see the red heart still, embroidered on the cuff!

She came and sat down beside me on the ground, I say, and spoke to me. I could not help reflecting how she was reverting, becoming savage. I thought this—but in my heart I knew she was not savage as myself.

"How are you coming on?" she said. "You sit up nicely—"

"Yes, and can stand, or walk, or ride," I added.

Her brown eyes were turned full on me. In the sunlight I could see the dark specks in their depths. I could see every shade of tan on her face.

"You are not to be foolish," she said.

"You stand all this nobly," I commented presently.

"Ah, you men—I love you, you men!" She said it suddenly and with perfect sincerity. "I love you all—you are so strong, so full of the desire to live, to win. It is wonderful, wonderful! Just look at those poor boys there—some of them are dying, almost, but they won't whimper. It is wonderful."

"It is the Plains," I said. "They have simply learned how little a thing is life."

"Yet it is sweet," she said.

"But for you, I see that you have changed again."

She spread her leather skirt down with her hands, as though to make it longer, and looked contemplatively at the fringed leggins below.

"You were four different women," I mused, "and now you are another, quite another."

At this she frowned a bit, and rose. "You are not to talk," she said, "nor to think that you are well; because you are not. I must go and see the others."

I lay back against the wagon bed, wondering in which garb she had been most beautiful—the filmy ball dress and the mocking mask, the gray gown and veil of the day after, the thin drapery of her hasty flight in the night, her half conventional costume of the day before— or this, the garb of some primeval woman. I knew I could never forget her again. The thought gave me pain, and perhaps this showed on my face, for my eyes followed her so that presently she turned and came back to me.

"Does the wound hurt you?" she asked. "Are you in pain?"

"Yes, Ellen Meriwether," I said, "I am in pain. I am in very great pain."

"Oh," she cried, "I am sorry! What can we do? What do you wish? But perhaps it will not be so bad after a while—it will be over soon."

"No, Ellen Meriwether," I said, "it will not be over soon. It will not go away at all."

Chapter Xx - Gordon Orme, Magician

We lay in our hot camp on the sandy valley for some days, and buried two more of our men who finally succumbed to their wounds. Gloom sat on us all, for fever now raged among our wounded. Pests of flies by day and mosquitoes by night became almost unbearable. The sun blistered us, the night froze us. Still not a sign of any white-topped wagon from the east, nor any dust-cloud of troopers from the west served to break the monotony of the shimmering waste that lay about us on every hand. We were growing gaunt now and haggard; but still we lay, waiting for our men to grow strong enough to travel, or to lose all strength and so be laid away.

We had no touch with the civilization of the outer world. At that time the first threads of the white man's occupancy were just beginning to cross the midway deserts. Near by our camp ran the recently erected line of telegraph, its shining cedar poles, stripped of their bark, offering wonder for savage and civilized man alike, for hundreds of miles across an uninhabited country. We could see the poles rubbed smooth at their base by the shoulders of the buffalo. Here and there a little tuft of hair clung to some untrimmed knot. High up in some of the naked poles we could see still sticking, the iron shod arrows of contemptuous tribesmen, who had thus sought to assail the "great medicine" of the white man. We heard the wires above us humming mysteriously in the wind, but if they bore messages east or west, we might not read them, nor might we send any message of our own.

At times old Auberry growled at this new feature of the landscape. "That was not here when I first came West," he said, "and I don't like its looks. The old ways were good enough. Now they are even talkin' of runnin' a railroad up the valley—as though horses couldn't carry in everything the West needs or bring out everything the East may want. No, the old ways were good enough for me."

Orme smiled at the old man.

"None the less," said he, "you will see the day before long, when not one railroad, but many, will cross these plains. As for the telegraph, if only we had a way of tapping these wires, we might find it extremely useful to us all right now."

"The old ways were good enough," insisted Auberry. "As fur telegraphin', it ain't new on these plains. The Injuns could always telegraph, and they didn't need no poles nor wires. The Sioux may be at both ends of this bend, for all we know. They may have cleaned up all the wagons coming west. They have planned for a general wipin' out of the whites, and you can be plumb certain that what has happened here is knowed all acrost this country to-day, clean to the big bend of the Missouri, and on the Yellowstone, and west to the Rockies."

"How could that be?" asked Orme, suddenly, with interest. "You talk as if there were something in this country like the old 'secret mail' of East India, where I once lived."

"I don't know what you mean by that," said Auberry, "but I do know that the Injuns in this country have ways of talkin' at long range. Why, onct a bunch of us had five men killed up on the Powder River by the Crows. That was ten o'clock in the morning. By two in the afternoon everyone in the Crow village, two hundred miles away, knowed all about the fight—how many whites was killed, how many Injuns—the whole shootin'-match. How they done it, I don't know, but they shore done it. Any Western man knows that much about Injun ways."

"That is rather extraordinary," commented Orme.

"Nothin' extraordinary about it," said Auberry, "it's just common. Maybe they done it by lookin'-glasses and smokes—fact is, I know that's one way they use a heap. But they've got other ways of talkin'. Looks like a Injun could set right down on a hill, and think good and hard, and some other Injun a hundred miles away'd know what he was thinkin' about. You talk about a prairie fire runnin' fast—it ain't nothin' to the way news travels amongst the tribes."

Belknap expressed his contempt for all this sort of thing, but the old man assured him he would know more of this sort of thing when he had been longer in the West. "I know they do telegraph," reiterated the plainsman.

"I can well believe that," remarked Orme, quietly.

"Whether you do or not," said Auberry, "Injuns is strange critters. A few of us has married among Injuns and lived among them, and we have seen things you wouldn't believe if I told you."

"Tell some of them," said Orme. "I, for one, might believe them."

"Well, now," said the plainsman, "I will tell you some things I have seen their medicine men do, and ye can believe me or not, the way ye feel about it."

"I have seen 'em hold a pow-wow for two or three days at a time, some of 'em settin' 'round, dreamin', as they call it all of 'em starvin', whole camp howlin', everybody eatin' medicine herbs. Then after while, they all come and set down just like it was right out here in the open. Somebody pulls a naked Injun boy right out in the middle of them. Old Mr. Medicine Man, he stands up in the plain daylight, and he draws his bow and shoots a arrer plum through that boy. Boy squirms a heap and Mr. Medicine Man socks another arrer through him, cool as you please—I have seen that done. Then the medicine man steps up, cuts off the boy's head with his knife—holds it up plain, so everybody can see it. That looked pretty hard to me first time I ever seen it. But now the old medicine man takes a blanket and throws it over this dead boy. He lifts up a corner of the blanket, chucks the boy's head under it, and pulls down the edges of the blanket and puts rocks on them. Then he begins to sing, and the whole bunch gets up and dances 'round the blanket. After while, say a few minutes, medicine man pulls off the blanket—and thar gets up the boy, good as new, his head growed on good and tight as ever, and not a sign of an arrer on him 'cept the scars where the wounds has plumb healed up!"

Belknap laughed long and hard at this old trapper's yarn, and weak as I was myself, I was disposed to join him. Orme was the only one who did not ridicule the story. Auberry himself was disgusted at the merriment. "I knowed you wouldn't believe it," he said. "There is no use tellin' a passel of tenderfeet anything they hain't seed for theirselves. But I could tell you a heap more things. Why, I have seen their buffalo callers call a thousand buffalo right in from the plains, and over the edge of a cut bank, where they'd pitch down and bust theirselves to pieces. I can show you bones Of a hundred such places. Buffalo don't do that when they are alone—thay have got to be *called*, I tell you.

"Injuns can talk with other animals—they can call them others, too. I have seed an old medicine man, right out on the plain ground in the middle of the village, go to dancin', and I have seed him call three full-sized beavers right up out'n the ground—seed them with my own *eyes*, I tell you! Yes, and I have seed them three old beavers standin' right there, turn into full-growed old men, gray haired. I have seed 'em sit down at a fire and smoke, too, and finally get up when they got through, and clean out—just disappear back into the ground. Now, how you all explain them there things, I don't pretend to say; but there can't no man call me a liar, fur I seed 'em and seed 'em unmistakable."

Belknap and the others only smiled, but Orme turned soberly toward Auberry. "I don't call you a liar, my man," said he. "On the contrary, what you say is very interesting. I quite believe it, although I never knew before that your natives in this country were possessed of these powers."

"It ain't all of 'em can do it," said Auberry, "only a few men of a few tribes can do them things; but them that can shore can, and that's all I know about it."

"Quite so," said Orme. "Now, as it chances, I have traveled a bit in my time in the old countries of the East. I have seen some wonderful things done there."

"I have read about the East Indian jugglers," said Belknap, interested. "Tell me, have you seen those feats? are they feats, or simply lies?"

"They are actual occurrences," said Orme. "I have seen them with my own eyes, just as Auberry has seen the things he describes; and it is no more right to accuse the one than the other of us of untruthfulness.

"For instance, I have seen an Indian juggler take a plain bowl, such as they use for rice, and hold it out in his hand in the open sunlight; and then I have seen a little bamboo tree start in it and grow two feet high, right in the middle of the bowl, within the space of a minute or so.

"You talk about the old story of 'Jack and the Bean Stalk'; I have seen an old fakir take a bamboo stick, no thicker than his finger, and thrust it down in the ground and start and climb up it, as if it were a tree, and keep on climbing till he was out of sight; and then there would come falling down out of the sky, legs and arms, his head, pieces of his body. When these struck the ground, they would reassemble and make the man all over again—just like Auberry's dead boy, you know.

"These tricks are so common in Asia that they do not excite any wonder. As to tribal telegraph, they have got it there. Time and again, when our forces were marching against the hill tribes of northwestern India, we found they knew all of our plans a hundred miles ahead of us—how, none of us could tell—only the fact was there, plain and unmistakable."

"They never do tell," broke in Auberry. "You couldn't get a red to explain any of this to you—not even a squaw you have lived with for years. They certainly do stand pat for keeps."

"Yet once in a while," smiled Orme, in his easy way, "a white man does pick up some of these tricks. I believe I could do a few of them myself, if I liked—in fact, I have sometimes learned some of the simpler ones for my own amusement."

General exclamations of surprise and doubt greeted him from our little circle, and this seemed to nettle him somewhat. "By Jove!" he went on, "if you doubt it, I don't mind trying a hand at it right now. Perhaps I have forgotten something of my old skill, but we'll see. Come, hen."

All arose now and gathered about him on the ground there in the full sunlight. He evinced no uneasiness or surprise, and he employed no mechanism or deception which we could detect.

"My good man," said he to Auberry, "let me take your knife." Auberry loosed the long hunting-knife at his belt and handed it to him. Taking it, Orme seated himself cross-legged on a white blanket, which he spread out on the sandy soil.

All at once Orme looked up with an expression of surprise on his face. "This was not the knife I wanted," he said. "I asked for a plain American hunting-knife, not this one. See, you have given me a Malay kris! I have not the slightest idea where you got it."

We all looked intently at him. There, held up in his hand, was full proof of what he had said—a long blade of wavy steel, with a little crooked, carved handle. From what I had read, I saw this to be a kris, a wavy bladed knife of the Malays. It did not shine or gleam in the sun, but threw back a dull reflection from its gray steel, as though lead and silver mingled in its make. The blade was about thirty inches long, whereas that of Auberry's knife could not have exceeded eight inches at the most.

"We did not know you had that thing around you!" exclaimed Belknap. "That is only sleight of hand."

"Is it, indeed?" said Orme, smiling. "I tell you, I did not have it with me. After all, you see it is the same knife."

We all gaped curiously, and there, as I am a living man, we saw that wavy kris, extended in his hand, turn back into the form of the plainsman's hunting-knife! A gasp of wonder and half terror came from the circle. Some of the men drew back. I heard an Irish private swear and saw him cross himself. I do not explain these things, I only say I saw them.

"I was mistaken," said Orme, politely, "in offering so simple a test as this; but now, if you still think I had the kris in my clothing—how that could be, I don't know, I'm sure—and if you still wish to call my little performance sleight of hand, then I'll do something to prove what I have said, and make it quite plain that all my friend here has said is true and more than true. Watch now, and you will see blood drip from the point of this blade—every drop of blood it ever drew, of man or animal. Look, now—watch it closely."

We looked, and again, as I am a living man, and an honest one, I hope, I saw, as the others did, running from the point of the steel blade, a little trickling stream of red blood! It dropped in a stream, I say, and fell on the white blanket upon which Orme was sitting. It stained the blanket entirely red. At this sight the entire group broke apart, only a few remaining to witness the rest of the scene.

I do not attempt to explain this illusion, or whatever it was. I do not know how long it lasted; but presently, as I may testify, I saw Orme rise and kick at the wetted, bloodstained blanket. He lifted it, heavy with dripping blood. I saw the blood fall from its corners upon the ground.

"Ah," he remarked, calmly, "it's getting dry now. Here is your knife, my good fellow."

I looked about me, almost disposed to rub my eyes, as were, perhaps, the others of our party. The same great plains were there, the same wide shimmering stream, rippling in the sunlight, the same groups of animals grazing on the bluff, the same sentinels outlined against the sky. Over all shone the blinding light of the Western mid-day sun. Yet, as Orme straightened out this blanket, it was white as it had been before! Auberry looked at his knife blade as though he would have preferred to throw it away, but he sheathed it and it fitted the sheath as before.

Orme smiled at us all pleasantly. "Do you believe in the Indian telegraph now?" he inquired.

I have told you many things of this strange man, Gordon Orme, and I shall need to tell yet others. Sometimes my friends smile at me even yet over these things. But since that day, I have not doubted the tales old Auberry told me of our own Indians. Since then, too, I have better understood Gordon Orme and his strange personality, the like of which I never knew in any land.

Chapter XXI - Two In The Desert

How long it was I hardly knew, for I had slink into a sort of dull apathy in which one day was much like another; but at last we gathered our crippled party together and broke camp, our wounded men in the wagons, and so slowly passed on westward, up the trail. We supposed, what later proved to be true, that the Sioux had raided in the valley on both sides of us, and that the scattered portions of the army had all they could do, while the freight trains were held back until the road was clear.

I wearied of the monotony of wagon travel, and without council with any, finally, weak as I was, called for my horse and rode on slowly with the walking teams. I had gone for some distance before I heard hoofs on the sand behind me.

"Guess who it is," called a voice. "Don't turn your head."

"I can't turn," I answered; "but I know who it is."

She rode up alongside, where I could see her; and fair enough she was to look upon, and glad enough I was to look. She was thinner now with this prairie life, and browner, and the ends of her hair were still yellowing, like that of outdoors men. She still was booted and gloved after the fashion of civilization, and still elsewise garbed in the aboriginal costume, which she filled and honored graciously. The metal cylinders on her leggins rattled as she rode.

"You ought not to ride," she said. "You are pale."

"You are beautiful," said I; "and I ride because you are beautiful."

Her eyes were busy with her gloves, but I saw a sidelong glance. "I do not understand you," she said, demurely.

"I could not sit back there in the wagon and think," said I. "I knew that you would be riding before long, and I guessed I might, perhaps, talk with you."

She bit her lip and half pulled up her horse as if to fall back. "That will depend," was her comment. But we rode on, side by side, knee to knee.

Many things I had studied before then, for certain mysteries had come to me, as to many men, who wish logically to know the causes of great phenomena. From boyhood I had pondered many things. I had lain on my back and looked up at the stars and wondered how far they were, and how far the farthest thing beyond them was. I had wondered at that indeterminate quotient in my sums, where the same figure came, always the same, running on and on. I used to wonder what was my soul, and I fancied that it was a pale, blue flaming oblate, somewhere near my back and in the middle of my body—such was my boyish guess of what they told me was a real thing. I had pondered on that compass of the skies by which the wild fowl guide themselves. I had wondered, as a child, how far the mountains ran. As I had grown older I had read the law, read of the birth of civilization, pondered on laws and customs. Declaring that I must know their reasons, I had read of marriages in many lands, and many times had studied into the questions of dowry and bride-price, and consent of parents, and consent of the bride—studied marriage as a covenant, a contract, as a human and a so-called divine thing. I had questioned the cause of the old myth that makes Cupid blind. I had delved deep as I might in law, and history and literature, seeking to solve, as I might—what?

Ah, witless! it was to solve this very riddle that rode by my side now, to answer the question of the Sphinx. What had come of all my studies? Not so much as I was learning now, here in the open, with this sweet savage woman whose leggins tinkled as she rode, whose tunic swelled softly, whose jaw was clean and brown. How weak the precepts of the social covenant seemed. How feeble and far away the old world we too had known. And how infinitely sweet, how compellingly necessary now seemed to me this new, sweet world that swept around us now.

We rode on, side by side, knee to knee. Her garments rustled and tinkled.

Her voice awoke me from my brooding. "I wish, Mr. Cowles," said she, "that if you are strong enough and can do so without discomfort, you would ride with me each day when I ride."

"Why?" I asked. That was the wish in my own mind; but I knew her reason was not the same as mine.

"Because," she said. She looked at me, but would not answer farther.

"You ought to tell me," I said quietly.

"Because it is prescribed for you."

"Not by my doctor." I shook my head. "Why, then?"

"Stupid—oh, very stupid officer and gentleman!" she aid, smiling slowly. "Lieutenant Belknap has his duties to look after; and as for Mr. Orme, I am not sure he is either officer or gentleman."

She spoke quietly but positively. I looked on straight up the valley and pondered. Then I put out a hand and touched the fringe of her sleeve.

"I am going to try to be a gentleman," said I. "But I wish some fate would tell me why it is a gentleman can be made from nothing but a man."

Chapter XXII - Mandy McGovern On Marriage

Our slow travel finally brought us near to the historic forks of the Platte where that shallow stream stretches out two arms, one running to the mountains far to the south, the other still reaching westward for a time. Between these two ran the Oregon Trail, pointing the way to the Pacific, and on this trail, somewhere to the west, lay Laramie. Before us now lay two alternatives. We could go up the beaten road to Laramie, or we could cross here and take an old trail on the north side of the river for a time. Auberry thought this latter would give better feed and water, and perhaps be safer as to Indians, so we held a little council over it.

The Platte even here was a wide, treacherous stream, its sandy bottom continuously shifting. At night the melted floods from the mountains came down and rendered it deeper than during the day, when for the most part it was scarcely more than knee deep. Yet here and there at any time, undiscoverable to the eye, were watery pitfalls where the sand was washed out, and in places there was shifting quicksand, dangerous for man or animal.

"We'll have to boat across," said Auberry finally. "We couldn't get the wagons over loaded." Wherefore we presently resorted to the old Plains makeshift of calking the wagon bodies and turning them into boats, it being thought probable that two or three days would be required to make the crossing in this way. By noon of the following day our rude boats were ready and our work began.

I was not yet strong enough to be of much assistance, so I sat on the bank watching the busy scene. Our men were stripped to the skin, some of the mountaineers brown almost as Indians, for even in those days white hunters often rode with no covering but the blanket, and not that when the sun was warm. They were now in, now out of the water, straining at the lines which steadied the rude boxes that bore our goods, pulling at the heads of the horses and mules, shouting, steadying, encouraging, always getting forward. It took them nearly an hour to make the first crossing, and presently we could see the fire of their farther camp, now occupied by some of those not engaged in the work.

As I sat thus I was joined by Mandy McGovern, who pulled out her contemplative pipe. "Did you see my boy, Andy Jackson?" she asked. "He went acrost with the first bunch—nary stitch of clothes on to him. He ain't much thicker'n a straw, but say—he was a-rastlin' them mules and a-swearin' like a full-growed man! I certainly have got hopes that boy's goin' to come out all right. Say, I heerd him tell the cook this mornin' he wasn't goin' to take no more sass off n him. I has hopes—I certainly has hopes, that Andrew Jackson '11 kill a man some time yit; and like enough it'll be right soon."

I gave my assent to this amiable hope, and presently Mandy went on.

"But say, man, you and me has got to get that girl acrost somehow, between us. You know her and me—and sometimes that Englishman—travels along in the amberlanch. She's allowed to me quiet that when the time come for her to go acrost, she'd ruther you and me went along. She's all ready now, if you air."

"Very good," said I, "we'll go now—they've got a fire there, and are cooking, I suppose."

Mandy left me, and I went for my own horse. Presently we three, all mounted, met at the bank. Taking the girl between us, Mandy and I started, and the three horses plunged down the bank. As it chanced, we struck a deep channel at the send-off, and the horses were at once separated. The girl was swept out of her saddle, but before I could render any assistance she called out not to be alarmed. I saw that she was swimming, down stream from the horse, with one hand on the pommel. Without much concern, she reached footing on the bar at which the horse scrambled up.

"Now I'm good and wet," laughed she. "It won't make any difference after this. I see now how the squaws do."

We plunged on across the stream, keeping our saddles for most of the way, sometimes in shallow water, sometimes on dry, sandy bars, and now and again in swift, swirling channels; but at last we got over and fell upon the steaks of buffalo and the hot coffee which we found at the fire. The girl presently left us to make such changes in her apparel as she might. Mandy and I were left alone once more.

"It seems to me like it certainly is too bad," said she bitterly, over her pipe stem, "that there don't seem to be no real man around nowhere fittin' to marry a real woman. That gal's good enough for a real man, like my first husband was."

"What could he do?" I asked her, smiling.

"Snuff a candle at fifty yards, or drive a nail at forty. He nach'elly scorned to bring home a squirrel shot back of the ears. He killed four men in fair knife fightin', an' each time come free in co'te. He was six foot in the clean, could hug like a bar, and he wa'n't skeered of anything that drawed the breath of life."

"Tell me, Aunt Mandy," I said, "tell me how he came courting you, anyway."

"He never did no great at co'tin'," said she, grinning. "He just come along, an' he sot eyes on me. Then he sot eyes on me again. I sot eyes on him, too."

"Yes?"

"One evenin', says he, 'Mandy, gal, I'm goin' to marry you all right soon.'

"Says I, 'No, you ain't!'

"Says he, 'Yes, I air!' I jest laughed at him then and started to run away, but he jumped and ketched me—I told you he could hug like a bar. Mebbe I wasn't hard to ketch. Then he holds me right tight, an' says he,' Gal, quit this here foolin'. I'm goin' to marry you, you hear!—then maybe he kisses me—law! I dunno! Whut business is it o' yourn, anyhow? That's about all there was to it. I didn't seem to keer. But that," she concluded, "was a real *man*. He shore had my other two men plumb faded."

"What became of your last husband, Mandy?" I asked, willing to be amused for a time. "Did he die?"

"Nope, didn't die."

"Divorced, eh?"

"Deevorced, hell! No, I tole you, I up an' left him."

"Didn't God join you in holy wedlock, Mandy?"

"No, it was the Jestice of the Peace."

"Ah?"

"Yep. And them ain't holy none—leastways in Missouri. But say, man, look yere, it ain't God that marries folks, and it ain't Jestices of the Peace—it's *theirselves*."

I pondered for a moment. "But your vow—your promise?"

"My promise? Whut's the word of a woman to a man? Whut's the word of a man to a woman? It ain't words, man, it's *feelin's*."

"In sickness or in health?" I quoted.

"That's all right, if your *feelin's* is all right. The Church is all right, too. I ain't got no kick. All I'm sayin' to you is, folks marries *theirselves*."

I pondered yet further. "Mandy," said I, "suppose you were a man, and your word was given to a girl, and you met another girl and couldn't get her out of your head, or out of your heart—you loved the new one most and knew you always would—what would you do?"

But the Sphinx of womanhood may lie under linsey-woolsey as well as silk. "Man," said she, rising and knocking her pipe against her bony knee, "you talk like a fool. If my first husband was alive, he might maybe answer that for you."

Chapter XXIII - Issue Joined

Later in the evening, Mandy McGovern having left me, perhaps for the purpose of assisting her protégée in the somewhat difficult art of drying buckskin clothing, I was again alone on the river bank, idly watching the men out on the bars, struggling with their teams and box boats. Orme had crossed the river some time earlier, and now he joined me at the edge of our disordered camp.

"How is the patient getting along?" he inquired. I replied, somewhat surlily, I fear, that I was doing very well, and thenceforth intended to ride horseback and to comport myself as though nothing had happened.

"I am somewhat sorry to hear that," said he, still smiling in his own way. "I was in hopes that you would be disposed to turn back down the river, if Belknap would spare you an escort east."

I looked at him in surprise. "I don't in the least understand why I should be going east, when my business lies in precisely the opposite direction," I remarked, coolly.

"Very well, then, I will make myself plain," he went on, seating himself beside me. "Granted that you will get well directly—which is very likely, for the equal of this Plains air for surgery does not exist in the world—I may perhaps point out to you that at least your injury might serve as an explanation—as an excuse—you might put it that way—for your going back home. I thought perhaps that your duty lay there as well."

"You become somewhat interested in my affairs, Mr. Orme?"

"Very much so, if you force me to say it."

"I think they need trouble you no farther."

"I thought that possibly you might be sensible of a certain obligation to me," he began.

"I am deeply sensible of it. Are you pleased to tell me what will settle this debt between us?"

He turned squarely toward me and looked me keenly in the eye. "I have told you. Turn about and go home. That is all."

"I do not understand you."

"But I understand your position perfectly."

"Meaning?"

"That your affections are engaged with a highly respectable young lady back at your home in Virginia. Wait—" he raised his hand as I turned toward him. "Meaning also," he went on, "that your affections are apparently also somewhat engaged with an equally respectable young lady who is not back home in Virginia. Therefore—"

He caught my wrist in a grip of steel as I would have struck him. I saw then that I still was weak.

"Wait," he said, smiling coldly. "Wait till you are stronger."

"You are right," I said, "but we shall settle these matters."

"That, of course. But in the meantime, I have only suggested to you that could you agree with me in my point of view our obligation as it stands would be settled."

"Orme," said I, suddenly, "your love is a disgrace to any woman."

"Usually," he admitted, calmly, "but not in this case. I propose to marry Miss Meriwether; and I tell you frankly, I do not propose to have anything stand in my way."

"Then, by God!" I cried, "take her. Why barter and dicker over any woman with another man? The field is open. Do what you can. I know that is the way I'd do."

"Oh, certainly; but one needs all his chances even in an open field, in a matter so doubtful as this. I thought that I would place it before you—knowing your situation back in Virginia—and ask you—"

"Orme," said I, "one question—Why did you not kill me the other day when you could? Your tracks would have been covered. As it is, I may later have to uncover some tracks for you."

"I preferred it the other way," he remarked, still smiling his inscrutable smile.

"You surely had no scruples about it."

"Not in the least. I'd as soon have killed you as to have taken a drink of water. But I simply love to play any kind of game that tests me, tries me, puts me to my utmost mettle. I played that game in my own way."

"I was never very subtle," I said to him simply.

"No, on the contrary, you are rather dull. I dared not kill you—it would have been a mistake in the game. It would have cost me her sympathy at once. Since I did not, and since, therefore, you owe me something for that fact, what do you say about it yourself, my friend?"

I thought for a long time, my head between my hands, before I answered him. "That I shall pay you some day Orme, but not in any such way as you suggest."

"Then it is to be war?" he asked, quietly.

I shrugged my shoulders. "You heard me."

"Very well!" he replied, calmly, after a while. "But listen. I don't forget. If I do not have my pay voluntarily in the way I ask, I shall some day collect it in my own fashion."

"As you like. But we Cowles men borrow no fears very far in advance."

Orme rose and stood beside me, his slender figure resembling less that of a man than of some fierce creature, animated by some uncanny spirit, whose motives did not parallel those of human beings. "Then, Mr. Cowles, you do not care to go back down the valley, and to return to the girl in Virginia?"

"You are a coward to make any such request."

His long white teeth showed as he answered. "Very well," he said. "It is the game. Let the best man win. Shall it then be war?"

"Let the best man win," I answered. "It is war."

We both smiled, each into the other's face.

Chapter XXIV - Forsaking All Others

When finally our entire party had been gotten across the Platte, and we had resumed our westward journey, the routine of travel was, for the time, broken, and our line of march became somewhat scattered across the low, hilly country to which we presently came. For my own part, our progress seemed too slow, and mounting my horse, I pushed on in advance of the column, careless of what risk this might mean in an Indian country. I wished to be alone; and yet I wished to be not alone. I hoped that might occur which presently actually did happen.

It was early in the afternoon when I heard her horse's feet coming up behind me as I rode. She passed me at a gallop; laughing back as though in challenge, and so we raced on for a time, until we quite left out of sight behind us the remainder of our party. Ellen Meriwether was a Virginia girl with Western experience, and it goes without saying that she rode well—of course in the cavalry saddle and with the cross seat. Her costume still was composed of the somewhat shriveled and wrinkled buckskins which had been so thoroughly wetted in crossing the river. I noticed that she had now even discarded her shoes, and wore the aboriginal costume almost in full, moccasins and all, her gloves and hat alone remaining to distinguish her in appearance at a distance from a native woman of the Plains. The voluminous and beruffled skirts of the period, and that feminine monstrosity of the day, the wide spreading crinoline, she had left far behind her at the Missouri River. Again the long curls, which civilization at that time decreed, had been forgotten. Her hair at the front and sides half-waved naturally, but now, instead of neck curls or the low dressing of the hair which in those days partly covered the fashionable forehead, she had, like a native woman, arranged her hair in two long braids. Her hat, no longer the flat straw or the flaring, rose-laden bonnet of the city, was now simply a man's cavalry hat, and almost her only mark of coquetry was the rakish cockade which confined it at one side. Long, heavy-hooped earrings such as women at that time wore, and which heretofore I had never known her to employ, she now disported.

Brown as her face was now becoming, one might indeed, at a little distance, have suspected her to be rather a daughter of the Plains than a belle of civilization. I made some comment on this. She responded by sitting the more erect in her saddle and drawing a long, deep breath.

"I think I shall throw away my gloves," she said, "and hunt up some brass bracelets. I grow more Indian every day. Isn't it glorious, here on the Plains? Isn't it *glorious*!"

It so seemed to me, and I so advised her, saying I wished the western journey might be twice as long.

"But Mr. Orme was saying that he rather thought you might take an escort and go back down the river."

"I wish Mr. Orme no disrespect," I answered, "but neither he nor any one else regulates my travel. I have already told you how necessary it was for me to see your father, Colonel Meriwether."

"Yes, I remember. But tell me, why did not your father himself come out?"

I did not answer her for a time. "My father is dead," I replied finally.

I saw her face flush in quick trouble and embarrassment. "Why did you not tell me? I am so sorry! I beg your pardon."

"No," I answered quietly, "we Quakers never wish to intrude our own griefs, or make any show of them. I should have told you, but there were many other things that prevented for the time." Then, briefly, I reviewed the happenings that had led to my journey into the West. Her sympathy was sweet to me.

"So now, you see, I ought indeed to return," I concluded, "but I can not. We shall be at Laramie now very soon. After that errand I shall go back to Virginia."

"And that will be your home?"

"Yes," I said bitterly. "I shall settle down and become a staid old farmer. I shall be utterly cheerless."

"You must not speak so. You are young."

"But you," I ventured, "will always live with the Army?"

"Why, our home is in Virginia, too, over in old Albemarle, though we don't often see it. I have been West since I came out of school, pretty much all the time, and unless there should be a war I suppose I shall stay always out here with my father. My mother died when I was very young."

"And you will never come back to quiet old Virginia, where plodding farmers go on as their fathers did a hundred years ago?"

She made no immediate answer, and when she did, apparently mused on other things. "The Plains," she said, "how big—how endless they are! Is it not all wild and free?"

Always she came back to that same word "free." Always she spoke of wildness, of freedom.

"For all one could tell, there might be lions and tigers and camels and gazelles out there." She gestured vaguely toward the wide horizon. "It is the desert."

We rode on for a time, silent, and I began to hum to myself the rest of the words of an old song, then commonly heard:

> "O come with me, and be my love,
> For thee the jungle's depths I'll rove.
> I'll chase the antelope over the plain,
> And the tiger's cub I'll bind with a chain,
> And the wild gazelle with the silvery feet
> I'll give to thee for a playmate sweet."

"Poets," said I, "can very well sing about such things, but perhaps they could not practice all they sing. They always —"

"Hush!" she whispered, drawing her horse gently down to a walk, and finally to a pause. "Look! Over there is one of the wild gazelles."

I followed the direction of her eyes and saw, peering curiously down at us from beyond the top of a little ridge, something like a hundred yards away, the head, horns, and neck of a prong-horn buck, standing facing us, and seeming not much thicker than a knife blade. Her keen eyes caught this first; my own, I fancy, being busy elsewhere. At once I slipped out of my saddle and freed the long, heavy rifle from its sling. I heard her voice, hard now with eagerness. I caught a glance at her face, brown between her braids. She was a savage woman!

"Quick!" she whispered. "He'll run."

Eager as she, but deliberately, I raised the long barrel to line and touched the trigger. I heard the thud of the ball against the antelope's shoulder, and had no doubt that we should pick it up dead, for it disappeared, apparently end over end, at the moment of the shot. Springing into the saddle, I raced with my companion to the top of the ridge. But, lo! there was the antelope two hundred yards away, and going as fast on three legs as our horses were on four.

"Ride!" she called. "Hurry!" And she spurred off at breakneck speed in pursuit, myself following, both of us now forgetting poesy, and quite become creatures of the chase.

The prong-horn, carrying lead as only the prong-horn can, kept ahead of us, ridge after ridge, farther and farther away, mile after mile, until our horses began to blow heavily, and our own faces were covered with perspiration. Still we raced on, neck and neck, she riding with hands low and weight slightly forward, workmanlike as a jockey. Now and again I heard her call out in eagerness.

We should perhaps have continued this chase until one or the other of the horses dropped, but now her horse picked up a pebble and went somewhat lame. She pulled up and told me to ride on alone. After a pause I slowly approached the top of the next ridge, and there, as I more than half suspected, I saw the antelope lying down, its head turned back. Eager to finish the chase, I sprang down, carelessly neglecting to throw the bridle rein over my horse's head. Dropping flat, I rested on my elbow and fired carefully once more. This time the animal rolled over dead. I rose, throwing up my hat with a shout of victory, and I heard, shrilling to me across the distance, her own cry of exultation, as that of some native woman applauding a red hunter.

Alas for our joy of victory! Our success was our undoing. The very motion of my throwing up my hat, boyish as it was, gave fright to my horse, already startled by the shot. He flung up his head high, snorted, and was off, fast as he could go. I followed him on foot, rapidly as I could, but he would none of that, and was all for keeping away from me at a safe distance. This the girl saw, and she rode up now, springing down and offering me her horse.

"Stay here," I called to her as I mounted. "I'll be back directly"; and then with such speed as I could spur out of my new mount, I started again after the fugitive.

It was useless. Her horse, already lame and weary, and further handicapped by my weight, could not close with the free animal, and without a rope to aid me in the capture, it would have been almost impossible to have stopped him, even had I been able to come alongside. I headed him time and again, and turned him, but it was to no purpose. At last I suddenly realized that I had no idea how far I had gone or in what direction. I must now think of my companion. Never was more welcome sight than when I saw her on a distant ridge, waving her hat. I gave up the chase and returned to her, finding that in her fatigue she had sunk to the ground exhausted. She herself had run far away from the spot where I had left 'her.

"I was afraid," she panted. "I followed. Can't you catch him?"

"No," said I, "he's gone. He probably will go back to the trail."

"No," she said, "they run wild, sometimes. But now what shall we do?"

I looked at her in anxiety. I had read all my life of being afoot on the Plains. Here was the reality.

"But you are hurt," she cried. "Look, your wound is bleeding."

I had not known it, but my neck was wet with blood.

"Get up and ride," she said. "We must be going." But I held the stirrup for her instead, smiling.

"Mount!" I said, and so I put her up.

"Shall we go back to camp?" she asked in some perturbation, apparently forgetting that there was no camp, and that by this time the wagons would be far to the west. For reasons of my own I thought it better to go back to the dead antelope, and so I told her.

"It is over there," she said, pointing in the direction from which she thought she had come. I differed with her, remembering I had ridden with the sun in my face when following it, and remembering the shape of the hilltop near by. Finally my guess proved correct, and we found the dead animal, nearly a mile from where she had waited for me. I hurried with the butchering, cutting the loin well forward, and rolling it all tight in the hide, bound the meat behind the saddle.

"Now, shall we go back?" she asked. "If we rode opposite to the sun, we might strike the trail. These hills look all alike."

"The river runs east and west," I said, "so we might perhaps better strike to the southward."

"But I heard them say that the river bends far to the south not far from where we crossed. We might parallel the river if we went straight south."

"But does not the trail cut off the bend, and run straight west?" I rejoined. Neither of us knew that the course of the north fork ran thence far to the northwest and quite away from the trail to Laramie.

Evidently our council was of little avail. We started southwest as nearly as we could determine it, and I admit that grave anxiety had now settled upon me. In that monotonous country only the sun and the stars might guide one. Now, hard as it was to admit the thought, I realized that we would be most fortunate if we saw the wagons again that night. I had my watch with me, and with this I made the traveler's compass, using the dial and the noon mark to orient myself; but this was of small assistance, for we were not certain of the direction of the compass in which the trail lay. As a matter of fact, it is probable that we went rather west than southwest, and so paralleled both the trail and the river for more than a dozen miles that afternoon. The girl's face was very grave, and now and again she watched me walking or trotting alongside at such speed as I could muster. My clothing was covered with blood from my wound.

I looked always for some little rivulet which I knew must lead us to the Platte, but we struck no running water until late that evening, and then could not be sure that we had found an actual water course. There were some pools of water standing in a coulee, at whose head grew a clump of wild plum trees and other straggly growth. At least here was water and some sort of shelter. I dared go no farther.

Over in the west I saw rising a low, black bank of clouds. A film was coming across the sky. Any way I looked I could see no break, no landmark, no trend of the land which could offer any sort of guidance. I wished myself all places in the world but there, and reproached myself bitterly that through my clumsiness I had brought the girl into such a situation.

"Miss Meriwether," I said to her finally, putting my hand on the pommel of her saddle as we halted, "it's no use. We might as well admit it; we are lost."

Chapter XXV - Cleaving Only Unto Her.

She made no great outcry. I saw her bend her face forward into her hands.

"What shall we do?" she asked at length.

"I do not know," said I to her soberly; "but since there is water here and a little shelter, it is my belief that we ought to stop here for the night."

She looked out across the gray monotony that surrounded us, toward the horizon now grown implacable and ominous. Her eyes were wide, and evidently she was pondering matters in her mind. At last she turned to me and held out her hands for me to assist her in dismounting.

"John Cowles, *of Virginia*," she said, "I am sorry we are lost."

I could make no answer, save to vow silently that if I lived she must be returned safely to her home, unhurt body and soul. I dared not ponder on conventions in a case so desperate as I knew ours yet might be. Silently I unsaddled the horse and hobbled it securely as I might with the bridle rein. Then I spread the saddle blanket for her to sit upon, and hurried about for Plains fuel. Water we drank from my hat, and were somewhat refreshed. Now we had food and water. We needed fire. But this, when I came to fumble in my pockets, seemed at first impossible, for I found not a match.

"I was afraid of that," she said, catching the meaning of my look. "What shall we do? We shall starve!"

"Not in the least," said I, stoutly. "We are good Indians enough to make a fire, I hope."

In my sheath was a heavy hunting knife; and now, searching about us on the side of the coulee bank, I found several flints, hard and white. Then I tore out a bit of my coat lining and moistened it a trifle, and saturated it with powder from my flask, rubbed in until it all was dry. This niter-soaked fabric I thought might serve as tinder for the spark. So then I struck flint and steel, and got the strange spark, hidden in the cold stone ages and ages there on the Plains; and presently the spark was a little flame, and then a good fire, and so we were more comfortable.

We roasted meat now, flat on the coals, the best we might, and so we ate, with no salt to aid us. The girl became a trifle more cheerful, though still distant and quiet. If I rose to leave the fire for an instant, I saw her eyes following me all the time. I knew her fears, though she did not complain.

Man is the most needful of all the animals, albeit the most resourceful. We needed shelter, and we had none. Night came on. The great gray wolves, haunters of the buffalo herds, roared their wild salute to us, savage enough to strike terror to any woman's soul. The girl edged close to me as the dark came down. We spoke but little. Our dangers had not yet made us other than conventional.

Now, worst of all, the dark bank of cloud arose and blotted out all the map of the stars. The sun scarce had sunk before a cold breath, silent, with no motion in its coming, swept across or settled down upon the Plains. The little grasses no longer stirred in the wind. The temperature mysteriously fell more and more, until it was cold, very cold. And those pale, heatless flames, icy as serpent tongues played along the darkening heavens, and mocked at us who craved warmth and shelter. I felt my own body shiver. She looked at me startled.

"You are cold," said she.

"No," I answered, "only angry because I am so weak." We sat silent for very long intervals. At length she raised her hand and pointed.

Even as dusk sank upon us, all the lower sky went black. An advancing roar came upon our ears. And then a blinding wave of rain drove across the surface of the earth, wiping out the day, beating down with remorseless strength and volume as though it would smother and drown us twain in its deluge—us, the last two human creatures of the world!

It caught us, that wave of damp and darkness, and rolled over us and crushed us down as we cowered. I caught up the blanket from the ground and pulled it around the girl's shoulders. I drew her tight to me as I lay with my own back to the storm, and pulled the saddle over her head, with this and my own body keeping out the tempest from her as much as I could. There was no other fence for her, and but for this she might perhaps have died; I do not know. I felt her strain at my arms first, then settle back and sink her head under the saddle flap and cower close like some little schoolfellow, all the curves of her body craving shelter, comfort, warmth. She shivered terribly. I heard her gasp and sob. Ah, how I pitied her that hour!

Colonel Meriweather Expresses His Thanks For The Rescue Of His Daughter

Orme Testifies That He Heard John And The Colonel Quarreling

Our fire was gone at the first sweep of the storm, which raged thunderously by, with heavy feet, over the echoing floor of the world. There came other fires, such blazes and explosions of pale balls of electricity as I had never dreamed might be, with these detonations of pent-up elemental wrath such as I never conceived might have existence under any sky. Night, death, storm, the strength of the elements, all the primeval factors of the world and life were upon us, testing us, seeking to destroy us, beating upon us, freezing, choking, blinding us, leaving us scarce animate.

Yet not destroying us. Still, somewhere under the huddle and draggle of it all burned on the human soul. The steel in my belt was cold, but it had held its fire. The ice in the flints about us held fire also in its depths. Fire was in our bodies, the fire of life—indomitable, yearning—in our two bodies. So that which made the storm test us and try us and seek to slay us, must perhaps have smiled grimly as it howled on and at length disappeared, baffled by the final success of the immutable and imperishable scheme. The fire in our two bodies still was there.

As the rain lessened, and the cold increased, I knew that rigors would soon come upon us. "We must walk," I said. "You shiver, you freeze."

"You tremble," she said. "You are cold. You are very cold."

"Walk, or we die," I gasped; and so I led her at last lower down the side of the ravine, where the wind was not so strong.

"We must run," I said, "or we shall die." I staggered as I ran. With all my soul I challenged my weakness, summoning to my aid that reserve of strength I had always known each hour in my life. Strangely I felt—how I cannot explain—that she must be saved, that she was I. Strange phrases ran through my brain. I remembered only one, "Cleaving only unto her"; and this, in my weakened frame of body and mind, I could not separate from my stern prayer to my own strength, once so ready, now so strangely departed from me.

We ran as we might, back and forward on the slippery mud, scrambled up and down, panting, until at length our hearts began to beat more quickly, and the love of life came back strongly, and the unknown, mysterious fire deep down somewhere, inscrutable, elemental, began to flicker up once more, and we were saved—saved, we two savages, we two primitive human beings, the only ones left alive after the deluge which had flooded all the earth—left alive to begin the world all over again.

Chapter XXVI - In Sickness And In Health

To the delirious or the perishing man, time has no measuring. I do not know how we spent the night, or how long it was. Some time it became morning, if morning might be called this gray and cheerless lifting of the gloom, revealing to us the sodden landscape, overcast with still drizzling skies which blotted out each ray of sunlight.

Search what way I might, I could find nothing to relieve our plight. I knew that Auberry would before this time have gone back to follow our trail, perhaps starting after us even before night had approached; but now the rain had blotted out all manner of trails, so rescue from that source was not to be expected. Not even we ourselves could tell where we had wandered, nor could we, using the best of our wits as we then had them, do more than vaguely guess where our fellow travelers by that time might be. Neither did we know distance nor direction of any settlement. What geography we thought right was altogether wrong. The desert, the wilderness, had us in its grip.

We sat, draggled and weary, at the shoulder of the little ravine, haggard and worn by the long strain. Her skin garments, again wet through, clung tight to her figure, uncomfortably. Now and again I could see a tremor running through her body from the chill. Yet as I looked at her I could not withhold my homage to her spirit. She was a splendid creature, so my soul swore to me, thoroughbred as any in all the world. Her chin was high, not drawn down in defeat. I caught sight of her small ear, flat to the head, pink with cold, but the ear of a game creature. Her nose, not aquiline, not masculine, still was not weak. Her chin, as I remember I noted even then, was strong, but lean and not over-laden with flesh. Her mouth, not thin-lipped and cold, yet not too loose and easy, was now plaintive as it was sweet in its full, red Cupid bow. Round and soft and gentle she seemed, yet all the lines of her figure, all the features of her face, betokened bone and breeding. The low-cut Indian shirt left her neck bare. I could see the brick red line of the sunburn creeping down; but most I noted, since ever it was my delight to trace good lineage in any creature, the splendid curve of her neck, not long and weak, not short and animal, but round and strong—perfect, I was willing to call that and every other thing about her.

She turned to me after a time and smiled wanly. "I am hungry," she said.

"We shall make a fire," I answered. "But first I must wait until my coat dries. The lining is wet, and we have no tinder. The bark is wet on the little trees; each spear of grass is wet."

Then I bethought me of an old expedient my father had once shown me. At the bandolier across my shoulder swung my bullet pouch and powder flask, in the former also some bits of tow along with the cleaning worm. I made a loose wad of the tow kept thus dry in the shelter of the pouch, and pushed this down the rifle barrel, after I had with some difficulty discharged the load already there. Then I rubbed a little more powder into another loose wad of tow, and fired the rifle into this. As luck would have it, some sparks still smoldered in the tow, and thus I was able once more to nurse up a tiny flame. I never knew before how comforting a fire might be. So now again we ate, and once more, as the hours advanced, we felt strength coming to us. Yet, in spite of the food, I was obliged to admit a strange aching in my head, and a hot fever burning in my bones.

"See the poor horse," she said, and pointed to our single steed, humped up in the wind, one hip high, his head low, all dejection.

"He must eat," said I, and so started to loosen his hobble. Thus engaged I thought to push on toward the top of the next ridge to see what might be beyond. What I saw was the worst thing that could have met my eyes. I sank down almost in despair.

There, on a flat valley nearly a mile away in its slow descent, stood the peaked tops of more than a score of Indian tepees. Horses were scattered all about. From the tops of the lodges little dribbles of smoke were coming. The wet of the morning kept the occupants within, but here and there a robed figure stalked among the horses.

I gazed through the fringe of grasses at the top of the ridge, feeling that now indeed our cup of danger well-nigh was full. For some moments I lay examining the camp, seeking to divine the intent of these people, whom I supposed to be Sioux. The size of the encampment disposed me to think that it was a hunting party and not an expedition out for war. I saw meat scaffolds, as I supposed, and strips of meat hanging over ropes strung here and there; although of this I could not be sure.

I turned as I heard a whisper at my shoulder. "What is it?" she asked me; and then the next moment, gazing as I did over the ridge, she saw. I felt her cower close to me in her instant terror. "My God!" she murmured, "what shall we do? They will find us; they will kill us!"

"Wait, now," said I. "They have not yet seen us. They may go away in quite the other direction. Do not be alarmed."

We lay there looking at this unwelcome sight for some moments, but at last I saw something which pleased me better.

The men among the horses stopped, looked, and began to hurry about, began to lead up their horses, to gesticulate. Then, far off upon the other side, I saw a blanket waving.

"It is the buffalo signal," I said to her. "They are going to hunt, and their hunt will be in the opposite direction from us. That is good."

We crept back from the top of the ridge, and I asked her to bring me the saddle blanket while I held the horse. This I bound fast around the horse's head.

"Why do you blind the poor fellow?" she inquired, "He cannot eat, he will starve. Besides, we ought to be getting away from here as fast as we can."

"I tie up his head so that he cannot see, or smell, and so fall to neighing to the other horses," I explained to her. "As to getting away, our trail would show plainly on this wet ground. All the trail we left yesterday has been wiped out; so that here is our very safest place, if they do not happen to run across the head of this little draw. Besides, we can still eat; and besides again—" perhaps I staggered a little as I stood.

"You are weak!" she exclaimed. "You are ill!"

"I must admit," said I, "that I could probably not travel far. If I dared tell you to go on alone and leave me, I would command you to do so."

Her face was pale. "What is wrong?" she asked. "Is it a fever? Is it your wound again?"

"It is fever," I answered thickly. "My head is bad. I do not see distinctly. If you please, I think I will lie down for a time."

I staggered blindly now as I walked. I felt her arm under mine. She led me to our little fireside, knelt on the wet ground beside me as I sat, my head hanging dully. I remember that her hands were clasped. I recall the agony on her face.

The day grew warmer as the sun arose. The clouds hung low and moved rapidly under the rising airs. Now and again I heard faint sounds, muffled, far off. "They are firing," I muttered. "They are among the buffalo. That is good. Soon they will go away."

I do not remember much of what I said after that, and recall only that my head throbbed heavily, and that I wanted to lie down and rest. And so, some time during that morning, I suppose, I did lie down, and once more laid hold upon the hand of Mystery.

I do not wish to speak of what followed after that. For me, a, merciful ignorance came; but what that poor girl must have suffered, hour after hour, night after night, day after day, alone, without shelter, almost without food, in such agony of terror as might have been natural even had her solitary protector been possessed of all his faculties—I say I cannot dwell upon that, because it makes the cold sweat stand on my face even now to think of it. So I will say only that one time I awoke. She told me later that she did not know whether it was two or three days we had been there thus. She told me that now and then she left me and crept to the top of the ridge to watch the Indian camp. She saw them come in from the chase, their horses loaded with meat. Then, as the sun came out, they went to drying meat, and the squaws began to scrape the hides. As they had abundant food they did not hunt more than that one day, and no one rode in our direction. Our horse she kept concealed and blindfolded until dark, when she allowed him to feed. This morning she had removed the blanket from his head, because now, as she told me with exultation, the Indians had broken camp, mounted and driven away, all of them, far off toward the west. She had cut and dried the remainder of our antelope meat, taking this hint from what we saw the Indians doing, and so most of our remaining meat had been saved.

I looked at her now, idly, dully. I saw that her belt was drawn tighter about a thinner waist. Her face was much thinner and browner, her eyes more sunken. The white strip of her lower neck was now brick red. I dared not ask her how she had gotten through the nights, because she had used the blanket to blindfold the horse. She had hollowed out a place for my hips to lie more easily, and pulled grasses for my bed. In all ways thoughtfulness and unselfishness had been hers. As I realized this, I put my hands over my face and groaned aloud. Then I felt her hand on my head.

"How did you eat?" I asked her. "You have no fire." "Once I had a fire," she said. "I made it with flint and steel as I saw you do. See," she added, and pointed to a ring of ashes, where there were bits of twigs and other fuel.

"Now you must eat," she said. "You are like a shadow. See, I have made you broth."

"Broth?" said I. "How?"

"In your hat," she said. "My father told me how the Indians boil water with hot stones. I tried it in my own hat first, but it is gone. A hot stone burned it through." Then I noticed that she was bareheaded. I lay still for a time, pondering feebly, as best I could, on the courage and resource of this girl, who now no doubt had saved my life, unworthy as it seemed to me. At last I looked up to her.

"After all, I may get well," I said. "Go now to the thicket at the head of the ravine, and see if there are any little cotton-wood trees. Auberry told me that the inner bark is bitter. It may act like quinine, and break the fever."

So presently she came back with my knife and her hands full of soft green bark which she had found. "It is bitter," said she, "but if I boil it it will spoil your broth." I drank of the crude preparation as best I might, and ate feebly as I might at some of the more tender meat thus softened. And then we boiled the bitter bark, and I drank that water, the only medicine we might have. Alas! it was our last use of my hat as a kettle, for now it, too, gave way.

"Now," she said to me, "I must leave you for a time. I am going over to the Indian camp to see what I can find."

She put my head in the saddle for a pillow, and gave me the remnant of her hat for a shade. I saw her go away, clad like an Indian woman, her long braids down her back, her head bare, her face brown, her moccasined feet slipping softly over the grasses, the metals of her leggins tinkling. My eyes followed her as long as she remained visible, and it seemed to me hours before she returned. I missed her.

She came back laughing and joyful. "See!" she exclaimed. "Many things! I have found a knife, and I have found a broken kettle; and here is an awl made from a bone; and here is something which I think their women use in scraping hides." She showed me all these things, last the saw-edged bone, or scraping hoe of the squaws, used for dressing hides, as she had thought.

172

"Now I am a squaw," she said, smiling oddly. She stood thoughtfully looking at these things for a time. "Yes," she said, "we are savages now."

I looked at her, but could see no despair on her face. "I do not believe you are afraid," I said to her. "You are a splendid creature. You are brave."

She looked down at me at length as I lay. "Have courage, John Cowles," she said. "Get well now soon, so that we may go and hunt. Our meat is nearly gone."

"But you do not despair," said I, wondering. She shook her head.

"Not yet. Are we not as well off as those?" she pointed toward the old encampment of the Indians. A faint tinge came to her cheeks. "It is strange," said she, "I feel as if the world had absolutely come to an end, and yet—"

"It is just beginning," said I to her. "We are alone. This is the first garden of the world. You are the first woman; I am the first cave man, and all the world depends on us. See," I said—perhaps still a trifle confused in my mind—"all the arts and letters of the future, all the paintings, all the money and goods of all the world; all the peace and war, and all the happiness and content of the world rest with us, just us two. We are the world, you and I."

She sat thoughtful and silent for a time, a faint pink, as I said, just showing on her cheeks.

"John Cowles, of Virginia," she said simply, "now tell me, how shall I mend this broken kettle?"

Chapter XXVII - With All My Worldly Goods I Thee Endow

Poor, indeed, in worldly goods must be those to whom the discarded refuse of an abandoned Indian camp seems wealth. Yet such was the case with us, two representatives of the higher civilization, thus removed from that civilization by no more than a few days' span. As soon as I was able to stand we removed our little encampment to the ground lately occupied by the Indian village.

We must have food, and I could not yet hunt. Here at the camp we found some bits of dried meat. We found a ragged and half-hairless robe, discarded by some squaw, and to us it seemed priceless, for now we had a house by day and a bed by night. A half-dozen broken lodge poles seemed riches to us. We hoarded some broken moccasins which had been thrown away. Like jackals we prowled around the filth and refuse of this savage encampment—-we, so lately used to all the comforts that civilization could give.

In the minds of us both came a thought new to both—a desire for food. Never before had we known how urgent is this desire. How few, indeed, ever really know what hunger is! If our great men, those who shape the destinies of a people, could know what hunger means, how different would be their acts! The trail of the lodge poles of these departing savages showed where they had gone farther in their own senseless pursuit of food, food. We also must eat. After that might begin all the deeds of the world. The surplus beyond the necessary provender of the hour is what constitutes the world's progress, its philosophy, its art, all its stored material gains. We who sat there under the shade of our ragged hide, gaunt, browned by the sun, hatless, ill-clad, animals freed from the yoke of society, none the less were not free from the yet more perpetual yoke of savagery.

For myself, weakened by sickness, such food as we had was of little service. I knew that I was starving, and feared that she was doing little better. I looked at her that morning, after we had propped up our little canopy of hide to break the sun. Her face was clean drawn now into hard lines of muscle. Her limbs lay straight and clean before her as she sat, her hands lying in her lap as she looked out across the plains. Her eyes were still brown and clear, her figure still was that of woman; she was still sweet to look upon, but her cheeks were growing hollow. I said to myself that she suffered, that she needed food. Upon us rested the fate of the earth, as it seemed to me. Unless presently I could arise and kill meat for her, then must the world roll void through the ether, unpeopled ever more.

It was at that time useless for us to think of making our way to any settlements or any human aid. The immediate burden of life was first to be supported. And yet we were unable to go out in search of food. I know not what thoughts came to her mind as we sat looking out on the pictures o; the mirage which the sun was painting on the desert landscape. But, finally, as we gazed, there seemed, among these weird images, one colossal tragic shape which moved, advanced, changed definitely. Now It stood in giant stature, and now dwindled, but always it came nearer. At last it darkened and denned and so disappeared beyond a blue ridge not half a mile away from us. We realized at last that it was a solitary buffalo bull, no doubt coming down to water at a little coulee just beyond us. I turned to look at her, and saw her eyes growing fierce. She reached back for my rifle, and I arose.

"Come," I said, and so we started. We dared not use the horse in stalking our game.

I could stand, I could walk a short way, but the weight of this great rifle, sixteen pounds or more, which I had never felt before, now seemed to crush me down. I saw that I was starved, that the sap was gone from my muscles. I could stagger but a few yards before I was obliged to stop and put down the rifle. She came and put her arm about me firmly, her face frowning and eager. But a tall man can ill be aided by a woman of her stature.

"Can you go?" she said.

"No," said I, "I cannot; but I must and I shall." I put away her arm from me, but in turn she caught up the rifle. Even for this I was still

175

too proud. "No," said I, "I have always carried my own weapons thus far."

"Come, then," she said, "this way"; and so caught the muzzle of the heavy barrel and walked on, leaving me the stock to support for my share of the weight. Thus we carried the great rifle between us, and so stumbled on, until at length the sun grew too warm for me, and I dropped, overcome with fatigue. Patiently she waited for me, and so we two, partners, mates, a man and a woman, primitive, the first, went on little by little.

I knew that the bull would in all likelihood stop near the rivulet, for his progress seemed to indicate that he was very old or else wounded. Finally I could see his huge black hump standing less than a quarter of a mile away from the ridge where I last paused. I motioned to her, and she crept to my side, like some desert creature. We were hunting animals now, the two sexes of Man—nothing more.

"Go," said I, motioning toward the rifle. "I am too weak. I might miss. I can get no farther."

She caught up the rifle barrel at its balancing point, looked to the lock as a man might have done, and leaned forward, eager as any man for the chase. There was no fear in her eye.

"Where shall I shoot it?" she whispered to me, as though it might overhear her.

"At the life, at the bare spot where his shoulder rubs, very low down," I said to her. "And when you shoot, drop and He still. He will soon lie down."

Lithe, brown, sinuous, she crept rapidly away, and presently was hid where the grass grew taller in the flat beyond. The bull moved forward a little also, and I lost sight of both for what seemed to me an unconscionable time. She told me later that she crept close to the water hole and waited there for the bull to come, but that he stood back and stared ahead stupidly and would not move. She said she trembled when at last he approached, so savage was his look. Even a man might be smitten with terror at the fierce aspect of one of these animals.

But at last I heard the bitter crack of the rifle and, raising my head, I saw her spring up and then drop down again. Then, staggering a short way up the opposite slope, I saw the slow bulk of the great black bull. He turned and looked back, his head low, his eyes straight ahead. Then slowly he kneeled down, and so died, with his forefeet doubled under him.

She came running back to me, full of savage joy at her Success, and put her arm under my shoulder and told me to come. Slowly, fast as I could, I went with her to our prey.

We butchered our buffalo as Auberry had showed me, from the backbone down, as he sat dead on his forearms, splitting the skin along the spine, and laying it out for the meat to rest upon. Again I made a fire by shooting a tow wad into such tinder as we could arrange from my coat lining, having dried this almost into flame by a burning-glass I made out of a watch crystal filled with water, not in the least a weak sort of lens. She ran for fuel, and for water, and now we cooked and ate, the fresh meat seeming excellent to me. Once more now we moved our camp, the girl returning for the horse and our scanty belongings.

Always now we ate, haggling out the hump ribs, the tongue, the rich back fat; so almost immediately we began to gain In strength. All the next day we worked as we could at drying the meat, and taking the things we needed from the carcass. We got loose one horn, drying one side of the head in the fire. I saved carefully all the sinews of the back, knowing we might need them. Then between us we scraped At the two halves of the hide, drying it in the sun, fleshing it with our little Indian hoe, and presently rubbing into it brains from the head of the carcass, as the hide grew drier in the sun. We were not yet skilled in tanning as the Indian women are, but we saw that now we would have a house and a bed apiece, and food, food. We broiled the ribs at our fire, boiled the broken leg bones in our little kettle. We made fillets of hide to shade our eyes, she thus binding back the long braids of her hair. We rested and were comforted. Each hour, it seemed to me, she rounded and became more beautiful, supple, young, strong—there, in the beginning of the world. We were rich in these, our belongings, which we shared.

Chapter XXVIII - Till Death Do Part

Hitherto, while I was weak, exhausted, and unable to reason beyond the vague factors of anxiety and dread, she had cared for me simply, as though she were a young boy and I an older man. The small details of our daily life she had assumed, because she still was the stronger. Without plot or plan, and simply through the stern command of necessity, our interests had been identical, our plans covered us both as one. At night, for the sake of warmth, we had slept closely, side by side, both too weary and worn out to reason regarding that or any other thing. Once, in the night, I know I felt her arm across my face, upon my head her hand — she still sleeping, and millions of miles away among the stars. I would not have waked her.

But now, behold the strange story of man's advance in what he calls civilization. Behold what property means in regard to what we call laws. We were rich now. We had two pieces of robe instead of one. We might be two creatures now, a man and a woman, a wall between, instead of two suffering, perishing animals, with but one common need, that of self-preservation. There were two houses now, two beds; because this might be and still allow us to survive. Our table was common, and that was all.

I grew stronger rapidly. In spite of my wish, my eyes rested upon her; and thus I noticed that she had changed. My little boy was no longer a little boy, but some strange creature — I knew hot what — like to nothing I had ever seen or known; like no woman of the towns, and no savage of the plains, but better than both and different from either, inscrutable, sweet, yes, and very sad. Often I saw tears in her eyes.

During that first night when we slept apart, the wolves came very close to our meat heaps and set up their usual roaring chorus. The terror of this she could not endure, and so she came creeping with her half robe to my side where I lay. That was necessary. Later that night when she awoke under the shelter of her half hide, she found me sitting awake, near the opening. But she would not have me put over her my portion of the robe. She made of our party two individuals, and that I must understand. I must understand now that society was beginning again, and law, and custom. My playfellow was gone. I liked scarce so well this new creature, with the face of a Sphinx, the form of a woman, the eyes of something hurt, that wept—that wept, because of these results of my own awkwardness and misfortunes.

I say that I was growing stronger. At night, in front of her poor shelter, I sat and thought, and looked out at the stars. The stars said to me that life and desire were one, that the world must go on, that all the future of the world rested with us two. But at this I rebelled. "Ah, prurient stars!" I cried, "and evil of mind! What matters it that you suffer or that I suffer? Let the world end, yes, let the world end before this strange new companion, gained in want, and poverty, and suffering, and now lost by reason of comforts and health, shall shed one tear of suffering!"

But sometimes, worn out by watching, I, too, must lie down. Again, in her sleep, I felt her arm rest upon my neck. Now, God give me what He listeth, but may not this thing come to me again.

For now, day by day, night by night, against all my will and wish, against all my mind and resolution, I knew that I was loving this new being with all my heart and all my soul, forsaking all others, and that this would be until death should us part. I knew that neither here nor elsewhere in the world was anything which could make me whole of this—no principles of duty or honor, no wish nor inclination nor resolve!

I had eaten. I loved. I saw what life is.

I saw the great deceit of Nature. I saw her plan, her wish, her merciless, pitiless desire; and seeing this, I smiled slowly in the dark at the mockery of what we call civilization, its fuss and flurry, its pretense, its misery. Indeed, we are small, but life is not small. We are small, but love is very large and strong, born as it is of the great necessity that man shall not forget the world, that woman shall not rob the race.

For myself, I accepted my station in this plan, saying nothing beyond my own soul. None the less, I said there to my own soul, that this must be now, till death should come to part us twain.

Chapter XXIX - The Garden

Soon now we would be able to travel; but whither, and for what purpose? I began to shrink from the thought of change. This wild world was enough for me. So long as we might eat and sleep thus, and so long as I might not lose sight of her, it seemed to me I could not anywhere gain in happiness and content. Elsewhere I must lose both.

None the less we must travel. We had been absent now from civilization some three weeks, and must have been given up long since. Our party must have passed far to the westward, and by this time our story was known at Laramie and elsewhere. Parties were no doubt in search of us at that time. But where should these search in that wilderness of the unknown Plains. How should it be known that we were almost within touch of the great highway of the West, now again thronging with wagon trains? By force of these strange circumstances which I have related we were utterly gone, blotted out; our old world no longer existed for us, nor we for it.

As I argued to myself again and again, the laws and customs of that forgotten world no longer belonged to us. We must build laws again, laws for the good of the greatest number. I can promise, who have been in place to know, that in one month's time civilization shall utterly fade away from the human heart, that a new state of life shall within that space enforce itself, so close lies the savage in us always to the skin. This vast scheme of organized selfishness, which is called civilization, shall within three weeks be forgot and found useless, be rescinded as a contract between remaining units of society. This vast fabric of waste and ruin known as wealth shall be swept away at a breath within one month. Then shall endure only the great things of life. Above those shall stand two things—a woman and a man. Without these society is not, these two, a woman and a man.

So I would sit at night, nodding under the stars, and vaguely dreaming of these matters, and things came to me sweetly, things unknown in our ignorance and evil of mind, as we live in what we call civilization. They would become clear underneath the stars; and then the dawn would come, and she would come and sit by me, looking out over the Plains at the shimmering pictures. "What do you see?" she would ask of me.

"I see the ruins of that dome known as the capitol of our nation," I said to her, "where they make laws. See, it is in ruins, and what I see beyond is better."

"Then what more do you see," she would ask.

"I see the ruins of tall buildings of brick and iron, prisons where souls are racked, and deeds of evil are done, and iron sunk into human hearts, and vice and crime, and oppression and wrong of life and love are wrought. These are in ruins, and what I see beyond is better." Humoring me, she would ask that I would tell her further what I saw.

"I see the ruins of tall spires, where the truth was offered by bold assertion. I see the ruins of religion, corrupt because done for gain.

"I see houses also, much crowded, where much traffic and bartering and evil was done, much sale of flesh and blood and love and happiness, ruin, unhappiness. And what I see now is far better than all that."

"And then—" she whispered faintly, her hand upon my sleeve, and looking out with me over the Plains, where the mirage was wavering.

"I see there," I said, and pointed it out to her, "only a Garden, a vast, sweet Garden. And there arises a Tree—-one Tree."

This was my world. But she, looking out over the Plains, still saw with the eye of yesterday. Upon woman the artificial imprint of heredity is set more deeply than with man. The commands of society are wrought into her soul.

Chapter XXX - They Twain

Even as we were putting together our small belongings for the resumption of our journey, I looked up and saw what I took to be a wolf, stalking along in the grass near the edge of our encampment. I would have shot it, but reflected that I must not waste a shot on wolves. Advancing closer toward it, as something about its motions attracted me, I saw it was a dog. It would not allow me to approach, but as Ellen came it lay down in the grass, and she got close to it.

"It is sick," she said, "or hurt," and she tossed it a bone.

"Quick," I called out to her, "get it! Tame it. It is worth more than riches to us, that dog."

So she, coaxing it, at last got her hands upon its head, though it would not wag its tail or make any sign of friendship. It was a wolfish mongrel Indian dog. One side of its head was cut or crushed, and it seemed that possibly some squaw had struck it, with intent perhaps to put it into the kettle, but with aim so bad that the victim had escaped.

To savage man, a dog is of nearly as much use as a horse. Now we had a horse and a dog, and food, and weapons, and shelter. It was time we should depart, and we now were well equipped to travel. But whither?

"It seems to me," said I, "that our safest plan is to keep away from the Platte, where the Indians are more apt to be. If we keep west until we reach the mountains, we certainly will be above Laramie, and then if we follow south along the mountains, we must strike the Platte again, and so find Laramie, if we do not meet any one before that time." It may be seen how vague was my geography in regard to a region then little known to any.

"My father will have out the whole Army looking for us," said Ellen Meriwether to me. "We may be found any day."

But for many a day we were not found. We traveled westward day after day, she upon the horse, I walking with the dog. We had a rude travois, which we forced our horse to draw, and our little belongings we carried in a leathern bag, slung between two lodge poles. The dog we did not yet load, although the rubbed hair on his shoulders showed that he was used to harness.

At times on these high rolling plains we saw the buffalo, and when our dried meat ran low I paused for food, not daring to risk waste of our scanty ammunition at such hard game as antelope. Once I lay at a path near a water hole in the pocket of a half-dried stream, and killed two buffalo cows. Here was abundant work for more than two days, cutting, drying, scraping, feasting. Life began to run keen in our veins, in spite of all. I heard her sing, that day, saw her smile. Now our worldly goods were increasing, so I cut down two lodge poles and made a little travois for the dog. We had hides enough now for a small tent, needing only sufficient poles.

"Soon," said she to me, "we will be at Laramie."

"Pray God," said I to myself, "that we never may see Laramie!" I have said that I would set down the truth. And this is the truth; I was becoming a savage. I truly wanted nothing better. I think this might happen to many a man, at least of that day.

We forded several streams, one a large one, which I now think must have been the North Platte; but no river ran as we fancied the Platte must run. So we kept on, until we came one day to a spot whence we saw something low and unmoving and purple, far off in the northwest. This we studied, and so at length saw that it was the mountains. At last our journeying would change, at least, perhaps terminate ere long. A few more days would bring us within touch of this distant range, which, as I suppose now, might possibly have been a spur of what then were still called the Black Hills, a name which applied to several ranges far to the west and south of the mountains now so called. Or perhaps these were peaks of the mountains later called the Laramie Range.

Then came a thing hard for us to bear. Our horse, hobbled as usual for the night, and, moreover, picketed on a long rope I had made from buffalo hides, managed some time in the night to break his hobbles and in some way to pull loose the picket pin. When we saw that he was gone we looked at each other blankly.

"What shall we do?" she asked me in horror. For the first time I saw her sit down in despair. "We are lost! What shall we do?" she wailed.

I trailed the missing horse for many miles, but could only tell he was going steadily, lined out for some distant point. I dared not pursue him farther and leave her behind. An hour after noon I returned and sullenly threw myself on the ground beside her at our little bivouac. I could not bear to think of her being reduced to foot travel over all these cruel miles. Yet, indeed, it now must come to that.

"We have the dog," said I at length. "We can carry a robe and a little meat, and walk slowly. I can carry a hundred pound pack if need be, and the dog can take twenty-five—"

"And I can carry something," she said, rising with her old courage. "It is my part." I made her a pack of ten pounds, and soon seeing that it was too heavy, I took it from her and threw it on my own.

"At least I shall carry the belt," she said. And so she took my belt, with its flask and bullet pouch, the latter now all too scantily filled.

Thus, sore at heart, and somewhat weary, we struggled on through that afternoon, and sank down beside a little water hole. And that night, when I reached to her for my belt that we might again make our fire, she went pale and cried aloud that she had lost it, and that now indeed we must die!

I could hardly comfort her by telling her that on the morrow I would certainly find it. I knew that in case I did not our plight indeed was serious. She wept that night, wept like a child, starting and moaning often in her sleep. That night, for the first time, I took her in my arms and tried to comfort her. I, being now a savage, prayed to the Great

Spirit, the Mystery, that my own blood might not be as water, that my heart might be strong — the old savage prayers of primitive man brought face to face with nature.

When morning came I told her I must go back on the trail. "See, now, what this dog has done for us," I said. "The scratches on the ground of his little travois poles will make a trail easy to be followed. I must take him with me and run back the trail. For you, stay here by the water and no matter what your fears, do not move from here in any case, even if I should not be back by night."

"But what if you should not come back!" she said, her terror showing in her eyes.

"But I will come back," I replied. "I will never leave you. I would rise from my grave to come back to you. But the time has not yet come to lie down and die. Be strong. We shall yet be safe."

So I was obliged to turn and leave her sitting alone there, the gray sweep of the merciless Plains all about her. Another woman would have gone mad.

But it was as I said. This dog was our savior. Without his nose I could not have traced out the little travois trail; but he, seeing what was needed, and finding me nosing along and doubling back and seeking on the hard ground, seemed to know what was required, or perhaps himself thought to go back to some old camp for food. So presently he trotted along, his ears up, his nose straight ahead; and I, a savage, depended upon a creature still a little lower in the order of life, and that creature proved a faithful servant.

We went on at a swinging walk, or trot, or lope, as the ground said, and ate up the distance at twice the speed we had used the day before. In a couple of hours I was close to where she had taken the belt, and so at last I saw the dog drop his nose and sniff. There were the missing riches, priceless beyond gold — the little leaden balls, the powder, dry in its horn, the little rolls of tow, the knife swung at the girdle! I knelt down there on the sand, I, John Cowles, once civilized and now heathen, and I raised my frayed and ragged hands toward the Mystery, and begged that I might be forever free of the great crime of thanklessness. Then, laughing at the dog, and loping on tireless as when I was a boy, I ran as though sickness and weakness had never been mine, and presently came back to the place where I had left her.

She saw me coming. She ran out to meet me, holding out her arms.... I say she came, holding out her arms to me.

"Sit down here by my side," I commanded her. "I must talk to you. I will—I will."

"Do not," she implored of me, seeing what was in my mind. "Ah, what shall I do! You are not fair!"

But I took her hands in mine. "I can endure it no longer," I said. "I will not endure it."

She looked at me with her eyes wide—looked me full in the face with such a gaze as I have never seen on any woman's face.

"I love you," I said to her. "I have never loved any one else. I can never love any one again but you." I say that I, John Cowles, had at that moment utterly forgotten all of life and all of the world except this, then and there. "I love you!" I said, over and over again to her.

She pushed away my arm. "They are all the same," she said, as though to herself.

"Yes, all the same," I said. "There is no man who would not love you, here or anywhere."

"To how many have you said that?" she asked me, frowning, as though absorbed, studious, intent on some problem.

"To some," I said to her, honestly. "But it was never thus."

She curled her lip, scorning the truth which she had asked now that she had it. "And if any other woman were here it would be the same. It is because I am here, because we are alone, because I am a woman—ah, that is neither wise nor brave nor good of you!"

"That is not true! Were it any other woman, yes, what you say might be true in one way. But I love you not because you are a woman. It is because you are Ellen. You would be the only woman in the world, no matter where we were nor how many were about us. Though I could choose from all the world, it would be the same!"

She listened with her eyes far away, thinking, thinking. "It is the old story," she sighed.

"Yes, the old story," I said. "It is the same story, the old one. There are the witnesses, the hills, the sky."

"You seem to have thought of such things," she said to me, slowly. "I have not thought. I have simply lived along, enjoying life, not thinking. Do we love because we are but creatures? I cannot be loved so—I will not be! I will not submit that what I have sometimes dreamed shall be so narrow as this. John Cowles, a woman must be loved for herself, not for her sex, by some one who is a man, but who is beside—"

"Oh, I have said all that. I loved you the first time I saw you—the first time, there at the dance."

"And forgot, and cared for another girl the next day.' She argued that all over again.

"That other girl was you," I once more reiterated.

"And again you forgot me."

"And again what made me forget you was yourself! Each time you were that other girl, that other woman. Each time I have seen you you have been different, and each time I have loved you over again.

Each day I see you now you are different, Ellen, and each day I love you more. How many times shall I solve this same problem, and come to the same answer. I tell you, the thing is ended and done for me."

"It is easy to think so here, with only the hills and skies to see and hear."

"No, it would be the same," I said. "It is not because of that."

"It is not because I am in your power?" she said. She turned and faced me, her hands on my shoulders, looking me full in the eye. The act a brave one.

"Because I am in your power, John Cowles?" she asked. "Because by accident you have learned that I am a comely woman, as you are a strong man, normal, because I am fit to love, not ill to look at? Because a cruel accident has put me where my name is jeopardized forever—in a situation out of which I can never, never come clean again—is *that* why? Do you figure that I am a woman because you are a man? Is that why? Is it because you know I am human, and young, and fit for love? Ah, I know that as well as you. But I am in your hands—I am in your power. That is why I say, John Cowles, that you must try to think, that you must do nothing which shall make me hate you or make you hate yourself."

"I thought you missed me when I was gone," I murmured faintly.

"I did miss you," she said. "The world seemed ended for me. I needed you, I wanted you—" I turned toward her swiftly. "Wanted me?"

"I was glad to see you come back. While you were gone I thought. Yes, you have been brave and you have been kind, and you have been strong. Now I am only asking you still to be brave, and kind, and strong."

"But do you love me, will you love me—can you—"

"Because we are here," she said, "I will not answer. What is right, John Cowles, that we should do."

Woman is strongest when armored in her own weakness. My hands fell to the ground beside me. The heats vanished from my blood. I shuddered. I could not smile without my mouth going crooked, I fear. But at last I smiled as best I could, and I said to her, "Ellen! Ellen!" That was all I could find to say.

Chapter XXXI - The Betrothal

Strength came to us as we had need, and gradually even the weaker of us two became able to complete the day's journey without the exhaustion it at first had cost her. Summer was now upon us, and the heat at midday was intense, although the nights, as usual, were cold. Deprived of all pack animals, except our dog, we were perforce reduced to the lightest of gear, and discomfort was our continual lot. Food, however, we could still secure, abundant meat, and sometimes the roots of plants which I dug up and tested, though I scarce knew what they were.

We moved steadily on toward the west and northwest, but although we crossed many old Indian trails, we saw no more of these travelers of the Plains. At that time the country which we were traversing had no white population, although the valley of the Platte had long been part of a dusty transcontinental highway. It was on this highway that the savages were that summer hanging, and even had we been certain of its exact location, I should have feared to enter the Platte valley, lest we should meet red men rather than white.

At times we lost the buffalo for days, more especially as we approached the foothills of the mountains, and although antelope became more numerous there, they were far more difficult to kill, and apt to cost us more of our precious ammunition. I planned to myself that if we did not presently escape I would see what might be done toward making a bow and arrows for use on small game, which we could not afford to purchase at the cost of precious powder and ball.

I was glad, therefore, when we saw the first timber of the foothills; still gladder, for many reasons, when I found that we were entering the winding course of a flattened, broken stream, which presently ran back into a shingly valley, hedged in by ranks of noble mountains, snow white on their peaks. Here life should prove easier to us for the time, the country offering abundant shelter and fuel, perhaps game, and certainly change from the monotony of the Plains.

Here, I said to myself, our westward journey must end. It would be bootless to pass beyond Laramie into the mountains, and our next course, I thought, must be toward the south. I did not know that we were then perhaps a hundred miles or more northwest of Laramie, deep in a mountain range far north of the transcontinental trail. For the time, however, it seemed wise to tarry here for rest and recruiting. I threw down the pack. "Now," said I to her, "we rest."

"Yes," she replied, turning her face to the south, "Laramie is that way now. If we stop here my father will come and find us. But then, how could he find us, little as we are, in this big country? Our trail would not be different from that of Indians, even if they found it fresh enough to read. Suppose they *never* found us!"

"Then," said I, "we should have to live here, forever and ever."

She looked at me curiously. "Could we?" she asked.

"Until I was too old to hunt, you too weak to sew the robes or cook the food."

"What would happen then?"

"We would die," said I. "The world would end, would have to begin all over again and wait twice ten million years until man again was evolved from the amoeba, the reptile, the ape. When we died, this dog here would be the only hope of the world."

She looked at the eternal hills in their snow, and made no answer. Presently we turned to our duties about the camp.

It was understood that we should stay here for at least two days, to mend our clothing and prepare food for the southern journey. I have said I was not happy at the thought of turning toward that world which I had missed so little. Could the wild freedom of this life have worked a similar spell on her? The next day she came to me as I sat by our meager fireside. Without leading of mine she began a manner of speech until now foreign to her.

"What is marriage, John Cowles?" she asked of me, abruptly, with no preface.

"It is the Plan," I answered, apathetically. She pondered for a time.

"Are we, then, only creatures, puppets, toys?"

"Yes," I said to her. "A man is a toy. Love was born before man was created, before animals or plants. Atom, ran to atom, seeking. It was love." She pondered yet a while.

"And what is it, then, John Cowles, that women call 'wrong'?"

"Very often what is right," I said to her, apathetically. "When two love the crime is that they shall not wed. When they do not love, the crime is when they do wed."

"But without marriage," she hesitated, "the home—"

"It is the old question," I said. "The home is built on woman's virtue; but virtue is not the same where there is no tome, no property, where there is no society—it is an artificial thing, born of compromise, and grown stronger by custom of the ages of property-owning man."

I saw a horror come across her eyes.

"What do you say to me, John Cowles? That what a woman prizes is not right, is not good? No, that I shall *not* think!" She drew apart from me.

"Because you think just as you do, I love you," I said.

"Yet you say so many things. I have taken life as it came, just as other girls do, not thinking. It is not nice, it is not *clean*, that girls should study over these things. That is not right."

"No, that is not right," said I, dully.

"Then tell me, what is marriage—that one thing a girl dreams of all her life. Is it of the church?"

"It is not of the church," I said.

"Then it is the law."

"It is not the law," I said.

"Then what is it?" she asked. "John Cowles, tell me, what makes a wedding between two who really and truly love. Can marriage be of but two?"

"Yes," said I.

"But there must be witnesses—there must be ceremony—else there is no marriage," she went on. Her woman's brain clung to the safe, sane groove which alone can guide progress and civilization and society—that great, cruel, kind, imperative compromise of marriage, without which all the advancement of the world would be as naught. I loved her for it. But for me, I say I had gone savage. I was at the beginning of all this, whereas it remained with her as she had left it.

"Witnesses?" I said. "Look at those!" I pointed to the mountains. "Marriages, many of them, have been made with no better witnesses than those."

My heart stopped when I saw how far she had jumped to her next speech.

"Then we two are all the people left in the world, John Cowles? When I am old, will you cast me off? When another woman comes into this valley, when I am bent and old, and cannot see, will you cast me off, and, being stronger than I am, will you go and leave me?"

I could not speak at first. "We have talked too much," I said to her presently. But now it was she who would not desist.

"You see, with a woman it is for better, for worse—but with a man"

"With a Saxon man," I said, "it is also for better, for worse. It is one woman."

She sat and thought for a long time. "Suppose," she said, "that no one ever came."

Now with swift remorse I could see that in her own courage she was feeling her way, haltingly, slowly, toward solution of problems which most women take ready solved from others. But, as I thank God, a filmy veil, softening, refining, always lay between her and reality. In her intentness she laid hold upon my arm, her two hands clasping.

"Suppose two were here, a man and a woman, and he swore before those eternal witnesses that he would not go away any time until she was dead and laid away up in the trees, to dry away and blow off into the air, and go back—"

"Into the flowers," I added, choking.

"Yes, into the trees and the flowers—so that when she was dead and he was dead, and they were both gone back into the flowers, they would still know each other for ever and ever and never be ashamed—would that be a marriage before God, John Cowles?"

What had I brought to this girl's creed of life, heretofore always so sweet and usual? I did not answer. She shook at my arm. "Tell me!" she said. But I would not tell her.

"Suppose they did not come," she said once more. "It is true, they may not find us. Suppose we two were to live here alone, all this winter—just as we are now—none of my people or yours near us. Could we go on?"

"God! Woman, have you no mercy!"

She sat and pondered for yet a time, as though seriously weighing some question in her mind.

"But you have taught me to think, John Cowles. It is you who have begun my thinking, so now I must think. I know we cannot tell what may happen. I ask you, 'John Cowles, if we were brought to that state which we both know might happen—if we were here all alone and no one came, and if you loved me—ah, then would you promise, forever and forever, to love me till death did us part—till I was gone back into the flowers? I remember what they say at weddings. They cling one to the other, forsaking all others, till death do them part. Could you promise me—in that way? Could you promise me, clean and solemn? Because, I would not promise you unless it was solemn, and clean, and unless it was forever."

Strange, indeed, these few days in the desert, which had so drawn apart the veil of things and left us both ready to see so far. She had not seen so far as I, but, womanlike, had reasoned more quickly.

As for me, it seemed that I saw into her heart. I dropped my hands from my eyes and looked at her strangely, my own brain in a whirl, my logic gone. All I knew was that then or elsewhere, whether or not rescue ever came for us, whether we died now or later, there or anywhere in all the world, I would, indeed, love her and her only, forsaking all others until, indeed, we were gone back into the sky and flowers, until we whispered again in the trees, one unto the other! Marriage or no marriage, together or apart, in sickness or in health—so there came to me the stern conviction—love could knock no more at my heart, where once she had stood in her courage and her cleanness. Reverence, I say, was now the one thing left in my heart. Still we sat, and watched the sun shine on the distant white-topped peaks. I turned to her slowly at length.

"Ellen," I said, "do you indeed love me?"

"How can I help it, John Cowles," she answered bravely. My heart stopped short, then raced on, bursting all control. It was long before I could be calm as she.

"You have helped it very long," I said at last, quietly. "But now I must know—would you love me anywhere, in any circumstances, in spite of all? I love you because you are You, not because you are here. I must be loved in the same way, always."

She looked at me now silently, and I leaned and kissed her full on the mouth.

Chapter XXXII - The Covenant

She did not rebel or draw away, but there was that on her face, I say, which left me only reverent. Her hand fell into mine. We sat there, plighted, plighted in our rags and misery and want and solitude. Though I should live twice the allotted span of man, never should I forget what came into my soul that hour.

After a time I turned from her, and from the hills, and from the sky, and looked about us at the poor belongings with which we were to begin our world. All at once my eye fell upon one of our lighter robes, now fairly white with much working. I drew it toward me, and with her still leaning against my shoulder, I took up a charred stick, and so, laboriously, I wrote upon the surface of the hide, these words of our covenant:

"I, John Cowles, take thee, Ellen Meriwether, to be my lawful, wedded wife, in sickness, and in health, for better of for worse, till death do us part."

And I signed it; and made a seal after my name.

"Write," said I to her. "Write as I have written."

She took a fresh brand, blackened at the end, and in lesser characters wrote slowly, letter by letter:

"I, Ellen Meriwether, take thee, John Cowles, to be my lawful, wedded husband—" She paused, but I would not urge her, and it was moments before she resumed —*"in sickness and in health, for better or for worse—"* Again she paused, thinking, thinking—and so concluded, *"till death do us part."*

"It means," she said to me, simply as a child, "until we have both gone back into the flowers and the trees."

I took her hand in mine. Mayhap book and bell and organ peal and vestured choir and high ceremony of the church may be more solemn; but I, who speak the truth from this very knowledge, think it could not be.

"When you have signed that, Ellen," I said to her at last, "we two are man and wife, now and forever, here and any place in the world. That is a binding ceremony, and it endows you with your share of all my property, small or large as that may be. It is a legal wedding, and it holds us with all the powers the law can have. It is a contract."

"Do not talk to me of contracts," she said. "I am thinking of nothing but our—wedding."

Still mystical, still enigma, still woman, she would have it that the stars, the mountains—-the witnesses—and not ourselves, made the wedding. I left it so, sure of nothing so much as that, whatever her way of thought might be, it was better than my own.

"But if I do not sign this?" she asked at length.

"Then we are not married."

She sighed and laid down the pen. "Then I shall not sign it—yet," she said.

I caught up her hand as though I would write for her.

"No," she said, "it shall be only our engagement, our troth between us. This will be our way. I have not yet been sufficiently wooed, John Cowles!"

I looked into her eyes and it seemed to me I saw there something of the same light I had seen when she was the masked coquette of the Army ball—the yearning, the melancholy, the mysticism, the challenge, the invitation and the doubting—ah, who shall say what there is in a woman's eye! But I saw also what had been in her eyes each time I had seen her since that hour. I left it so, knowing that her way would be best.

"When we have escaped," she went on, "if ever we do escape, then this will still be our troth, will it not, John Cowles?"

"Yes, and our marriage, when you have signed, now or any other time."

"But if you had ever signed words like these with any *other* woman, then it would not be our marriage nor our troth, would it, John Cowles?"

"No," I said. *And, then I felt my face grow ashy cold and pale in one sudden breath!*

"But why do you look so sad?" she asked of me, suddenly. "Is it not well to wait?"

"Yes, it is well to wait," I said. She was so absorbed that she did not look at me closely at that instant.

Again she took up the charred stick in her little hand, and hesitated. "See," she said, "I shall sign one letter of my name each week, until all my name is written! Till that last letter we shall be engaged. After the last letter, when I have signed it of my own free will, and clean, and solemn—clean and solemn, John Cowles—then we will be—Oh, take me home—take me to my father, John Cowles! This is a hard place for a girl to be."

Suddenly she dropped her face into her hands, sobbing.

She hid her head on my breast, sore distressed now. She was glad that she might now be more free, needing some manner of friend; but she was still—what? Still woman! Poor Saxon I must have been had I not sworn to love her fiercely and singly all my life. But yet—

I looked at the robe, now fallen loose upon the ground, and saw that she had affixed one letter of her name and stopped. She smiled wanly. "Your name would be shorter to sign a little at a time," she said; "but a girl must have time. She must wait. And see," she said, "I have no ring. A girl always has a ring."

This lack I could not solve, for I had none.

"Take mine," she said, removing the ring with the rose seal. "Put it on the other finger—the—the right one."

I did so; and I kissed her. But yet—

She was weary and strained now. A pathetic droop came to the corners of her mouth. The palm of her little hand turned up loosely, as though she had been tired and now was resting. "We must wait," she said, as though to herself.

But what of me that night? When I had taken my own house and bed beyond a little thicket, that she might be alone, that night I found myself breathing hard in terror and dread, gazing up at the stars in agony, beating my hands on the ground at the thought of the ruin I had wrought, the crime that I had done in gaining this I had sought.

I had written covenants before! I have said that I would tell simply the truth in these pages, and this is the truth, the only extenuation I may claim. The strength and sweetness of all this strange new life with her had utterly wiped out my past, had put away, as though forever, the world I once had known. Until the moment Ellen Meriwether began the signing of her name, I swear I had forgotten that ever in the world was another by name of Grace Sheraton! I may not be believed—I ought not to be believed; but this is the truth and the truth by what measure my love for Ellen Meriwether was bright and fixed, as much as my promise to the other had been ill-advised and wrong.

A forsworn man, I lay there, thinking of her, sweet, simple, serious and trusting, who had promised to love me, an utterly unworthy man, until we two should go back into the flowers.

Far rather had I been beneath the sod that moment; for I knew, since I loved Ellen Meriwether, *she must not complete the signing of her name upon the scroll of our covenant!*

Chapter XXXIII - The Flaming Sword

The question of food ever arose for settlement, and early the next morning I set out upon a short exploring expedition through our new country, to learn what I might of its resources. There were trout in our little mountain stream, and although we had no hooks or lines I managed to take a few of these in my hands, chasing them under the stones. Also I found many berries now beginning to ripen, and as the forest growth offered us new supplies, I gathered certain barks, thinking that we might make some sort of drink, medicinal if not pleasant. Tracks of deer were abundant; I saw a few antelope, and supposed that possibly these bolder slopes might hold mountain sheep. None of these smaller animals was so useful to us as the buffalo, for each would cost as much expenditure of precious ammunition, and yield less return in bulk. I shook the bullet pouch at my belt, and found it light. We had barely two dozen bullets left; and few hunters would promise themselves over a dozen head of big game for twice as many shots.

I cast about me in search of red cedar that I might make a bow. I searched the willow thicket for arrow shafts, and prowled among little flints and pointed stones on the shores of our stream, seeking arrow points. It finally appeared to me that we might rest here for a time and be fairly safe to make a living in some way. Then, as I was obliged to admit, we would need to hurry on to the southward.

But again fate had its way with us, setting aside all plans. When I returned to our encampment, instead of seeing Ellen come out to meet me as I expected, I found her lying in the shade of the little tepee.

"You are hurt!" I cried. "What has happened?"

"My foot," said she, "I think it is broken!" She was unable to stand.

As she could, catching her breath, she told me how this accident had happened. Walking along the stony creek bank, she had slipped, and her moccasined foot, caught in the narrow crack between two rocks, had been held fast as she fell forward. It pained her now almost unbearably. Tears stood in her eyes.

So now it was my term to be surgeon. Tenderly as I might, I examined the foot, now badly swollen and rapidly becoming discolored. In spite of her protest—although I know it hurt me more than herself—I flexed the joints and found the ankle at least safe. Alas! a little grating in the smaller bones, just below the instep, told me of a fracture.

"Ellen," said I to her, "the foot is broken here—two bones, I think, are gone."

She sank back upon her robe with an exclamation as much of horror as pain.

"What shall we do!" she murmured. "I shall be crippled! I cannot walk—we shall perish!"

"No," I said to her, "we shall mend it. In time you will not know it has happened." Thus we gave courage to each other.

All that morning I poured water from a little height upon the bared foot, so that presently the inflammation and the pain lessened. Then I set out to secure flat splints and some soft bark, and so presently splintered and bound the foot, skillfully as I knew how; and this must have brought the broken bones in good juxtaposition, for at least I know that eventually nature was kind enough to heal this hurt and leave no trace of it.

Now, when she was thus helpless and suffering, needing all her strength, how could I find it in my heart to tell her that secret which it was my duty to tell? How could I inflict upon her a still more poignant suffering than this physical one? Each morning I said to myself, "To-day, if she is better, I will tell her of Grace Sheraton; she must know." But each time I saw her face I could not tell her.

Each day she placed a clean white pebble in a little pile at her side. Presently there were seven.

"John Cowles," she said to me that morning, "bring me our writing, and bring me my pen. To-day I must sign another letter." And, smiling, she did so, looking up into my face with love showing on her own. Had the charcoal been living flame, and had she written on my bare heart, she could not have hurt me more.

Of course, all the simple duties of our life now devolved upon myself. I must hunt, and keep the camp, and cook, and bring the fuel; so that much of the time I was by necessity away from her. Feverishly I explored all our little valley and exulted that here nature was so kind to us. I trapped hares in little runways. I made me a bow and some arrows, and very often I killed stupid grouse with these or even with stones or sticks, as they sat in the trees; and in bark baskets that I made I brought home many berries, now beginning to ripen fully. Roots and bulbs as I found them I experimented with, though not with much success. Occasionally I found fungi which made food. Flowers also I brought to her, flowers of the early autumn, because now the snows were beginning to come down lower on the mountains. In two months winter would be upon us. In one month we would have snow in the valley.

The little pile of white stones at her side again grew, slowly, slowly. Letter by letter her name grew invisible form on the scroll of our covenant—her name, already written, and more deeply, on my heart. On the fifth week she called once more for her charcoal pen, and signed the last letter of her Christian name!

"See, there," she said, "it is all my girl name, E-l-l-e-n." I looked at it, her hand in mine.

"'Ellen!'" I murmured. "It is signature enough, because you are the only Ellen in the world." But she put away my hand gently and said, "Wait."

She asked me now to get her some sort of cut branch for a crutch, saying she was going to walk. And walk she did, though resting her foot very little on the ground. After that, daily she went farther and farther, watched me as I guddled for trout in the stream, aided me as I picked berries in the thickets, helped me with the deer I brought into camp.

"You are very good to me," she said, "and you hunt well. You work. You are a man, John Cowles. I love you."

'Out Thar In Californy The Hills Are Full Of Gold'

But hearing words so sweet as these to me, still I did not tell her what secret was in my soul. Each day I said to myself that presently she would be strong enough to bear it, and that then I would tell her. Each day that other world seemed vaguer and farther away. But each day passed and I could not speak. Each day it seemed less worth while to speak. Now I could not endure the thought of losing her. I say that I could not. Let none judge me too harshly who have not known the full measure of this world and that.

There was much sign of bears in our thickets, and I warned her not to go out alone after berries where these long-footed beasts now fed regularly. Sometimes we went there together, with our vessels of bark, and filled them slowly, as she hobbled along. Our little dog was now always with us, having become far more tamed and docile with us than is ever the case of an Indian dog in savagery. One day we wandered in a dense berry thicket, out of which rose here and there chokecherry trees, and we began to gather some of these sour fruits for use in the pemmican which we planned to manufacture. All at once we came to a spot where the cherry trees were torn down, pulled over, ripped up by the roots. The torn earth was very fresh, and I knew that the bear that had done the work could not be far away.

All at once our dog began to growl and erect his hair, sniffing not at the foot scent, but looking directly into the thicket just ahead. He began then to bark, and as he did so there rose, with a sullen sort of grunt and a champing of jaws like a great hog, a vast yellow-gray object, whose head topped the bushes that grew densely all about. The girl at my side uttered a cry of terror and turned to run as best she might, but she fell, and lay there cowering.

The grizzly stood looking at me vindictively with little eyes, its ears back, its jaws working, its paws swinging loosely at its side, the claws white at the lower end, as though newly sharpened for slaughtering. I saw then that it was angered by the sight of the dog, and would not leave us. Each moment I expected to hear it crash through the bush in its charge. Once down in the brush, there would be small chance of delivering a fatal shot; whereas now, as it swung its broad head slightly to one side, the best possible opportunity for killing it presented itself immediately. Without hesitation I swung up the heavy barrel, and drew the small silver bead directly on the base of the ear, where the side bones of a bear's head are flatter and thinner, directly alongside the brain. The vicious crack of the rifle sounded loud there in the thicket; but there came no answer in response to it save a crashing and slipping and a breaking down of the bushes as the vast carcass fell at full length. The little ball had done its work and found the brain.

I knew the bear was dead, but for a time did not venture closely. I looked about and saw the girl slowly rising on her elbow, her face uncovered now, but white in terror. I motioned for her to lie still, and having reloaded, I pushed quietly through the undergrowth. I saw a vast gray, grizzled heap lying there, shapeless, motionless. Then I shouted aloud and went back and picked her up and carried her through the broken thicket, and placed her on the dead body of the grizzly, seating myself at her side.

We were two savages, successful now in the chase—successful, indeed, in winning the capital prize of all savages; for few Indians will attack the grizzly if it can be avoided. She laid her hand wonderingly upon the barrel of the rifle, looking at it curiously, that it had been so deadly as to slay a creature so vast as this. Then she leaned contentedly against my side, and so we sat there for a time. "John Cowles," she said, "you are brave. You are very much a man. I am not afraid when you are with me." I put my arm about her. The world seemed wild and fair and sweet to me. Life, savage, stern, swept through all my veins.

The skinning of the bear was a task of some moment, and as we did this we exulted that we would now have so fine a robe. The coarse meat we could not use, but the fat I took off in flakes and strips, and hung upon the bushes around us for later carrying into camp. In this work she assisted me, hobbling about as best she might.

We were busy at this, both of us greasy and bloody to our elbows, when all at once we stopped and looked at each other in silence. We had heard a sound. To me it sounded like a rifle shot. We listened. It came again, with others. There was a volley of several shots, sounds certain beyond any manner of question.

My heart stopped. She looked at me, some strange thought written upon her face. It was not joy, nor exultation, nor relief. Her eyes were large and startled. There was no smile on her face. These things I noted. I caught her bloody hand in my bloody one, and for an instant I believed we both meditated flight deeper into the wilderness. Yet I reasoned that since these shots were fired on our trail, we must be in

209

all likelihood found in any case, even were these chance hunters coming into our valley, and not a party searching for us.

"It may not be any one we know," I said. "It may be Indians."

"No," said she, "it is my father. They have found us. We must go! John"—she turned toward me and put her hands on my breast—"John!" I saw terror, and regret, and resolve look out of her eyes, but not joy at this deliverance. No, it was not joy that shone in her eyes. None the less, the ancient yoke of society being offered, we bowed our necks again, fools and slaves, surrendering freedom, joy, content, as though that were our duty.

Chapter XXXIV - The Loss Of Paradise

Silently we made our way toward the edge of the thicket where it faced upon the open valley. All about me I could hear the tinkling and crashing of fairy crystal walls, the ruins of that vision house I had builded in my soul. At the edge of the thicket we crouched low, waiting and looking out over the valley, two savages, laired, suspicious.

Almost as we paused I saw coming forward the stooping figure of an Indian trailer, half naked, beleggined, moccasined, following our fresh tracks at a trot. I covered him with the little silver bead, minded to end his quest. But before I could estimate his errand, or prepare to receive him, closely in case he proved an enemy, I saw approaching around a little point of timber other men, white men, a half dozen of them, one a tall man in dusty garments, with boots, and hat, and gloves.

And then I saw her, my promised wife, leave my side, and limp and stagger forward, her arms outstretched. I saw the yoke of submission, the covenant of society, once more accepted.

"Father!" she cried.

They gathered about us. I saw him look down at her with half horror on his face. Then I noticed that she was, clad in fringed skins, that her head covering was a bit of hide, that her hair was burned yellow at the ends, that her foot coverings were uncouth, that her hands and arms were brown, where not stained red by the blood in which they had dabbled. I looked down also at myself, and saw then that I was tall, brown, gaunt, bearded, ragged, my clothing of wool well-nigh gone, my limbs wound in puttee bands of hide, my hands large, horny, blackened, rough. I reeked with grime. I was a savage new drawn from my cave. I dragged behind me the great grizzled hide of the dead bear, clutched in one hairy hand. And somber and sullen as any savage, brutal and silent in resentment at being disturbed, I stared at them.

"Who are you?" demanded the tall man of me sternly; but still I did not answer. The girl's hands tugged at his shoulders. "It is my friend," she said. "He saved me. It is Mr. John Cowles, father, of the Virginia Cowles family. He has come to see you—" But he did not hear her, or show that he heard. His arm about her, supporting her as she limped, he turned back down the valley, and we others followed slowly.

Presently he came to the rude shelter which had been our home. Without speaking he walked about the camp, pushed open the door of the little ragged tepee and looked within. The floor was very narrow. There was one meager bed of hides. There was one fire.

"Come with me," he said at length to me. And so I followed him apart, where a little thicket gave us more privacy.

His was a strong face, keen under heavy gray brows, with hair that rose stiff and gray over a high forehead, so that he seemed like some Osage chief, taller by a third than most men, and naturally a commander among others.

"You are John Cowles, sir, then?" he said to me at length, quietly. "Lieutenant Belknap told me something of this when he came in with his men from the East." I nodded and waited.

"Are you aware, sir, of the seriousness of what you have done?" he broke out. "Why did you not come on to the settlements? What reason was there for you not coming back at once to the valley of the Platte—here you are, a hundred miles out of your way, where a man of any intelligence, it seems to me, would naturally have turned back to the great trail. Hundreds of wagons pass there every day. There is a stage line with daily coaches, stations, houses. A telegraph line runs from one end of the valley to the other. You could not have missed all this had you struck south. A fool would have known that. But you took my girl—" he choked up, and pointed to me, ragged and uncouth.

"Good God! Colonel Meriwether," I cried out at length, "you are not regretting that I brought her through?"

"Almost, sir," he said, setting his lips together. "Almost!"

"Do you regret then that she brought me through—that I owe my life to her?"

"Almost, sir," he repeated. "I almost regret it."

"Then go back—leave us—report us dead!" I broke out, savagely. It was moments before I could accept this old life again offered me.

"She is a splendid girl, a noble being," I said to him, slowly, at last. "She saved me when I was sick and unable to travel. There is nothing I could do that would pay the debt I owe to her. She is a noble woman, a princess among women, body and soul."

"She is like her mother," said he, quietly. "She was too good for this. Sir, you have done my family a grievous wrong. You have ruined my daughter's life."

Now at last I could talk. I struck my hand hard on his shoulder and looked him full in the eye. "Colonel Meriwether," I said to him, "I am ashamed of you."

"What do you mean?" He frowned sternly and shook off my hand.

"I brought her through," I said, "and if it would do any good, I would lie down here and die for her. If what I say is not true, draw up your men for a firing squad and let us end it. I don't care to go back to Laramie."

"What good would that do?" said he. "It's the girl's *name* that's compromised, man! Why, the news of this is all over the country— the wires have carried it both sides of the mountains; the papers are full of it in the East. You have been gone nearly three months together, and all the world knows it. Don't you suppose all the world will *talk*? Did I not see—" he motioned his hand toward our encampment.

He babbled of such things, small, unimportant, to me, late from large things in life. I interrupted long enough to tell him briefly of our journey, of our hardships, of what we had gone through, of how my sickness had rendered it impossible for us to return at once, of how we had wandered, with what little judgment remained to us, how we had lived in the meantime.

He shook his head. "I know men," said he.

"Yes," said I, "I would have been no man worth the name had I not loved your daughter. And I admit to you that I shall never love another woman, not in all my life."

In answer he flung down on the ground in front of me something that he carried—the scroll of our covenant, signed by my name and in part by hers.

"What does this mean?" he asked.

"It means," said I, "what it says; that here or anywhere, in sickness or in health, in adversity or prosperity, until I lie down to die and she beside me in her time, we two are in the eye of God married; and in the eye of man would have been, here or wherever else we might be."

I saw his face pale; but a somber flame came into his eyes. "And you say this—you, *after all I know regarding you!*"

Again I felt that old chill of terror and self-reproach strike to my heart. I saw my guilt once more, horrible as though an actual presence. I remembered what Ellen Meriwether had said to me regarding any other or earlier covenant. I recalled my troth, plighted earlier, before I had ever seen her,—my faith, pledged in another world. So, seeing myself utterly ruined in my own sight and his and hers, I turned to him at length, with no pride in my bearing.

"So I presume Gordon Orme has told you," I said to him. "You know of Grace Sheraton, back there?"

His lips but closed the tighter. "Have you told her—have you told this to my girl?" he asked, finally.

"Draw up your file!" I cried, springing to my feet. "Execute me! I deserve it. No, I have not told her. I planned to do so—I should never have allowed her to sign her name there before I had told her everything—been fair to her as I could. But her accident left her weak—I could not tell her—a thousand things delayed it. Yes, it was my fault."

He looked me over with contempt. "You are not fit to touch the shoe on my girl's foot," he said slowly. "But now, since this thing has begun, since you have thus involved her and compromised her, and as I imagine in some foul way have engaged her affections—now, I say, it must go on. When we get to Laramie, by God! sir, you shall marry that girl. And then out you go, and never see her face again. She is too good for you, but where you can be of use to her, for this reason, you shall be used."

I seated myself, my head in my hands, and pondered. He was commanding me to do that which was my dearest wish in life. But he was commanding me to complete my own folly. "Colonel Meriwether," said I to him, finally, "if it would do her any good I would give up my life for her. But her father can neither tell me how nor when my marriage ceremony runs; nor can he tell me when to leave the side of the woman who is my wife. I am subject to the orders of no man in the world."

"You refuse to do what you have planned to do? Sir, that shows you as you are. You proposed to—to live with her here, but not be bound to her elsewhere!"

"It is not true!" I said to him in somber anger. "I proposed to put before her the fact of my own weakness, of my own self-deception, which also was deception of her. I propose to do that now."

"If you did, she would refuse to look at you again."

"I know it, but it must be done. I must take my chances."

"And your chances mean this alternative—either that my girl's reputation shall be ruined all over the country—all through the Army, where she is known and loved—or else that her heart must be broken. This is what it means, Mr. Cowles. This is what you have brought to my family."

"Yes," I said to him, slowly, "this is what I have brought."

"Then which do you choose, sir?" he demanded of me.

"I choose to break her heart!" I answered. "Because that is the truth, and that is right. I only know one way to ride, and that is straight."

He smiled at me coldly in his frosty beard. "That sounds well from you!" he said bitterly. "Ellen!" he raised his voice. "Ellen, I say, come here at once!"

It was my ear which first heard the rustling of her footsteps at the edge of the thicket as she approached. She came before us slowly, halting, leaning on her crutch. A soft flush shone through the brown upon her cheeks.

I shall not forget in all my life the picture of her as she stood. Neither shall I forget the change which came across her face as she saw us sitting there silent, cold, staring at her. Then, lovable in her rags, beautiful in her savagery, the gentleness of generations of culture in all her mien in spite of her rude surroundings, she stepped up and laid her hand upon her father's shoulder, one finger half pointing at the ragged scroll of hide which lay upon the ground before us. I loved her—ah, how I loved her then!

"I signed that, father," she said gently. "I was going to sign it, little by little, a letter each week. We were engaged—nothing more. But here or anywhere, some time, I intend to marry Mr. Cowles. This I have promised of my own free will. He has been both man and gentleman, father. I love him."

I heard the groan which came from his throat. She sprang back. "What is it?" she said. The old fire of her disposition again broke out.

"What!" she cried. "You object? Listen, I will sign my name now—I will finish it—give me—give me—" She sought about on the ground for something which would leave a mark. "I say I have not been his, but will be, father—as I like, when I like—now, this very night if I choose—forever! He has done everything for me—I trust him—I know he is a man of honor, that he—" Her voice broke as she looked at my face.

"But what—what *is* it?" she demanded, brokenly, in her own eyes something of the horror which sat in mine. I say I see her picture now, tall, straight, sweet, her hands on her lifting bosom, eagerness and anxiety fighting on her face.

"Ellen, child, Mr. Cowles has something to tell you."

Then some one, in a voice which sounded like mine, but was not mine, told her—told her the truth, which sounded so like a lie. Some one, myself, yet not myself, went on, cruelly, blackening all the sweet blue sky for her. Some one—I suppose it was myself, late free—felt the damp of an iron yoke upon his neck.

I saw her knees sink beneath her, but she shrank back when I would have reached out an arm as of old.

"I hate that woman!" she blazed. "Suppose she does love you—do I not love you more? Let her lose—some one must lose!" But at the next moment her anger had changed to doubt, to horror. I saw her face change, saw her hand drop to her side.

"It is not that you loved another girl," she whispered, "but that you have deceived *me*—here, when I was in your power. Oh, it was not right! How could you! Oh, how could you!"

Then once more she changed. The flame of her thoroughbred soul came back to her. Her courage saved her from shame. Her face flushed, she stood straight. "I hate *you!*" she cried to me. "Go! I will never see you any more."

Still the bright sun shone on. A little bird trilled in the thicket near.

Chapter XXXV - The Yoke

When we started to the south on the following morning, I rode far at the rear, under guard. I recall little of our journey toward Laramie, save that after a day or two we swung out from the foothills into a short grass country, and so finally struck the steady upward sweep of a valley along which lay the great transcontinental trail. I do not know whether we traveled two days, or three, or four, since all the days seemed night to me, and all the nights were uniform in torture. Finally, we drove down into a dusty plain, and so presently came to the old frontier fort. Here, then, was civilization—the stage coach, the new telegraph wire, men and women, weekly or daily touch with the world, that prying curiosity regarding the affairs of others which we call news. To me it seemed tawdry, sordid, worthless, after that which I had left. The noise seemed insupportable, the food distasteful. I could tolerate no roof, and in my own ragged robes slept on the ground within the old stockade.

I was still guarded as a prisoner; I was approached by none and had conversation with none until evening of the day after my arrival. When I ate, it was at no gentleman's table, but in the barracks. I resented judgment, sentence and punishment, thus executed in one.

Evening gun had sounded, and the flag had been furled on my second day at Laramie, when finally Colonel Meriwether sent for me to come to his office quarters. He got swiftly enough to the matters on his mind.

"Mr. Cowles," said he, "it is time now that you and I had a talk. Presently you will be leaving Laramie. I can not try you by court martial, for you are a civilian. In short, all I can say to you is to go, with the hope that you may never again cross our lives."

I looked at him a time, silently, hating not him personally as much as I hated all the world. But presently I asked him, "Have you no word for me from her?"

"Miss Meriwether has no word for you," he answered, sternly, "nor ever will have. You are no longer necessary in her plans."

"Ah, then," said I, "you have changed your own mind mightily."

He set his lips together in his grim fashion. "Yes," said he, "I have changed my mind absolutely. I have just come from a very trying interview. It is not necessary for me to explain to you the full nature of it—"

"Then she has sent for me?"

"She will never send for you, I have said."

"But listen. At least, I have brought her back to you safe and sound. Setting aside all my own acts in other matters, why can you not remember at least so much as that? Yet you treat me like a dog. I tell you, I shall not leave without word from her, and when I leave I shall make no promises as to when I shall or shall not come back. So long as one chance remains—"

"I tell you that there is no longer any chance, no longer the ghost of a chance. It is my duty to inform you, sir, that a proper suitor long ago applied for my daughter's hand, that he has renewed his suit, and that now she has accepted him."

For a time I sat staring stupidly at him. "You need speak nothing but the truth with me," I said at last. "Colonel Meriwether, I have never given bonds to be gentle when abused."

"I am telling you the truth," he said. "By God, sir! Miss Meriwether is engaged to Lieutenant Lawrence Belknap of the Ninth Dragoons! You feel your honor too deeply touched? Perhaps at a later time Lieutenant Belknap will do himself the disgrace of accommodating you."

All these things seemed to dull and stupefy me rather than excite. I could not understand.

"If I killed him," said I, finally, "how would it better her case? Moreover, before I could take any more risk, I must go back to Virginia. My mother needs me there most sadly."

"Yes, and Miss Grace Sheraton needs you there sadly, as well," he retorted. "Go back, then, and mend your promises, and do some of those duties which you now begin to remember. You have proved yourself a man of no honor. I stigmatize you now as a coward."

There seemed no tinder left in my spirit to flame at this spark. "You speak freely to your prisoner, Colonel Meriwether," I said, slowly, at length. "There is time yet for many risks—chances for many things. But now I think you owe it to me to tell me how this matter was arranged."

"Very well, then. Belknap asked me for permission to try his chance long ago—before I came west to Laramie. I assigned him to bring her through to me. He was distracted at his failure to do so. He has been out with parties all the summer, searching for you both, and has not been back at Laramie more than ten days. Oh, we all knew why you did not come back to the settlements. When we came in he guessed all that you know. He knew that all the world would talk. And like a man he asked the right to silence all that talk forever."

"And she agreed? Ellen Meriwether accepted him on such terms?"

"It is arranged," said he, not answering me directly, "and it removes at once all necessity for any other arrangement. As for you, you disappear. It will be announced all through the Army that she and Lieutenant Belknap were married at Leavenworth before they started West, and that it was they two, and not you and my daughter, who were lost."

"And Belknap was content to do this?" I mused. "He would do this after Ellen told him that she loved me—"

"Stop!" thundered Colonel Meriwether. "I have told you all that is necessary. I will add that he said to me, like the gentleman he is, that in case my daughter asked it, *he* would marry her and leave her at once, until she of her own free will asked him to return. There is abundant opportunity for swift changes in the Army. What seems to you absurd will work out in perfectly practical fashion."

"Yes," said I, "in fashion perfectly practical for the ruin of her life. You may leave mine out of the question."

"I do, sir," was his icy reply. "She told you to your face, and in my hearing, that you had deceived her, that you must go."

"Yes," I said, dully, "I did deceive her, and there is no punishment on earth great enough to give me for that—except to have no word from her!"

"You are to go at once. I put it beyond you to understand Belknap's conduct in this matter."

"He is a gentleman," I said, "and fit to love her. I think none of us needs praise or blame for that."

He choked up. "She's my girl," he said. "Yes, all my boys in the Army love her—there isn't one of them that wouldn't be proud to marry her on any terms she would lay down. And there isn't a man in the Army, married or single, that wouldn't challenge you if you breathed a word of what has gone between you and her."

I looked at him and made no motion. It seemed to me go unspeakably sad, so incredible, that one should be so unbelievably underestimated.

"Now, finally," resumed Colonel Meriwether, after a time, ceasing his walking up and down, "I must close up what remains between you and me. My daughter said to me that you wanted to see me on some business matter. Of course you had some reason for coming out here."

"That was my only reason for coming," I rejoined. "I wanted to see you upon an important business matter. I was sent here by the last message my father gave any one—by the last words he spoke in his life. He told me I should come to you."

"Well, well, if you have any favor to ask of me, out with it, and let us end it all at one sitting."

"Sir," I said, "I would see you damned in hell before I would ask a crust or a cup of water of you, though I were starving and burning. I have heard enough."

"Orderly!" he called out. "Show this man to the gate."

Chapter XXXVI - The Goad

It was at last borne in upon me that I must leave without any word from Ellen. She was hedged about by all the stern and cold machinery of an Army Post, out of whose calculations I was left as much as though I belonged to a different world. I cannot express what this meant for me. For weeks now, for months, indeed, we two had been together each hour of the day. I had come to expect her greeting in the morning, to turn to her a thousand times in the day with some query or answer. I had made no plan from which she was absent. I had come to accept myself, with her, as fit part of an appointed and happy scheme. Now, in a twinkling, all that had been subverted. I was robbed of her exquisite dependence upon me, of those tender defects of nature that rendered her most dear. I was to miss now her fineness, her weakness and trustfulness, which had been a continual delight. I could no longer see her eyes nor touch her hands, nor sit silent at her feet, dreaming of days to come. Her voice was gone from my listening ears. Always I waited to hear her footstep, but it came no longer, rustling in the grasses. It seemed to me that by some hard decree I had been deprived of all my senses; for not one was left which did not crave and cry aloud for her.

It was thus that I, dulled, bereft; I, having lived, now dead; I, late free, now bound again, turned away sullenly, and began my journey back to the life I had known before I met her.

As I passed East by the Denver stage, I met hurrying throngs always coming westward, a wavelike migration of population now even denser than it had been the preceding spring. It was as Colonel Meriwether said, the wagons almost touched from the Platte to the Rockies. They came on, a vast, continuous stream of hope, confidence and youth. I, who stemmed that current, alone was unlike it in all ways.

One thing only quickened my laggard heart, and that was the all prevalent talk of war. The debates of Lincoln and Douglas, the consequences of Lincoln's possible election, the growing dissensions in the Army over Buchanan's practically overt acts of war—these made the sole topics of conversation. I heard my own section, my own State, criticised bitterly, and all Southerners called traitors to that flag I had seen flying over the frontiers of the West. At times, I say, these things caused my blood to stir once more, though perhaps it was not all through patriotism.

At last, after weeks of travel across a disturbed country, I finally reached the angry hive of political dissension at Washington. Here I was near home, but did not tarry, and passed thence by stage to Leesburg, in Virginia; and so finally came back into our little valley and the quiet town of Wallingford. I had gone away the victim of misfortune; I returned home with a broken word and an unfinished promise and a shaken heart. That was my return.

I got me a horse at Wallingford barns, and rode out to Cowles' Farms. At the gate I halted and looked in over the wide lawns. It seemed to me I noted a change in them as in myself. The grass was unkempt, the flower beds showed little attention. The very seats upon the distant gallery seemed unfamiliar, as though arranged by some careless hand. I opened the gate for myself, rode up to the old stoop and dismounted, for the first time in my life there without a boy to take my horse. I walked slowly up the steps to the great front door of the old house. No servant came to meet me, grinning. I, grandson of the man who built that house, my father's home and mine, lifted the brazen knocker of the door and heard no footstep anticipate my knock. The place sounded empty.

Finally there came a shuffling footfall and the door was opened, but there stood before me no one that I recognized. It was a smallish, oldish, grayish man who opened the door and smiled in query at me.

"I am John Cowles, sir," I said, hesitating. "Yourself I do not seem to know—"

"My name is Halliday, Mr. Cowles," he replied. A flush of humiliation came to my face.

"I should know you. You were my father's creditor."

"Yes, sir, my firm was the holder of certain obligations at the time of your father's death. You have been gone very long without word to us. Meantime, pending any action—"

"You have moved in!"

"I have ventured to take possession, Mr. Cowles. That was as your mother wished. She waived all her rights and surrendered everything, said all the debts must be paid—"

"Of course—"

"And all we could prevail upon her to do was to take up her quarters there in one of the little houses."

He pointed with this euphemism toward our old servants' quarters. So there was my mother, a woman gently reared, tenderly cared for all her life, living in a cabin where once slaves had lived. And I had come back to her, to tell a story such as mine!

"I hope," said he, hesitating, "that all these matters may presently be adjusted. But first I ask you to influence your mother to come back into the place and take up her residence."

I smiled slowly. "You hardly understand her," I said. "I doubt if my influence will suffice for that. But I shall meet you again." I was turning away.

"Your mother, I believe, is not here—she went over to Wallingford. I think it is the day when she goes to the little church—"

"Yes, I know. If you will excuse me I shall ride over to see if I can find her." He bowed. Presently I was hurrying down the road again. It seemed to me that I could never tolerate the sight of a stranger as master at Cowles' Farms.

Chapter XXXVII - The Furrow

I Found her at the churchyard of the old meetinghouse. She was just turning toward the gate in the low sandstone wall which surrounded the burying ground and separated it from the space immediately about the little stone church. It was a beautiful spot, here where the sun came through the great oaks that had never known an ax, resting upon blue grass that had never known a plow—a spot virgin as it was before old Lord Fairfax ever claimed it hi his loose ownership. Everything about it spoke of quiet and gentleness.

I knew what it was that she looked upon as she turned back toward that spot—it was one more low mound, simple, unpretentious, added to the many which had been placed there this last century and a half; one more little gray sandstone head-mark, cut simply with the name and dates of him who rested there, last in a long roll of our others. The slight figure in the dove-colored gown looked back lingeringly. It gave a new ache to my heart to see her there.

She did not notice me as I slipped down from my saddle and fastened my horse at the long rack. But when I called she turned and came to me with open arms.

"Jack!" she cried. "My son, how I have missed thee! Now thee has come back to thy mother." She put her forehead on my shoulder, but presently took up a mother's scrutiny. Her hand stroked my hair, my unshaven beard, took in each line of my face.

"Thee has a button from thy coat," she said, reprovingly. "And what is this scar on thy neck—thee did not tell me when thee wrote, Jack, what ails thee?" She looked at me closely. "Thee is changed. Thee is older—what has come to thee, my son?"

"Come," I said to her at length, and led her toward the steps of the little church.

Then I broke out bitterly and railed against our ill-fortune, and cursed at the man who would allow her to live in servants' quarters—indeed, railed at all of life.

"Thee must learn to subdue thyself, my son," she said. "It is only so that strength comes to us—when we bend the back to the furrow God sets for us. I am quite content in my little rooms. I have made them very clean; and I have with me a few things of my own—a few, not many."

"But your neighbors, mother, the Sheratons—"

"Oh, certainly, they asked me to live with them. But I was not moved to do that. You see, I know each rose bush and each apple tree on our old place. I did not like to leave them.

"Besides, as to the Sheratons, Jack," she began again—"I do not wish to say one word to hurt thy feelings, but Miss Grace—"

"What about Miss Grace?"

"Mr. Orme, the gentleman who once stopped with us a few days—"

"Oh, Orme! Is he here again? He was all through the West with me—I met him everywhere there. Now I meet him here!"

"He returned last summer, and for most of his time has been living at the Sheratons'. He and Colonel Sheraton agree very well. And he and Miss Grace—I do not like to say these things to thee, my son, but they also seem to agree."

"Go on," I demanded, bitterly.

"Whether Miss Grace's fancy has changed, I do not know, but thy mother ought to tell thee this, so that if she should jilt thee, why, then—"

"Yes," said I, slowly, "it would be hard for me to speak the first word as to a release."

"But if she does not love thee, surely she will speak that word. So then say good-by to her and set about thy business."

I could not at that moment find it in my heart to speak further. We rose and walked down to the street of the little town, and at the tavern barn I secured a conveyance which took us both back to what had once been our home. It was my mother's hands which, at a blackened old fireplace, in a former slave's cabin, prepared what we ate that evening. Then, as the sun sank in a warm glow beyond the old Blue Ridge, and our little valley lay there warm and peaceful as of old, I drew her to the rude porch of the whitewashed cabin, and we looked out, and talked of things which must be mentioned. I told her—told her all my sad and bitter story, from end to end.

"This, then," I concluded, more than an hour after I had begun, "is what I have brought back to you—failure, failure, nothing but failure."

We sat in silence, looking out into the starry night, how long I do not know. Then I heard her pray, openly, as was not the custom of her people. "Lord, this is not my will. Is this Thy will?"

After a time she put her hand upon mine. "My son, now let us reason what is the law. From the law no man may escape. Let us see who is the criminal. And if that be thee, then let my son have his punishment."

I allowed the edge of her gentle words to bite into my soul, but I could not speak.

"But one thing I know," she concluded, "thee is John Cowles, the son of my husband, John; and thee at the last will do what is right, what thy heart says to thee is right."

She kissed me on the cheek and so arose. All that night I felt her prayers.

Chapter XXXVIII - Hearts Hypothecated

The next morning at the proper hour I started for the Sheraton mansion. This time it was not my old horse Satan that I rode. My mother told me that Satan had been given over under the blanket chattel mortgage, and sold at the town livery stable to some purchaser, whom she did not know, who had taken the horse out of the country. I reflected bitterly upon the changes in my fortunes since the last time I rode this way.

At least I was not so much coward as to turn about. So presently I rode up the little pitch from the trough road and pulled the gate latch with my riding crop. And then, as though it were by appointment, precisely as I saw her that morning last spring—a hundred years ago it seemed to me—I saw Grace Sheraton coming down the walk toward me, tall, thin. Alas! she did not fill my eye. She was elegantly clad, as usual. I had liefer seen dress of skins. Her dainty boots clicked on the gravel. A moccasin would not.

I threw my rein over the hook at the iron arm of the stone gate pillar and, hat in hand, I went to meet her. I was an older man now. I was done with roystering and fighting, and the kissing of country girls all across the land. I did not prison Grace Sheraton against the stone gate pillar now, and kiss her against her will until she became willing. All I did was to lift her hand and kiss her finger tips.

She was changed. I felt that rather than saw it. If anything, she was thinner, her face had a deeper olive tint, her eyes were darker. Her expression was gay, feverish, yet not natural, as she approached. What was it that sat upon her face—melancholy, or fear, or sorrow, or resentment? I was never very bright of mind. I do not know.

"I am glad to see you," she said to me at length, awkwardly.

"And I to see you, of course." I misdoubt we both lied.

"It is very sad, your home-coming thus," she added; at which clue I caught gladly.

"Yes, matters could hardly be worse for us."

"Your mother would not come to us. We asked her. We feel deeply mortified. But now—we hope you both will come."

"We are beggars now, Miss Grace," I said. "I need time to look around, to hit upon some plan of life. I must make another home for myself, and for—"

"For me?" She faced me squarely now, eye to eye. A smile was on her lips, and it seemed to me a bitter one, but I could not guess what was hidden in her mind. I saw her cheek flush slowly, deeper than was usual with a Sheraton girl.

"For my wife, as soon as that may be," I answered, as red as she.

"I learn that you did not see Colonel Meriwether," she went on politely.

"How did you know it?"

"Through Captain Orme."

"Yes," said I, quietly, "I have heard of Captain Orme—much of him—very much." Still I could not read her face.

"He was with us a long time this summer," she resumed, presently. "Some two weeks ago he left, for Charleston, I think. He has much business about the country."

"Much business," I assented, "in many parts of the country. But most of all with men of the Army. So Captain Orme—since we must call him Captain and not minister—was so good as to inform you of my private matters."

"Yes." Again she looked at me squarely, with defiance. "I know all about it. I know all about that girl."

So there it was! But I kept myself under whip hand still. "I am very glad. It will save me telling you of myself. It is not always that one has the good fortune of such early messengers."

"Go on," she said bitterly, "tell me about her."

"I have no praises to sound for her. I do not wish to speak of this, if you prefer to hear it from others than myself."

She only smiled enigmatically, her mouth crooking in some confidence she held with herself, but not with me. "It was natural," she said at last, slowly. "Doubtless I would have done as she did. Doubtless any other man would have done precisely as you did. That is the way with men. After all, I suppose the world is the world, and that we are as we are. The girl who is closest to a man has the best chance with him. Opportunity is much, very much. Secrecy is everything."

I found nothing which suited me to say; but presently she went on, again leaning on the ivy-covered stone pillar of the gate, her hat held by its strings at her side, her body not imprisoned by my arms.

"Why should you not both have done so?" she resumed, bitterly. "We are all human."

"Why should we not have done what—what is it that you mean?" I demanded of her.

"Why, there was she, engaged to Mr. Belknap, as I am told; and there were you, engaged to a certain young lady by the name of Grace Sheraton, very far away. And you were conveniently lost—very conveniently—and you found each other's society agreeable. You kept away for some weeks or months, both of you forgetting. It was idyllic—ideal. You were not precisely babes in the woods. You were a man and a woman. I presume you enjoyed yourselves, after a very possible little fashion—I do not blame you—I say I might have done the same. I should like to know it for a time myself—freedom! I do not blame you. Only," she said slowly, "in society we do not have freedom. Here it is different. I suppose different laws apply, different customs!"

"Miss Grace," said I, "I do not in the least understand you. You are not the same girl I left."

"No, I am not. But that is not my fault. Can not a woman be free as much as a man? Have I not right as much as you? Have you not been free?"

"One thing only I want to say," I rejoined, "and it is this, which I ought not to say at all. If you mean anything regarding Ellen Meriwether, I have to tell you, or any one, that she is clean—mind, body, soul, heart—as clean as when I saw her first."

"Do you know, I like you for saying that!" she retorted. "I would never marry a man who knew nothing of other women—I don't want a milksop; and I would not marry a man who would not lie for the sake of a sweetheart. You lie beautifully! Do you know, Jack, I believe you are a bit of a gentleman, after all!

"But tell me, when is the wedding to be?" This last with obvious effort.

"You have not advised me."

"Oh, I beg your pardon. I meant your marriage with Ellen Meriwether. I supposed of course you had quite forgotten me!"

"Ellen Meriwether is already married," I said to her, with a calmness which surprised myself. But what surprised me most was the change which came upon her face at the words—the flush—the gleam of triumph, of satisfaction. I guessed this much and no more—that she had had certain plans, and that now she had other plans, changed with lightning swiftness, and by reason of my words.

"Lieutenant Lawrence Belknap and Miss Ellen Meriwether were married, I presume, some time after I started for the East," I went on. "But they were never engaged before our return to the settlements. It was all very suddenly arranged."

"How like a story-book! So he forgot her little incidents with you — all summer — side by side — day and night! How romantic! I don't know that I could have done so much, had I been a man, and myself not guilty of the same incidents. At least, he kept his promise."

"There had never been any promise at all between them."

"Then Captain Orme was quite mistaken?"

"Captain Orme does not trouble himself always to be accurate."

"At least, then, you are unmarried, Jack?"

"Yes, and likely to be for some years."

Now her face changed once more. Whether by plan of her own or not, I cannot say, but it softened to a more gentle — shall I say a more beseeching look? Was it that I again was at her side, that old associations awakened? Or was it because she was keen, shrewd and in control of herself, able to make plans to her own advantage? I cannot tell as to that. But I saw her face soften, and her voice was gentle when she spoke.

"What do you mean, Jack?" she asked.

If there was not love and caress in her tones, then I could not detect the counterfeit. I reiterate, if I should live a thousand years, I should know nothing of women, nothing. We men are but toys with them. As in life and in sex man is in nature's plan no master, no chooser, but merely an incident; so, indeed, I believe that he is thus always with a woman — only an incident. With women we are toys. They play with us. We never read them. They are the mystery of the world. When they would deceive us it is beyond all our art to read them. Never shall man, even the wisest, fathom the shallowest depths of a woman's heart. Their superiors? God! we are their slaves, and the stronger we are as men, the more are we enslaved.

Had it been left to my judgment to pronounce, I should have called her emotion now a genuine one. Mocking, cynical, contemptuous she might have been, and it would have suited my own mood. But what was it now on the face of Grace Sheraton, girl of a proud family, woman I once had kissed here at this very place until she blushed—kissed until she warmed—until she—

But now I know she changed once again, and I know that this time I read her look aright. It was pathos on her face, and terror. Her eye was that of the stricken antelope in dread of the pursuer.

"Jack," she whispered, "don't leave me! Jack, *I shall need you!*"

Before I could resolve any questions in my mind, I heard behind us the sound of approaching hoofs, and there rode up to the gate her brother, Harry Sheraton, who dismounted and hitched his horse near mine, saluting me as he pushed open the great gate. It was the first time I had seen him since my return.

"Am I intruding?" he asked. "I'm awfully glad to see you, Cowles—I heard below you were home. You've had a long journey."

"Yes," I answered, "longer than I had planned, by many weeks. And now I am glad to be back once more. No—" in answer to his turning toward his horse as though he would leave us. "You are looking well, Harry. Indeed, everything in old Virginia is good to see again."

"Wish I could be as polite with you. Have you been sick? And, I say, you did meet the savages, didn't you?"

I knew he meant the scar on the side of my neck, which still was rather evident, but I did not care to repeat the old story again. "Yes," I answered a bit shortly, "rather a near thing of it. I presume Captain Orme told you?" I turned to Miss Grace, who then admitted that she had heard something of the surgery which had thus left its mark. Harry seemed puzzled, so I saw it was news to him. Miss Grace relieved the situation somewhat by turning toward the house.

"I am sure you will want to talk with Jack," she said to him. "And listen, Harry, you must have him and Mrs. Cowles over here this very evening—we cannot think of her living alone at the old place. I shall send Cato down with, the carriage directly, and you may drive over after Mrs. Cowles." She held out her hand to me. "At dinner tonight, then?"

I bowed, saying that we would be very happy, by which I meant that we would be very miserable.

This, then, was all that had been determined by my visit. I was still an engaged man. Evidently nothing otherwise had been discussed in the Sheraton family councils, if any such had been held. If never suitor in Old Virginia rode up in sorrier case than mine that morning, as I came to call upon my fiancée, certainly did never one depart in more uncertain frame of mind than mine at this very moment. I presume that young Sheraton felt something of this, for he began awkwardly to speak of matters related thereto.

"It's awfully hard," he began, "to see strangers there in your own house—I know it must be hard. But I say, your father must have plunged heavily on those lands over West in the mountains. I've heard they're very rich in coal, and that all that was necessary was simply cash or credit enough to tide the deal over till next year's crops."

"My father always said there was a great fortune in the lands," I replied. "Yes, I think another year would have seen him through; but that year was not to come for him."

"But couldn't funds be raised somehow, even yet?"

I shook my head. "It is going to be hard in these times to raise funds in any way. Values are bad now, and if the Republican party elects

Lincoln next month, there will be no such things as values left in Virginia. I don't see how anything can save our property."

"Well, I'm not so sure," he went on, embarrassed. "My father and I have been talking over these matters, and we concluded to ask you if we might not take a hand in this. At least, we have agreed all along that—in this case you know—you and my sister—we have planned definitely that you should live in your old place. We're going to take that over. The redemption time has plenty of margin, and we can't allow those people to come in here and steal one of the old Virginia places in that way. We are going to arrange to hold that for you and my sister, and we thought that perhaps in time something could be worked out of the rest of the property in the same way. That is, unless Colonel Meriwether, your father's partner, shall offer some better solution. I suppose you talked it over with him?"

"I did not talk with him about it at all," said I, dully. For many reasons I did not care to repeat all of my story to him. I had told it often enough already. "None the less, it seems very generous of you and your father to take this interest in me. It would be very churlish of me if I did not appreciate it. But I trust nothing has been done as yet—"

"You trust not? Why, Cowles, you speak as though you did not want us to do it."

"I do not," said I.

"Oh, then—"

"You know our family well enough."

"That's true. But you won't be offended if I suggest to you that there are two sides to this, and two prides. All the country knows of your engagement, and now that you have returned, it will be expected that my sister will set the day before long. Of course, we shouldn't want my sister to begin too far down—oh, damn it, Cowles, you know what I mean."

"I presume so," said I to him, slowly. "But suppose that your sister should offer to her friends the explanation that the change in my fortunes no longer leaves desirable this alliance with my family?"

"Do you suggest that?"

"I have not done so."

"Has she suggested it?"

"We have not talked of it, yet it might be hard for your sister to share a lot so humble and so uncertain."

"That I presume will be for her to decide," he said slowly. "I admit it is a hard question all around. But, of course, in a matter of this kind, the man has to carry the heavy end of the log if there is one. If that falls to you, we know you will not complain."

"No," said I, "I hope not."

His forehead still remained furrowed with the old Sheraton wrinkles. He seemed uneasy. "By Jove," he broke out at length, flushing as he turned to me, "it is hard for a fellow to tell sometimes what's right, isn't it? Jack, you remember Jennie Williams, across under Catoctin?"

I nodded. "I thought you two were going to make a match of it sometime," I said.

"Prettiest girl in the valley," he assented; "but her family is hardly what we would call the best, you know." I looked at him very hard.

"Then why did you go there so often all last year?" I asked him. "Might she not think—"

He flushed still more, his mouth twitching now. "Jack," he said, "it's all through. I want to ask you. I ought to marry Jennie Williams, but—"

Now I looked at him full and hard, and guessed. Perhaps my face was grave. I was beginning to wonder whether there was one clean thing in all the world.

"Oh, she can marry," went on Harry. "No difficulty about that. She has another beau who loves her to distraction, and who doesn't in the least suspect—a decent sort of a fellow, a young farmer of her own class."

"And, in your belief, that wedding should go on?"

He shifted uneasily.

"When is this wedding to be?" I asked.

"Oh, naturally, very soon," he answered. "I am doing as handsome a thing as I know how by her. Sometimes it's mighty hard to do the handsome thing—even mighty hard to know what is the handsome thing itself."

"Yes," said I. But who was I that I should judge him?

"If you were just where I am," asked Harry Sheraton, slowly, "what would you do? I'd like to do what is right, you know."

"Oh no, you don't, Harry," I broke out. "You want to do what is easiest. If you wanted to do what is right, you'd never ask me nor any one else. Don't ask me, because I don't know. Suppose you were in the case of that other young man who loves her? Suppose he did not know—or suppose he *did* know. What would be right for him?"

"Heavy end of the log for him," admitted he, grimly. "That's true, sure as you're born."

"When one does not love a girl, and sees no happiness in the thought of living with her all his life, what squares that, Harry, in your opinion?"

"I've just asked you," he rejoined. "Why do you ask me? You say one ought to know what is right in his own case without any such asking, and I say that isn't always true. Oh, damn it all, anyway. Why are we made the way we are?"

"If only the girl in each case would be content by having the handsome thing done by her!" said I, bitterly.

Chapter XXXIX - The Uncovering Of Gordon Orme

It is not necessary for me to state that dinner in the Sheraton hall, with its dull mahogany and its shining silver and glass, was barely better than a nightmare to me, who should have been most happy. At least there remained the topic of politics and war; and never was I more glad to plunge into such matters than upon that evening. In some way the dinner hour passed. Miss Grace pleaded a headache and left us; my mother asked leave; and presently our hostess and host departed. Harry and I remained to stare at each other moodily. I admit I was glad when finally he announced his intention of retiring.

A servant showed me my own room, and some time before midnight I went up, hoping that I might sleep. My long life in the open air had made all rooms and roofs seem confining and distasteful to me, and I slept badly in the best of beds. Now my restlessness so grew upon me that, some time past midnight, not having made any attempt to prepare for sleep, I arose, went quietly down the stair and out at the front door, to see if I could find more peace in the open air. I sat down on the grass with my back against one of the big oaks, and so continued brooding moodily over my affairs, confused as they had now become.

By this time every one of the household had retired. I was surprised, therefore, when I saw a faint streak of light from one of the windows flash out across the lawn. Not wishing to intrude, I rose quietly and changed my position, passing around the tree. Almost at that instant I saw the figure of a man appear from the shrubbery and walk directly toward the house, apparently headed for the window from which emerged the light.

I watched him advance, and when I saw him reach the heavily barred trellis which ran up to the second gallery, I felt confirmed in my suspicion that he was a burglar. Approaching carefully in the shadow, I made a rapid run at him, and as his head was turned at the time, managed to catch him about the neck by an arm. His face, thus thrown back, was illuminated by the flare of light. I saw him plainly. It was Gordon Orme!

The light disappeared. There was no cry from above. The great house, lying dark and silent, heard no alarm. I did not stop to reason about this, but tightened my grip upon him in so fell a fashion that all his arts in wrestling could avail him nothing. I had caught him from behind, and now I held him with a hand on each of his arms above the elbow. No man could escape me when I had that hold.

He did not speak, but struggled silently with all his power. At length he relaxed a trifle. I stood close to him, slipped my left arm under his left along his back, and caught his right arm in my left hand. Then I took from his pocket a pistol, which I put into my own. I felt in his clothing, and finally discovered a knife, hidden in a scabbard at the back of his neck. I drew it out—a long-bladed, ivory thing I found it later, with gold let into the hilt and woven into the steel.

He eased himself in my grip as much as he could, waiting; as I knew, for his chance to twist and grapple with me. I could feel him breathing deeply and easily, resting, waiting for his time, using his brains to aid his body with perfect deliberation.

"It's no use, Orme," I said to him, finally. "I can wring your neck, or break your back, or twist your arms off, and by God! I've a notion to do them all. If you make any attempt to get away I'm going to kill you. Now come along."

I shoved him ahead of me, his arms pinioned, until we found a seat far away in a dark portion of the great front yard. Here I pushed him down and took the other end of the seat, covering him with his own pistol.

"Now," I demanded, "tell me what you are doing here."

"You have your privilege at guessing," he sneered, in his easy, mocking way. "Have you never taken a little adventure of this sort yourself?"

"Ah, some servant girl—at your host's house. Excellent adventure. But this is your last one," I said to him.

"Is it so," he sneered. "Then let me make my prayers!" He mocked at me, and had no fear of me whatever.

"In Virginia we keep the shotgun for men who prowl around houses at night. What are you doing here?"

"You have no right to ask. It is not your house."

"There was a light," said I. "For that reason I have a right to ask. I am a guest, and a guest has duties as well as a host."

A certain change in mood seized him. "If I give you parole," he asked, "will you believe me, and let us talk freely?"

"Yes," said I at length, slowly. "You are a liar; but I do not think you will break parole."

"You gauge me with perfect accuracy," he answered. "That is why I wish to talk."

I threw the pistol on the seat between us. "What is it you want to know," I asked. "And again I ask you, why are you here, when you are supposed to be in South Carolina?"

"I have business here. You cost me my chance out there in the West," he answered, slowly. "In turn I cost you your chance there. I shall cost you other things here. I said you should pay my debt." He motioned toward my neck with his slim finger.

"Yes, you saved my life," I said, "and I have hated you for that ever since."

"Will you make me one promise?" he asked.

"Perhaps, but not in advance."

"And will you keep it?"

"If I make it."

"Will you promise me to do one thing you have already promised to do?"

"Orme, I am in no mood to sit here and gossip like an old woman."

"Oh, don't cut up ugly. You're done out of it all around, in any case. Belknap, it seems, was to beat both you and me. Then why should not you and I try to forget? But now as to this little promise. I was only going to ask you to do as much as Belknap, or less."

"Very well, then."

"I want you to promise to marry Grace Sheraton."

I laughed in his face. "I thought you knew me better than that, Orme. I'll attend to my own matters for myself. I shall not even ask you why you want so puerile a promise. I am much of a mind to shoot you. Tell me, who are you, and what are you, and what are you doing in this country?"

"Do you really want to know?" he smiled.

"Assuredly I do. I demand it."

"I believe I will tell you, then," he said quietly. He mused for a time before he raised his head and went on.

"I am Charles Gordon Orme, Marquis of Bute and Rayne. Once I lived in England. For good reasons I have since lived elsewhere. I am what is known as a black sheep—a very, very black one."

"Yes, you are a retrograde, a renegade, a blackguard and a murderer," I said to him, calmly.

"All of those things, and much more," he admitted, cheerfully and calmly. "I am two persons, or more than two. I can't in the least make all this plain to you in your grade of intelligence. Perhaps you have heard of exchangeable personalities?"

"I have heard of double personalities, and double lives," I said, "but I have never admired them."

"We will waive your admiration. Let me say that I can exchange my personality. The Jews used to say that men of certain mentality were possessed of a devil. I only say that I was a student in India. One phrase is good as another. The Swami Hamadata was my teacher."

"It would have been far better for you had you never known him, and better for many others," was my answer to his astonishing discourse.

"Perhaps; but I am only explaining as you have requested. I am a Raja Yogi. I have taken the eight mystic steps. For years, even here in this country, I have kept up the sacred exercises of breath, of posture, of thought."

"All that means nothing to me," I admitted simply.

"No, it means nothing for me to tell you that I have learned Yama, Niyama, Asana, Pranayama, Pratyahara, Dharana, Dyhana and Samadhi! Yes, I was something of an adept once. I learned calm, meditation, contemplation, introspection, super-conscious reasoning—how to cast my own mind to a distance, how to bring other minds close up to me. But,"—he smiled with all his old mockery—"mostly I failed on Pratyahara, which says the senses must be quelled, subdued and set aside! All religions are alike to me, but they must not intrude on my own religion. I'd liefer die than not enjoy. My religion, I say, is to play the great games—to adventure, and above all, to enjoy! That is why I am in this country, also why I am in these grounds to-night."

"You are playing some deeper game than I know?"

"I always am! How could you be expected to understand what it took me years to learn? But I suppose in your case you need a few practical and concrete proofs. Let me show you a few things. Here, put your hand on my heart."

I obeyed. "You feel it beat?" he said. "Now it stops beating, does it not?" And as I live, it *had slopped*!

"Feel on the opposite side," he commanded. I did so, and there was his heart, clear across his body, and beating as before! "Now I shall stop it again," he remarked, calmly. And I swear it did stop, and resumed when he liked!

"Put your hand upon my abdomen," he said. I did so. All at once his body seemed thin and empty, as a spent cocoon.

"I draw all the organs into the thorax," he explained. "When one has studied under the Swami, as I have, he gains control over all his different muscles, voluntary and involuntary. He can, to a great extent, cut off or increase the nerve force in any muscle. Simple tricks in magic become easy to him. He gains, as you may suppose, a certain influence over men, and more especially over women, if that be a part of his religion. It was not with the Swami. It is with me!"

"You are a strange man, Orme," I said, drawing a long breath. "The most dangerous man, the most singular, the most immoral I ever knew."

"No," he said, reaching for his cigar case, "I was only born without what you call morals. They are not necessary in abstruse thought. Yet in some ways I retain the old influences of my own country. For instance, I lie as readily as I speak the truth, because it is more convenient; but though I am a liar, I do not break my word of honor. I am a renegade, but I am still an English officer! You have caught that distinction."

"Yes, I would trust you," I said, "if you gave me your word of honor."

He turned full upon me. "By Jove, old chap," he said, with a queer note in his voice, "you touch me awfully close. You're like men of my own family—you stir something in me that I used to know. The word of a fighting man—that's the same for yours and mine; and that's why I've always admired you. That's the sort of man that wins with the best sort of women."

"You were not worth the best sort of woman," I said to him. "You had no chance with Ellen Meriwether."

"No, but at least every fellow is worth his own fight with himself. I wanted to be a gentleman once more. Oh, a man may mate with a woman of any color—he does, all over the world. He may find a mistress in any nationality of his own color, or a wife in any class similar to his own—he does, all over the world. But a sweetheart, and a wife, and a woman—when a fellow even like myself finds himself honestly gone like that—when he begins to fight inside himself, old India against old England, renegade against gentleman—say, that's awfully bitter—when he sees the other fellow win. You won—"

"No," said I, "I did not win. You know that perfectly well. There is no way in the world that I can win. All I can do is to keep parole— well, with myself, I suppose."

"You touch me awfully close," he mused again. "You play big and fair. You're a fighting man and a gentleman and—excuse me, but it's true—an awful ass all in one. You're such an ass I almost hesitate to play the game with you."

"Thank you," said I. "But now take a very stupid fellow's advice. Leave this country, and don't be seen about here again, for if so, you will be killed."

"Precisely," he admitted. "In fact, I was just intending to arrange a permanent departure. That was why I was asking you to promise me to—in short, to keep your own promise. There's going to be war next spring. The dreams of this strange new man Lincoln, out in the West, are going to come true—there will be catastrophies here. That is why I am here. War, one of the great games, is something that one must sometimes cross the globe to play. I will be here to have a hand in this one."

"You have had much of a hand in it already," I hazarded. He smiled frankly.

"Yes," he said, "one must live. I admit I have been what you call a secret agent. There is much money behind me, big politics, big commercial interests. I love the big games, and my game and my task—my duty to my masters, has been to split this country along a clean line from east to west, from ocean to ocean—to make two countries of it! You will see that happen, my friend."

"No one will ever see it happen," I said to him, soberly.

"Under which flag, then, for you?" he asked quickly.

"The flag you saw on the frontier, Orme," I answered him. "That is the flag of America, and will be. The frontier is free. It will make America free forever."

"Oh, well," he said, "the argument will be obvious enough by next spring—in April, I should guess. And whatever you or I may think, the game will be big, very big—the biggest until you have your real war between black and white, and your yet bigger one between yellow and white. I imagine old England will be in that with you, or with one of you, if you make two countries here. But I may be a wandering Jew on some other planet before that time."

He sat for a time, his chin dropped on his breast. Finally he reached me his hand.

"Let me go," he said. "I promise you to leave."

"To leave the State?"

"No, I will not promise that."

"To leave the County?"

"Yes, unless war should bring me here in the course of my duty. But I will promise to leave this town, this residence—this girl—in short, I must do that. And you are such an ass that I was going to ask you to promise to keep your promise—up there." He motioned toward the window where the light lately had been.

"You do not ask that now?" I queried.

"You are a fighting man," he said, suddenly. "Let all these questions answer themselves when their time comes. After all, I suppose a woman is a woman in the greatest of the Barnes, and one takes one's chances. Suppose we leave the debt unsettled until we meet some time? You know, you may be claiming debt of me."

"Will you be ready?" I asked him.

"Always. You know that. Now, may I go? Is my parole ended?"

"It ends at the gate," I said to him, and handed him his pistol. The knife I retained, forgetfully; but when I turned to offer it to him he was gone.

Chapter XL - A Confusion In Covenants

During the next morning Harry Sheraton galloped down to the village after the morning's mail. On his return he handed me two letters. One was from Captain Matthew Stevenson, dated at Fort Henry, and informed me that he had been transferred to the East from Jefferson Barracks, in company with other officers. He hinted at many changes in the disposition of the Army of late. His present purpose in writing, as he explained, was to promise us that, in case he came our way, he would certainly look us up.

This letter I put aside quickly, for the other seemed to me to have a more immediate importance. I glanced it over, and presently found occasion to request a word or so with Colonel Sheraton. We withdrew to his library, and then I handed him the letter.

"This," I explained, "is from Jennings & Jennings, my father's agents at Huntington, on whose advice he went into his coal speculations."

"I see. Their advice seems to have been rather disastrous."

"At first it seemed so," I answered, "but now they advise me by no means to allow foreclosure to be completed if it can be avoided. The lands are worth many times the price paid for them."

"I see—and they have some sort of an offer as well—eh?"

"A half loaf is better than no bread," I assented. "I think I ought to go out there and examine all this in detail."

"But one thing I don't understand about this," began Colonel Sheraton, "your father's partner, Colonel Meriwether, was on joint paper with him. What did he say to you when you saw him?"

"Nothing," I replied. "We did not discuss the matter."

"What? That was the sole reason why you went out to see him!"

"Other matters came up," said I. "This was not brought up at all between us."

Colonel Sheraton looked at me keenly. "I must admit, Mr. Cowles," said he, slowly weighing his words, that of late certain things have seemed more than a little strange to me. If you will allow me so to express myself, there is in my own house, since you came, a sort of atmosphere of indefiniteness. Now, why was it you did not take up these matters with Colonel Meriwether? Certainly they were important to you; and under the circumstances they have a certain interest to myself. What are you trying to cover up?"

"Nothing from you of a business nature, sir; and nothing from Miss Grace of any nature which I think she ought to know."

On His Way Back Home John Finds His Mother And Grace, Who
Have Come To Meet Him

He turned on me swiftly. "Young man, what do you propose to do in regard to my daughter? I confess I have contemplated certain plans in your benefit. I feel it is time to mention these matters with you."

John's Mother Hears That His Mission Has Been A Failure "I've Failed. Mother!"

"It is time," I answered. "But if you please, it seems to me Miss Grace and I should first take them up together. Has she spoken to you in any way that might lead you to think she would prefer our engagement to be broken?"

"No, sir. There has only been a vagueness and indefiniteness which I did not like."

"Had my affairs not mended, Colonel Sheraton, I could not have blamed any of you for breaking the engagement. If conditions prove to be practically the same now as then, it is she who must decide her course and mine."

"That is perfectly honorable. I have no criticism to offer. I have only her happiness at heart."

"Then, if you please, sir, since I am rather awkwardly situated here, I should like very much to see Miss Grace this morning."

He bowed in his lofty way and left me. Within a half hour a servant brought me word that Miss Grace would see me in the drawing-room.

She was seated in a wide, low chair near the sunny window, half hid by the leafy plants that grew in the boxes there. She was clad in loose morning wear over ample crinoline, her dark hair drawn in broad bands over the temples, half confined by a broad gold comb, save two long curls which hung down her neck at either side. It seemed to me she was very thin—thinner and darker than ever. Under her wide eyes were heavy circles. She held out her hand to me, and it lay cold and lifeless in my own. I made some pleasant talk of small matters as I might, and soon as I could arrived at the business of the letter I had received.

"Perhaps I have been a little hurried, after all, in classing myself as an absolute pauper," I explained as she read. "You see, I must go out there and look into these things."

"Going away again?" She looked up at me, startled.

"For a couple of weeks. And when I come back, Miss Grace—"

So now I was up to the verge of that same old, definite question.

She sat up in the chair as though pulling herself together in some sudden resolve, and looked me straight in the face.

"Jack," she said, "why should we wait?"

"To be sure," said I. "Only I do not want you to marry a pauper if any act of my own can make him better than a pauper in the meantime."

"You temporize," she said, bitterly. "You are not glad. Yet you came to me only last spring, and you—"

"I come to you now, Miss Grace," I said.

"Ah, what a difference between then and now!" she sighed.

For a time we could find nothing fit to say. At last I was forced to bring up one thing I did not like to mention.

"Miss Grace," said I, seating myself beside her, "last night, or rather this morning, after midnight, I found a man prowling around in the yard."

She sprang up as though shocked, her face gray, her eyes full of terror.

"You have told!" she exclaimed, "My father knows that Captain Orme—"

It was my own turn to feel surprise, which perhaps I showed.

"I have told no one. It seemed to me that first I ought to come to you and ask you about this. Why was Orme there?"

She stared at me. "He told me he would come back some time," she admitted at length. All the while she was fighting with herself, striving, exactly as Orme had done, to husband her powers for an impending struggle. "You see," she added, "he has secret business all over the country—I will own I believe him to be in the secret service of the inner circle of a number of Southern congressmen and business men. He is in with the Southern circle—of New Orleans, of Charleston—Washington. For this reason he could not always choose his hours of going and coming."

"Does your father know of his peculiar hours?"

"I presume so, of course."

"I saw a light at a window," I began, "whose window I do not know, doubtless some servant's. It could not have been a signal?"

"A *signal*? What do you mean? Do you suspect me of putting out a beacon light for a cheap night adventure with some man? Do you expect me to tolerate that sort of thing from you?"

"I ask you to tolerate nothing," I said. "I am not in the habit of suspecting ladies. But I ask you if you can explain the light on that side of the house."

"Jack," she said, flinging out a hand, "forgive me. I admit that Captain Orme and I carried on a bit of a flirtation, after he came back—after he had told me about you. But why should that—why, he did not know you were here."

"No," said I, dryly, "I don't think he did. I am glad to know that you found something to amuse you in my absence."

"Let us not speak of amusements in the absence of each other," she said bitterly. "Think of your own. But when you came back, it was all as it was last spring. I could love no other man but you, Jack, and you know it. After all, if we are quits, let us stay quits, and forgive, and forget—let us forget, Jack."

I sat looking at her as she turned to me, pleading, imploring in her face, her gesture.

"Jack," she went on, "a woman needs some one to take care of her, to love her. I want you to take care of me—you wouldn't throw me over for just a little thing—when all the time you yourself—"

"The light shone for miles across the valley," said I.

"Precisely, and that was how he happened to come up, I do not doubt. He thought we were still up about the place. My father has always told him to make this his home, and not to go to the tavern. They are friends politically, in many ways, as you know."

"The light then was that of some servant?"

"Certainly it was. I know nothing of it. It was an accident, and yet you blame me as though—why, it was all accident that you met Captain Orme. Tell me, Jack, did you quarrel? What did he tell you?"

"Many things. He is no fit man for you to know, nor for any woman."

"Do I not know that? I will never see him again."

"No, he will never come back here again, that is fairly sure. He has promised that; and he asked me to promise one thing, by the way."

"What was that?"

"To keep my promise with you. He asked me to marry you! Why?"

Infinite wit of woman! What chance have we men against such weapons? It was coquetry she forced to her face, and nothing else, when she answered: "So, then, he was hard hit, after all! I did not know that. How tender of him, to wish me married to another than himself! The conceit of you men is something wondrous."

"Mr. Orme was so kind as to inform me that I was a gentleman, and likewise a very great ass."

"Did you promise him to keep your promise, Jack?" She put both her hands on mine as it lay on the chair arm. Her eyes looked into mine straight and full. It would have taken more imagination than mine to suspect the slightest flickering in their lids. "Jack," she murmured over and over again. "I love you! I have never loved any other man."

"So now," I resumed, "I have come to you to tell you of all these things, and to decide definitely and finally in regard to our next plans."

"But you believe me, Jack? You do promise to keep your promise? You do love me?"

"I doubt no woman whom I wed," I answered. "I shall be gone for two or three weeks. As matters are at this moment it would be folly for either of us to do more than let everything stand precisely as it is until we have had time to think. I shall come back, Miss Grace, and I shall ask your answer."

"Jack, I'm sure of that," she murmured. "It is a grand thing for a woman to have the promise of a man who knows what a promise is."

I winced at this, as I had winced a thousand times at similar thrusts unconsciously delivered by so many. "No," said I, "I think Orme is right. I am only a very stupid ass."

She reached out her hand. I felt her fingers close cold and hard on mine, as though loth to let me go. I kissed her fingers and withdrew, myself at least very glad to be away.

I retired presently to my room to arrange my portmanteaus for an early journey. And there, filling up one-half of the greater valise, was a roll of hide, ragged about its edge. I drew it out, and spread it flat upon the bed before me, whitened and roughened with bone, reddened with blood, written on with rude stylus, bearing certain words which all the time, day and night, rang, yes, and sang, in my brain.

"I, John Cowles—I, Ellen Meriwether—take thee, for better, for worse—till death—" I saw her name, E-l-l-e-n.

Chapter XLI - Ellen Or Grace

Presently once more I departed. My mother also ended her visit at Dixiana, preferring to return to the quiet of her two little whitewashed rooms, and the old fireplace, and the sooty pot-hooks which our people's slaves had used for two generations in the past.

As to what I learned at Huntington, which place I reached after some days of travel, I need say no more than that I began to see fully verified my father's daring and his foresight. The matter of the coal land speculation was proved perfectly feasible. Indeed, my conference with our agents made it clear that little remained excepting the questions of a partition of interests, or of joint action between Colonel Meriwether and my father's estate. The right of redemption still remained, and there offered a definite alternative of selling a part of the lands and retaining the remainder clear of incumbrance. We wrote Colonel Meriwether all these facts from Huntington, requesting his immediate attention. After this, I set out for home, not ill-pleased with the outlook of my material affairs.

All these details of surveying and locating lands, of measuring shafts and drifts, and estimating cubic yards in coal, and determining the status of tenures and fees, had occupied me longer than I had anticipated. I had been gone two days beyond a month, when finally, somewhat wearied with stage travel, I pulled up at Wallingford.

As I approached the little tavern I heard much laughing, talking, footfalls, hurrying, as men came or went on one errand or another. A large party had evidently arrived on a conveyance earlier than my own. I leaned against the front rail of the tavern gallery and waited for some stable-boy to come. The postmaster carried away his mail sack, the loungers at the stoop gradually disappeared, and so presently I began to look about me. I found my eyes resting upon a long figure at the farther end of the gallery, sitting in the shade of the steep hill which came down, almost sharp as a house roof, back of the tavern, and so cut off the evening sun. It was apparently a woman, tall and thin, clad in a loose, stayless gown, her face hid in an extraordinarily long, green sun-bonnet. Her arms were folded, and she was motionless. But now and then there came a puff of smoke from within the caverns of the sun-bonnet, accompanied with the fragrant odor of natural leaf, whose presence brooked no debate by the human nose. I looked at this stranger again and yet again, then slowly walked up and held out my hand. No one in all the world who could counterfeit Mandy McGovern, even so far away, and under conditions seemingly impossible for her presence!

Mandy's pipe well-nigh fell from her lips. "Well, good God A'mighty! If it ain't you, son!" she exclaimed.

"Yes," I smiled.

"They told me you-all lived somewheres around here."

"Aunt Mandy," I interrupted. "Tell me, what in the world are you doing here?"

"Why, me and the folks just come down to look around. Her and her Pa was comin', and I come, too."

"*Who* came with you, Aunt Mandy?"

"Still askin' fool questions like you didn't know! Why, you know who it was. The Colonel's ordered to jine his rigiment at Fort Henry. Gal come along o' him, o' course. I come along with the gal, o' course. My boy and my husband come along with me, o' course."

"Your son, Andrew Jackson?"

"Uh-huh. He's somewheres 'round, I reckon. I see him lickin' a nigger a few minutes ago. Say, that boy's come out to be the fightenest feller I ever did see. Him allowin' he got that there Injun, day we had the fight down on the Platte, it just made a new man out'n him. 'Fore long he whupped a teamster that got sassy with him. Then he taken a rock and lammed the cook 'cause he looked like he was laffin' at him. Not long atter that, he killed a Injun he 'lowed was crawlin' 'round our place—done kilt him and taken his skulp 'fore I had time to explain to him that like enough that Injun was plum peaceful, and only comin' in to get a loaf o' bread."

"Bread? Aunt Mandy, where was all this?"

"Where d'ye suppose it was unlessen at our *hotel*? My man and me seen there was a good openin' there on the trail this side o' the south fork, and we set up a hotel in a dugout. Them *emigrants* would give you anything you aste for a piece o' pie, or a real baked loaf o' bread. We may go back there some time. We could make our pile in a couple o' years. I got over three hundred dollars right here in my pocket."

"But I don't quite understand about the man—your husband—"

"Yep, my lastest one. Didn't you know I married ole man Auberry? He's 'round here somewheres, lookin' fer a drink o' licker, I reckon. Colonel Meriwether 'lowed there'd be some fightin' 'round these parts afore long. My man and my son 'lowed the West was gettin' right quiet for them, and they'd just take a chanct down here, to see a little life in other parts."

"I hadn't heard of this last marriage of yours, Aunt Mandy," I ventured.

"Oh, yes, me and him hooked up right soon atter you and the gal got lost. Don't see how you missed our place when you come East. We done took at least six bits off'n every other man, woman or child that come through there, east or west, all summer long. You see I was tired of that lazy husband o' mine back home, and Auberry he couldn't see nothin' to that woman o' his'n atter he found out how I could bake pie and bread. So we both seem' the chanct there was there on the trail, we done set up in business. Say, I didn't know there was so many people in the whole world as they was of them *emigrants*. Preacher come along in a wagon one day—broke, like most preachers is. We kep' him overnight, free, and he married us next mornin' for nothin'. Turn about's fair play, I reckon."

I scarcely heard her querulous confidences. "Where is Colonel Meriwether?" I asked her at last.

"Inside," she motioned with her pipe. "Him and the gal, too. But say, who's that a-comin' down the street there in that little sawed-off wagon?"

I looked. It was my fiancée, Grace Sheraton!

By her side was my friend, Captain Stevenson, and at the other end of the seat was a fluttering and animated figure that could be no one else but Kitty. So then I guessed that Stevenson and his wife had come on during my absence and were visiting at Dixiana. No doubt they had driven down now for the evening mail.

Could anything have lacked now to set in worse snarl my already tangled skein of evil fortune! Out of all the thousand ways in which we several actors in this human comedy might have gone without crossing each other's paths, why should Fate have chosen the only one to bring us thus together?

Kitty seemed first to spy me, and greeted me with an enthusiastic waving of her gloves, parasol, veil and handkerchief, all held confusedly, after her fashion, in one hand. "P-r-r-r-t!" she trilled, school-girl-like, to attract my attention meanwhile. "Howdy, you man! If it isn't John Cowles I'm a sinner. Matt, look at him, isn't he old, and sour, and solemn?"

Stevenson jumped out and came up to me, smiling, as I passed down the steps. I assisted his vivacious helpmeet to alight. I knew that all this tangle would presently force itself one way or the other. So I only smiled, and urged her and her husband rapidly as I might up the steps and in at the door, where I knew they would immediately be surprised and fully occupied. Then again I approached Grace Sheraton where she still sat, somewhat discomfited at not being included in these plans, yet not unwilling to have a word with me alone.

"You sent me no word," began she, hurriedly. "I was not expecting you to-day; but you have been gone more than two weeks longer than you said you would be." The reproach of her voice was not lost to me.

Stevenson had run on into the tavern after his first greeting to me, and presently I heard his voice raised in surprise, and Kitty's excited chatter. I heard Colonel Meriwether's voice answering. I heard another voice.

"Who is in there?" asked Grace Sheraton of me, curiously. I looked her slowly and fully in the face.

"It is Colonel Meriwether," I answered. "He has come on unexpectedly from the West. His daughter is there also, I think. I have not yet seen her."

"That woman!" breathed Grace Sheraton, sinking back upon her seat. Her eye glittered as she turned to me. "Oh, I see it all now—you have been with them—*you have met her again!* My God! I could kill you both—I could—I say I could!"

"Listen," I whispered to her, putting a hand on her wrist firmly. "You are out of your head. Pull up at once. I have not seen or heard from either of them. I did not know they were coming, I tell you."

"Oh, I say, Cowles," sang out Stevenson, at that moment running out, flushed and laughing. "What do you think, here's my Colonel come and caught me at my leave of absence! He's going across the mountains, over to his home in Albemarle. We're all to be at Henry together. But I suppose you met them—"

"No, not yet," I said. "I've just got in myself."

We both turned to the girl sitting pale and limp upon the seat of the wagonette. I was glad for her sake that the twilight was coming.

The courage of her family did not forsake Grace Sheraton. I saw her force her lips to smile, compel her face to brighten as she spoke to Captain Stevenson.

"I have never met any of the Meriwethers. Will you gentlemen present me?"

I assisted her to alight, and at that time a servant came and stood at the horse's head. Stevenson stepped back to the door, not having as yet mentioned my presence there.

There came out upon the gallery as he entered that other whose presence I had for some moments known, whom I knew within the moment I must meet — Ellen!

Her eyes fell upon me. She stepped back with a faint exclamation, leaning against the wall, her hands at her cheeks as she stared. I do not know after that who or what our spectators were. I presume Stevenson went on into the house to talk with Colonel Meriwether, whom I did not see at all at that time.

The first to speak was Grace Sheraton. Tall, thin, darker than ever, it seemed to me, and now with eyes which flickered and glittered as I had never seen them, she approached the girl who stood there shrinking. "It is Miss Meriwether? I believe I should know you," she began, holding out her hand.

"This is Miss Grace Sheraton," I said to Ellen, and stopped. Then I drew them both away from the door and from the gallery, walking to the shadows of the long row of elms which shaded the street, where we would be less observed.

For the first time in my life I saw the two together and might compare them. Without my will or wish I found my eyes resting upon Ellen. Without my will or wish, fate, nature, love, I know not what, made selection.

Ellen had not as yet spoken. "Miss Sheraton," I repeated to her finally, "is the lady to whom I am engaged to be married."

The vicious Sheraton temper broke bounds. There was more than half a sneer on my fiancée's face. "I should easily know who this lady is," she said.

Ellen, flushed, perturbed, would have returned to the gallery, but I raised my hand. Grace Sheraton went on. "An engagement is little. You and he, I am advised, lived as man and wife, forgetting that he and I were already pledged as man and wife."

"That is not true!" broke in Ellen, her voice low and even. She at least had herself in hand and would tolerate no vulgar scene.

"I could not blame either of you for denying it."

"It was Gordon Orme that told her," I said to Ellen.

She would not speak or commit herself, except to shake her head, and to beat her hands softly together as I had seen her do before when in distress.

"A gentleman must lie like a gentleman," went on Grace Sheraton, mercilessly. "I am here to congratulate you both."

I saw a drop of blood spring from Ellen's bitten lip.

"What she says is true," I went on to Ellen. "It is just as Gordon Orme told your father, and as I admitted to you. I was engaged to be married to Miss Sheraton, and I am still so engaged."

Still her small hands beat together softly, but she would not cry out, she would not exclaim, protest, accuse. I went on with the accusation against myself.

"I did not tell you. I had and have no excuse except that I loved you. I am here now for my punishment. You two shall decide it."

At last Ellen spoke to my fiancée. "It is true," said she. "I thought myself engaged to Mr. Cowles. I did not know of you—did not know that he had deceived me, too. But fortunately, my father found us before it was too late."

"Let us spare ourselves details," rejoined Grace Sheraton. "He has wronged both of us."

"Yes, he has done wrong," I heard Ellen say. "Perhaps all men do—I do not want to know. Perhaps they are not always to blame—I do not want to know."

The measure of the two women was there in those words, and I felt it.

"Could you want such a man?" asked Grace Sheraton, bitterly. I saw Ellen shake her head slowly. I heard her lips answer slowly. "No," she said. "Could you?"

I looked to Grace Sheraton for her answer, and as I looked I saw a strange and ghastly change come over her face. "My God!" she exclaimed, reaching out a hand against a tree trunk to steady herself, "Your leavings? No! But what is to become of me!"

"You wish him?" asked Ellen. "You are entirely free. But now, if you please, I see no reason why I should trouble you both. Please, now, I shall go."

But Grace Sheraton sprang to her side as she turned. I was amazed at her look. It was entreaty on her face, not anger! She held out her hands to Ellen, her face strangely distorted. And then I saw Ellen's face also change. She put out her hand in turn.

"There," she said, "time mends very much. Let us hope—" Then I saw her throat work oddly, and her words stop.

No man may know the speech with which women exchange thought. I saw the two pass a few paces apart, saw Grace Sheraton stoop and whisper something.

It was her last desperate resource, a hazard handsomely taken. It won, as courage should, or at least as much as a lie may win at any time; for it was a bitter, daring, desperate shaming lie she whispered to Ellen.

As Ellen's face turned toward me again I saw a slow, deep scorn invade it. "If I were free," she said to me, "if you were the last man on earth, I would not look at you again. You deceived me—but that was only a broken word, and not a broken life! This girl—indeed she may ask what will become of her!"

"I am tired of all these riddles," I broke out, my own anger now arising, and myself not caring to be made thus sport of petticoats.

"Your duty is clear," went on my new accuser, flashing out at me. "If you have a trace of manhood left, then let the marriage be at once— to-morrow. How dare you delay so long!" She choked in her own anger, humiliation, scorn—I know not what, blushed in her own shame.

Orme was right. I have always been a stupid ass. It took me moments to grasp the amazing truth, to understand the daring stroke by which Grace Sheraton had won her game. It had cost her much. I saw her standing there trembling, tearful, suffering, her eyes wet. She turned to me, waiting for me to save her or leave her damned.

I would not do it. All the world will say that I was a fool, that I was in no way bound to any abhorrent compact, that last that any man could tolerate. Most will say that I should have turned and walked away from both. But I, who have always been simple and slow of wit, I fear, and perhaps foolish as to certain principles, now felt ice pass through all my veins as my resolution came to me.

I could not declare against the woman who had thus sworn against me. With horror I saw what grotesque injustice was done to me. I broke out into a horrible laughter.

I had said that I had come for my punishment, and here it was for me to take. I had told Orme that one day I would pay him for my life. Here now was Orme's price to be paid! If this girl had not sinned with me, she had done so by reason of me. It was my fault; and a gentleman pays for his fault in one way or another. There seemed to me, I say, but one way in which I could pay, I being ever simple and slow of wit. I, John Cowles, without thinking so far as the swift consequences, must now act as the shield of the girl who stood there trembling, the girl who had confessed to her rival her own bitter sin, but who had lied as to her accomplice in her sin!

"It is true," I said, turning to Ellen. "I am guilty. I told you I deserved no mercy, and I ask none. I have not asked Miss Sheraton to release me from my engagement. I shall feel honored if she will now accept my hand. I shall be glad if she will set the date early as may be."

Night was now coming swiftly from the hills.

Ellen turned to pass back toward the door. "Your pardon!" I exclaimed to Grace Sheraton, and sprang after Ellen.

"Good-by," I said, and held out my hand to her. "Let us end all these heroics, and do our best. Where is your husband? I want to congratulate him."

"My husband!" she said in wonder. "What do you mean?"

Night, I say, was dropping quickly, like a shroud spread by a mighty hand.

"Belknap—" I began.

"Ah," she said bitterly. "You rate me low—as low as I do you!"

"But your father told me himself you two were to be married," I broke out, surprise, wonder, dread, rebellion now in every fiber of my body and soul.

"My father loves me dearly," she replied slowly. "But he cannot marry me until I wish. No, I am not married, and I never will be. Good-by."

Again I heard my own horrible laughter.

Night had fallen thick and heavy from the mountains, like a dark, black shroud.

Chapter XLII - Face To Face

I did not see Colonel Meriwether. He passed on through to his seat in Albemarle without stopping in our valley longer than over night. Part of the next morning I spent in writing a letter to my agents at Huntington, with the request that they should inform Colonel Meriwether at once on the business situation, since now he was in touch by mail. The alternative was offered him of taking over my father's interests through these creditors, accepting them as partners, or purchasing their rights; or of doing what my father had planned to do for him, which was to care individually for the joint account, and then to allot each partner a dividend interest, carrying a clear title.

All these matters I explained to my mother. Then I told her fully what had occurred at the village the night previous between Ellen Meriwether and my fiancée. She sat silent.

"In any case," I concluded, "it would suit me better if you and I could leave this place forever, and begin again somewhere else."

She looked out of the little window across our pleasant valley to its edge, where lay the little church of the Society of Friends. Then she turned to me slowly, with a smile upon her face. "Whatever thee says," was her answer. "I shall not ask thee to try to mend what cannot be mended. Thee is like thy father," she said. "I shall not try to change thee. Go, then, thy own way. Only hear me, thee cannot mend the unmendable by such a wrongful marriage."

But I went; and under my arm I bore a certain roll of crinkled, hairy parchment.

This was on the morning of Wednesday, in November, the day following the national election in the year 1860. News traveled more slowly then, but we in our valley might expect word from Washington by noon of that day. If Lincoln won, then the South would secede. Two nations would inevitably be formed, and if necessary, issue would be joined between them as soon as the leaders could formulate their plans for war. This much was generally conceded; and it was conceded also that the South would start in, if war should come, with an army well supplied with munitions of war and led by the ablest men who ever served under the old flag—men such as Lee, Jackson, Early, Smith, Stuart—scores and hundreds trained in arms at West Point or at the Virginia Military Institute at Lexington—men who would be loyal to their States and to the South at any cost.

Our State was divided, our valley especially so, peace sentiment there being strong. The entire country was a magazine needing but a spark to cause explosion. It was conceded that by noon we should know whether or not this explosion was to come. Few of us there, whether Unionists or not, had much better than contempt for the uncouth man from the West, Lincoln, that most pathetic figure of our history, later loved by North and South alike as greatest of our great men. We did not know him in our valley. All of us there, Unionists or Secessionists, for peace or for war, dreaded to hear of his election.

Colonel Sheraton met me at the door, his face flushed, his brow frowning. He was all politics. "Have you any news?" he demanded. "Have you heard from Leesburg, Washington?"

"Not as yet," I answered, "but there should be messages from Leesburg within the next few hours." We had no telegraph in our valley at that time.

"I have arranged with the postmaster to let us all know up here, the instant he gets word," said Sheraton. "If that black abolitionist, Lincoln, wins, they're going to fire one anvil shot in the street, and we can hear it up this valley this far. If the South wins, then two anvils, as fast as they can load. So, Mr. Cowles, if we hear a single shot, it is war—*war*, I tell you!

"But come in," he added hastily. "I keep you waiting. I am glad to see you this morning, sir. From my daughter I learn that you have returned from a somewhat successful journey—that matters seem to mend for you. We are all pleased to learn it. I offer you my hand, sir. My daughter has advised me of her decision and your own. Your conduct throughout, Mr. Cowles, has been most manly, quite above reproach. I could want no better son to join my family." His words, spoken in ignorance, cut me unbearably.

"Colonel Sheraton," I said to him, "there is but one way for a man to ride, and that is straight. I say to you; my conduct has not been in the least above reproach, and your daughter has not told you all that she ought to have told."

We had entered the great dining room as we talked, and he was drawing me to his great sideboard, with hospitable intent to which at that moment I could not yield. Now, however, we were interrupted.

A door opened at the side of the room, where a narrow stairway ran down from the second floor, and there appeared the short, stocky figure, the iron gray mane, of our friend, Dr. Samuel Bond, physician for two counties thereabout, bachelor, benefactor, man of charity, despite his lancet, his quinine and his calomel.

"Ah, Doctor," began Colonel Sheraton, "here is our young friend back from his travels again. I'm going to tell you now, as I think I may without much risk, that there is every hope the Cowles family will win in this legal tangle which has threatened them lately—win handsomely, too. We shall not lose our neighbors, after all, nor have any strangers breaking in where they don't belong. Old Virginia, as she was, and forever, gentlemen! Join us, Doctor. You see, Mr. Cowles," he added to me, "Doctor Bond has stopped in as he passed by, for a look at my daughter. Miss Grace seems just a trifle indisposed this morning—nothing in the least serious, of course."

We all turned again, as the front door opened. Harry Sheraton entered.

"Come, son," exclaimed his father. "Draw up, draw up with us. Pour us a drink around, son, for the success of our two families. You, Doctor, are glad as I am, that I know."

We stood now where we had slowly advanced toward the sideboard. But Doctor Bond did not seem glad. He paused, looking strangely at me and at our host. "Harry," said he, "suppose you go look in the hall for my saddle-bags—I have left my medicine case."

The young man turned, but for no reason apparently, stopped at the door, and presently joined us again.

"May I ask for Miss Grace this morning, Doctor," I began, politely.

"Yes," interjected Colonel Sheraton. "How's the girl? She ought to be with us this minute—a moment like this, you know."

Doctor Bond looked at us still gravely. He turned from me to Colonel Sheraton, and again to Harry Sheraton. "Harry," said he, sternly. "Didn't you hear me? Get out!"

We three were left alone. "Jack, I must see you a moment alone," said Doctor Bond to me.

"What's up," demanded Colonel Sheraton. "What's the mystery? It seems to me I'm interested in everything proper here. What's wrong, Doctor? Is my girl sick?"

"Yes," said the physician.

"What's wrong?"

"She needs aid," said the old wire-hair slowly.

"Can you not give it, then? Isn't that your business?"

"No, sir. It belongs to another profession," said Doctor. Bond, dryly, taking snuff and brushing his nose with his immense red kerchief.

Colonel Sheraton looked at him for the space of a full minute, but got no further word. "Damn your soul, sir!" he thundered, "explain yourself, or I'll make you wish you had. What do you mean?" He turned fiercely upon me.

"By God, sir, there's only one meaning that I can guess. You, sir, what's wrong? *Are you to blame?*"

I faced him fairly now. "I am so accused by her," I answered slowly.

"What! *What!*" He stood as though frozen.

"I shall not lie about it. It is not necessary for me to accuse a girl of falsehood. I only say, let us have this wedding, and have it soon. I so agreed with Miss Grace last night."

The old man sprang at me like a maddened tiger now, his eyes glaring about the room for a weapon. He saw it—a long knife with ivory handle and inlaid blade, lying on the ledge where I myself had placed it when I last was there. Doctor Bond sprang between him and the knife. I also caught Colonel Sheraton and held him fast.

"Wait," I said. "Wait! Let us have it all understood plainly. Then let us take it up in any way you Sheratons prefer."

"Stop, I say," cried the stern-faced doctor—as honest a man, I think, as ever drew the breath of life. He hurled his sinewy form against Colonel Sheraton again as I released him. "That boy is lying to us both, I tell you. I say he's not to blame, and I know it. I *know* it, I say. I'm her physician. Listen, you, Sheraton—you shall not harm a man who has lied like this, like a gentleman, to *save* you and your girl."

"Damn you both," sobbed the struggling man. "Let me go! Let me alone! Didn't I *hear* him—didn't you hear him *admit* it?" He broke free and stood panting in the center of the room, we between him and the weapon. "Harry!" he called out sharply. The door burst open.

"A gun—my pistol—get me something, boy! Arm yourself—we'll kill these—"

"Harry," I called out to him in turn. "Do nothing of the sort! You'll have me to handle in this. Some things I'll endure, but not all things always—I swear I'll stand this no longer, from all of you or any of you. Listen to me. Listen I say—it is as Doctor Bond says."

So now they did listen, silently.

"I am guiltless of any harm or wish of harm to any woman of this family," I went on. "Search your own hearts. Put blame where it belongs. But don't think you can crowd me, or force me to do what I do not freely offer."

"It is true," said Doctor Bond. "I tell you, what he says could not by any possibility be anything else but true. He's just back home. *He has been gone all summer.*"

Colonel Sheraton felt about him for a chair and sank down, his gray face dropped in his hands. He was a proud man, and one of courage. It irked him sore that revenge must wait.

"Now," said I, "I have something to add to the record. I hoped that a part of my story could be hid forever, except for Miss Grace and me alone. I have not been blameless. For that reason, I was willing, freely—not through force—to do what I could in the way of punishment to myself and salvation for her. But now as this thing comes up, I can no longer shield her, or myself, or any of you. We'll have to go to the bottom now."

I flung out on the table the roll which I had brought with me to show that morning to Grace Sheraton—the ragged hide, holding writings placed there by my hand and that of another.

"This," I said, "must be shown to you all. Colonel Sheraton, I have been very gravely at fault. I was alone for some months in the wilderness with another woman. I loved her very much. I forgot your daughter at that time, because I found I loved her less. Through force of circumstances I lived with this other woman very closely for some months. We foresaw no immediate release. I loved her, and she

275

loved me—the only time I knew what love really meant, I admit it. We made this contract of marriage between us. It was never enforced. We never were married, because that contract was never signed by us both. Here it is. Examine it."

It lay there before us. I saw its words again stare up at me. I saw again the old pictures of the great mountains; and the cloudless sky, and the cities of peace wavering on the far horizon. I gazed once more upon that different and more happy world, when I saw, blurring before my eyes, the words—"I, John Cowles—I, Ellen Meriwether—take thee—take thee—for better, for worse—till death do us part." I saw her name, "E-l-l-e-n."

"Harry," said I, turning on him swiftly. "Your father is old. This is for you and me, I think. I shall be at your service soon."

His face paled. But that of his father was now gray, very old and gray.

"Treachery!" he murmured. "Treachery! You slighted my girl. My God, sir, she should not marry you though she died! This—" he put out his hand toward the hide scroll.

"No," I said to him. "This is mine. The record of my fault belongs to me. The question for you is only in regard to the punishment.

"We are four men here," I added, presently, "and it seems to me that first of all we owe protection to the woman who needs it. Moreover, I repeat, that though her error is not mine, it was perhaps pride or sorrow or anger with me which led her to her own fault. It was Gordon Orme who told her that I was false to her, and added lies about me and this other woman. It was Gordon Orme, Colonel Sheraton, I do not doubt—sir, *I found him in your yard, here, at midnight*, when I last was here. And, sir, there was a light—a light—" I tried to smile, though I fear my face was only distorted. "I agreed with your daughter that it was without question a light that some servant had left by chance at a window."

I wish never to hear again such a groan as broke from that old man's lips. He was sunken and broken when he put out his hand to me. "Boy," said he, "have mercy. Forgive. Can you—could you—"

"Can you yourself forgive this?" I answered, pointing to the scroll. "I admit to you I love Ellen Meriwether yet, and always will. Sir, if I married your daughter, it could only be to leave her within the hour."

Silence fell upon all of us. Harry set down his glass, and the clink on the silver tray sounded loud. None moved but Doctor Bond, who, glasses upon nose, bent over the blurred hide, studying it.

"Colonel Sheraton," said he at length, "it seems to me that we have no quarrel here among ourselves. We all want to do what is best done now to make amends for what has not always been best done. Mr. Cowles has given every proof we could ask—we could not ask more of any man—you have no right to ask so much. He wishes, at great cost to himself, I think, to do what he can to save your girl's happiness and honor. He admits his own fault." He looked at me, savagely shaking a finger, but went on.

"Perhaps I, a physician, unfortunately condemned to see much of the inner side of human nature, am as well equipped as any to call him more guiltless than society might call him. I say with him, let him who is without guilt first cast a stone. Few of us are all we ought to be, but why? We speak of double lives—why, we all lead double lives—the entire world leads a double life; that of sex and of society, that of nature and of property. I say to you, gentlemen, that all the world is double. So let us be careful how we adjudge punishment; and let us be as fair to our neighbor as we are to ourselves. This is only the old, old question of love and the law.

"But wait a minute—" he raised a hand as Colonel Sheraton stirred. "I have something else to say. As it chances, I am curious in other professions than my own sometimes—I read in the law sometimes, again in theology, literature. I wish to be an educated man so far as I may be, since a university education was denied me. Now, I say to you, from my reading in the law, a strong question arises whether the two who wrote this covenant of marriage are not at this moment *man and wife!*" He rapped a finger on the parchment.

A sigh broke in concert from all within that room. The next moment, I know not how, we were all four of us bending above the scroll. "See there," went on the old doctor. "There is a definite, mutual promise, a consideration moving from each side, the same consideration in each case, the promise from each bearing the same intent and value, and having the same qualifying clauses. The contract is definite; it is dated. It is evidently the record of a unanimous intent, an identical frame of mind between the two making it at that time. It is signed and sealed in full by one party, no doubt in his own hand. It is written and acknowledged by the other party in her own hand—"

"But not *signed!*" I broke in. "See, it is not *signed*. She said she would sign it one letter each week—weeks and weeks—until at last, this, which was only our engagement, should with the last letter make our marriage. Gentlemen," I said to them, "it was an honest contract. It was all the formality we could have, all the ceremony we could have. It was all that we could do. I stand before you promised to two women. Before God I was promised to one. I loved her. I could do no more—"

"It was enough," said Doctor Bond, dryly, taking snuff. "It was a wedding."

"Impossible!" declared Colonel Sheraton.

"Impossible? Not in the least," said the doctor. "It can be invalid only upon one ground. It might be urged that the marriage was not consummated. But in the courts that would be a matter of proof. Whatever our young friend here might say, a court would say that consummation was very probable.

"I say, as this stands, the contract is a definite one, agreeing to do a definite thing, namely, to enter into the state of marriage. The question of the uncompleted signature does not invalidate it, nor indeed come into the matter at all. It is only a question whether the signature, so far as it goes, means the identity of the Ellen Meriwether who wrote the clause preceding it. It is a question of identification solely. Nothing appears on this contract stipulating that she must sign her full name before the marriage can take place. That verbal agreement, which Mr. Cowles mentions, of signing it letter by letter, does not in law affect a written agreement. This written contract must, in the law, be construed just as It stands, and under its own phrasing, by its own inherent evidence. The obvious and apparent evidence is that the person beginning this signature was Ellen Meriwether—the same who wrote the last clause of the contract. The handwriting is the same—the supposition is that it is the same, and the burden of proof would lie on the one denying it.

"Gentlemen," he went on, taking a turn, hands behind back, his big red kerchief hanging from his coat tails, "I take Mr. Cowles' word as to acts before and after this contract. I think he has shown to us that he is a gentleman. In that world, very different from this world, he acted like a gentleman. In that life he was for the time freed of the covenant of society. Now, in this life, thrown again under the laws of society, he again shows to us that he is a gentleman, here as much as there. We cannot reason from that world to this. I say—yes, I hope I am big enough man to say—that we cannot blame him, arguing from that world to this. We can exact of a man that he shall be a gentleman in either one of those worlds; but we cannot exact it of him to be the *same* gentleman in *both*!

"Now, the question comes, to which of these worlds belongs John Cowles? The court will say that this bit of hide is a wedding ceremony. Gentlemen," he smiled grimly, "we need all the professions here to-day—medicine, ministry and law! At least, Colonel Sheraton, I think we need legal counsel before we go on with any more weddings for this young man here."

"But there is no record of this," I said. "There is no execution in duplicate."

"No," said the doctor. "It is only a question of which world you elect." I looked at him, and he added, "It is also only a question of morals. If this record here should be destroyed, you would leave the other party with no proof on her side of the case."

He brushed off his nose again, and took another short turn from the table, his head dropped in thought. "It is customary," he said as he turned to me, "to give the wife the wedding certificate. The law, the ministry, and the profession of medicine, all unite in their estimate of the relative value of marital faithfulness as between the sexes. It is the *woman* who needs the proof. All nature shields the woman's sex. She is the apple of Nature's eye, and even the law knows that."

I walked to the mantel and took up the knife that lay there. I returned to the table, and with a long stroke I ripped the hide in two. I threw the two pieces into the grate.

"That is my proof," said I, "that Ellen Meriwether needs no marriage certificate! I am the certificate for that, and for her!"

Colonel Sheraton staggered to me, his hand trembling, outstretched. "You're free to marry my poor girl—" he began.

"It is proof also," I went on, "that I shall never see Ellen Meriwether again, any more than I shall see Grace Sheraton again after I have married her. What happens after that is not my business. It is my business, Colonel Sheraton, and yours—possibly even your son's"—I smiled at Harry—"to find Gordon Orme. I claim him first. If I do not kill him, then you—and you last, Harry, because you are least fit."

"Gentlemen, is it all agreed?" I asked. I tossed the knife back on the mantel, and turned my back to it and them.

"Jack," said my old wire-hair, Doctor Bond, "I pray God I may never see this done again to any man. I thank God the woman I loved died years ago. She was too good—they're all too good—I, a physician, say they are all too good. Only in that gap between them and us lies any margin which permits you to lie to yourself at the altar. To care for them—to shield them—they, the apple of the Eye—that is why we men are here." He turned away, his face working.

"Is it agreed?" I asked of Colonel Sheraton, sternly.

His trembling hand sought mine. "Yes," he said. "Our quarrel is discharged, and more than so. Harry, shake hands with Mr. Cowles. By God! men, our quarrel now runs to Gordon Orme. To-morrow we start for Carolina, where we had his last address. Mr. Cowles, my heart bleeds, it bleeds, sir, for you. But for her also—for her up there. The courts shall free you quickly and quietly, as soon as it can be done. It is you who have freed us all. You have been tried hard. You have proved yourself a man."

But it was not the courts that freed us. None of us ever sought actual knowledge of what agency really freed us. Indeed, the time came swiftly for us all to draw the cloak of secrecy about one figure of this story, and to shield her in it forever.

Again we were interrupted. The door at the stair burst open. A black maid, breathless, broke into the room.

"She's a-settin' there—Miss Grace just a-settin' there—" she began, and choked and stammered.

"What is it?" cried Doctor Bond, sharply, and sprang at the door. I heard him go up the stairs lightly as though he were a boy. We all followed, plying the girl with questions.

"I went in to make up the room," blubbered she, "an' she was just settin' there, an' I spoke to her an' she didn't answer—an' I called to her, an' she didn't answer—she's just a-settin' there right *now*."

When The Way Of Women Passeth A Man's Understanding

As a cloud sweeps over a gray, broken moor, so now horror swept upon us in our distress and grief. We paused one moment to listen, then went on to see what we knew we must see.

I say that we men of Virginia were slow to suspect a woman. I hope we are still slower to gossip regarding one. Not one of us ever asked Doctor Bond a question, fearing lest we might learn what perhaps he knew.

He stood beyond her now, his head bowed, his hand touching her wrist, feeling for the pulse that was no longer there. The solemnity of his face was louder than speech. It seemed to me that I heard his silent demand that we should all hold our peace forever.

Grace Sheraton, her lips just parted in a little crooked smile, such as she might have worn when she was a child, sat at a low dressing table, staring directly into the wide mirror which swung before her at its back. Her left arm lay at length along the table. Her right, with its hand under her cheek and chin, supported her head, which leaned but slightly to one side. She gazed into her own face, into her own heart, into the mystery of human life and its double worlds, I doubt not. She could not tell us what she had learned.

Her father stepped to her side, opposite the old doctor. I heard sobs as they placed her upon her little white bed, still with that little crooked smile upon her face, as though, she were young, very young again.

I went to the window, and Harry, I think, was close behind me. Before me lay the long reaches of our valley, shimmering in the midday autumn sun. It seemed a scene of peace and not of tragedy.

But even as I looked, there came rolling up our valley, slowly, almost as though visible, the low, deep boom of the signal gun from the village below. It carried news, the news from America!

We started, all of us. I saw Colonel Sheraton half look up as he stood, bent over the bed. Thus, stunned by horror as we were, we waited. It was a long time, an interminable time, moments, minutes, it seemed to me, until there must have been thrice time for the repetition of the signal, if there was to be one.

There was no second sound. The signal was alone, single; ominous.

"Thank God! Thank God!" cried Colonel Sheraton; swinging his hands aloft, tears rolling down his old gray cheeks. "*It is war*! Now we may find forgetfulness!"

Chapter XLIII - The Reckoning

So it was war. We drew apart into hostile camps. By midwinter South Carolina, Mississippi, Georgia, Alabama, Florida, Louisiana, Texas, had withdrawn from the Union. There arose two capitals, each claiming a government, each planning war: Washington and Richmond.

As for me, I had seen the flag on our far frontiers, in wide, free lands. It was a time when each must choose for himself. I knew with whom my own lot must be cast. I pledged myself to follow the flag of the frontier, wherever it might go.

During the winter I busied myself, and when the gun of Sumpter came on that sad day of April, I was ready with a company of volunteers who had known some months of drill, at least, and who had been good enough to elect me for their captain. Most of my men came from the mountains of Western Virginia, where geography made loyalty, and loyalty later made a State. I heard, remotely, that Colonel Meriwether would not join the Confederacy. Some men of Western Virginia and Eastern Kentucky remained with the older flag. Both the Sheratons, the old Colonel and his son Harry, were of course for the South, and early in January they both left home for Richmond. On the other hand, again, our friend Captain Stevenson stood for the Federal government; and so I heard, also indirectly, did young Belknap of the Ninth Dragoons, Regulars, a gallant boy who swiftly reached distinction, and died a gallant man's death at Shiloh later on.

My mother, all for peace, was gray and silent over these hurrying events. She wept when she saw me in uniform and belt. "See," she said, "we freed our slaves long ago. We thought as the North thinks. This war is not for the Society of Friends." But she saw my father's blood in me again, and sighed. "Go, then," she said.

All over the country, North and South, came the same sighed consent of the women, "Go, then." And so we went out to kill each other, we who should all have been brothers. None of us would listen. The armies formed, facing each other on Virginia soil. Soon in our trampled fields, and broken herds, and ruined crops, in our desolated homes and hearts, we, brothers in America, learned the significance of war.

They crossed our little valley, passing through Alexandria, coming from Harper's Ferry, these raw ninety-day men of McDowell and Patterson, who thought to end the Confederacy that spring. Northern politics drove them into battle before they had learned arms. By midsummer all the world knew that they would presently encounter, somewhere near Manassas, to the south and west, the forces of Beauregard and Johnston, then lying within practical touch of each other by rail.

My men, most of them young fellows used to horse and arms, were brigaded as infantry with one of the four divisions of McDowell's men, who converged along different lines toward Fairfax. For nearly a week we lay near the front of the advance, moving on in snail-like fashion, which ill-suited most of us Virginians, who saw no virtue in postponing fight, since we were there for fighting. We scattered our forces, we did not unite, we did not entrench, we did not advance; we made all the mistakes a young army could, worst of all the mistake of hesitancy.

It was not until the twentieth of July that our leaders determined upon a flanking movement to our right, which was to cross Bull Run at the Sudley Ford. Even so, we dallied along until every one knew our plans. Back of us, the battle opened on the following day, a regiment at a time, with no concert, no *plan*. My men were with this right wing, which made the turning movement, but four brigades in all. Four other brigades, those of Howard, Burnside, Keyes and Schenck, were lost somewhere to the rear of us. Finally, we crossed and reached the left flank of the Confederates under Beauregard, and swung south along Bull Run. Our attack was scattering and ill-planned, but by three o'clock of the next day we were in the thickest of the fighting around the slopes which led up to the Henry House, back of which lay the Confederate headquarters.

I saw the batteries of Rickett and Griffin of our Regulars advance and take this height against the steadily thickening line of the Confederates, who had now had full time to concentrate. There came a hot cavalry charge upon the Zouave regiment on my left, and I saw the Zouaves lie down in the woods and melt the line of that charge with their fire, and save the battery for a time. Then in turn I saw that blunder by which the battery commander allowed Cummings' men—the Thirty-third Virginia, I think it was—deliberately to march within stone's throw of them, mistaken for Federal troops. I saw them pour a volley at short range into the guns, which wiped out their handlers, and let through the charging lines now converging rapidly upon us. Then, though it was but my first battle, I knew that our movement must fail, that our extended line, lying upon nothing, supported by nothing, must roll back in retreat along a trough road, where the horses and guns would mow us down.

Stuart's men came on, riding through us as we broke and scattered. Wheat's Louisiana Tigers came through our remnants as well. We had no support. We did not know that back of the hill the Confederate recruits were breaking badly as ourselves, and running to the rear. We were all new in war. We of the invading forces caught the full terror of that awful panic which the next day set the North in mourning, and the South aflame with a red exultation.

All around us our lines wavered, turned and fled. But to some, who knew the danger of the country back of us, it seemed safer to stay than to run. To that fact I owe my life, and at least a little satisfaction that some of us Virginians held our line for a time, even against those other Virginians who came on at us.

We were scattered in a thin line in cover of heavy timber, and when the pursuit came over us we killed a score of their men after they had passed. Such was the confusion and the madness of the pursuit, that they rolled beyond our broken line like a wave, scarce knowing we were there. Why I escaped I do not know, for I was now easily visible, mounted on a horse which I had caught as it came through the wood riderless. I was passing along our little front, up and down, as best I could in the tangle.

The pursuit went through us strung out, scattered, as disorganized as our own flight. They were practically over us and gone when, as I rode to the right flank of the remaining splinter of my little company, I saw, riding down upon us, a splendid soldier, almost alone, and apparently endeavoring to reach his command after some delay at the rear. He was mounted on a fine horse—a great black animal. His tall figure was clad in the gray uniform of the Confederates, with a black hat sweeping back from his forehead. He wore cavalry boots and deep gauntleted gloves, and in all made a gallant martial figure as he rode. A few of our men, half witless with their terror, crossed his path. I saw him half rise, once, twice, four times, standing in the stirrups to enforce his saber cuts, each one of which dropped a man. He and his horse moved together, a splendid engine of ruthless, butchery.

"Look out, Cap!" I heard a squeaking voice behind me call, and looking down, I saw one of my men, his left arm hanging loose, resting his gun across a log with his right. "Git out 'o the way," he repeated. "I'm goin' to kill him." It was that new-made warrior, Andrew Jackson McGovern, who had drifted back into our valley from some place, and joined my company soon after its organization. I ordered the boy now to drop his gun. "Leave him alone!" I cried. "He belongs to me."

It was Gordon Orme. At last, fate had relented for me. My enemy was at hand. No man but Orme could thus ride my old horse, Satan. Now I saw where the horse had gone, and who it was that owned him, and why Orme was here.

I rode out to meet him. The keenness of the coming, encounter for the time almost caused me to forget my anger. I seem never to have thought but that fate had brought me there for that one purpose. He saw me advance, and whirled in my direction, eager as myself; and presently I saw also that he recognized me, as I did him.

This is to be said of Gordon Orme, that he feared no man or thing on earth. He smiled at me now, showing his long, narrow teeth, as he came, lightly twirling his long blade. Two pistols lay in my holsters, and both were freshly loaded, but without thought I had drawn my sword for a weapon, I suppose because he was using his. He was a master of the sword, I but a beginner with it.

We rode straight in, and I heard the whistle of his blade as he circled it about his head like a band of light. As we joined he made a cut to the left, easily, gently, as he leaned forward; but it came with such swiftness that had it landed I doubt not my neck would have been shorn like a robin's. But at least I could ride as well as he or any other man. I dropped and swerved, pulling out of line a few inches as we passed. My own blow, back-handed, was fruitless as his.

We wheeled and came on again, and yet again, and each time he put me on defense, and each time I learned more of what was before me to do. My old servant, Satan, was now his servant, and the great black horse was savage against me as was his rider. Wishing nothing so much as to kill his own rival, he came each time with his ears back and his mouth open, wicked in the old blood lust that I knew. It was the fury of his horse that saved me, I suppose, for as that mad beast bored in, striving to overthrow my own horse, the latter would flinch away in spite of all I could do, so that I needed to give him small attention when we met in these short, desperate charges. I escaped with nothing more than a rip across the shoulder, a touch on the cheek, on the arm, where his point reached me lightly, as my horse swerved away from the encounters. I could not reach Orme at all.

At last, I know not how, we clashed front on, and his horse bore mine back, with a scream fastening his teeth in the crest of my mount, as a dog seizes his prey. I saw Orme's sword turn lightly, easily again around his head, saw his wrist turn gently, smoothly down and extend in a cut which was aimed to catch me full across the head. There was no parry I could think, but the full counter in kind. My blade met his with a shock that jarred my arm to the shoulder.

I saw him give back, pull off his mad horse and look at his hand, where his own sword was broken off, a foot above the hilt. Smiling, he saluted with it, reigning back his horse, and no more afraid of me than if I were a child. He did not speak, nor did I. I pulled up my own horse, not wishing to take the advantage that now was mine, but knowing that he would not yield—that I must kill him.

He did so at his own peril who took Orme for a dullard. I watched him closely. He saluted again with his broken sword, and made as though to toss it from him, as indeed he did. Then like a flash his hand dropped to his holster.

I read his thought, I presume, when he made his second salute. His motion of tossing away the sword hilt gave me the fraction of time which sometimes is the difference between life and death. Our fire was almost at the same instant, but not quite. His bullet cut the epaulet clean from my left shoulder; but he did not fire again, nor did I. I saw him straighten up in his saddle, precisely as I had once seen an Indian chieftain do under Orme's own fire. He looked at me with a startled expression on his face.

At that moment there came from the edge of the woods the crack of a musket. The great horse Satan pitched his head forward and dropped limp, sinking to his knees. As he rolled he caught his rider under him. I myself sprung down, shouting out some command toward the edge of the wood, that they should leave this man to me.

Whether my men heard me or not I do not know. Perhaps they heard rather the hoarse shouts of a fresh column in gray which came up in the pursuit, fagged with its own running. When these new men passed me all they saw was a bit of wood torn with shot and ball, and in the open two figures, both dusty and gray, one helping the other from what seemed to be a fall of his horse. Scenes like that were common. We were not disturbed by the men of either side. We were alone presently, Gordon Orme and I.

I stooped and caught hold of the hind leg of the great black horse, and even as I had once turned a dead bull, so now I turned this carcass on its back. I picked up the fallen rider and carried him to the woods, and there I propped his body against a tree. Slowly he opened his eyes, even pulled himself up more fully against the support.

"Thank you, old man," he said. "The horse was deucedly heavy—spoiled that leg, I think." He pointed to his boot, where his foot lay turned to one side. "I suffer badly. Be a good fellow and end it."

I answered him by tossing down one of his own pistols, both of which I had secured against need. He looked at it, but shook his head.

"Let's talk it over a bit first," he said. "I'm done. I'll not make any trouble. Did you ever know me to break parole?"

"No," said I, and I threw down the other weapon on the ground. "In mercy to us both, Orme, die. I do not want to kill you now; and you shall not live."

"I'm safe enough," he said. "It's through the liver and stomach. I can't possibly get over it."

He stared straight ahead of him, as though summoning his will. "*Swami!*" I heard him mutter, as though addressing some one.

"There, that's better," he said finally. He sat almost erect, smiling at me. "It is *Asana*, the art of posture," he said. "I rest my body on my ribs, my soul on the air. Feel my heart."

I did so, and drew away my hand almost in terror. It stopped beating at his will, and began again! His uncanny art was still under his control!

"I shall be master here for a little while," he said. "So—I move those hurt organs to ease the flow. But I can't stop the holes, nor mend them. We can't get at the tissues to sew them fast. After a while I shall die." He spoke clearly, with utter calmness, dispassionately. I never saw his like among men.

I stood by him silently. He put his own hand on his chest. "Poor old heart," he said. "Feel it work! Enormous pumping engine, tremendous thing, the heart. Think what it does in seventy years—and all for what—that we may live and enjoy, and so maybe die. What few minutes I have now I owe to having trained what most folk call an involuntary muscle. I command my heart to beat, and so it does."

I looked down at a strange, fascinating soul, a fearsome personality, whose like I never knew in all my life.

"Will you make me a promise?" he said, smiling at me, mocking at me.

"No," I answered.

"I was going to ask you, after my death to take my heart and send it back to my people at Orme Castle, Gordon Arms, in England—you know where. It would be a kindness to the family." I gazed at him in a sort of horror, but he smiled and went on. "We're mediaeval to-day as ever we were. Some of us are always making trouble, one corner or the other of the world, and until the last Gordon heart comes home to rest, there's no peace for that generation. Hundreds of years, they've traveled all over the world, and been lost, and stolen, and hidden. My father's is lost now, somewhere. Had it come back home to rest, my own life might have been different. I say, Cowles, couldn't you do that for me? We've nearly always had some last friend that would—we Gordons."

"I would do nothing for you as a favor," I answered.

"Then do it because it is right. I'd rather it should be you. You've a wrist like steel, and a mind like steel when you set yourself to do a thing."

"I say, old man," he went on, a trifle weary now, "you've won. I'm jolly well accounted for, and it was fair. I hope they'll not bag you when you try to get out of this. But won't you promise what I've asked? Won't you promise?"

It is not for me to say whether or not I made a promise to Gordon Orme, or to say whether or not things mediaeval or occult belong with us to-day. Neither do I expect many to believe the strange truth about Gordon Orme. I only say it is hard to deny those about to die.

"Orme," I said, "I wish you had laid out your life differently. You are a wonderful man."

"The great games," he smiled—"sport, love, war!" Then his face saddened. "I say, have you kept your other promise to me?" he asked. "Did you marry that girl—what was her name—Miss Sheraton?"

"Miss Sheraton is dead."

"Married?" he asked.

"No. She died within two months after the night I caught you in the yard. I should have killed you then, Orme."

He nodded. "Yes, but at least I showed some sort of remorse—the first time, I think. Not a bad sort, that girl, but madly jealous. Fighting blood, I imagine, in that family!"

"Yes," I said, "her father and brother and I, all three, swore the same oath."

"The same spirit was in the girl," he said, nodding again. "Revenge—that was what she wanted. That's why it all happened. It was what I wanted, too! You blocked me with the only woman—"

"Do not speak her name," I said to him, quietly. "The nails on your fingers are growing blue, Orme. Go with some sort of squaring of your own accounts. Try to think."

He shrugged a shoulder. "My Swami said we do not die—we only change worlds or forms. What! I, Gordon Orme, to be blotted out—to lose my mind and soul and body and senses—not to be able to *enjoy*. No, Cowles, somewhere there are other worlds, with women in them. I do not die—I transfer." But sweat stood on his forehead.

"As to going, no ways are better than this," he mused, presently. "I swear I'm rather comfortable now; a trifle numb—but we—I say, we must all—all go some time, you know. Did you hear me?" he repeated, smiling. "I was just saying that we must all go, one way or another, you know."

"I heard you," I said. "You are going now."

"Yes," he admitted, "one can't hold together forever under a pull like this. You're an awfully decent sort. Give me a bit of paper. I want to write." I found him a pencil and some pages of my notebook.

"To please you, I'll try to square some things," he said. "You've been so deuced square and straight with me, all along. I'm—I'm Gordon, now, I'm English. Word of a fighting man, my—my *friend*."

He leaned forward, peering down at the paper as though he did not clearly see; but he wrote slowly for a time, absorbed in thought.

In all the death scenes which our country knew in thousands during those years, I doubt if any more unbelievable than this ever had occurrence. I saw the blood soaking all his garments, lying black on the ground about him. I saw his face grow gray and his nails grow blue, his pallor deepen as the veins lost their contents. I saw him die. But I swear that he still sat there, calm as though he did not suffer, and forced his body to do his will. And—though I ask a rough man's pardon for intruding my own beliefs—since he used his last superb reserves to leave the truth behind him, I myself thought that there must be somewhere an undying instinct of truth and justice, governing even such as Gordon Orme; yes, I hope, governing such as myself as well. Since then I have felt that somewhere there must be a great religion written on the earth and in the sky. As to what this could offer in peace to Gordon Orme I do not say. His was a vast debt. Perhaps Truth never accepted it as paid. I do not know.

There he sat, at last smiling again as he looked up. "Fingers getting dreadfully stiff. Tongue will go next. Muscles still under the power for a little time. Here, take this. You're going to live, and this is the only thing—it'll make you miserable, but happy, too. Good-by. I'll not stop longer, I think."

Like a flash his hand shot out to the weapon that lay near him on the ground. I shrank back, expecting the ball full in my face. Instead, it passed through his own brain!

His will was broken as that physical instrument, the brain, wonder seat of the mysteries of the mind, was rent apart. His splendid mind no longer ruled his splendid body. His body itself, relaxing, sank forward, his head at one side, his hand dropping limp. A smile drew down the corner of his mouth—a smile horrible in its pathos; mocking, and yet beseeching.

* * * * *

At last I rubbed the blood from my own face and stooped to read what he had written. Then I thanked God that he was dead, knowing how impossible it would have been elsewise for me to stay my hand. These were the words:

"I, Gordon Orme, dying July 21, 1861, confess that I killed John Cowles, Senior, in the month of April, 1860, at the road near Wallingford. I wanted the horse, but had to kill Cowles. Later took the money. I was a secret agent, detailed for work among U.S. Army men.

"I, Gordon Orme, having seduced Grace Sheraton, asked John Cowles to marry her to cover up that act.

"I, Gordon Orme, appoint John Cowles my executor. I ask him to fulfill last request. I give him what property I have on my person for his own. Further, I say not; and being long ago held as dead, I make no bequests as to other property whatsoever.—Gordon Orme. In Virginia, U.S.A."

It was he, then, who had in cold blood killed my father! That horrid riddle at last was read. In that confession I saw only his intent to give me his last touch of misery and pain. It was some moments before I could read all the puzzle of his speech, half of which had promised me wretchedness, and half happiness. Then slowly I realized what I held in my hand. It was the proof of his guilt, of my innocence. He had robbed me of my father. He had given me—what? At least he had given me a chance. Perhaps Ellen Meriwether would believe!

* * * * *

It was my duty to care for the personal belongings of Gordon Orme; but regarding these matters a soldier does not care to speak. I took from his coat a long, folded leather book. It was hours later, indeed late the following morning, before I looked into it. During the night I was busy making my escape from that fated field. As I came from the rear, mounted, I was supposed to be of the Confederate forces, and so I got through the weary and scattered columns of pursuit, already overloaded with prisoners. By morning I was far on my way toward the Potomac. Then I felt in my pockets, and opened the wallet I had found en Orme's body.

It held various memoranda, certain writings in cipher, others in foreign characters, pieces of drawings, maps and the like, all of which I destroyed. It contained also, in thin foreign notes, a sum large beyond the belief of what an ordinary officer would carry into battle; and this money, for the time, I felt justified in retaining.

Orme was no ordinary officer. He had his own ways, and his own errand. His secret, however great it was—and at different times I have had reason to believe that men high in power on both sides knew how great it was, and how important to be kept a secret—

never became fully known. In all likelihood it was not his business actually to join in the fighting ranks. But so at least it happened that his secret went into the unknown with himself. He was lost as utterly as though he were a dark vision passing into a darker and engulfing night. If I learned more than most regarding him, I am not free to speak. He named no heirs beyond myself. I doubt not it was his wish that he should indeed be held as one who long ago had died.

Should Gordon Orme arise from his grave and front me now, I should hardly feel surprise, for mortal conditions scarce seem to give his dimensions. But should I see him now, I should fear him no more than when I saw him last. His page then was closed in my life forever. It was not for me to understand him. It is not for me to judge him.

Chapter XLIV - This Indenture Witnesseth

Within the few days following the battle, the newspapers paused in their warnings and rebukes on the one side, their paeans of victory on the other, and turned to the sober business of printing the long lists of the dead. Then, presently, each section but the more resolved, the North and South again joined issue, and the war went on.

As for myself, I was busy with my work, for now my superiors were good enough to advance me for what they called valor on the field. Before autumn ended I was one of the youngest colonels of volunteers in the Federal Army. Thus it was easy for me to find a brief furlough when we passed near Leesburg on our way to the Blue Ridge Gap, and I then ran down for a look at our little valley.

The women now were taking ranks steadfastly as the men. My mother greeted me, and in spite of all her sorrow, in spite of all the ruin that lay around us there, I think she felt a certain pride. I doubt if she would have suffered me to lay aside my uniform. It hung in our home long after the war was ended, and my Quaker mother, bless her! kept it whole and clean.

There were some business matters to be attended to with our friend Dr. Samuel Bond, who had been charged to handle our estate matters during my absence. He himself, too old and too busy to serve in either army, had remained at home, where certainly he had enough to do before the end of the war, as first one army and then the other swept across Wallingford.

I found Doctor Bond in his little brick office at the top of the hill overlooking the village. It was he who first showed me the Richmond papers with lists of the Confederate dead. Colonel Sheraton's name was among the first I saw. He had been with Cumming's forces, closely opposed to my own position at Bull Run. He himself was instantly killed, and his son Harry, practically at his side, seriously, possibly fatally wounded, was now in hospital at Richmond. Even by this time we were learning the dullness to surprise and shock which war always brings. We had not time to grieve.

I showed Doctor Bond the last writing of Gordon Orme, and put before him the Bank of England notes which I had found on Orme's person, and which, by the terms of his testament, I thought might perhaps belong to me.

"Could I use any of this money with clean conscience?" I asked. "Could it honorably be employed in the discharging of the debt Orme left on my family?"

"A part of that debt you have already caused him to discharge," the old doctor answered, slowly. "You would be doing a wrong if you did not oblige him to discharge the rest."

I counted out and laid on the desk before him the amount of the funds which my father's memoranda showed had been taken from him by Orme that fatal night more than a year ago. The balance of the notes I tossed into the little grate, and with no more ado we burned them there.

We concluded our conference in regard to my business matters. I learned that the coal lands had been redeemed from foreclosure, Colonel Meriwether having advanced the necessary funds; and as this now left our debt running to him, I instructed Doctor Bond to take steps to cancel it immediately, and to have the property partitioned as Colonel Meriwether should determine.

"And now, Jack," said my wire-haired old friend to me at last, "when do you ride to Albemarle? There is something in this slip of paper"—he pointed to Orme's last will and confession—"which a certain person ought to see."

"My duties do not permit me to go and come as I like these days," I answered evasively. But Dr. Samuel Bond was a hard man to evade.

"Jack," said he, fumbling in his dusty desk, "here's something *you* ought to see. I saved it for you, over there, the morning you threw it into the fireplace."

He spread out on the top of the desk a folded bit of hide. Familiar enough it was to me.

"You saved but half," I said. "The other half is gone!"

He pushed a flake of snuff far up his long nose. "Yes," said he quietly. "I sent it to her some three months ago."

"What did she say?"

"Nothing, you fool. What did you expect?"

"Listen," he went on presently. "Your brain is dull. What say the words of the law? 'This Indenture Witnesseth!' Now what is an 'indenture'? The old Romans and the old English knew. They wrote a contract on parchment, and cut it in two with an indented line, and they gave each party a half. When the court saw that these two halves fitted—as no other portions could—then indeed the indenture witnessed. It was its own proof.

"Now, my son," he concluded savagely, "if you ever dreamed of marrying any other woman, damn me if I wouldn't come into court and make this indenture witness for you *both*—for her as well as you! Go on away now, and don't bother me any more."

Chapter XLV - Ellen

Our forces passed up the valley of Virginia and rolled through the old Rockfish Gap—where once the Knights of the Golden Horn paused and took possession, in the name of King Charles, of all the land thence to the South Sea. We overspread all the Piedmont Valley and passed down to the old town of Charlottesville. It was nearly deserted now. The gay Southern boys who in the past rode there with their negro servants, and set at naught good Thomas Jefferson's intent of simplicity in the narrow little chambers of the old University of Virginia, now were gone with their horses and their servants. To-day you may see their names in bronze on the tablets at the University doors.

I quartered my men about the quiet old place, and myself hunted up an office-room on one of the rambling streets that wandered beneath the trees. I was well toward the finish of my morning's work when I heard the voice of my sentry challenge, and caught an answering word of indignation in a woman's voice. I stepped to the door.

A low, single-seated cart was halted near the curb, and one of its occupants was apparently much angered. I saw heir clutch the long brown rifle barrel which extended out at the rear over the top of the seat. "You git out'n the road, man," repeated she, "or I'll take a shot at you for luck! We done come this fur, and I reckon we c'n go the rest the way."

That could be no one but old Mandy McGovern! For the sake of amusement I should have left her to make her own argument with the guard, had I not in the same glance caught sight of her companion, a trim figure in close fitting corduroy of golden brown, a wide hat of russet straw shading her face, wide gauntlet gloves drawn over her little hands.

Women were not usual within the Army lines. Women such as this were not usual anywhere. It was Ellen!

Her face went rosy red as I hastened to the side of the cart and put down Mandy's arm. She stammered, unable to speak more connectedly than I myself. Mandy could not forget her anger, and insisted that she wanted to see the "boss."

"I am the Colonel in command right here, Aunt Mandy," I said. "Won't I do?"

"You a kunnel?" she retorted. "Looks to me like kunnels is mighty easy made if you'll do. No, we're atter Ginral Meriwether, who's comin' here to be the real boss of all you folks. Say, man, you taken away my man and my boy. Where they at?"

"With me here," I was glad to answer, "safe, and somewhere not far away. The boy is wounded, but his arm is nearly well."

"Ain't got his bellyful o' fightin' yit?"

"No, both he and Auberry seem to be just beginning."

"Humph! Reackon they're happy, then. If a man's gettin' three squares a day and plenty o' fightin', don't see whut more he kin ask."

"Corporal," I called to my sentry, who was now pacing back and forth before the door, hiding his mouth behind his hand, "put this woman under arrest, and hold her until I return. She's looking for privates Auberry and McGovern, G Company, First Virginia Volunteers. Keep her in my office while they're sent for. Bring me my bag from the table."

It was really a pretty fight, that between Mandy and the corporal. The latter was obliged to call out the guard for aid. "Sick 'em, Pete!" cried Mandy, when she found her arms pinioned; and at once there darted out from under the cart a hairy little demon of a dog, mute, mongrelish, pink-eared, which began silent havoc with the corporal's legs.

I looked again at that dog. I was ready to take it in my arms and cry out that it was my friend! It was the little Indian dog that Ellen and I had tamed! Why, then, had she kept it, why had she brought it home with her? I doubt which way the contest would have gone, had not Mandy seen me climb into her vacated seat and take up the reins. "Pete" then stolidly took up his place under the cart.

We turned and drove back up the shady street, Ellen and I. I saw her fingers twisting together in her lap, but as yet she had not spoken. The flush on her cheek was deeper now. She beat her hands together softly, confused, half frightened; but she did not beg me to leave her.

"If you could get away," she began at last, "I would ask you to drive me back home. Aunt Mandy and I are living there together. Kitty Stevenson's visiting me—you'll—you'll want to call on Kitty. My father has been in East Kentucky, but I understand he's ordered here this week. Major Stevenson is with him. We thought we might get word, and so came on through the lines."

"You had no right to do so. The pickets should have stopped you," I said. "At the same time, I am very glad they didn't."

"So you are a Colonel," she said after a time, with an Army girl's nice reading of insignia.

"Yes," I answered, "I am an officer. Now if I could only be a gentleman!"

"Don't!" she whispered. "Don't talk in that way, please."

"Do you think I could be?"

"I think you have been," she whispered, all her face rosy now.

We were now near the line of our own pickets on this edge of the town. Making myself known, I passed through and drove out into the country roads, along the edge of the hills, now glorious in their autumn hues. It was a scene fair as Paradise to me. Presently Ellen pointed to a mansion house on a far off hill—such a house as can be found nowhere in America but in this very valley; an old family seat, lying, reserved and full of dignity, at a hilltop shielded with great oaks. I bethought me again of the cities of peace I had seen on the far horizons of another land than this.

"That is our home," she said. "We have not often been here since grandfather died, and then my mother. But this is the place that we Meriwethers all call home."

Then I saw again what appeal the profession of arms makes to a man—how strong is its fascination. It had taken the master of a home like this from a life like this, and plunged him into the hardships and dangers of frontier war, again into the still more difficult and dangerous conflicts between great armies. Not for months, for years, had he set foot on his own sod—sod like ours in Loudoun, never broken by a plow.

As we approached the gate I heard behind us the sound of galloping horses. There came up the road a mounted officer, with his personal escort, an orderly, several troopers, and a grinning body servant.

"Look—there he comes—it is my father!" exclaimed Ellen; and in a moment she was out of the cart and running down the road to meet him, taking his hand, resting her cheek against his dusty thigh, as he sat in saddle.

The officer saluted me sharply. "You are outside the lines," said he. "Have you leave?"

I saluted also, and caught the twinkle in his eye as I looked into his face.

"On detached service this morning, General," I said. "If you please, I shall report to you within the hour."

He wheeled his horse and spurred on up along his own grounds, fit master for their stateliness. But he entered, leaving the gate wide open for us to pass.

"Shut the gate, Benjie," said Ellen as I tossed down a coin to the grinning black. And then to me, "You don't know Benjie? Yes, he's married again to Kitty's old cook, Annie. They're both here."

An orderly took our horse when finally we drove up; but at the time I did not go into the house. I did not ask for Mrs. Kitty Stevenson. A wide seat lay beneath one of the oaks. We wandered thither, Ellen and I. The little dog, mute, watchful, kept close at her side.

"Ellen," said I to her, "the time has come now. I am not going to wait any longer. Read this." I put into her hand Gordon Orme's confession.

She read, with horror starting on her face. "What a scoundrel—what a criminal!" she said. "The man was a demon. He killed your father!"

"Yes, and in turn I killed him," I said, slowly. Her eyes flashed. She was savage again, as I had seen her. My soul leaped out to see her fierce, relentless, exulting that I had fought and won, careless that I had slain.

"Orme did all he could to ruin me in every way," I added. "Read on." Then I saw her face change to pity as she came to the next clause. So now she knew the truth about Grace Sheraton, and, I hoped, the truth about John Cowles.

"Can you forgive me?" she said, brokenly, her dark eyes swimming in tears, as she turned toward me.

"That is not the question," I answered, slowly. "It is, can *you* forgive *me*?" Her hand fell on my arm imploringly.

"I have no doubt that I was much to blame for that poor girl's act," I continued. "The question only is, has my punishment been enough, or can it be enough? Do you forgive me? We all make mistakes. Am I good enough for you, Ellen? answer me."

But she would not yet answer. So I went on.

"I killed Gordon Orme myself, in fair fight; but he wrote this of his own free will. He himself told me it would be proof. Is it proof?"

She put the paper gently to one side of her on the long seat. "I do not need it," she said. "If it came to question of proof, we have learned much of these matters, my father and I, since we last met you. But I have never needed it; not even that night we said good-by. Ah! how I wanted you back after you had gone!"

"And your father?" I asked of her, my hand falling on hers.

"He knows as much as I. Lately he has heard from your friend, Doctor Bond—we have both learned a great many things. We are sorry. I am sorry. I have *always* been sorry."

"But what more?" I asked. "Ellen!"

She put out her hands in a sort of terror. "Don't," she said. "I have put all this away for so long that now—I can't begin again. I can't! I can't! I am afraid. Do not ask me. Do not. No—no!"

She started from the seat as though she would have fled in a swift panic. But now I caught her.

"Stop!" I exclaimed, rage in all my heart. "I've been a fool long enough, and now I will have no more of foolishness. I will try no more to figure niceties. I'll not try to understand a woman. But gentleman or not, I swear by God! if we were alone again, we two, out there—then I'd not use you the same the second time whatever you said, or asked, or pleaded, or argued, I would not listen—not a word would I listen to—you should do as I said, as I desired. And I say now you *must*, you *shall*!"

Anger may have been in my face—I do not know. I crushed her back into the seat.

And she—Ellen—the girl I had seen and loved in the desert silences?

She sank back against the rail with a little sigh as of content, a little smile as of a child caught in mischief and barred from escape. Oh, though I lived a thousand years, never would I say I understood a woman!

"Now we will end all this," I said, frowning. I caught her by the arm and led her to the gallery, where I picked up the bag I had left at the driveway. I myself rang at the door, not allowing her to lead me in. The orderly came.

"My compliments to General Meriwether," I said, "and Colonel Cowles would like to speak with him."

He came, that tall man, master of the mansion, dusty with his travel, stern of face, maned like a gray bear of the hills; but he smiled and reached out his hand. "Come in, sir," he said. And now we entered.

"It seems you have brought back my girl again. I hope my welcome will be warmer than it was at Laramie!" He looked at us, from one to the other, the brown skin about his keen eyes wrinkling.

"I have certain things to say, General," I began. We were walking into the hall. As soon as I might, I handed to him the confession of Gordon Orme. He read it with shut lips.

"Part of this I knew already," he said, finally, "but not this as to your father. You have my sympathy—and, sir, my congratulations on your accounting for such a fiend. There, at least, justice has been served." He hesitated before continuing.

"As to some details, I regret that my daughter has been brought into such matters," he said, slowly. "I regret also that I have made many other matters worse; but I am very glad that they have now been made plain. Dr. Samuel Bond, of Wallingford, your father's friend, has cleared up much of all this. I infer that he has advised you of the condition of our joint business matters?"

"Our estate is in your debt General," I said, "but I can now adjust that. We shall pay our share. After that, the lands shall be divided, or held jointly as yourself shall say."

"Why could they not remain as they are?" He smiled at me. "Let me hope so."

I turned to Ellen. "Please," I said, "bring me the other half of this."

I flung open my bag and spread upon the nearest table my half of the record of our covenant, done, as it had seemed to me, long years ago. Colonel Meriwether and I bent over the half rigid parchment. I saw that Ellen had gone; but presently she came again, hesitating, flushing red, and put into my hands the other half of our indenture. She carried Pete, the little dog, under her arm, his legs projecting stiffly; and now a wail of protest broke from Pete, squeezed too tightly in her unconscious clasp.

I placed the pieces edge to edge upon the table. The old familiar words looked up at me again, solemnly. Again I felt my heart choke my throat as I read: "*I, John Cowles—I, Ellen Meriwether—take thee— take thee—until death do us part.*"

I handed her a pencil. She wrote slowly, freakishly, having her maiden will; and it seemed to me still a week to a letter as she signed. But at last her name stood in full—*E-l-l-e-n M-e-r-i-w-e-t-h-e-r*.

"General," I said, "this indenture witnesseth! We two are bound by it. We have 'consented together in holy wedlock.' We have 'witnessed the same before God.' We have 'pledged our faith, either to other.'"

He dashed his hand across his eyes; then, with a swift motion, he placed our hands together. "My boy," said he, "I've always wanted my girl to be taken by an Army man—an officer and a gentleman. Damn it, sir! I beg your pardon, Ellen—give me that pencil. I'll sign my own name—I'll witness this myself! There's a regimental chaplain with our command—if we can't find a preacher left in Charlottesville."

"Orderly!" I called, with a gesture asking permission of my superior.

"Yes, orderly," he finished for me, "get ready to ride to town. We have an errand there." He turned to us and motioned us as though to ownership, bowing with grave courtesy as he himself left the room. I heard the chatter of Mrs. Kitty greet him. I was conscious of a grinning black face peering in at a window—Annie, perhaps. They all loved Ellen.

But Ellen and I, as though by instinct, stepped toward the open door, so that we might again see the mountain tops.

I admit I kissed her!

Lightning Source UK Ltd.
Milton Keynes UK
UKHW011005231120
373921UK00001B/215